PRAISE FOR HEATHER BURCH

"Burch weaves the challenges of family and the hope life can bring into a book that will touch readers' hearts in the most enduring ways."

—*Booklist* on *In the Light of the Garden*

"Digging deep into the issues of loss and healing, this novel will take readers on a journey of rich emotions, deeply woven secrets, and the long-forgotten magic of childhood. The characters are dynamic, and their stories are utterly moving. This is a terrific story by Burch."

—*RT Book Reviews* on *In the Light of the Garden*

"An engrossing coming-into-her-own tale with an intriguing magical twist, *In the Light of the Garden* expands the idea of what it means to be abandoned and then tenderly explores the wonder of being found."

—Serena Chase, *USA Today*'s *Happy Ever After* blog

"Heather Burch has proven herself to have such an exceptional storytelling range that one might be tempted to call her 'the Mariah Carey of romance fiction.' *One Lavender Ribbon* blew my expectations out of the water and then swept me away on a wave of sweet romance. Don't miss this one."

—Serena Chase, *USA Today*'s *Happy Ever After* blog

"Burch's latest combines a sweet, nostalgic, poignant tale of a true love of the past with the discovery of true love in the present . . . Burch's lyrical, contemporary storytelling, down-to-earth characters, and intricate plot make this one story that will delight the heart."

—*RT Book Reviews* on *One Lavender Ribbon*, 4.5 Stars

"Heather Burch draws you into the story from page one and captures your attention, your emotions, and your heart strings until the very end. She reaches into your very soul with a story that is so real that it stays with you for weeks after the last page is turned, the last sigh has floated away, the last giggle has played out, and the last tear is shed."
—Carolyn Brown, *New York Times* and *USA Today* bestselling author
on *Along the Broken Road*

something
like
family

ALSO BY HEATHER BURCH

Adult Fiction

One Lavender Ribbon
In the Light of the Garden

The Roads to River Rock

Along the Broken Road
Down the Hidden Path

Young Adult Fiction

Summer by Summer

Halflings

Halflings
Guardian
Avenger

something
like
family

A Novel

Heather Burch

LAKE UNION
PUBLISHING

Published by Lake Union Publishing, Seattle

www.apub.com

Amazon, the Amazon logo, and Lake Union Publishing are trademarks of Amazon.com, Inc., or its affiliates.

ISBN-13: 9781542045780
ISBN-10: 1542045789

Cover design by Laura Klynstra

Printed in the United States of America

For the men and women of the Johns Creek Veterans Association. Thank you for your service and for being an inspiration. I shall never tire of hearing your stories.

Off in the distance, burning bright
One flickering candle lights the night.
Its flame is small but ever true
It points the way for me and you.
For we were warriors in our day
Until the fight took us away.
A whisper on the quiet air
Says leave behind your empty chair.

CHAPTER 1

As an old man, there were certain things Tuck Wayne could no longer do. He couldn't read the paper without bifocals, he could no longer please a woman, and he couldn't eat the fire-spicy food he loved. As far as regrets went, he—like all men coming to the end of their lives—had some. But there was one that never let him rest. One deep regret that continually gnawed at his gut. One regret that kept him awake at night. And it was one of the few things he could try to remedy.

Tuck walked to his back door and shoved the slider open. Lake Tears sprawled before him, the remnants of fog burning off her edges and evaporating in the warm Smoky Mountain morning sun. He used to go out on the boat on mornings like this. Now he only went when he knew the crappie were biting. This had been Millie's favorite time of day. Beautiful Tennessee mornings when the mountains glistened with dew and the lake shimmered with life.

He still missed Millie. Tuck felt the familiar tightening in his throat. It always came when his thoughts dwelled on her. But this time of year was the worst. This time of year, he could look out the back windows and practically see her stooped over a freshly added tomato plant in the garden. Sometimes, he'd catch her telling a tomato hornworm that though she had no hatred for the creature, he was a trespasser and not of good character so she'd not again make the mistake of sending him out. She'd be forced to end his life. But she'd never been able to follow through. Tuck wondered how many insects she'd carried to the edge of the lake. He smiled at the memory.

Tuck stepped out, turned to close the slider behind him, and caught a glimpse of himself in the mirror on the dining room wall. Sometimes it shocked him to see an old man staring back. Like anyone in his seventies, he'd been aging for years, but he never really saw it until lately, when the age spots had darkened and the lines of his face intensified. He placed his hands on his cheeks, making sure that was him. Yes. It was no trick of the mirror. Tuck Wayne, old and feeble, glared back at him with bushy white brows and springy, thinning hair. The skin around his eyes seemed to be pulling away, and the flesh of his body was loose, muscle tone he'd had since grade school lost to the rigidity of time.

But that was OK. It was all OK, because he'd lived a life to be proud of. Mostly. Loved a woman who lit the sun. How he'd ever snagged a looker like Millie, he still didn't know. He used to ask her what horrible thing she'd done in a past life to pay penance like this in the present one—being saddled with a man like him. She'd swat at his shoulder and he'd pull her into an embrace, and she'd squeal and pretend to fight. And they'd end up on the floor laughing.

From the slider door, Tuck stared at the dining room floor. It was going to be one of those days. A memory day, he liked to call them. A time when he'd graciously let Millie's ghost roam the house, landing here and there and drawing him away from whatever task he'd begun. Into the eyes of the old man in the mirror Tuck said, "I miss you, Millie."

He blinked several times, but the tears still filled his eyes. Somewhere deep inside, Tuck knew what he had to do. It's what Millie would want. It's what he wanted. "Not sure I can make this right, but I'll do what

I can." He told himself this because there wasn't any other human to talk to. He talked to Bullet plenty, but Bullet was a dog, and though his giant brown eyes were usually full of understanding, he rarely gave an opinion. A true friend, but not always the most helpful one in times like these.

Tuck turned away from both the mirror and the memories and gave his attention to the shoreline, hands splayed on the rotting wooden banister. One day, he'd replace those boards. He yelled for Bullet, using his sharp, military voice because it carried across the entire lake and echoed back to him. It was oddly comforting to hear that voice—even though it came from Tuck himself. It reminded him of a time when he was strong, at the peak of his life physically, and knowing that at least a remnant of that man was left gave him hope. No matter where Bullet had gone off to, the voice would bring him home. The German shepherd came jetting out of the woods, making an arc as he ran into the wind along the shore, his feet moving so fast, Tuck could see the spray of water at the edge of the lake being kicked up by massive paws. He shook his head but had to smile. "You'll be soaked by the time you get back here." He didn't really mind. At least Bullet could still move with the ease and agility of his youth.

Bullet bolted up the back steps, taking them two at a time. Tuck reached down and scrubbed at his ears. Bullet instantly turned to putty, leaning in and groaning. His fur was peppered with dirt and water, but his shepherd undercoat was dry. "Come on," Tuck said, and Bullet followed him to the door. "Dry your feet."

Bullet lifted and dropped his front paws before entering the house.

Without taking time to think about it, Tuck grabbed the phone from its cradle on the kitchen wall while the scent of lake-wet dog rose around him. He dialed one of the only numbers he knew by heart. "Hey, Phil. You still got the information on that PI?"

Tuck heard Phil riffle through papers. "Sure."

"Tell him to find my grandson."

There was a pause. "You sure about that, Tuck? There could be repercussions."

Maybe there would be. He could live with that. But the uncertainty of a grandchild living out there somewhere and Tuck not knowing him . . . well, it was getting where Tuck *couldn't* live with *that*. Repercussions or no, he needed to reach out.

"We might not find what you want to hear." The words were deathly soft. Cautious words for a battle-hardened attorney.

"He might be dead is what you're sayin'. I'm an old man, Phil. Not a fool. I know the kind of life his mother led. I need to know what happened. Either way." Tuck left no room for discussion. This was his call. His call alone, because alone he'd lived with the guilt and regret of not doing this sooner.

"Long as you understand. When Vin finds him, I'll go myself to talk to him."

A flash of emotion surprised Tuck. "I'd sure appreciate that."

Tuck hung up the phone and waited for Millie's ghost to tell him he'd done the right thing.

∞

Tampa, Florida
Two weeks later

Rave Wayne sat at a booth in the greasy spoon where he'd worked the last year. His friend Allen sat across from him, talking about starting a band. Rave had gotten off at ten, but they served until eleven and he'd told Stacey, the waitress, he could hang around in case they got a late-night rush. But he had to leave at eleven, busy or not. He had big plans when he got home.

My birthday is tomorrow. He willed the words into the air silently because almost no one knew, but if they did, they'd do something for him. A candle in one of the diner's blackberry pie slices or a match in a Twinkie. He figured his roommates would buy him a case of beer, but with rent overdue, they'd all share it. That's what you were supposed to do on your birthday, wasn't it? Drink with your friends. He'd be twenty-two.

Allen went on about the band. "So, you in?" Allen looked expectant. Rave was about to ruin his day.

"Sorry, dude." Rave swigged the last of his Coke. The ice had melted, but he'd sweated out so much water during his shift washing dishes, he didn't mind the taste and lack of fizz. "I promised Ashley I wouldn't join any more bands."

Allen made a face. "Dude, it's not like she's your wife."

Rave stood, annoyed at Allen and annoyed by a couple a few tables over who wouldn't stop arguing in low voices. He'd listened to the cutting tone of the man, whose eyes, red with anger, stabbed holes in his girlfriend. Whining and fighting tears with each rise and fall of her chest, the girl just sat there and took it. *Get up. Walk away,* Rave wanted to tell her. *He doesn't own you.* But he kept quiet. None of his business.

Rave hoped the argument wouldn't escalate.

"Rave, sit down. I haven't told you the best part."

"If it was the best part, you would have started with it." But Rave indulged his friend and dropped back into the booth. He was tired. He just wanted to go home. It had been a long night, and he'd woke to no hot water, making it impossible to take a decent shower.

Near them, the man noisily shoved his chair out and tossed some money on the table.

"My cousin knows this guy down in Miami who works at a studio. If we can get some decent tracks down and send them, he'll get them to the studio for us."

"Dude. Not interested." Rave hated being so blunt. Well, actually, he didn't. He wished the rest of the world said what it meant instead of softening everything. People needed to toughen up. *Allen* needed to toughen up if the wounded look entering his eyes was any indication.

"You're a jerk, man." Allen slid out of the seat. "I'm offering you a real opportunity."

Rave bit back a laugh and raised his arms. "What? Something better than all this?"

Allen huffed and followed the couple out the door. The girl was being dragged along, and Rave couldn't stop watching them as they continued to argue at the side of a newer-model Honda. He drove a '98 Accord himself. It was battered, but it still got him down the road.

He imagined what they were fighting about. The guy had probably accused her of sleeping around. That's what always happened between his mom and her string of loser boyfriends.

When Rave saw the guy bring his hand back, he jumped to his feet. It was either a warning or the prestrike. When the man's flattened hand connected hard with the girl's cheek, Rave burst through the café door. Gravel crunched beneath his feet, and he saw the girl's head of brown hair snap to one side. Rave reached, grabbed the guy by the shirt, and planted a fist in his face. That's all he remembered until people were dragging him off.

His shirt and knuckles were bloody. His front tooth felt a little loose, so the guy must have landed at least one punch. It would tighten up. He'd had loose teeth before. He ran a tongue along the top and bottom teeth. None missing, so that was good.

When the blue lights lit up the landscape in front of the café, Rave's heart sank. He didn't need this. Especially now. He was doin' good. Around him, the parking lot was littered with people and the hushed tones and accusatory looks that always accompanied scenes like this.

The sheriff talked to the couple—united in their despair—before coming over to Rave. Stacey, the night shift server, had wrapped some ice in a kitchen towel and handed it to him. When he stared at it, she cupped his hand and lifted it to his right eye. Oh. Shiner. That'd be great for his birthday tomorrow. His eye stung the minute the towel hit it.

Sheriff Parker stopped at his feet. "Evening, Rave."

"Evening, Dick."

"You can call me Sheriff Parker."

Rave swallowed the bits of dirt that had been caught between his teeth. "I thought we were closer than that. First-name basis."

"Stand up, Rave."

When Parker reached behind him for his cuffs, Rave huffed. "Seriously? You're arresting me?"

"He said you attacked him."

"Did he also tell you he was knocking around his girlfriend? He hit her in the face, Parker."

Sheriff Parker sighed. Honestly, he didn't look like he wanted to arrest Rave any more than Rave wanted to be arrested. "Turn around."

He'd be in jail for his birthday. *Happy birthday to me.*

Parker cuffed him and left him standing beside the patrol car while he went back to talk to the couple again.

Allen materialized from the side of the building, smoking a cigarette. "Saw the whole thing, man. This sucks."

"Allen, tell Parker what happened. Otherwise, it's my word against theirs. Look at them." He nodded toward the couple, who were obviously corroborating each other's stories.

Allen took a long draw. "I'd like to think you can count on me. Just like I can count on you for the band."

Rave sighed. Closed his eyes. He'd made a promise, and with all the things that were out of his control, keeping his word was one within his power. "I'm not joining your band."

"Too bad." Allen flicked his cigarette butt at Rave's feet. "Good luck." He disappeared beyond the dark corner of the building.

Sheriff Parker reappeared and placed a hand over Rave's head as he lowered him into the backseat of his patrol car. The lights shone, blue swirls running along the café windows, lighting the darkened street, and disappearing only to reappear and follow the same track again. Thirty-six times per minute. Rave had counted. It was almost a beat.

Parker sat in the front seat, doing paperwork while Rave remained silent.

"Doesn't seem that long ago when I picked you up last. You told me you were changing things. I thought we'd had a good talk."

"Yeah." Rave dropped the side of his head to the window.

"Hey, you're almost twenty-two. Happy birthday." Sharp eyes looked into the rearview, making contact with Rave. Whether it was sarcasm or sentiment, Rave wasn't sure, so he didn't answer.

"If memory serves, Judge Gavin gave you a final warning. If I haul you in tonight, you're going away."

Rave could hear him clicking a pen. "If?"

"I told the guy it was in his best interest not to press charges."

"Why would you do that?" It was Rave, not the other guy, sitting in the back of the cop car.

"I could see the welts on his girlfriend's cheek. As much as I hate to say it, Rave, you did the right thing. If it wasn't at the tail end of a lengthy string of wrong things, I'd even be buying you a cup of coffee."

"But you're not because if a bad kid does something good, no one cares. If a good kid does, he's a flippin' hero."

Parker pivoted on the seat so he could look Rave in the eye. "Son, the world doesn't owe you squat, and the sooner you figure that out, the better your life will be."

"Yeah, life's what you make of it. I get it. That's always easy for people to say who had something to start with. I didn't have jack, Parker. So don't act like you get me or understand me or even care."

Parker rummaged for the keys. "I've seen a million just like you. Boy, you got two roads in front of you. One is leading to nothing but pain. One—maybe, just maybe, if you're strong enough—might lead you to some form of happiness. But it's two roads. And cowards always take the easy road. And they line the street with words like 'Life hasn't given me jack.'"

Rave didn't know why his nose tingled or why the skin around his eyes suddenly felt hot. Maybe because this was one of the longest conversations he'd had with any man trying to help him—and in his heart, he knew that's what Parker was doing.

Parker's voice softened. "Tonight, I didn't see a good kid or a bad kid. I saw a young man stand up for what was right." He opened the back door and helped Rave out. "That's what's in you, Rave. Under all the anger and the hurt." He shoved a finger into Rave's chest. "That's what's in you. What you do with it is your choice."

He unlocked the cuffs, and Rave ran his hands over the reddened areas on his wrists. He started to walk away in the direction of his apartment because he didn't trust his voice to speak.

Parker stopped him. "Hey!"

Rave turned, uncertain.

"I meant it about the happy birthday."

Rave walked the rest of the way home because he was saving his gas money so he could take Ashley and Daniel to the aquarium the following weekend. Daniel was four and had become obsessed with stingrays in the last few months. There were stingray tanks at the aquarium and already, Rave could see in his mind's eye what the bright-eyed little guy's reaction would be. Rave had caught stingrays in the Gulf, but the ones at the aquarium had the barbs removed, making them safe for little hands.

Otherwise, he'd take Daniel fishing. Plus, Ashley had been all over him to act more like a grown-up. He was trying. He really was. But with not much of a role model, he wasn't certain what *grown-up* looked like.

The apartment he shared with three other twenty-somethings smelled like stale beer and sweat. Ashley always threw open the windows when she arrived, so when he started up the two cracked concrete steps to his front door, he knew she and Daniel were there. A rust-red curtain danced in the open window. *SpongeBob* music wafted out to him.

Why wasn't there a stingray character in *SpongeBob*? That's what Daniel had asked him at least a hundred times.

The front door flew open, and Ashley stared at him, tight-lipped. "You're late."

"Sorry, Ash." His cheek was throbbing.

She took one long look at him, her heavily lined eyes going from head to toe. "You were fighting?"

Before he could answer or explain, she spun from the door and started gathering Daniel's things. The small suitcase hung from her hand, his blanket—no, wait, he was a big boy now and didn't want anyone calling it a blanket; his *tent*—draped over her forearm.

Panic set in. "Ashley, what are you doing?"

Daniel looked up from the TV, a giant smile forming on his face. "Rave!" He stood on the couch and jumped into Rave's arms.

"Hey there, Rock Star." Daniel hugged him hard and was mumbling about the awesome weekend they were going to have while his mom was gone. Words like *beach* and *park* and *McDonald's* all flew at him with unrestrained little-boy glee.

Rave nodded at every request while keeping one eye on Ashley. She was mumbling, too. Her voice rising with each word. "Tonight. You pick tonight of all nights to get into a fight."

"There're fudge pops in the freezer," he told Daniel, who squirmed out of his arms to help himself.

"It's not like I planned it, Ash." He tried to reach for her hand, but she jerked away from him. "I didn't have a choice."

She stopped at his feet, blue eyes blazing. She'd curled her long, blonde hair. "You always have a choice, Rave. And you *always* make the wrong one."

A long breath left his lips. "I understand why you're mad, but please, don't take it out on Daniel. He's really been excited about staying the weekend."

Her shoulders lowered marginally. Her eyes found his. "You left me no choice."

Usually, he could soften her up, at least a little. But the determination stayed right in her gaze, creating a firewall between them.

"Rave, I can't leave town wondering if the cops are going to pick you up. They'd call social services. It's hard enough taking care of him—I don't need some caseworker breathing down my neck, too."

A wave of regret washed over him. She was right. He was making things worse for her. She'd gotten pregnant at seventeen and had opted to keep the child rather than abort. Rave had been part of that decision. He'd encouraged her, told her he'd be there for her. She'd become an adult almost overnight, and he'd continued to be a kid. Until last year, when they started dating and went from friends to lovers. He'd started making better choices. For her and for Daniel. But old habits were hard to break. And old friends came around even though you asked them not to, and fights happened whether you were looking for them or not.

Ashley had gathered everything in her arms and was standing near the front door. She pulled a deep breath and stared above her head where the remnant of an old leak still marred the ceiling tile. Her breathing slowed, followed by a long silence as her delicate shoulders rose and fell. He hoped she was changing her mind. But when she focused on him, her face a mix of apology and determination, he knew she hadn't. And what she planned to say was far worse than missing a weekend with Daniel. "Rave, we need to talk."

Something cold slithered over his neck and back.

She dumped everything at her feet and moved to stand near him, her long hair a shield, her gaze locked on the floor.

He knew this posture. Knew that tone. It meant nothing good, and Rave tried to prepare himself.

"I don't want you to see Daniel anymore."

Shock, followed by anger, then confusion, took turns eroding his remaining composure. "What? Over a *fight*?"

In answer, she crossed her arms and lifted her chin, a face of flint.

Not see Daniel? That was ridiculous. He'd been part of Daniel's life since Ashley was three months pregnant and had confided in him. "Ashley."

She stepped away when he moved toward her. "I need to move on."

His chest tightened, and he wondered if this was what a heart attack felt like. His heart hurt, a single hand fisted in his blood-splattered shirt. "Listen, I shouldn't have fought. I won't. I swear, I won't. Just don't . . ." But his voice gave out.

She shook her head.

"Please." The word was all breath, a silent plea. And it did little good. Rave shot a glance into the kitchen, where Daniel was happily finishing a fudge pop. He tried to imagine his life without the little blond-headed ball of sunshine in it. He couldn't. But his gaze went back to Ashley, and he realized this wasn't a snap decision. She was too resolved, too calm. Too emotionless. "How long have you been planning this?"

That's when tears filled her eyes. He'd not expected that. She'd seemed so calculated a few moments ago. "I didn't want to tell you like this."

He tried to swallow the cotton in his throat. "Tell me what?" Now it was his turn to sound calm regardless of the runaway train in his chest.

"Do you remember Barry?"

"Yeah, the guy you had it bad for and who left town without even—" That's when it all started falling into place for Rave. He'd heard from someone that Barry's father had reopened his car lot in the next town over.

She lowered her voice. "Rave, I think he may be Daniel's father."

Rave swallowed the words, though he didn't want to. Daniel's father.

"We were hoping to take some time and—"

"You've talked to him? When were you going to mention this, Ashley? You're dating me, remember?"

There was hurt in her eyes. "Don't make this any harder. He didn't know about Daniel. He's willing to take a paternity test. Rave, he wants us in his life."

"So do I, Ashley. But apparently that only matters when there's no better offer."

She leaned closer and whispered, "Rave. He may be Daniel's *biological* father."

"And that gives him rights why? He walked out on you, Ash."

"He has money. He can give things to Daniel I'd never be able to on my own."

Rave gripped her upper arm. "*We* can. Someday. Together. I can work while you go to school. I know you'd like to."

She pulled away from him. "With Barry, I won't have to." The words were quiet, but their force rocked him from his head to his feet. The punches he'd suffered tonight paled by comparison. This was a real beating.

CHAPTER 2

"Tampa, Florida."

Tuck cradled the phone against his ear. "Are you sayin' what I think, Phil?"

The attorney cleared his throat. "Yes, I am. Not really that far from here. A day's drive."

"So he's . . ."

"He's alive, Tuck. Alive and working in a greasy-spoon café. Single and staying in a rundown apartment with some other youngsters."

Tuck placed a hand to his heart and willed the world to stop spinning. "If it's only a day's drive, maybe I should—"

"Stubborn old man. I know what you're thinking, and the answer is no. Besides, your doctor would shoot me."

The edge in Tuck's voice appeared. "My doctor doesn't run my life."

Phil chuckled. "Like I said, stubborn. Let me go alone, Tuck. We don't know what the reception is going to be. Let me soften things a bit. I'll invite him here to meet you. If I don't get anywhere, I'll come back, load you in the car, and drive you there myself."

Tuck looked around his ranch house. Stacks of pans littered the kitchen; they were clean, but there was no room in the cupboards for them, so they remained on the counters and table. He didn't need much room, but if he was having a guest, his grandson, he'd need to clear some space. "He's alive."

"Yes. Looks rough around the edges from the photos Vin sent, but none the worse for wear. Looks like you, Tuck."

But all Tuck could think about was that his grandson was alive. And maybe—if God still listened to the prayers of old men—he was going to get to meet him before he passed from this life to the next.

Tuck got off the phone, surprised by how much energy had seemed to drain out of him from talking to Phil. He followed the path through all the junk he'd collected in the past forty years. He'd always been a pack rat, but after Millie died, it'd gotten out of hand. Stacks of old magazines in one corner, boxes of books in another. Books he'd never read. Books he had no real intention of reading. Boxes and bins of small appliances lined the path to the front door. A retired electrician by trade, he was handy with gadgets and had thought to repair them and then sell them for a few cents. Keep busy. He'd go to the auctions and come home with a new truckload of things, but rarely did he dive into fixing any of them. He'd gotten a good toaster out of the deal and the cordless phone he'd used for several years. And a few other odds and ends. That was about all he had to show for the many truckloads of junk that decorated his home.

And that's what he'd started to call it. Junk. 'Cause junk was stuff that might be good if someone fixed it. Now it was time to start hauling. If he was lucky—and after all, that's what the guys in his army unit had called him—he was going to have a houseguest.

He'd need to get a room ready. He glanced around his aging four-bedroom ranch. For a place with more than twenty-two hundred square feet, it looked like a cramped little box. He propped the front door open. An early April breeze drifted into the stuffy living space. He'd open windows, he'd clean. But first, he grabbed the closest box and hauled it out. The withering container was filled with lawn mower parts and odd pieces of silverware that rattled and clinked as he walked. He could store everything in the barn and bring things back one box at a time.

Something about that felt good. Right, in fact. But he needed to conserve his strength because tonight was the memorial. And guest or no, nothing got in the way of that.

$\sim\!\!9$

"Rave Wayne?"

Rave stopped busing a table near the front door of the café. Marco, his boss, had been mad at him about last night's fight, and right now, the last thing Rave needed was some attorney drawing attention to him. And the guy in the gray suit with the bad comb-over and sweaty forehead was definitely an attorney. "Yeah?"

The man motioned to the seat across from him. "Could I have a few moments of your time?"

Rave chewed his cheek. "Sorry, all my moments are spoken for." Dishes clanged together as he took the full bin into the kitchen, then tried to make a quick escape. Rave headed out the front door, still untying the dingy white apron around his hips. The night air was warm but fresh. Early spring in Tampa had temperatures in the eighties, but he didn't mind. He had parked at the end of the building because his car was a heap, and Marco preferred that it not sit in the front. Or in the light of the street lamp.

He knew, the second the guy rushed out of the café to follow him. At least they could have their conversation outside. "Mr. Wayne?"

Rave nearly laughed out loud. He propped his weight against his car door. The tired old girl groaned a little when he did. "Yes?"

"I was sent here by Tuck Wayne. Do you know that name?"

"Nope," Rave said, but his heartbeat quickened. Other than his mother, he didn't know anyone who shared his last name.

"He hired me to find you. He's your grandfather. He'd very much like to meet you."

The world swirled around Rave, and he was thankful for the metal car door behind him. He shook his head. "I don't have any living relatives. If I did, I'd know it." His hands were sweating, and Rave felt a fight-or-flight instinct coming on. He opted for flight and got into his car before the man could stop him.

Through the closed window, he heard muffled words. "How would you know, Rave? From your mother? She was a sick woman, delusional, even. Isn't there the smallest chance she could have lied—"

Seriously? This guy he just met wanted to stand at his window and pass judgment on Rave's mom? No. Rave flew out of the car and grabbed the attorney's shirt. "You don't know anything about my mother." But then a thought struck him, and he let the man go. "Do you? Is there news about her?" He knew there wasn't. In his heart, he knew his mother was dead.

"No. I have no news of her whereabouts or status. But what I do have is an invitation from the man who raised your mother. He would very much like to get to know you, Rave. You're all the family he has left."

The words spiked through his system. Leaving jagged slivers as they went.

The man added, "And *he's* all the family *you* have."

The pain of knowing there had been someone out there all those years while his mother dragged him from town to town rushed over him. There was someone—someone *well*—who could have helped them? Rave's hands clenched at his sides. "You wasted a trip. I don't want to have anything to do with him."

The man considered him for a long while. Then, he slipped a business card from his jacket pocket and placed it beneath one of the windshield wiper blades on Rave's car. "I'll be here in town for a week. Please, reconsider. Tuck is a good man. He just wants to meet you."

The man walked away, angling toward the roach motel across the street.

Rave took the business card and stared at it. Then he tossed it on the ground and drove home.

∽

Barton, Tennessee

"I did it, Millie. I found him." Tuck stood in the last room on the second floor. It's where he'd found her all those years ago. It was the one area of the house he hadn't filled with boxes from the auction barn.

It's where he felt close to her. She'd been planning to fix up that room. Turn it into a sitting room where she could invite the ladies in town to come over and have tea. Millie didn't know much about tea—or about ladies—but she'd always wanted to be one of those finely dressed women in magazines where the room behind them was as impeccable as their hairdos. She'd gone all the way to Gatlinburg once to get one of those hairdos herself and had returned home with what he'd thought looked like a hairy mushroom on her head. She'd stood a little taller, tilted her mushroom head just so, pursed her mouth like a schoolmarm.

He'd had to suffer through manners and decorum for the whole night. By the next morning, while she worked the garden, Millie had cursed the hair and the hairspray that had mingled with her sweat and ran into her eyes.

She'd dropped her fists to her denim-covered hips and told Tuck, "I guess proper ladies don't till the ground. I guess proper ladies don't sweat."

Tuck had rubbed at the scruff on his chin and told her, "I guess I wouldn't have much use for a proper lady, then."

She'd showered and returned to her task, clean-faced and with a floppy hat on her wet head.

Memories were elusive things, kissing him with joy one moment, pain the next. Tuck sat down on the armchair. It faced the wall where Millie's handiwork had been left in process. "So many things I done wrong over the years, Millie." He rubbed one hand over the other, his elbows propped on the arms of Millie's favorite chair. He'd been content to sit in that chair and watch her paint the walls. She loved to paint. He hated it.

But he didn't mind watching her, all excitement and enthusiasm, talking about the great things she could use the room for once it was freshly coated. She'd always been a visionary. Never in his life had he known anyone else with her optimism. No one but her could simply paint a room and suddenly make it become the Taj Mahal. That's how Millie saw things. None of the brokenness. All the possibilities. It was right here on the floor where he'd found her. A brain hemorrhage had stolen her from him. Ten years ago.

It occurred to him that perhaps he'd started collecting junk as a tribute to Millie. He'd never thought of it before. But that first night he'd left the house—because the memories and the sadness were too much—he'd found the auction barn. It'd been like a church calling an old sinner home. It was a lighthouse hailing a lost ship. He'd stepped inside, and when the first lot of things that no one wanted was taken out a back door, he'd asked what would happen to the items. The guy beside him told him they'd be tossed into a garbage truck and hauled to the dump.

The chair squeaked as he moved, readjusting his old bones on the broken-down cushion. Beside the windowsill sat a drinking glass, its contents long gone, but a ring of calcium and other minerals etching the lower quarter of the glass.

All these years. All these long years, and they had a grandson out there, alive. "I hope he'll like me." Tuck was surprised by the desperation in his voice. "Wish you were here instead of me. You'd know what to do." Millie always knew what to do.

If he tried hard enough, he could see her standing there in the corner, blue paint on her cheek, admonishment on her lips. *Tuck Wayne, what have you done to my sitting room?*

"Nothing, Millie. Left it just the way it was."

So I see. It's incomplete, Tuck. You could have at least finished painting it.

"No. As long as it's like this, you'll keep coming back to get after me."

Stubborn old man.

"Our grandson is coming, Millie. I know in my heart he's going to."

Then finish the room.

Tuck leaned forward in the chair waiting for Millie to say more. But she was gone. When the squares of sunshine through the window turned into long strips of shadow, he left and closed the door behind him. Tuck used the new doorknob he'd purchased and installed. The key to the lock hung from a chain on his neck—not unlike the dog tags he'd worn so long ago. Before going downstairs, he removed the chain, the shiny key between his fingers. Instead of finishing the room, Tuck locked the door.

Tampa, Florida

If anyone had told Rave he'd be knocking on the hotel room door of an attorney two days after the announcement that he had a long-lost relative, he'd have said they were crazy. But here he was.

Phil Ratzlaff, the attorney, now dressed in khaki pants and a T-shirt, looked surprised to see him. A smile grew on his face, and he motioned for Rave to come in while he dabbed at his mouth with a paper napkin.

The room smelled like Chinese takeout. He spied the greasy bag on the edge of a small table. "Mr. Yong's?"

"Yes. My cardiologist is going to kill me, but Lord willing and the creek don't rise, I'm eating this at least once a day while I'm here."

Rave hovered just inside the doorway. His stomach roiled. Too much beer—he'd had to buy it himself since his roommates made no mention of his birthday, and then with the fiasco at the café, he felt like everything in his gut was attempting a reappearance. Plus, he hadn't eaten much since yesterday, but what was there wasn't happy.

The attorney pointed a pair of chopsticks at him. "You OK? You look a little green around the gills."

"Yeah. I guess being fired doesn't agree with me."

The attorney had started to eat but replaced the small, square box on the table. Concern edged his eyes. "You were fired?"

Rave tossed a nod behind him. "Just now."

The man slid a set of glasses onto his nose. "Was there justification for the dismissal?"

"He thinks so. The guy I beat up the other night came to him with a complaint. In the end, Marco decided I wasn't good for business."

Phil Ratzlaff folded his arms over his chest and used an index finger to brush at his own cheek. "Is that where you got the black eye?"

"Yep."

"I'm sorry about your job." He looked at Rave over the top of his dark-rimmed glasses. "Have you changed your mind about Tuck's offer?"

Rave dropped into a nearby chair. He was tired. So tired of everything. And the fact that Ashley was keeping Daniel from him cut him to the root of his being. Daniel was the only bright spot in his world. "I just . . . have questions."

"Fire away." Ratzlaff went back to feasting on Mr. Yong's orange chicken.

Rave could tell the man was trying to make him feel comfortable, keep things friendly, social.

Ratzlaff paused at the small fridge. "Beer?"

"No." He'd spew for sure. "I'll take a water." He was dehydrated after work and his party for one. And everything was rolling around in his stomach like he'd ridden the Mad Tea Party Tea Cups at Disney. He'd been there once. Lived in Florida, not more than an hour away and had only been to Disney World once. But most of his friends had never been, so he felt privileged. His mom had scored some tickets. Or maybe stolen them.

You could be a kid at Disney. A kid all day long, not wondering if there'd be a place to sleep that night or if there'd be food. There was an abundance of food everywhere, it seemed. You only had to walk to the table as people left and sit down. They'd stayed at a cheap hotel down the road from the park. It had been one of the best days of his life with his mom. Except the Tea Cups. Those made him puke.

"Why is he doing this? What does he get out of it?"

Ratzlaff shrugged one shoulder. "He gets to know you. You favor him, Rave. That blond hair. 'Course his is white now, but I've known him for a long time. He had your same personality at your age. I was just a kid back then."

"Is he like rich or something?"

Rave knew the instant Ratzlaff went on alert. It was there, in his light-brown eyes. He chuckled. "No. He's not rich."

"Rich enough to send his attorney to get me. And unless you happened across my name on Facebook—which I know you didn't, 'cause I'm not on there—he hired someone else to find me."

"How do you know he didn't hire me to find you?" This was becoming a battle of wills.

"Big-shot attorney. Two hundred dollars an hour. Nah. Private investigators can be locked in for not much more than that a day. How long were you looking for me?"

"A couple weeks. And I'd do well to make two hundred an hour. Rave, your grandfather is my friend as well as my client. You might say I'm protective."

Rave snickered. "So, the dude sent to collect me is now warning me not to take advantage of the old man?"

Ratzlaff raised his hands and dropped them. "Guilty as charged. Tuck's a good man."

"You keep saying that."

"It's true."

Rave rubbed his hands on his jeans. "Maybe." He stood to leave.

"No more questions?" Ratzlaff followed him to the door.

"For now." Rave stepped out into the hot, windy night. Across the palm-tree-lined road, he could see the lights of the café. Less than a mile from here, the salt breezes of the Gulf of Mexico rushed the shoreline.

Behind him, he heard Ratzlaff counting. "Three, four, five." He held a wad of cash out to Rave.

"What's that?"

"Tuck asked me to give it to you. No strings. He said that if you decide to come, that'd be more than enough for a plane ticket or gas in your car. But regardless, he wanted you to have it. Do with it what you want. Of course, he's hoping you'll come. At least for a while."

Rave chuckled. Right. He was hardly *family pride* material. He was a young man more concerned with survival than making something of himself. Not that he wouldn't like to be more than he was. But life was already hard, and there was little time to chase dreams. "Yeah, if he meets me, he might change his mind."

Ratzlaff reached out and placed a hand on Rave's shoulder. He would have moved away, but the stack of cash was between them, and it was too much to resist.

"I know how things must have been for you when your mom was around. I know you've been on your own since you were sixteen or seventeen, and she abandoned you here. And from the state it sounds like she was in, I understand why you assume she's dead. Fact is, son, if you could change anything for her, wouldn't you go back and do it?"

"I'm not like my mother." But the comparison burned.

"I'm counting on that." Ratzlaff handed him the hundreds and closed the door of his room.

It was more money than Rave had seen in a while. He fanned the bills, realizing that with them there was another one of Ratzlaff's business cards and a slip of paper with an address. "Barton, Tennessee." Rave shoved it all in his pocket and drove straight to Walmart. He bought Daniel the Ninja bicycle he'd asked for last Christmas. They'd pooled enough cash to get him a secondhand Schwinn, but Rave had nearly taken the entire thing apart to repair all the rust spots and fix the broken spokes. It was a nightmare. But Daniel had been happy.

After wheeling the Ninja to the front, he hit the food aisles and bought Daniel every kind of food he loved, from cheddar potato chips to fresh carrots. That kid could eat carrots until his skin turned orange. He bought him the newest superhero movie and a card. He wrote inside, "Sorry for everything, Ash. Take care of Daniel. Please make sure he knows I still love him."

After loading the groceries into his car, he laid the bike on its side and rubbed it against the asphalt until it scuffed the paint. Daniel would never notice or care. But the damage would keep Ashley from returning the bike for cash. As much as he'd always cared for her, Ashley had a way of working the angles. Working people. He loved her, but sometimes he wondered if she was missing a sensitivity card.

Then, he drove to her place in the hopes he'd get to say one last good-bye.

But less than an hour later, he was on the road, heading out of town and fighting back the tears. Ashley had refused to let him see Daniel.

CHAPTER 3

Barton, Tennessee

"Here, Tuck, let me get you a fresh cup." Becca Johnson took his mug into the kitchen of Sustenance, the local coffee shop, and dumped the cold brew in the empty side of the sink. She'd been watching Tuck for a few minutes as he'd stared into the cup but had only taken a couple of sips. Not like him to let his coffee get cold. Tuck preferred his coffee hot. Trini liked her coffee scalding, and Mrs. Fletcher—who always took time to drop into the coffee shop on Fridays—liked her coffee lukewarm. Becca took notice of these kinds of things.

Tuck reminded her of her late grandfather, and that made Becca miss the man who'd taught her how to climb trees and whittle, how to make sarsaparilla tea and the best grilled cheese sandwiches in the world. Sometimes she felt so much older than she was. Like she'd lived two lifetimes. Sometimes she felt like a twenty-something. But not as often as she probably should.

Alexandra, Becca's boss, watched her dump the mug. She was hunched over the steaming, soapy water on the other side of the sink scrubbing dishes. "Hey?"

Becca chuckled. Alexandra took it as a personal insult when people didn't appreciate her coffee. "Tuck. Not sure he's feeling well. He doesn't seem himself."

Alexandra brushed her upper arm over her sweat-glistening forehead. Clumps of suds ran toward her elbow. "Well, since it's Tuck. By the way, have you decided if you're going to the concert with me?"

Becca drew in a long breath. "I appreciate the invitation. Honestly. But, no, I don't think so."

Alexandra propped her hip on the stainless steel sink. "It's going to be awesome."

Becca smiled. Nodded—pleasantly, noncommittally.

"Becca. You're in your early twenties, but I can't drag you away from the coffee shop long enough to have some fun. It's unholy."

Becca laughed. Of all the people she knew, concert-going, ripped-jeans-and-T-shirt-wearing, forty-year-old, self-proclaimed rebel Alexandra was not the likeliest authority on what was holy. "I'll think about it."

Alexandra fancied herself an outsider. Even though she'd been in Barton for nearly seven years and not only did she know everyone, she knew their business. Except Tuck. He kept to himself. It wasn't that Tuck was standoffish. He just didn't share his private life. "Go take care of Tuck. If he's not feeling well, maybe you can brighten his day."

Becca returned to his table with the mug filled to its rim with fresh, hot coffee, Alexandra's blend called Life's Too Short, Drink Good Coffee.

"Thank you, Becca," Tuck said, rubbing a hand over the springy hairs on his head.

"You want cream?" Why she found it impossible to leave him alone, she couldn't say. But there was something different about Tuck today.

A far-off loneliness hunched his shoulders, and a pinched frown corrugated his brow.

"Nah. Cream's for sissies. But thanks for the offer." He gave her a smile, along with the kind of dead-on look that hinted at a bit of respect. Probably because she helped Trini with housework on Sundays and because Tuck and Trini were friends. Becca liked older people. She always had. She'd been close to her grandparents while they were living, and now that they were gone, she'd surrogated those relationships. Trini was her stand-in grandma. Tuck . . . well, he'd be good grandpa material if he ever opened up.

Just as she was turning to leave his table, he caught her by the wrist. The motion seemed to startle him as much as her, and when she offered a tentative "Yes?" he released her.

Tuck's gaze went from her face to the store window. Outside, downtown Barton was busy with shops and people and dogs on leashes. Tuck's voice was soft when he asked, "Do you believe in second chances?"

Such a strange question for a seventy-something man to ask a twenty-something girl. Becca pulled out the seat across from him and sank into it. "I want to believe in second chances. If there aren't any, how are we ever supposed to learn? So, yes, I do."

Tuck's contemplative eyes roamed the street beyond the window. He nodded gently. "I do, too. Believe in them, that is."

Maybe that was why she was drawn to Tuck. They were both people desperate for a second chance. It wasn't that Becca didn't like her life. She did. She loved Sustenance, loved being the smiling face that greeted the patrons, loved knowing she was helping her family. But sometimes she wondered if there was a "for Becca" aspect of her life. Something that was hers and hers alone. So much was outward-based. Sometimes she longed for that one thing that was inward. Still, Becca felt honored that Tuck had shared something personal. He'd chosen her, and that made her heart happy. Even if she didn't have a clue what they were talking about. She reached behind her to a counter where a container of freshly made whipped cream sat. She held it over his mug.

"Don't ruin it," Tuck warned.

"Trust me." With that, she squeezed the handle and crowned Tuck's coffee.

He scowled and took a drink. Bushy brows shot up, and then his throat made a deep, growling sound. "That's pretty good."

Becca replaced the container. "Not just for sissies." That was all the conversation that passed between her and Tuck.

Later that night, as she and Alexandra worked to clean the coffee shop, Becca propped her arm on the top of the mop. "Have you ever met someone that you were strangely drawn to?"

Alexandra brushed a hand through the spikes of her pixie haircut. "Every time I meet a hot single guy."

Becca waved a hand in her direction. "No. Not like that. Someone you feel like you're supposed to watch out for?"

Alexandra's cheek slanted into a wry grin. "Besides you?"

Becca went back to mopping.

"Don't pout. Who do you think you're supposed to watch out for?"

Being asked the direct question made Becca uncomfortable. But she was in it now. "Tuck."

Alexandra moved across the coffee shop to face her. "Then he's got a great guardian angel. Now go change clothes. We're going to the concert."

$\sim$

All day Tuck had fought the summer flies that slipped into the house each time he left the door open and the screen door propped. When the last of the sunrays disappeared beyond the mountainside, he closed the door. Once, when he and Millie left the front open after dark, an owl flew into their house. Right through the front door and landed on the mantel, pretty as a picture, and ready to call the place home. With broom in hand, they'd finally shooed it out. After that, Tuck didn't leave the front door open after dark. Today he'd cleared and cleaned and was ready for a quiet evening when he heard the knock on the door. He rose slowly because everyone who stopped by knew it took him a few seconds to get his body in gear.

Tuck opened the door to find a young man on the other side. The sandy hair and dark eyes were unmistakably Wayne blood. Tuck tried to breathe, but there was no air. His grandson. This was his grandson. His hands fidgeted at his sides because he didn't want to scare the boy, and though Tuck wasn't a hugger, he itched to reach out—just to make sure the boy was really there. It was late. Maybe he'd fallen asleep in the recliner, and this was just a dream. He'd been exhausted after spending the bulk of his energy working and clearing a path in one of the upstairs bedrooms. Tuck smacked his hands across his craggy face and felt the sting. Definitely awake. "You . . . you came." The young man on the other side of the door—almost a reflection of Tuck himself at a younger age—rejuvenated Tuck's entire being. The exhaustion slipped away, draining like water through a sieve. Excitement surged into him. How to begin? What to say? He steadied himself by clasping a fidgety hand on the door frame. "I'm Tuck."

The boy chewed his cheek. "Rave."

"Come in. Please, come in. I have some stew in the icebox. Made it last night. You must be hungry." He continued to study the planes of the young face before him.

They almost looked eye to eye. If Tuck's spine hadn't succumbed to arthritis, they'd stand the same, six foot one. Emotions suddenly welled in Tuck, and he had to grip the other side of the door frame as well. "You're a nice-looking fella. A bit on the thin side, but you got your mother's angelic face." Maybe he was saying too much. Maybe he was babbling. This was his *grandson*. "I'm happy you came."

Rave glanced inside the house, his brows rising on a smooth forehead.

Tuck realized he was still blocking the door. "Oh, I'm sorry. Come in." This time he stepped aside for the young man.

Eyes the color of a moonless night bounced around the living room. "You've got a lot of stuff here."

Tuck had been clearing out, but it seemed the more he cleared, the more showed up. "I didn't realize how cluttered it had become." He grinned. "I like to go to auctions."

Rave perked up a little. "Like car auctions?"

Tuck scratched his chin. "I got a few cars in the back barn. All need fixin' but some humdingers."

Rave seemed to be trying to hide a smile. "Humdingers, huh?"

"I mean, they're not much to look at right now, but one day I'm gonna fix them up."

Rave rested his arms over his chest. "One day?"

Tuck nodded and motioned for the boy to follow him into the kitchen.

"How long you had those cars you're going to fix up?"

Tuck scratched his jaw. "Aw, about twenty years, I'd guess."

A single laugh escaped Rave's mouth.

"Are you in the mood for stew? Or I've got some steaks I can pull out of the freezer. Also got venison, neighbor uses my land for hunting, so he always brings me some venison steaks and sausage. I like to save the steaks for special occasions."

"I'm not hungry. I stopped off at McDonald's when I realized how far out in the boonies I was headed." A moment later he added, "You feel like this is a special occasion?"

Tuck slowly turned to face him. Rave had sat down at his table, and although he was trying to keep cool, keep things light, there was a deep yearning in the boy's eyes. Tuck lowered himself onto the seat across from his grandson. His voice was soft, almost a whisper, when he said, "It is for me, Rave. Years ago, Millie and I made peace with the fact that you were likely gone forever. Millie was your grandmother's name. She died ten years back."

Uncertainty entered Rave's gaze. "Did you think I was dead?"

"We didn't know what happened to you. We . . . we knew your mother wasn't capable of taking care of you in the state she was in."

"But you knew I existed. You knew my mother had me."

Tuck swallowed. "Yes, I did. And I wish to heaven I'd have searched for you a long time ago."

Rave stood. "Why didn't you?"

Tuck's hands were trembling. They needed to have this conversation, but he'd hoped it wouldn't happen this quickly. Fear of losing the boy before ever getting to know him shot through his system and choked his words. "I spent a good portion of my life trying to help your mother. But she'd run. She ran her whole life, and the only thing I can pray for her now is that she found peace. Lord knows there was no peace in this life for her. Millie got sick after your mother left. I think it was mostly grief, but sometimes Millie wouldn't even bother to eat. My focus went to getting her healthy. And I did, finally. But by then, so much time had passed, I had no idea where to start looking for you."

The boy's eyes glistened. Talk of his mother must be the one thing that cut straight to his heart. Rave spoke. "Mom told me you were dead. She told me she lost her mother at age twenty and her father just before I was born. Why'd she do that?"

"I don't know," Tuck lied. "Why'd your momma do most of the things she did?"

The kitchen was quiet except for their breathing. Outside, a gentle mountain wind swayed the trees, rustling their leaves. Tuck looked to the mountains beyond the kitchen for strength. He and those mountains had seen a lot of heartache. They'd weathered it all together. They'd manage this storm, too.

"Why now?" Rave said.

Tuck filled his lungs with air. "I had a dream that you were alive. And alone. You were laying on your side and it was your birthday and no one knew. You were holding a gold cross in your hand. I believe it had belonged to your momma."

Rave turned white. Either the dream hit close to home, or the boy was coming down with a sudden flu. He studied the table between them. "I *was* alone for my birthday. But you'd already been searching for me for two weeks. That suggests you had the dream two weeks before it happened."

Tuck leaned forward. "It *really* happened?" He'd assumed the dream was symbolic.

Rave's eyes narrowed. "Yeah. And maybe you know that because you had your voyeur spying on me through my bedroom window."

Tuck shook his head. "No. That's not . . . I sent Phil to speak to you after Vin Mitchum found you. Vin confirmed your identity and sent everything to Phil. Phil wouldn't spy, he's a . . ."

"A good man?"

"Yes, he is."

"Said the same about you. Repeatedly. Like a warning."

Tuck frowned. "Why would he be warning you? He didn't mention that to me."

"He was just looking out for you, Tuck. Scared the young thug would come and take advantage of the old man."

Tuck rested his forearms on the table. "As long as you're here, everything is as much yours as mine. You need the truck to go to town, take it. You need cash? The cookie jar is on the counter." He pulled a breath before saying the rest. "You're my grandson. My kin. Only family I got."

"And how do you know I'm not here to take your money, rob you blind, and hit the road?"

Tuck gave him a dead-on stare. "It's the same thing I told your momma. But her demons were too big to silence. I didn't know how to help her. Didn't even know how to help myself. But I loved her.

Unconditionally." *And I love you the same.* That was unspoken, but just as loud.

"You don't know anything about me. So, you're either too trusting or just plain stupid."

Tuck threw his head back and laughed. "And for a young man planning to rob me, you sure seem concerned about my well-being."

Rave grinned.

"My hope is in you, boy. If you let me down, you let me down." He pointed a crooked finger and closed one eye. "That's on you."

A frown flashed across Rave's face.

"But if I don't take this opportunity to invest in my own flesh and blood . . . well, that's on me. It took me a long time to make peace with how I handled things with your momma. Age and time have a way of humbling a man. I believe second chances are rare. I got one. I'm gonna do my best to not mess it up. Phil can mind his own business."

Rave laughed again, easily, this time, like maybe the wildcat in him was starting to calm. "I can stay for a week or so."

Tuck's nose tingled. He brushed it with his fingertips, then rubbed his entire face because it seemed a tidal wave of nerve endings were throbbing there, pushing him closer and closer to tears. Relief tears. A week or two was all he could ask for. After all, this was a young man whose world had probably been built only to be ripped apart, then built again on hopes and promises from a mother who'd lie to get out of any situation. Tuck had long ago given up hope that Sharon had ever changed. If she had, she'd have found her way home. There could only be a nominal amount of trust in her child. Rave thought it a big deal that Tuck was opening his home. Much more important, and with infinitely more on the line, Rave was opening his heart. And that showed the kind of character Tuck hoped for. His throat was constricted when he said, "In that case, let's get your things unloaded."

∽

Rave stepped out the front door and into the evening breeze. It was colder here in Tennessee—the wind had a chill he wasn't used to. But he'd be lying if he said he didn't like it. The green mountains and rolling hills. Everything was lush, not brown and dry, dead from the unforgiving Florida sun. He grabbed a hoodie and slipped it on. He had a few trash bags of stuff in his backseat and his guitar in the trunk. But a giant mound of fur appeared and practically knocked him off his feet. Before he could respond, large paws were on his shoulders, and a wet tongue was sampling his cheek.

"Bullet, get down!" Tuck used a voice so solid, it surprised Rave. Tuck grabbed the dog by the scruff of the neck. "He doesn't usually take to strangers so quick."

Rave scratched the dog's neck and head. "Nice to meet you, Bullet."

When they'd unloaded the bags, Rave opened the trunk, which contained nothing but his guitar case. "This all of it?" Tuck asked.

"All I own."

Something flashed across the old man's face. Like some tragedy had just played out in his mind. Rave didn't know what the big deal was. He had everything he needed. When he did need something, and he didn't have it, the item usually found its way to him. It was easier to travel light.

Of course, he wouldn't expect Tuck to understand that. He had boxes of small appliances that were older than Rave. And car parts. And magazines.

"You play guitar?" Tuck asked.

It had been Rave's first love. It was the one thing that used to quiet even the worst of nights. And the loneliest of mornings. For years, it had been light in the dark, freedom in prison. He used his free hand to close the trunk. "I play a little." But lately, he'd been playing less and less. Maybe he'd lost his passion for it, or maybe he'd just lost passion in general. He didn't know. But neither scenario made him happy.

The screen door creaked as Tuck pulled it open. "I gotta get some WD-40 on those hinges."

They carried his stuff upstairs, Tuck flipping lights on as they went. "You can have whatever room you want. I cleared some things out of this first room. It has a nice view of the lake, and at night you can open the window and get a good breeze. Also, it's the biggest room. If you like it, we'll clear out the rest of this junk. There's another room next door, but it's beside mine, and I snore like a skill saw."

"What about the room across the hall?"

Tuck turned away as he said, "That was Millie's sitting room. Stays locked."

Millie and Tuck. Rave's grandparents. It still felt surreal. Rave entered the room Tuck offered and looked around. It was a big space, but loaded. Old monitors and thousands of miles of cords peeked out from the boxes without lids. "What is all of this?"

"This here's the computer room."

"You know a lot about computers, Tuck?" Rave dropped his trash bag in the corner.

"Nope. Figured I'd start tearing into one and learn."

Rave lifted the edge of a box and peered into the hopeless stack of out-of-date floppy discs and keyboards. "How'd that work out for you?"

Tuck scratched his head. "Well, nothing's compatible. I swear, the computer industry must be moving at a fierce pace."

Rave cleared his throat. "Uh, yeah. You could say that." He propped his weight on one of the stacks. "Did you know that the computers it took to put a man on the moon originally took up an entire room?"

Tuck nodded. "Makes sense."

"And did you know that a computer with the same amount of capability now sits in virtually every household in the country?"

Tuck's mouth fell open. "You don't say." He walked over to a box and looked in. "That's almost unbelievable. I guess this stuff really is out of date, huh?"

"Yeah." Rave dug a little deeper in the box. "I might be able to find a few things, but most of this is—"

"Big paperweights?"

"Yes. Sorry."

"Well, at least I won't feel bad about throwing them out. For now, whatever's in your way can be relocated to the next room."

Rave bit back a smile. "Or I could haul them downstairs and out to the trash."

Tuck frowned. "You sure they're no good?"

"Trust me."

"All right, then. Tomorrow, that's what we'll do . . ." Tuck opened the bedroom window and wiggled the screen until it came loose. He maneuvered it into the house and set it by the wall. He grabbed the first thing he could reach—a narrow speaker—and held it up. "No good?"

Rave shook his head. "No good."

Tuck tossed it out the window, and they both watched as it flew, a quivering cord following it like a kite tail until it slammed into the ground and broke into pieces. The old man gave Rave a crooked grin. "That was something."

Rave rubbed the back of his neck. He hadn't expected the old man to do something so spontaneous. Or violent. Cool. "It might be easier to carry everything down."

"My way's more fun."

"No argument there." Rave realized he was smiling. A real smile. An I'm-letting-my-guard-down-too-quickly smile. It didn't matter. He'd made the decision to come, but he still wasn't certain what he'd hoped to find by making the trip from Tampa to Barton. If things hadn't happened the way they had—Ashley refusing to let him see Daniel anymore and losing his job at the café—he wouldn't have come. And what did that really say about his character? If everything hadn't gone wrong, he'd still be in Florida. Now he was committed to staying with Tuck for a week. He could do that. Sure he could. He wasn't like his mother.

The truck was a newer-model crew cab with a sweet stereo system and CD player. It was also Bluetooth compatible, but Rave didn't have a cell phone, so there was nothing for him to connect. What he did have was a stack of heavy-metal CDs. He'd popped one in at Tuck's and drove with the wind from the air conditioner blowing in his face and the music pounding in his ears.

The weather was amazing in Tennessee. Still April, and things were blooming, but the mornings were cool, chilly even, to his Florida-acclimated system. By now, Tampa would be climbing into the mid-eighties by day and not much cooler than that by night.

He'd slept well last night with the window open and a breeze wafting over the bed. He'd slept well each of the nights he'd stayed at Tuck's. This wasn't as bad as he'd thought. In fact, Tuck seemed to constantly find opportunities to make Rave feel welcome. Feel like family. Today, he'd sent him to town in his Chevy.

In the six days Rave had been there, he'd even gotten to pluck at his guitar each night before bed. Tuck turned in early most evenings, leaving Rave alone with his thoughts. He'd mostly dwelled on Ashley and Daniel. He missed them so fiercely it could only be likened to slow death.

One thing had surprised him—playing his guitar and how it made him feel. Before coming to Barton, his guitar had always been his escape. He could strum a few chords, close his eyes, and drift away on the reverb and the tone and the melody. Disappear into the sound, the way the music filled the silence, the way it cocooned the mind. Here, he'd play, but his mind would stray, reliving the day, bouncing from moment to moment, making note of the things that mattered, allowing the rest to drift away. He'd found it odd and amusing that Tuck had an array of hot sauces in the fridge. Dutifully, he'd set them out each night at dinner, but he never opened a bottle. Tuck also wiped down the back slider door with a paper towel and window cleaner each day whether it was dirty or not. Funny little things Rave noticed, and he'd think on them as he played his guitar late at night.

"So, this is town. If that's what you could call it," he mumbled. The small town square was lined with some kind of flowering trees and rows of midcentury buildings. At the center was a fountain and wrought iron benches. On one corner sat a diner—not unlike the café he worked in back home. Home. Was that home? He'd been there longer than anywhere else. But home was a place where you had roots.

Rave had been at Tuck's for less than a week, and the two of them had emptied the freezer stock of steaks and venison. They'd cleared his room of the electronic components, and Tuck had told him he could paint it if he wanted to. Right after that offer, Tuck had grown pensive, his hand falling to his chest, where it gathered the material of his shirt. The mention of painting a room seemed to sadden Tuck, so Rave asked why. But Tuck only gave him a distant smile and told him he'd never know what it meant to have Rave there. Later, he'd found Tuck in the hallway with his hand flattened against the door at the end of the hall. A key on a chain hung from the doorknob. Strange, Rave thought, to live alone but keep a room locked. That had caused the first hint of flight syndrome. It wasn't safe to get too comfortable, especially with people who harbored secrets. He'd planned on leaving in a week. But, if he were honest with himself, he had nowhere to go. There was nothing waiting for him back in Florida.

This morning, Tuck had asked if he wanted to check out town and hit the grocery store. He'd said sure, thinking Tuck would drive. Instead, Tuck peeled off a hundred from the roll he kept in his front pocket and handed him the truck keys.

Rave shrugged, then mumbled, "Cool." He grabbed the food list off the refrigerator door, which made Tuck smile, and left.

And that's where the dilemma began. Should he buy food for one or for two? He'd been there six days. Was he going to leave? He should. He would. That's what he decided when he entered the run-down grocery store. It smelled like old produce and meat. Everything looked fresh enough—really fresh, in fact. But the faint smell was nauseating. He put some fresh vegetables in his cart and meandered through the rest of the store. By the time he was checking out, the smell was gone. A guy his age stood at the checkout counter and another bagged the groceries.

The checker stopped pushing the items across the belt. "You new around here?"

Rave glanced up from his wallet, expecting a challenge in the guy's eyes. Instead, he found a wide, toothy smile. "Yeah."

"Nice truck. Tuck Wayne's got a truck like that. Never heard it blastin' music that loud, though."

The grocery sacker laughed. "Never heard Tuck blasting music at all."

"He's my—" Grandpa? Grandfather? Rave realized these were words he'd never said. "I'm staying with him."

"You his grandson? Phil told my mom Tuck was havin' company. His grandson from Florida. You staying through summer?"

It was weird—and disconcerting—to think they knew anything about him. He typically kept to himself. Especially in a new town. He'd learned from his mother it was best to not make waves. Fly under the radar. Of course that was because she was usually setting someone up. Under the radar was safer. Silent entrance. Speedy exit.

But he didn't have to do that. He wasn't out to hurt anyone or steal anything. "I don't know how long I'll be here."

The one across the counter nodded. "Yeah, man. I get it. Keeping it real." He went on punching bar codes from the produce into an archaic computer. Maybe Tuck had been right. Maybe there was a market for floppy discs. They could sell them, along with VCRs and Walkmans—a thing Rave wasn't too familiar with, although his mom had sung the praises of the Walkman when she'd spotted a broken one at a flea market once.

The guy checking his groceries slid the last of the produce toward the sacker. "Every Friday and Saturday morning there's a swap meet on the square. James Harper sets up on the corner. He has CDs, and that's about the only place around here you can find any decent death metal."

Rave's brows shot up. "You listen to death metal?"

"Yeah. And country. I'm Buck." He pointed to the sacker, a kid with a buzz cut and dark-blue eyes. "This here is Rowdy."

Rave shook hands with the sacker, who added, "Real name is Randall, but everyone calls me Rowdy."

"Thanks for the info about the swap meet." He knew there was a quizzical look on his face. Of course there was. He'd just stepped into the Twilight Zone. He took his change from Buck. "I'm Rave."

Rowdy placed the last bag in the cart. "Dude. That's a cool name. Is it a nickname or—"

"Nope. On my birth certificate." He didn't mention the rest of the story. How his mom named him that because she'd gotten pregnant at a rave.

Buck shook his hand next. "Maybe see you Friday? I'm usually there. I help my dad at his booth." He rolled his eyes. "You know, farmers."

No. Rave didn't know farmers. Or farm boys who listened to death metal. Or guys his age who were this friendly unless they were after something. "Maybe."

He left through the slow-moving automatic door. Outside, he turned and glanced back. Buck and the other kid were flipping through a hunting magazine. Rave shook his head to clear it. Then he started up the truck and turned onto the road, letting the air conditioner vents fill the truck with the perfect temperature—a blend of cool and comfortable—something he knew was a dangerous combination.

When he realized the truck was low on gas, he wheeled into a station and started counting what money he had left. Before he could step out, there was someone knocking on his window. He jumped and lost count of the change. He had at least a ten and a five. In the window, another face about his age, this one littered with pimples over ghostly white skin. It reminded him of the tourists back home. Walkers, he liked to call them, because their dead-white flesh looked painted on.

The kid's brows rose. "How much?"

Rave put the window down. "How much what?"

The boy smiled. "How much gas? Tuck usually fills it."

Confused, Rave glanced up at the station window. FULL SERVICE. "Oh, uh, I've just got fifteen."

"You Tuck's grandkid? You look like him. I mean, don't take that wrong, just family resemblance." The guy started filling the tank but kept talking. "I was hoping Tuck's grandkid would be a girl."

"Sorry to disappoint you." Rave leaned out the window and noticed the kid wasn't even watching the pump. "Dude. Only fifteen, remember?"

He brushed a hand through the air and left the pump running while he took a squeegee and cleaned the windshield. "Tuck's got a tab here. He'll settle up."

Rave looked down at the cash in his hand, then at the floorboard of Tuck's truck. It was littered with trash and speckled with dirt. "Is there a car wash in town?"

The kid pointed across the road, then finished pumping the gas. "If it was a snake, it would have bit cha."

"Thanks." Rave started to drive off, but first he handed the kid a five for a tip.

⁂

Time got away from Rave while he cleaned the truck. It felt good to scrub the thing, the red paint gleaming, the wheels shining. He dried it by hand because the gravel road Tuck lived down would make it a mud mess if he didn't.

Adjacent to the car wash was a snow cone stand. There was sweat on his brow, but it wasn't uncomfortable. Not like home, where this much exertion would leave every pore running like a miniature faucet. Still, he could do with something cold so he rummaged through the ashtray and found four bucks in quarters. He'd used all the cash to wash, vacuum, and wax Tuck's Chevy. He parked by the stand and walked up. There were two rows of picnic tables, six in all, in front of the stand. He ordered a Tiger's Blood, and when he turned around to have a seat, he stopped.

There, at the last picnic table, sat a girl. She had long, red hair that she'd pulled over one shoulder. Waves of the deep auburn stuff caught the sun, and he wondered for a moment if it would feel as soft as it looked. A small nose that fit her delicate features was stuck in a book. He glanced behind him at the woman running the snow cone shop, then back to the girl. No way had she been sitting there when he pulled up. He'd have noticed her—the pretty face, the soft-looking skin. But she wasn't eating a snow cone, so why was she there?

He sat directly across from her, one table down. Rave scraped at the top of his snow cone, stealing glances at her. She wore a white sundress and cowboy boots. Behind him he heard the woman yell, "It's ready."

The girl stood, walked past him, tan legs taking long strides and that skirt teasing the breeze. It seemed her skirt and hair were competing for attention. Behind him, he heard, "Thanks, Elsie."

She sat back down and opened her book, taking the occasional bite of a melting snow cone.

He opened his mouth twice to say something, but nothing came out. He probably shouldn't be staring, but he was, in that way guys did when they were interested in someone of the opposite sex. Of course, he wasn't interested in this girl. He couldn't be. Ashley was still in his system. Where the redhead was concerned, he was curious, nothing more. Still, he couldn't deny the quick shot of instant attraction that settled in his stomach. It was normal, a guy noticing a pretty girl. One of his sweaty hands wrapped around his snow cone cup. It cooled his fingers.

She finished her snow cone and rose to leave.

Before he could form a thought, he said to her, "Wait."

She paused, then turned around, one brow peaked. "Yes?"

Oh, that was smooth. Words. He needed words. He was usually confident with girls. "Uh, I'm Rave." It wasn't just that she was pretty. There was something . . . settled about her. Like she knew exactly where she was headed, and life needed only to stay out of her way.

"Hello." She turned around and started to step away from him.

"Wait."

Again, she turned, faced him, this time cocking her hip. She held the book to her chest. Bright-green eyes locked on him.

"I, um, I think I read that." He pointed to the book.

Her mouth became an *o*. "Really? Most guys aren't into life-affirming chick lit. Good for you. Break down those gender walls." Her tone was just playful enough to make the sarcasm alluring.

He dropped his head. "Is that what that is?"

She nodded. "Mm-hmm."

Rave brushed a hand through his hair. "I might have just been trying to get you into a conversation so I could find out your name."

"Or you could have just asked me my name." There was a hint of a smile on her face.

"What's your name?"

"Rebecca. Friends call me Becca or sometimes Bec."

"You live here?" The snow cone had helped cool him down, but that seemed lost now.

"All my life." She cast a glance behind her. "I have to get back to work, Rave. Welcome to Barton. By the way, I've never seen Tuck's truck look so clean."

By the time he'd gone from looking over at the gleaming red Chevy to back at her, she'd made it halfway to the road. "Bye, Rebecca," he hollered.

"You can call me Becca," she said, then jogged across the road. He watched her slip into a coffee shop on the corner called Sustenance. Whatever that meant.

With a goofy smile planted on his face, Rave drove home.

⁓

Rave had never washed a new vehicle. His whole life, all he or his mother had ever owned were secondhand beaters with as many dents as rust spots. Those, he'd run a hose over a few times a year, because, let's face it, they looked about the same, clean or dirty.

"She sure is shining," Tuck said when Rave encouraged him to slip into the driver's seat.

"I detailed the trim work, too." Rave pointed out the spots that had been the grimiest—the coffee cup holder, the area around the radio, the steering wheel. "All the dust from the dirt road will be a constant battle, but at least she can breathe for a while."

"Driveway," Tuck said.

"What?"

"It's a driveway, not a road. No other cars, no other houses, and it's on my property, so that makes it a driveway, doesn't it?"

Rave nodded. "Guess so. How much property do you have?"

"Quite a few acres."

Rave laughed. "Great. If you ever decide to sell, you can put up a sign that says Quite a Few Acres for Sale."

Tuck grinned. "For the price, we can say, 'quite a bit.'"

Rave nodded and used the hem of his T-shirt to wipe at the inside door frame. He'd missed a spot.

"Proud of your work, aren't you?" Seated in the cab, Tuck was eye to eye.

"Guess so." That wasn't all. He liked taking the truck and making it look new again. He liked the ranch house and the barn. He liked the idea of wandering through a swap meet with Tuck on the weekend. In fact, he had some other ideas about the swap meet.

Tuck worked the muscle in his jaw. "I had some maps on the floor. Need those. Where are they?"

"They were covered with mud and something had spilled on them. They're in the trash, Tuck."

The jaw crunching intensified. Rave watched him lower his fingers from the steering wheel and wring his hands. His eyes darted around the cab. What was happiness quickly turned to something else. Despair, maybe.

"Was there something special about the maps?" He could go back to the car wash. They'd be near the top of the garbage can he'd tossed them in.

"No. No, I just . . ."

Rave almost wanted to calm him. He started to reach for Tuck but stopped himself. "We'll buy new maps."

Tuck focused in on him. The frown softened. "OK. New maps."

"Something else I was thinking about . . ." Rave let the words fall away, carried on the wind to be lost on the lake behind the house because he wasn't sure about this. He hadn't thought this through, and it seemed maybe he couldn't think it through without hearing it out loud. "I met a kid at the store today. Buck or something. And he said there's a swap meet in town on weekends. I was thinking we could load up some of the junk you've got inside and sell it. Not a lot, the first week or two. Maybe just a few boxes, but if people like what we have, we could add more."

Tuck's eyes widened. "A week or two. That'd mean you're staying for a while."

45

"Guess I'll have to. Make sure you keep taking care of Ruby."

When Tuck gave him a quizzical look, Rave added, "The truck."

"Oh, Ruby. Suits her. I guess I have been negligent. Old arthritic fingers don't relish holding a scrub brush."

That made Rave feel bad. He hadn't meant to point out any shortcomings of Tuck's. "I'd like to stay for a few more weeks. See how things go."

"Live here?"

"If that'd be OK."

"Son, nothing would make me happier." He raised a finger. "But, every first and third Saturday night is the memorial. If you live here, you don't miss the memorial. Ever. You ever do, and I'll have to ask you to leave."

Seriously? This old man had done everything in his power to get Rave there and to make him a place where he'd want to stay, but miss a memorial—whatever that was—and he'd be out? He'd just started thinking maybe this place was different. Maybe this man was different, but just like everyone else who'd ever entered Rave's life, he came with stipulations. Rave should have known not to let his guard down. "Fine. Whatever." He'd stay until he had a better place to go. Then he'd load his car and hit the road. And never look back. The one thing he'd learned from his mom.

CHAPTER 4

Rave watched Tuck rise from his recliner when the phone rang. It was late on Friday night and for once, Rave thought he might follow Tuck's lead and turn in early. A couple of hours before, they'd finished dinner—steaks on the grill, again. He'd never eaten so much steak in his life. Rave had spent the day poking through boxes to find stuff for the first swap meet. From the living room, he could hear Tuck. It sounded like he was trying to calm someone down. When Tuck stepped around the kitchen door and Rave saw the fire in his eyes, he put down the antique transistor radio and gave Tuck his full attention.

Tuck passed him and went to a cabinet on the far wall. He opened a drawer and before Rave could inquire, he'd strapped a pistol to his waist.

"Whoa. What's happening?"

Tuck checked the pistol for ammo and then pointed above the mantel. "Grab the shotgun."

Rave did as instructed. He'd fired a couple of guns in his lifetime, but he wasn't good with them. Tuck took the pump-action shotgun, checked it, clicked the safety, and grunted, "Come on."

They left Tuck's property and turned onto a dirt road less than a quarter of a mile down the main road away from town. "Trini Barton's place. Some kids are partying out on her land, and the sheriff's not answering her calls."

Her last name was the same as the town. But that wasn't the detail that interested Rave right now. "So, we're going to go—what?—murder them?"

Tuck gave him a disgusted look. "No. Run 'em off if we have to. Let 'em know they can't be there disrupting an old woman."

Rave forced his head to bob. "OK, man. I'm in." The shotgun sat between them, the pistol hung on Tuck's right side. If this went sideways, and he got arrested . . . with his *grandfather* . . . he'd never live it down. There were some things you couldn't recover from. This had to be one of them.

Rave had to admit, this whole toting-guns-in-the-truck thing had him nervous, and the bumpy road to their destination wasn't helping soothe the anxiety. Trini Barton's house was a long, skinny ranch that had yellow paint and white shutters. There was a giant street lamp in her front yard that illuminated an oblong swatch of her property. It looked out of place there in the country rather than lining the homes of a neighborhood. "Almost daytime with that giant streetlight."

Tuck nodded. "Yeah. City put it in for her. She'd called the sheriff one too many times about intruders. Come to find out, a family of raccoons had taken up residence under her front porch. She'd hear them at night. Scared the daylights out of her."

"Is she not used to being alone?" It looked like she'd lived there forever.

"Has been here since her husband died over eight years ago. Being alone never bothered Trini until someone broke into her house. He was a drifter. Druggie. Lookin' for cash or some dope. Anyway, Trini's never been fond of guns, but she chased him out with a baseball bat."

They pulled in alongside a tan SUV, and as soon as they stepped from the truck, Rave could hear music and voices in the distance.

Trini burst through the front door. "Thanks for coming, Tuck. Last time, those hooligans tore up half my pasture."

"You get ahold of the sheriff?" Tuck stopped at the bottom of the steps. Rave stayed beside him.

Trini was petite, about Tuck's age, with her hair pulled back and her light-brown eyes framed with brackets of concern. "I did. He's gone over to Shelby County. Deputy's working an accident out on the highway. I let Sheriff Cogdill know you were handling things here."

Tuck closed his eyes. He clapped a hand on Rave's back. "This here's my grandson, Rave. He's staying with me."

Trini stepped closer. "Is this Sharon's boy? Goodness, he looks like her."

The woman came down the steps but stopped on the bottom where she could look Rave in the eye. She placed her hands on his cheeks. Her fingertips were soft and warm against his skin. She smelled like baby powder. "Welcome to Barton."

"Thank you, ma'am." He itched to get away.

"We'll take a drive over to the pasture, Trini. Get those kids off your land." Tuck hooked his hand on his pistol, very Old West, John Wayne style.

Her gaze lingered on Tuck. "I'd be much obliged."

They got in the truck and bounced down a road that was little more than a path, but Tuck knew the way. More than once, he cranked the wheel to follow the road when it seemed like it would disappear in the tall grass that the headlights illuminated. This would be easier in the daytime.

When they came to a large fallen tree blocking the way, Tuck shoved the truck into Park and got out, mumbling. Rave followed.

Tuck inspected the road, the tree, and the edges of the path where dense foliage would prevent them from going around.

Beyond the tree, he could make out several bodies moving around in the headlights. "They dragged this tree here. Blocked the path to Trini's."

The oak was massive. Tuck pointed out a long fresh scar on the trunk. "Wrapped a chain around it. Probably got a vehicle blocking the main road. I told Trini years ago she needed a gate at the top of that road. It leads right to her hayfield."

If they went to this much trouble to block a back way, Rave didn't think a gate would stop them.

"Well," Tuck said. "Guess we'll have to have a conversation with them from right here."

They went back to the truck, and Tuck reached inside. "Close your ears."

Rave wondered if he was going to fire off a round, but instead, he flattened his hand against the steering wheel, and the horn blared. For a good fifteen seconds, it vibrated over the mountains and echoed back to them. The music stopped.

Tuck yelled over the tree trunk, "You're on private property. Go home."

Rave couldn't imagine anyone going to this much trouble, then packing it up just because an old man yelled and blew a horn at them.

When the music started again, accompanied by laughter, Tuck hit the horn again until the music stopped. "I'm giving you to the count of ten, then I'm taking aim. That pretty little Tacoma with the lift kit—I'm shooting out your windshield first. Now pack it up so I don't have to destroy your trucks."

Rave stared at Tuck. His voice didn't even sound the same. It carried over the pasture, almost as loud as the truck horn had been. Even his posture was different. Standing taller, eyes on alert. Face frozen. The music didn't return—an admission that they were at least considering if the screaming man was serious or not—but there were also no engines starting. The laughter and voices had melted into muted tones that Rave couldn't make out from the distance.

"You leave me no choice." Tuck's voice echoed over the land. He took the shotgun from the cab of the truck.

Over the felled log, Rave saw a single set of taillights. "Hey, one's leaving." And really, he didn't want to get arrested for shooting at teenagers. He'd thought coming to Barton would be boring. So far, it had been anything but that.

Tuck's face was hard. "One's not enough."

The sound of Tuck pumping the shotgun was intensified by the tension-thick air. Rave watched as Tuck slowly raised the barrel until it was aimed at the sky. "Tuck, are you really going to—"

The crack of the gun stopped Rave's words. His hands flew to his ears. They were ringing. Not boring. Definitely not boring. Back in Tampa there were lots of guys who talked tough about carrying guns. In all the time he'd lived there—and even in the rough crowd he'd been trying to stay away from—he'd never seen anyone draw a gun. And certainly not fire one.

Across the pasture, car and truck engines started up. Some yelled at him, but there was no conviction in their words. They were leaving. First vehicle in the parade was the lifted Tacoma.

Tuck grinned. The hardness gone. "Look at 'em. Hightailing it outta here."

Rave had no words. Had they really just done this? Tuck seemed perfectly calm. Like maybe this was a common occurrence. Rave's nerve endings were raw and zinging. Silently, he got in the truck. Tuck offered a grin, turned the truck around, and drove back to Trini's.

Trini was waving at them as they neared her house. Standing on the front porch, with her free hand propped against a broom, she hollered, "That'll teach 'em." Whether she was prepared to sweep the porch or use the broom as a weapon if needed, Rave couldn't say. It all felt a little unreal to him—like maybe he was being punked, and a camera crew would leap out of the woods at any moment.

Rave started to get out of the truck. Tuck stopped him. "You all right?" Thick, bushy brows rode high on Tuck's face.

Rave nodded, but he knew there was no color in his cheeks. "Yeah. I'm good."

They visited with Trini on her porch for a few minutes. Then she disappeared into the house and returned with something that smelled like heaven on Christmas Day. "Blackberry pie. Best in the state."

Rave's mouth watered. Tuck took the pie and headed for the truck. "Thanks, Trini. We'll have it for breakfast."

Rave followed Tuck and the pie, because, hey, what else was there to do? He leaned his head against the headrest as Tuck shifted the Chevy and drove home. The sudden rush of excitement had finally worked its way out of Rave's system, leaving him tired and ready for bed. Of all the adrenaline-laced moments he'd had in his life, this was one he'd not soon forget.

Bullet scratched at his bedroom door early the next morning. Rave opened it and let the dog—tail wagging, mouth panting—come in.

"Hey, Furball." It'd taken Rave a long time to fall asleep after the visit to Trini's. And the sleep he'd had was restless. He just wasn't accustomed to old men drawing guns on teenagers. Rave fell back on the bed and curled under the covers. He'd left his window open, and the chill in the air surprised him. Shouldn't it be warmer out? Back in Florida, late-spring and summer nights were no cooler than the days. If it was eighty-five in the afternoon, it'd feel like eighty-five at midnight. He hadn't acclimated to mountain weather yet.

Bullet jumped onto the bed and landed, paws first, on Rave's stomach. A large muzzle found its way to his neck and a cold nose plant had

Rave laughing. "Get off me." He shoved, but the dog's tail went into spasms, and he barked once and pounced again, this time sending a dripping wet tongue from Rave's armpit to his jaw.

Rave grabbed the dog's head and shoved him away. Bullet rebounded, squared his massive shoulders over Rave—his prey—and barked again, daring him to move.

This time, Rave football tackled him and rolled the dog onto his back. Bullet squirmed but finally calmed, content to have Rave holding him down. "You're all bark," Rave said before letting him loose. Bullet stayed.

"Big baby." Rave dug his fingertips into the thick hair at Bullet's ribs and the dog went still, head lolled to the side, tongue hanging out. It was interesting to Rave that Bullet was careful with Tuck, but with Rave, he could just let go, be the big, hundred-pound bruiser that he was.

"Where's Tuck this morning?" Rave asked the dog. "Have you been out yet?"

Rave pulled on a T-shirt and his jeans, which were crumpled on the bedroom floor. Bullet watched in awe as if he'd never seen anyone dress before. The dog's tail was in perpetual motion until Rave said, "Go outside?"

The big dog spun around twice—there was room to do it now, since they'd cleared out all the computer parts—and ran out of the room with Rave following him and telling him to slow down.

A knock sent Rave to the front door. He'd planned on letting Bullet out the back—like Tuck always did—but when he pulled the door open, the dog shot out, scraping past a man in uniform. Rave's eyes focused in on the sheriff's car first, then on the man.

"I'm here for Tuck Wayne. Is he home?"

Last night's adventure played through Rave's mind. "I'm not sure."

The man removed his sunglasses and sized up Rave. "You his grandson?"

He nodded.

"I'm Sheriff Cogdill. Need to speak to Tuck."

Rave played it cool. This wasn't his first time. Though the sheriff seemed all business, he wasn't coming off as a jerk, so Rave would try to handle this and save Tuck the embarrassment. "I don't think he's feeling well. He's been in bed for a couple days. Maybe I could help you."

The sheriff's eyes narrowed. "Felt good enough to shoot at some kids last night over at the Barton farm."

Rave shook his head. "That wasn't him. That was m—"

From behind him Tuck hollered, "Hey, Martin. What brings you out this early?"

Cogdill stepped past Rave and over to Tuck. The two men met in the center of the living room and gave each other a backslap hug. "You look good, Tuck. How you feeling?"

Rave watched.

"Feel like a million bucks."

Cogdill put his hands on his waist. "And how does a million bucks feel?"

Tuck's shoulders bounced with the laughter as he said, "Like I could attract a million does." What were they laughing at? Then Rave got it. Bucks and does. As in deer. A million bucks and a million does. Was there no end to the redneck humor?

"You want some blackberry pie? Trini sent us home with it last night. It was all I could do to stay out of it and save it for breakfast."

"Trini. That's why I'm here, Tuck." Cogdill followed him into the kitchen, and Rave called for Bullet to come in. The dog ignored him at first, but when he sharpened his tone—the way Tuck did—Bullet stopped his trajectory and turned. He ran full speed into the house.

In the kitchen Tuck put the coffee on and dished up three generous helpings of blackberry pie. Rave's mouth watered.

They sat at the table and ate half the pie before Cogdill continued. "Tuck, you know you can't go off shooting at innocent kids."

"Weren't no innocent kids. They were trespassers. And a person's got a right to protect his property when the law doesn't show up." He spied Cogdill over a heaping spoonful of pie.

The man dropped his spoon to his plate. "I was out of town, Tuck. I would have taken care of it when I returned. You know I always do."

"And Trini is supposed to let them wreck her pasture in the meantime? That ain't the way to handle things, Cogdill. You of all folks should know that."

Cogdill released a surrendering sigh. "The law is the law."

"And yet you show up at my door. Who's the law protecting? The innocent? Or the trespassing criminals?" Tuck stood from the table. "I'm not apologizing for what I did. And if Trini calls, I'll do it again. Arrest me. Don't. That's up to you. But I won't have teenagers terrorizing my neighbors and sit aside and watch. You know me, Cogdill."

The man scraped the fork over his plate, back and forth as if considering his options or possibly considering more pie. "Then we've got to find another way to protect Trini's land. This happens again, and one of the parents issues a complaint, I'll have to take you in."

Tuck sat back in his chair. "Then take me in."

It was a challenge. Rave split his glances between the two men. Cogdill didn't appreciate the defiance. Rave needed to do something. "Tuck, didn't you say a gate might keep them out?"

"At the main road. They won't drive past Trini's house to get to the pasture because she'd be able to get all their license plate numbers. We block that entrance, it might be enough."

Rave sat up. "If all you need is license plate numbers, I could get those. We know some of the makes of vehicles that were there last night. The small hatchback that left first. Couldn't tell the color. Then there was the lifted Tacoma. It was white, no doubt about that one."

The sheriff dropped his fork to his plate. It clanged and splattered blackberry goo over the table. The air in the room changed, and Rave knew he'd said the wrong thing, but he didn't know what that was. The tension between Tuck and Cogdill thickened.

Cogdill broke the silence. "You know there's a kid in the next county with the same truck as Glen, Tuck."

"Yeah," Tuck agreed and rubbed a hand over his chin. "Seems a far way to come to cause trouble but not impossible."

"Glen was home watching a movie. He told me."

Tuck nodded but didn't look convinced. "No one's accusing him, Martin."

Cogdill chewed his cheek. "I'll talk to the guys at the logging company. See if we can't get a heavy-duty gate out there for Trini. Don't know what it'll cost, but I'll chip in."

"Me, too. See what the guys can do, and let me know."

They stood, and Tuck led Cogdill to the door. "In the meantime, keep your firearms at home, Tuck."

"You know I got a legal right to carry."

"A right. Doesn't mean a license to use them to scare kids. I know you weren't firing at them. If I thought you were, I'd confiscate the weapons and haul you to jail." He added, "Thanks for the pie. Might be Trini's best. Pass the word to her for me, would you?"

Tuck opened the door, letting a mountain breeze fly inside. "Will do."

When Tuck closed the door and turned around, he said to Rave, "You've got that confused look on your face again."

Rave shook his head. "Just weird. Like *Mayberry* meets *Fargo*."

"What do you know about *Mayberry*? Isn't that a little before your time?"

"Yeah. But my girlfriend's son watches this channel on cable that has all the old black-and-white shows. He's crazy about them. *I Love Lucy*, *Andy Griffith*, especially that one with the talking horse."

"*Mister Ed*," Tuck said.

"Yeah. He used to watch *Twilight Zone*, but it was giving him nightmares, so his mom made him stop."

"Kids these days." Tuck motioned for Rave to follow him out back. They took their coffee and sat on the back porch, where they could watch the fish jump in the lake. A single boat skated across the silvery, smooth water.

Tuck was unusually thoughtful today. Hands together on his lap, one thumb ran over the bumpy skin of the other. Rave watched, splitting his time between Tuck and the small runabout gliding over the water. "We've got the memorial this evening. Don't forget."

It must be important to Tuck because at the mention, it seemed like a lifetime of memories played across his face. Intense enough to keep Rave from asking too many questions about the thing, though every cell of his body wanted to. "I won't forget," Rave answered. "Tuck?"

It took a moment for him to acknowledge. "Yes?"

Not *too many* questions, but he'd like an idea about what he was in for. "Is the memorial for someone? Grandma Millie, maybe?"

Tuck shrunk a little in his chair. "No. Not for Millie."

The weight of old sorrow was thick enough to cut. Rave opted for a subject change. He'd know about the memorial soon enough. "What line of work were you in before you retired?"

"After the army I came here and became an electrician. Ended up with my own crews and eventually my own company. When I retired, I sold it to Albert Brine. He's still here in town."

Rave's mind toyed with the new knowledge. He needed a skill. Now that he had a roof over his head, maybe he could consider taking some classes.

It was a moment before he realized Tuck's full attention had shifted to him. "Why do you ask?"

Rave lifted and dropped one shoulder. "I was just thinking that it's time I learn a skill. You think I'd be good at electrical work?"

All of Tuck's face smiled. It was as if each wrinkle had its own intent—and all were thrilled at this new possibility. "Yes, sir, I do."

Rave chewed his cheek. "If I decide to stick around, is that something you could start teaching me?"

Tuck was nodding before Rave could finish. "I'd love that. And when you're ready, I'll give Albert a call and see if we can't get you on as an apprentice."

Rave raised a finger. "If I stay."

Tuck slowly nodded. "If you stay."

Before them, the lake shimmered with the morning sun. A breeze trickled over the smooth expanse of the water, giving it ripples that stretched from the bank to the far side of the shore.

Several minutes passed before Tuck said, "You never mentioned you have a girl back in Florida."

Raven leaned his head back. "That's because I don't. She dumped me for a guy she thinks could be her son's father."

"How old is the boy?" Tuck mimicked him, resting his head on his chair.

"He's four. Really smart. Man, he's got a smile as bright as daytime."

Tuck's fingers unthreaded on his lap. "Miss him, don't you?"

Rave looked away. "Yeah."

"There's plenty of cash in the cookie jar if you want to go visit."

If only things were that easy. "I can't. His mom doesn't want me around him. Said it's too confusing, since she's trying to build a relationship with the dad."

Tuck sighed. "That's a tough break. You talk to her lately?"

"No." It was just too painful. He'd gone to her house that night. Daniel was already in bed, and she refused to wake him up to let Rave say good-bye. He'd left the items with her and drove away fighting the tears and wishing he could have given Daniel one last hug.

When Tuck stood to go inside, Rave swiped at his cheek. A procession of ducks rose from the water and took flight. Tuck was gone for only a moment, then returned and hovered over Rave's shoulder. "You know the worst part about growing old?"

Rave shook his head but didn't look up.

"Living with regret." He placed a hand on Rave's shoulder and squeezed. A moment later, he dropped a cordless phone into Rave's lap. Then he went inside and closed the slider door.

Rave rolled the phone over and over in his hand until the cool plastic had warmed. Ash would likely be home. It was her day off. Saturday, so Daniel would be home, too. It wasn't too early, so he wouldn't wake them if he called. All in all, he couldn't have picked a better time to reach out. He turned on the phone, listened to the buzz, shut it off before dialing.

What was his problem? But that was easy enough to answer. He was in love with Ashley. Even hearing her voice—and the new distance and aggravation in it since Barry showed up—hurt. It hurt so deep in his heart, he almost couldn't bear it.

But what if she let him talk to Daniel? He could explain why he was gone. Not the part about Ashley making him leave, but that he had a grandpa he needed to visit. Daniel would understand that. The smart four-year-old had asked Rave where his mommy and daddy were and if he had a grandpa like on *The Waltons*. Daniel had only watched a few episodes of that show before losing interest in the in-depth story lines. It was no *Mister Ed*.

Rave turned on the phone, dialed Ashley's cell, and held the receiver tightly against his ear.

She answered with a groggy, "Hello?"

"Ash, it's Rave."

In the background, he could hear sheets and blankets moving. Her voice was bedroom soft when she yawned and it made him ache to be there. To hold her. She was probably in the oversize T-shirt she slept in and fuzzy socks. The memory made him smile.

"Rave, why are you calling?"

He closed his eyes. She didn't sound mad, just uncertain. "Are you in your favorite sleep shirt?"

A long, surrendering sigh came through the phone line, so close he could almost feel her breath. "You shouldn't be calling." But there was no conviction in her words. He'd caught her in a weakened state, fresh out of sleep.

"Dark-pink fuzzy socks? And a full glass of water sitting on your nightstand."

She giggled but stifled it. "I dreamed about you last night."

Those words caused Rave's throat to close. "I dream about you every night, Ash. I miss you."

I miss you, too. He willed the words from her lips, but she only sighed again.

Rave cleared his throat. "How are things with Barry?"

A long pause. That was a good sign. "He's talking about moving in here."

A poker stabbed Rave's heart. "That's kind of fast, isn't it?"

"It's not like we just met. We dated before. Plus, his dad is going to turn over one of the car lots to Barry, the little one on Main Street. He just bought it. Anyway, it's just logistically easier if he lives here."

Rave bit his tongue until it bled. "How is he with Daniel?"

Another long pause had Rave's heart pounding.

"He doesn't really know him yet. And Daniel doesn't help matters by constantly saying, 'That's not how Rave does it.' I swear, Rave, if I didn't know better, I'd think you were coaching my son how to get rid of Barry."

The smile that spread across Rave's face calmed his aching nerves. *He doesn't belong there. I do. Don't blame Daniel for understanding that.*

The sheets hummed as Ashley moved around. "Barry's father really likes us. Barry said that was good. Once the car lot is turned over, his dad is going to help us buy a house."

The thought sat in Rave's stomach like a rock. "Ash, I know the future was scary. But are you sure this is the right—"

She cut him off. "The right thing? I don't know, Rave. How does anyone know if they're doing the right thing? What I do know is that near the end of every week I have to add water to the gallon of milk in the fridge so Daniel can have cereal. I count out hot dogs and days till my next paycheck. I'm being offered a chance, a real chance. How can I not take it?"

"Do you love him, Ash?" It was a simple question.

"I'll love not having to wonder if we'll have gas money. I'll love being able to buy Daniel new school clothes. You should be happy for Daniel."

A rustling sound came over the line. "Mommy, who's on the phone?"

Rave closed his eyes. Hearing Daniel's soft morning voice—even from so far away—shredded his heart.

"Go watch TV, Daniel, I'll be out in a few minutes."

"Do we have Pop-Tarts?" His sweet little Muppet voice. Rave pressed the phone harder to his ear, hoping to capture—to remember—every word.

"Yes, I'll make you some in a minute."

"'Kay, Mommy." Rave heard little feet shuffling, growing farther and farther away.

"Let me talk to him." It was a desperate plea.

"No, Rave," she hissed. "Barry's coming over to get us in an hour. The last thing I need is Daniel ratting me out."

"Ash, listen . . ." *Think fast.* "I can tell him to give Barry a chance. Tell him not to keep talking about me."

"Why would you do that?" Suspicion laced her words.

His hand fisted over his chest. "Because I love you, Ash. And I want you to be happy."

Time seemed to stop. There was no noise on the other end of the line. Rave wondered if he'd gone too far until he heard Ashley call Daniel to the phone.

Rave stood up on the porch, nervous energy driving him out of his seat. He waited.

"Rave?" Little-boy excitement crackled through the line.

"Hey, buddy. I miss you."

"I miss you, too, Rave. When are you coming home? Will you be back in a jiffy?"

Rave glanced into the house. There at the table, Tuck was setting out breakfast plates. They'd already filled up on pie. "That's just it, Rock Star. I've got to stay here."

"Forever?" His small voice dropped.

"For a while. I want you to do me a favor. But first, I have a question for you about Mommy's new friend. Daniel, is he nice to you?"

"He's OK. He doesn't yell or anything, and he bought me a new Ninja bicycle. How'd he know that was the one I wanted for almost forever?"

Rave bit down hard. "He did that, huh?"

"It was here when I woke up one morning."

Rave squeezed his eyes shut. "Daniel, as long as he's good to you, it's better not to talk about me."

"What if he stops being good to me?"

Rave opened his mouth, and the words left before he could stop them. "If that ever happens, you tell him I'm your guardian angel. You tell him I'm always watching, and if he ever hurts you, I'll hunt him down and—"

That's when Ashley grabbed the phone. She put her palm over the receiver, but Rave could still hear a muffled request for Daniel to go watch cartoons. "Good job, Rave. I should have known you'd try to sabotage us."

"You told him the bike was from Barry." How could she have done that? He knew Ashley was trying to build a future with the guy, but to sell out Rave to Daniel in the process . . . it just wasn't right.

"I had no choice," she huffed. "You're already one cloud lower than Jesus himself in Daniel's eyes. Did you really think I'd give Daniel more reason to go on about how you walk on water?"

Loyalty was something Daniel understood. His mom could learn from him. "I'm sorry." He didn't want Daniel to think he walked on water, but he did want him to know Rave would always be there for him. Always.

"I have to go."

"Bye, Ash. I love you." The phone clicked so quickly, Rave was certain she hadn't heard.

CHAPTER 5

Rave came down the stairs a few minutes before eight o'clock Saturday evening. Tuck had told him the memorial began at eight, and if Tuck's demeanor was any indication of the seriousness of the occasion, he'd best be on time.

Most of the lamps were off except in the dining room, where the light from overhead spilled onto the table. There, Tuck was setting out multiple shot glasses. "Need a hand?" Rave asked, less because he thought Tuck needed one and more because he was hoping Tuck would explain. A bottle of whiskey sat in the center of the table.

"Nope," Tuck answered as he unscrewed the top of the bottle.

"Are we expecting company?" Rave glanced through the darkened house. "I can turn on the porch light."

Tuck motioned for him to sit on a chair he'd pulled up to the table. He also noticed there was no shot glass in front of his chair. Or Tuck's, for that matter.

"Company's already here." Tuck used an open palm to gesture toward the table. "Boys, meet Rave. Rave, meet the boys."

Alarm slid down Rave's spine.

Tuck laughed. "Ah, don't be looking at me like I lost my marbles. Sit down, son. It'll make sense soon enough."

Rave did as instructed, the quiet of the house surrounding him. Tuck sat as well and moved the bottle of whiskey until it touched the first shot glass. He poured to the rim as he said, "In honor of you, Private First Class Sam Louden, in memory of your heroic acts during the Vietnam War."

Rave swallowed hard but opted to breathe shallow, for it seemed that even a deep intake of air would disrupt the ghosts in the room.

Tuck's face glowed in the single light, the brackets framing his eyes, deep caverns of memory. "Sam was from Kentucky. He loved football, farming, and a girl named Bella Reece. He always said she was too good for him, but a finer soldier you'd never hope to meet. You saved my bacon one night, didn't you, Sam? We were both laid up in a MASH unit, and some VC crazy snuck past the guards. I woke up to find a knife to my throat. You knocked that guy in the head with a bedpan, of all things. A bedpan saved my life." Tuck chuckled, his eyes far away and glistening with nostalgia.

Rave knew the night would be a long one. He didn't want to be here. He didn't want to see Tuck so vulnerable. And that's how he looked to Rave—vulnerable, breakable, easy to fell. The masks Tuck usually wore—so readily worn by so many people, especially men—fell away as he spoke, half the time to a man who wasn't there and half the time in memory of his fallen friend. Each new story made Rave feel a little more exposed, as if in sharing the memories, he'd somehow become a part of them. He didn't want to hear how these men had suffered. How they'd died. Because to know meant a certain amount of responsibility.

Tuck continued. "I was with you the day you died. The sun rose like any other day, the heat scorched our heads, and we worked our way through that steam room of a jungle. We'd gotten bad intel. Just recon, they'd told us. The enemy camp was supposed to be empty. You'd taken point. I remember the look you gave me, right before swinging your rifle around and starting off ahead of the rest of us. I'll never forget that look, Sam. It was like you knew. It was like you knew you were going to die. Do you remember that moment?"

Rave forced his eyes closed for a few seconds.

"You looked up at the sky and said, 'One day we'll all go home.' That's what you told me. Bullets started flying not two minutes later. I tried to get to you, Sam. I belly-crawled over half the field, but they kept pushing us back. When I finally got to you, you were gone. Flat on your back and staring up at that same sky. We carried you out. Took turns because the landing zone was a couple clicks away. All the way back to the chopper, I heard you saying over and over in my head, 'One day we'll all go home.'"

Tuck reached over and took the full shot glass. He raised it high. "Rest, my friend. You are not forgotten." Tuck downed the drink and replaced the glass. He turned to the next seat. "Corporal Manny Hernandez. Manny was from New York, and what we didn't know about big-city living, he happily shared with all us yokels."

Tuck went on talking until late in the night. Rave sat quietly. There were no words that could be spoken without interrupting something he didn't even feel like he should be watching. There had been five full glasses. By the time Tuck had drank the last one, his speech was slurred and his eyes glassy. When Tuck stood and stumbled, Rave caught him. Bullet, who'd remained faithfully at Tuck's feet, moved out of their way. "Let me help you get to bed," Rave told Tuck. How Tuck could even have the energy to stand up was astounding after all the memories he'd relived in the last few hours.

Tuck slung his arm over Rave's shoulder. "You're a good boy."

Rave grinned. "You're a really good old man." He meant it. What kind of man put himself through that kind of torture for the sake of remembering friends?

"Do you know what REST means?" Tuck's voice was low.

"Nope."

"It's an acrorym—acrome—no wait, it's an acronym."

Rave flipped on lights as they made their way up the stairs and down the long hall to Tuck's bedroom.

"It means Remember Every Soldier Today. REST."

Rave deposited Tuck on the bed.

Tuck leaned up as Rave unlaced his grandfather's boots. "That's what we do at the memorial. We remember every soldier."

"It's a nice tribute, Tuck." And something he did twice a month. Rave was exhausted just experiencing this once. No way could he do this again in two weeks.

"They were my men." A distinct hint of responsibility rang in those words. "Even though they're gone, they're still my boys. I'm still watching over them."

Rave sat down on the edge of the bed and pulled the covers over his grandfather. "And who watches over you, Tuck?"

Tuck pulled at the blankets until they were under his chin. He blinked once, but it looked like a struggle to coax his lids to reopen. "Millie does."

When Rave heard the deep-chested rumble of sleep, he stood. "Now I do, too," he whispered too quietly for Tuck to hear. Still, he couldn't explain the smile that appeared on Tuck's face after the words drifted from his mouth and landed like butterflies after a storm.

Bullet sat outside Tuck's door. Rave motioned to the dog. "Come on, let's clean up."

⁂

Rave was quiet as he worked the next morning. The memorial weighed heavily on his mind. Last night, he'd watched a man empty out the contents of his heart. He'd heard stories that rocked him, stripped him to his core, and left him both sad and confused about Tuck's incredible young men and what they'd accomplished in their duty to their country. Many of them would have been younger than Rave was right now. Death, he supposed, didn't take age into account when doling out its offerings.

He figured Tuck would sleep it off for the better part of the day. Instead, Rave had found him in the kitchen making coffee. Tuck silently drank a cup while staring into the deep unknown of the kitchen wall. The air around them still felt electric with the raw emotion of the previous night. Every time Rave opened his mouth to speak, the words stalled. He decided to change the tone of the day. He was curious about the girl he'd met in town, so he turned the conversation to Rebecca and asked Tuck about her. He learned that she helped Trini—who was practically family to Rebecca—on Sunday afternoons. That was a morsel of information he couldn't ignore.

As late morning shifted to early afternoon, Rave gave Tuck space. He supposed the older man wasn't accustomed to having a visitor there for the memorial. But it had been Tuck who'd insisted. Still, the runaway emotions must be raw. All Rave's sufferings paled when compared to what Tuck had experienced in the war.

For three hours, Rave worked to organize the next bedroom. Though a daybed took up one corner, the sewing table and other items along the far wall suggested that the room had once been used by Millie. And yet, it was the bedroom across the hall that stayed locked. Rave was careful as he chose items for the next swap meet even though Tuck had given him the go-ahead to clear the room. Anything that seemed of a personal nature, he left alone. He didn't touch the closet, which still had hand-decorated sweaters folded on the shelf and pairs of tennis shoes on the floor. They must belong to Millie, his grandmother. It still felt surreal to Rave that he had grandparents, even if Millie was gone. She'd lived, and the evidence of her life surrounded him. At one moment, he'd reached into the closet and lifted one of the sweaters to his nose. It smelled like rose water and wet newspapers. Faint, but unmistakably a personal scent that must be his grandmother's. Eyes closed, he imagined her. A face decayed by years; thin, soft hair; a grandma pooch of a stomach.

Rave closed the closet door, leaving Millie inside. One day, he'd ask Tuck about her. But not today. There were enough ghosts in the house after the memorial.

He'd worked up a sweat cleaning, so Rave showered, used some Aqua Velva, because that's what Tuck had in the medicine cabinet, and changed into clean jeans and a white T-shirt. He had a plan. With the cleaned pie pan on his passenger seat, Rave drove his car over to Trini's house.

His palms grew sweaty as soon as he knocked on Trini's front door. He heard movement inside, and when the door swung open, he found himself smiling.

Rebecca had a bandana wrapped around her forehead, and there was sweat on her brow and a mop in her free hand. It was a moment before she said, "City boy."

His brow went up, and he fought the urge to look down at her tan legs beneath the jeans shorts she wore. "Redneck girl."

A smile almost formed on her face. "Are you here for Trini?"

Not really. "Yeah," he lied. "Returning the pie pan. And wondering if her pasture was OK after Friday night."

Rebecca cocked her head and rested her palm on the top of the mop. "What happened Friday night?"

He motioned behind him. "Some people were out here partying."

Rebecca's eyes narrowed. "Again?" A bevy of emotions ran over her features, turning her green eyes to angry emeralds. There was a smattering of freckles across her tanned nose and cheeks, like spilled salt on a table—no real pattern but an undeniable design.

He nodded, content to stand there and watch the play of reactions on her face. It was entertaining, no doubt. When she spun away from him and propped her mop on the doorjamb, he glanced over her legs. *Nice. Tan. Long.*

She twisted her feet into a nearby pair of tennis shoes that had once been white but were stained a dingy shade of gray. Her butt wiggled back and forth, and Rave enjoyed the display while she wrestled the shoes onto her feet. She yelled, "Be right back, Trini."

There was a grunt from somewhere deep in the house.

She barreled past him out the front door. When he didn't follow, she turned. "Are you comin'?"

Maybe Rave had missed part of the conversation. She hadn't said anything, right? Or had she, and he'd been distracted watching her rear end shift from side to side, the muscles in her upper thighs flexing and—"Where are we going?"

She stopped at the base of the steps. "To check the pasture. Why you came, remember?"

"Yeah." He set the pie pan on the porch swing by the front door and followed her.

They started down the path where Tuck had driven three nights before. It was easy to see the way in the daylight, unlike the nighttime twists and turns they'd taken on Friday.

Rebecca ran a hand over the tops of the tall grass as they walked. "Why hadn't you visited Tuck before?"

The trees quivered with a soft breeze that caused the grass blades to whistle. "I didn't know about him."

Rebecca stopped and turned to look at Rave, her eyes catching fire from the sun above. "You didn't know you had a grandfather? How does that happen?"

"My mom told me all our relatives were dead."

Rebecca sucked in a breath. "Why would she do that?"

Rave rolled his shoulder. "She had a lot of problems."

Rebecca held his gaze. "What kind of problems?"

What was she fishing for? "I don't know. Problems. Drugs, guys, mental problems. She lied a lot."

"Where is she now?"

He opened his mouth, but nothing came out.

Rebecca put her hands on her hips and angled into the sun. "I'm sorry. I'm too nosy. Ask too many questions. But it feels like I don't get a real picture of someone without giving them the third degree."

Rave moved a little closer to her. "Are you trying to get a real picture of me?"

A quizzical look flashed over her face. "I do with everyone. You're not special, city boy."

"How do you know?"

She shook her head. "I've met guys like you."

"You realize what a contradiction that is, don't you? In one breath you're trying to figure me out, and in the next you're suggesting you know all about me."

She crossed her arms. "I do. I know you're from the city. Somewhere warmer than here, because you tend to react to the breeze by hunching your shoulders and squeezing your arms to your sides. There are sun streaks running through the blond in your hair. Also, you've got a dark tan—not a farmer tan, either. So, my bet would be a coastline. Florida, maybe."

"Why not California?"

Her gaze drifted over him from his face to his shoes and back. "No. Not California."

She was pretty good.

"How can you tell?"

She grinned. "Your car has a Florida license plate."

He laughed. "Nice. You're observant for a redneck."

"And you're gullible for a city boy." Her smile faded. "You didn't answer me. Where's your mom now?"

"Dead, I think."

"Oh, wow, Rave. I'm sorry." New emotions played in her features.

"I don't know for sure, but I mean I think she would have made her way back to Tampa if she was still alive." He started walking, the fallen tree coming into view ahead.

The breeze caught Rebecca's hair, and she gathered it over one shoulder. It smelled like strawberries. "How long has it been since you've seen her?"

"Over five years." The sorrow for him was palpable. "She said she was going to the store one day and never came back."

"She just left?" Becca's bright-green eyes widened, catching afternoon sun rays.

"She was a drug addict. We moved around a lot while I was growing up. Georgia, Alabama, and finally Florida. Those are the states I remember. She always talked about going to Texas. We never had a real home, just places to sleep. Houses or apartments, but no place to call our own."

"That had to be a really rough way to grow up."

"It could have been worse. I always knew she loved me. At least, until she left. When I was small, I thought everyone lived like we did. I didn't know how bad things were until I went to school and realized some kids had lived in their houses since they were born. My favorite place to live was Tampa. It felt more like home than anywhere else."

"I've never been there. What's it like?"

"It's awesome. Great music scene, lots of stuff to do. It's a fairly big city, though, so a person can get taken if they're not careful."

She stepped around the tree trunk. "I'd probably be there like five minutes and get robbed blind."

"Nah, you seem pretty tough. Haven't you traveled much?"

"Hardly." They'd walked a few yards from the downed tree. "I got to go to New York once. With my marching band. Really cool, but not like I'd imagined."

"What do you mean?"

She paused. "I'd heard so much about it—the screaming cabbies, the loud Italian accents everywhere, people being rude, and lots of pickpockets. It didn't seem like that at all. People there were . . . just people. Our cabdriver was really friendly."

Rave listened, content to watch the way her fingers touched the runaway strands of her hair.

"In my mind I'd created this almost alien place. But New York was normal." She tilted her head back and forth. "Kind of normal."

"Would you go back?"

She stared up at the gathering clouds. "I'd go anywhere." There was a sadness in her tone.

"Why don't you?"

Her eyes dropped to his. "Because I live here. My life is here. My world is here."

"That doesn't mean you can't travel."

She swallowed, and the vein in her throat moved. "Sometimes it does." Rebecca walked on, closing off the conversation.

They inspected the field, but Rave had no idea what they were looking for, so he walked around, stomping the ground and digging his toe into the soft earth every now and again when Rebecca glanced at him.

She lifted her shoulders and dropped them. "Everything looks OK."

Rave agreed.

"From her yard, Trini can keep an eye on the road if she stands near that giant tree. Did you notice it? The massive, green, witch-hat-shaped blob?"

"The one that looks like a Christmas tree?"

Rebecca nodded and turned him by the shoulders. There, far off in the background, the top of the large pine reached toward the sky. "She decorates it every year. A billion or more lights."

The pressure of her hands on his shoulders warmed him. "That's a lot of electricity."

"People from all around come to see it. It's cool."

Would he see it? It was spring now. Rave toyed with the idea of sticking around that long. He knew he wouldn't. Still, it was kind of neat to make a plan, even if it wasn't going to happen.

When they made it back to Trini's, he planted a hand on the porch banister. If he didn't say what was on his mind, he'd chicken out. "You want to go out sometime?"

She was halfway to the door and stopped midstep. "No."

That hadn't gone the way he'd hoped. "Why not? City boy, redneck girl. Seems like a perfect match."

She turned to face him. "I broke up with someone not that long ago. Summer is right around the corner, and that's a really busy time for me."

"I just broke up with someone, too. Or, she broke up with me. I'm not looking for a girlfriend, Becca. I'm not looking to consume a huge chunk of your space, just—you know, go out sometime."

She was going to say yes. He could sense it. "Thanks, Rave. But no. I'll give Trini the pie pan."

She left him standing on the steps. He stared at the heavy wooden door that had closed behind her. He still loved Ash. That, he knew. But having someone to talk to who was near his own age would be nice. "Not giving up on you, redneck girl," he hollered at the closed door. He instantly felt silly until a blind in the front window moved and her face appeared. She shook her head at him, but the grin was impossible to hide. "Go home," she mouthed through the glass.

He turned and headed to his car, passing the giant pine tree. Christmas wasn't *that* far away.

☙

Tuck was happy to see Phil when he arrived at a quarter past nine. More than a week had passed since the memorial, but Tuck and Rave hadn't spoken of it. Tuck knew it had left Rave with a lot to think about. Phil had come to take Tuck to the doctor. That had been his habit for the last six months or so, after Dr. Rice and Phil ganged up on him. That's how he thought of it, anyway. And Julius Morehound, down at the pharmacy, was a coconspirator. All of them. Traitors. What seventy-six-year-old man needed heart medicine? In Tuck's mind, a ticker was supposed to just give out one day. That's how it was meant to be. You didn't go dousing it with medication, trying to slow the inevitable. He'd reluctantly added the heart pills to his other medications. But he was an unwilling participant. This was his body, after all. It ought to be *his* choice. At the same time, now that Rave was there, he was glad he had friends who cared. He could overlook their busybody ways.

Phil shook Rave's hand as he stepped inside. "Good to see you, young man. Looks like Tuck is fattening you up a bit."

Filled out, Rave called it. He sure looked better than when he'd arrived. Less stress framing his eyes. It was too much for a young man to carry. Of course, at that tender age, Tuck had carried a good bit as well.

Rave smiled and started to say something, but the phone in the kitchen rang. "I'll grab that so you two can get going."

He disappeared into the other room. A moment later, Rave's head popped back in, excitement lighting his eyes. "It's Ash. Ashley. She's calling from Tampa."

Tuck's heart swelled a bit. Rave had wanted to share that news before they left for the doctor. Wanted to share it with *him*. His grandfather.

Phil hooked a thumb toward the kitchen. "That boy looks happy."

Tuck nodded. "That's his girl back in Tampa. He's got it bad for her."

Phil slapped him on the back. "You ought to feel pretty special. Boy's giving up time with a girl to hang out with you."

It was special. It was an honor. Even if Rave and the girl were on the rocks. "Well, it isn't that simple. She's got a young son and is trying to reconcile with the father."

"You know, an old friend once told me, things always work out. And when you think it's the darkest hour, you know the sun is getting ready to rise."

That's what Millie used to say. Tuck grabbed his light jacket from the back of the chair as Phil stepped outside. Tuck was always cold these days. Old-man cold. Like life was slipping away from him, escaping from the inside out. It left a chill in its wake. He supposed the rest of his days, be they few years or many, he'd continue to get colder and colder until one day they'd lower him into the stony ground, and the transition from warm-blooded being to chilled and lifeless statue would be complete.

That was all right with him. He was ready to cross that beautiful river and take Millie's hand. That's how he'd dreamed it once. The most beautiful place imaginable, a lush garden with brilliantly colored flowers and a crystal river. Millie was in her favorite church dress, her feet bare, and she was as young and beautiful as the day he'd married her. All those years ago when he'd felt like life was done.

They'd met by accident. She was kicking a flat tire on the side of the road. He had been home from the war for three months, spending his days in Gatlinburg with the family and his nights laying outside on a sleeping bag on the back porch because the house felt too small, too tight, like it was about to fall in on him. One day he'd gone for a drive and ended up deep in the mountains near Gatlinburg. When he reached the crossroads, rather than follow the sign home he'd turned and headed south.

He'd not been right in the head. That he knew. And life was waiting. But he wasn't ready to live it. And then, he'd seen Millie.

CHAPTER 6

1975

"Stupid, stupid car." Her hands were fisted, and she pounded on the hood.

Keep driving, Tuck's mind warned him. *You know hostile territory when you see it. Nothin' but danger there.*

But the blonde looked up as his car slowed. The sun glinted off the gold in her hair. Long, gorgeous locks he'd like to sink his hands into because there was nothing that felt better than fingers in a woman's hair. It was one of the things he missed most while serving. The heat of a woman's flesh, the scent of her skin. Tuck closed his eyes for a few moments as his car came to a stop a few yards before hers.

She leaned into the passenger window, propping her forearms on the sill. Already, a scent like mint and fresh berries entered his nose. If he was like Mack, he'd say something brilliant about the car being a worthy opponent in a boxing match but hard to beat. Mack always had a line for the ladies. He'd tried to teach the other guys in the unit, but it became more of a game than anything. "Mack, what do you say to a woman who gets dumped and left in a bar?" "Mack, how do you pick up a woman who's out with her girlfriends?" "Mack, how do you—" It went on and on for months. The situations became outlandish. The pickup lines hilarious. And right now, with the pretty blonde staring at him, Tuck couldn't access a single one.

"Are—are you going my way?" As soon as the words left his mouth, he shrank. *Goin' my way?* That was the best he could do?

He hadn't really made eye contact with her yet, so he mustered his energy and looked over. Into a sea of feminine perfection. Straight blonde hair, parted in the middle, framed her face in a flawless A shape. Her lips were full, her flesh moist from the sun and the battle with the car. Her midriff top showed off a flat, tanned belly. High-waist sailor shorts with oversize white buttons drew more attention than they should, and Tuck knew he was blushing.

When his eyes returned to hers, there was a smile on her face. A knowing smile, a Cheshire smile. She had a white peace sign painted on her cheek. Faded, as if it'd suffered through a full night.

Finally, she answered him. "I don't know. Which way are you going?" She angled her head and stared down the long road before them.

Well, that was the question, wasn't it? *Which way are you going?* If he'd only had an answer that worked. An answer that fit, that made sense. He'd taken a road leading south. Instead of home—that's all he knew. Tuck tapped the steering wheel with his thumb. "I don't know." He needed to explain, give her something logical, or she'd think he was a lunatic. At the same time, something in her demeanor begged for honesty. "All I know is, I'm not ready to go back."

She stood. Her hands folded over her stomach. Her slender arms rose and fell with each of her breaths. Over the drone of his engine, he thought he heard her say, "Good. Let's not go back together." A moment later, she reached in, pulled up the lock on his '68 Oldsmobile

442, and opened the door. Tan legs entered his car first, and Tuck felt his temperature rise.

"I'm Millicent, but everyone calls me Millie." She held her hand out to him.

"I'm Tuck. Everyone calls me Tuck." Her fingers were warm velvet, but when she shook his hand—firmly, not daintily like a lady should— he knew there was some granite at her core.

"Answer me three questions, Tuck." She tilted on the seat so she could look at him fully.

"Fire away."

"Are you a crazed maniac who means me harm?" The intensity of her gaze vibrated through the air between them, causing it to feel electric.

"No. I am not."

"Have you ever hurt a woman?"

Tuck swallowed hard. A hut flashed before his eyes, a woman screaming, a misplaced bullet. Tuck closed off the image. "No."

"Do you promise not to hurt me?"

Tuck placed a hand over his heart because that was a vow he could keep. So many he'd not been able to while he was in Vietnam. *We're getting outta this, I promise.* He couldn't count how many times he'd held the hand of a dying soldier, telling him he was going to be OK. Telling him he was going home. "I swear, Millicent. I will never, ever harm you."

She smiled, her cheeks moving the edges of her hair. She mimicked his posture and placed a hand over her heart. "Then I promise to do the same. I won't hurt you, either, Tuck." The depths of her blue eyes darkened. Her word was as solid as his own, of that he was sure.

"Where are we headed?" He hooked a thumb behind him. "And what about your car, Millie?"

She glanced back. "It's not mine. I'm not even supposed to be driving it. I don't have a license. It belongs to the guy who broke my heart by spending the night with one of my friends."

"You stole his car?" Tuck had to grin at that one.

"No, I stole his keys, the car just came along for the ride."

"So, where to, auto thief?"

She turned on the radio, and Elton John's voice singing about Bennie and the Jets filled the silence. "I don't care. Just drive."

⁓

Rave slipped out the back door and sat on a lounge chair where he could look out over the lake and imagine Ashley beside him. His hand had gone sweaty holding the phone. "How's Daniel?"

"He's fine, sleeping in this morning. Still misses you. Still talks about you, but not to Barry. Not that it matters much now." Her words were breathy, filled with concern or distraction or some other thing Rave couldn't put his finger on.

"What's wrong, Ash?" Just hearing her voice, just listening to her made the ache in his chest that much stronger.

"Nothing." Too cheery. Something was off. "I don't want to talk about things here. Tell me about you, Rave. Tell me what it's like seeing your grandfather."

He had to pull a few calming breaths before continuing because this was how it should be. How it was supposed to be. The two of them talking about everything. "It's kind of great."

"So, he didn't want you to come to help pay his bills or put you to work or something?"

An eagle swooped over the glass-calm lake, wings tipping against the wind. "No. Not at all. He's kind of a pack rat, so we've been clearing out boxes of junk and mostly storing them in the barn."

"A barn? Is he a farmer?"

"Not really. He's got a large plot of land—quite a few acres." Saying that made Rave grin. "I don't know if he ever really worked the land here. He was an electrician by trade until he retired. I know my grand-mother Millie had a vegetable garden."

"That sounds really nice. Electricians make a lot of money." Money was something Ash had always been preoccupied with. If you had money, you were a little higher on her importance list. It was a character flaw Rave found easy to overlook, since she'd never had money. He hadn't, either, but Ash had to take care of Daniel, not just herself. That was a big responsibility. He understood why she envied people who'd never had to worry about their cash flow.

"How are *you* doing?" he asked.

Ashley sighed. There was a distinct sadness to her tone.

"Ash. What's going on? This is me. I know when you're upset."

"I just—I'm a little bit worried about the bills. Barry made me think he'd be willing to cover half, and we're not together now."

Rave swallowed. "What happened?"

"He said it was all moving too fast. He's not even here, Rave. He left town with some friends—headed to the Keys for a few days, and I'm stuck with the bills. If I would have known he wasn't going to hold up his end of the bargain, I'd have been more careful budgeting."

Rave stood and went into the kitchen. His eyes landed on the cookie jar on the counter. "How much would you need to get by?" Tuck had told him that if he needed cash, it was there. He could talk to Tuck when he got home, but right now, Ash and Daniel needed help. Tuck would understand. Rave could work off the money. He slid the large round jar closer and opened the lid, uncertain about what he'd find. Change, ones, a few fives and tens. When he reached in and pulled out the first wad of cash, he whistled. "Holy crap." Fifties and hundreds. Lots and lots of them. Some wadded up, some wrapped, some in seal-able bags and labeled with a hand scrawled amount.

"Rave? What is it?" Ashley's voice sharpened.

"Nothing. You didn't answer me, Ash. How much do you need to get by?"

"Four hundred would cover rent and utilities. I was counting on Barry for five hundred so I could buy a bunch of groceries."

Tuck would never miss a few hundreds. There were dozens in the jar. But he didn't plan on stealing the cash. "I can wire five hundred to you. No problem."

"Rave! How can you do that? Are you working there? Is your grandfather rich or something?"

"No, he's not rich, but he's not poor, either. Look, it's all good. I've got it handled. I can send the money in an hour. You'll be able to pick it up at Walmart. I'll call you later today and make sure you got it."

"Oh, actually, don't call me until Monday. My sister is coming to town, and she'll be here all weekend. I've really been neglecting family, so I promised her I'd give her my full attention." There was a long pause. "Is that OK, Rave?"

"Sure. Whatever you need. But Monday, I really want to talk to Daniel, all right?"

"He'll be looking forward to it all weekend."

So would Rave.

❧

1975

There was a sadness in Millie—something Tuck understood. Though he didn't know the origin of her pain, he commiserated with it. It reached out to him, intertwining with his own loss.

They'd made their way to his uncle's cabin in Barton, Tennessee, with little more than the music and the road noise to keep them company. At one point in the trip, she'd stretched out over the front seat and put her head in Tuck's lap while he drove. There, she'd slept for an hour, the failing peace sign staring up at him and her long legs bent, knees against her chest.

The cabin was in the middle of the woods, but in good repair, and Tuck wondered if Uncle Iven still used it for hunting or if he simply kept it up so it wouldn't be absorbed by the forest.

They'd stopped at the grocer's and picked up a few staples because even people with no destination and no clues about the future got hungry and needed nourishment. Behind the cabin, a rock-bed river ran the length of this section of Iven's property. It emptied into Lake Tears near the main house. This had always been Tuck's favorite part of the land. He couldn't explain why he hadn't thought to come here before picking up Millie. But it was when she'd said, "I don't care, just drive," that the destination crystalized in his mind. Iven was gone for the summer. He always returned to England at this time of year to visit his mother and extended family.

They cooked hot dogs on the open fire in the pit out back with the remnants of a picnic surrounding them. Millie watched him prepare a fishing pole while she broke off bites of the bun-encased hot dog and popped them into her mouth.

"Ever fish?" he asked her when her gaze on him became intense.

"Nope. Not in a hurry to learn, either. Seems like we should leave the poor fish alone. They aren't harming anyone."

He chuckled. "In that case, we shouldn't eat the hot dogs, either. Or the bologna we bought or the potatoes."

"The potatoes?"

"Poor helpless vegetables. They don't even have fins to swim away when a predator comes near."

"Fish predator. Maybe that's what I'll call you."

But when he glanced up to see if she was serious, she was grinning. Tuck lowered the fishing pole and moved to sit beside her. They were near the riverbank, and the cool water created a haze of fog on the ground. Instead of moving away, Millie moved closer, scooting her bottom until her hip was against his. Her head tipped back, and her eyes closed.

Tuck's chest tightened. She was beautiful. Her tanned throat elongated, her shoulders bare. Her profile stunning. Without realizing what he was doing, his fingertip came up and grazed the peace sign on her cheek.

At his touch, her eyes flew open.

"Sorry," he said. "Just wondering what that's about."

Her finger came up between them and touched the peeling face paint. "I was going to go to this rally about getting the last of our soldiers out of Vietnam. I never made it there because I found my boyfriend at my friend's house."

"Do that a lot, do you? Go to rallies?"

She shook her head. "My first. But we still have boys there. Seems like they should come home. Don't you agree?"

It's not much better here, he wanted to tell her. Coming home was nothing like the grand stories he'd heard from Uncle Iven, a decorated veteran of World War II. Iven had returned to a parade and fanfare. He'd returned a hero.

"Don't you agree?" Millie repeated.

Before them, the river splashed over smooth rocks, cutting its own path from the mountain above, where the water gathered and ran downhill. Tuck glanced at her. "What's your favorite kind of cake?"

She blinked twice and answered, "My mother makes the best red velvet cake on the planet."

"What would you say to your mother if she only baked it halfway, then pulled it out of the oven and expected you to eat it?"

"I'd say it's not done. All her hard work was for nothing. The cake's ruined."

"Yeah. Anyone would say that, wouldn't they?"

Millie's legs were stretched out in front of her. She crossed them at the ankle, bare feet grazing the grass at the riverbank. "Are you saying the soldiers should stay?"

Tuck pulled a long breath. "I'm saying it's madness to begin making a cake if you're not going to finish it. Once you're baking it, you should see it through."

"When did you return from Vietnam?" Her blue eyes filled with understanding.

He hadn't told her he was a soldier. He hadn't planned to. "A few months back."

"I bet you're sick of talking about being there, what it was really like."

No one asked. Even his family. They didn't want to know what it was like because they'd all drawn their conclusions from photographs and newsprint of journalists trying to make a name for themselves—at the expense of the American soldier.

"It wasn't like in the pictures you see. We didn't run around dragging people out of huts and killing men, women, and children."

"Then what was it like, Tuck?"

Deep in her blue eyes, he found something he'd been missing for all the months he'd been home. Compassion. Tuck didn't know what to do with that. He wasn't certain how one was supposed to answer, so he opted for the truth. "Like any war, I guess. Lots of downtime, then a mission and walking along, and all of a sudden you're in a gunfight. Not those big, epic battles like we had during World War Two. These were fast—you never knew where the enemy was or where they'd come from. All of a sudden, they're shooting your guys and you're firing back. And you can smell the spent bullets and blood, ammonia on the air, then it's over. And quiet. Deathly quiet. I can't explain it, really."

"Keep going," Millie said, slipping her hand into his.

"There were a few major battles we were involved in. I remember one specifically where we killed over a hundred of the enemy. But the papers only told about the US losses. I guess you could say we were destined to lose that war whether we won or not. When we found out, we started to feel like America's dirty little secret. Like somehow the nation blamed us for the war. We were just following orders. Drafted, so most of us hadn't chosen to be there. When I got home, I felt the sting of how deeply our nation had wounded us."

"Did you like being a soldier?"

"I liked the missions where we were sent out to accompany medical teams. We would go into villages and take care of ailments and injuries. I liked the days we spent painting and fixing schools."

Millie tilted her head. "I didn't know you did those things."

"Yeah, that doesn't make for great journalism. It was far more compelling to show a mutilated young Viet Cong soldier naked and laying in a ditch."

Millie nodded. "I guess it humanized the enemy."

"Yeah. And demonized us." This was the most he'd talked about it in the time he'd been home. Already the world felt a little lighter. The weight he'd been carrying on his shoulders lifted as if perhaps it wouldn't eventually flatten him.

Millie placed her free hand on top of their interlocked fingers. "Was it hard to kill the enemy?"

Tuck looked over the river and considered her question. They were brutal. A ruthless force. "We hardly ever shot first. Most times we were defending ourselves. And they were ghosts that came out of nowhere. Firing back was easy. But taking a life. Knowing you'd stopped someone's heart from beating. Yeah, that was hard."

"Is that why you told me in the car you weren't ready to go back? Did you mean go home?"

"Yeah. The silence was eating me up inside. My mother looks at me with this mistrust in her eyes. Or maybe confusion, not knowing what I've done. I don't understand why no one just asks me. I'd tell them the truth. But I don't even know if they'd believe me."

Beyond the river, the sun was sinking behind a cluster of mountains, creating a rainbow sunset. "I believe you, Tuck."

The force of those four words hit him in the chest. He reached to her cheek and brushed his fingers along the peace sign.

She chuckled. "Will you wash that off for me?" She moved onto her knees and scooted to the edge of the river.

Tuck grabbed a checkered cloth they'd brought from the cabin and doused it. He lifted it to her cheek. Cold water ran in rivulets down her jaw and throat. The water was chilled from its mountain trek, but heat rose between their bodies. Millie kept her eyes shut while he washed, then doused the cloth again and again. Her cheek was red from the cold and the friction. But she looked beautiful, angelic even, her hands tucked between her knees while he cleaned her.

There was not a trace of the paint left. "Good as new."

Millie opened her eyes but didn't move away. He'd rolled onto his knees as well, and now they were face-to-face, his breath mingling with hers. She bit her lower lip. Before Tuck could think of all the reasons not to, he leaned in and kissed her, his lips finding the soft pink flesh of hers. The instant was an eternity. Lips and tongues mingled, then he leaned forward, causing her head to tip back. He eased her into a deeper kiss, delving, longing for more. It was fire and ice, mixing, cracking, exploding. It was warmth and shivers, it was perfection and weakness because he knew—*he knew*—that once he'd tasted Millie, he'd never be able to get enough.

Tuck was ruined.

Rave watched outside the front window, wondering what manner of conversation would have Tuck and Phil in such deep concentration. It was early afternoon, and Tuck and Phil had returned home from the doctor's office, but no one had bothered to come inside. For several minutes they stood by Phil's Lincoln. Finally, Tuck made his way to the front door. Bullet greeted him, but Tuck walked right past without acknowledging the dog. The long morning must have tired him out. Tuck didn't seem himself.

"I took money out of the cookie jar," Rave confessed.

"OK." Tuck walked right by him and into the kitchen.

Rave frowned and followed his grandfather. "I used it to send to Ashley. She was tight on cash."

Tuck stopped at the coffeepot. His hands were spread across the counter, and his head went down.

Rave stood behind him. "I'll work off the money."

Tuck stared up at the ceiling. "I don't care about the money. I need to talk to you."

Rave lifted a hand to Tuck's shoulder but stopped short. He wasn't good at empathy when it was man to man. "Sure, Tuck."

Tuck turned and motioned for him to sit down. The kitchen chair scraped as he pulled it, the sound intensified by the tension-thick air.

Rave leaned forward. "Like I said, I can work it off—"

Tuck's eyes reddened, and he seemed like he might explode, but it wasn't exactly anger Rave was picking up on; it was something else, something almost hopeless about the angle of his head, the slant of his jaw. Tuck's hands fisted on the table. "You need to forgive your mother, boy."

At first, Rave thought he must have heard wrong. They rarely spoke of Rave's mother, and never in the same sentence with the word *forgiveness*.

Tuck's mouth pressed into a tight line. It looked like there were dozens more words vying to spew from between his lips, but he wouldn't allow them. The battle was evident. His cheeks twitched, his eyes darted from one side of the kitchen to the other. "That's all. You need to forgive her." It was the shortened tone he used when calling Bullet.

Rave bit back the anger rising from the basement of his heart. "Forgive her?" He had to repeat the words to make certain they were real. Air hissed from his nose. "I don't forgive your daughter. She abandoned me. Do you know what that feels like, Tuck? To have the only person you've known your whole life wave good-bye to you? To not even have the decency to admit she wasn't coming back?"

Tuck slammed a fist on the table, causing Raven's flesh to tighten. He didn't react, though, but held his ground as solidly as Tuck. This was an impassable road, and one Tuck had no right veering down. "No matter what she's done, you just have to. That's it."

A humorless laugh escaped from Rave. "So, bringing me here, opening your home, was about forgiving *her*?" Rave leaned forward in his seat, eyes spitting fire. "She *abandoned* me. I was barely seventeen years old." He wiped a sudden tear from his cheek.

Tuck's eye softened, if only for a moment. "But she—"

"She was sick? She was an addict. Is that supposed to excuse what she did? She wasn't an addict at the end. Mom was getting her life cleaned up. Drug-free for weeks." Rave had to stop talking to breathe, or he'd explode. "She gave me just enough hope to nearly destroy me. So, no. I won't forgive her. As long as I live."

Tuck stood. "You've got to let go of your anger toward her." He paced the kitchen floor like a caged animal, like a criminal facing execution. He spun and pointed at Rave. "You'll never be free to move on with your life until you forgive her."

Rave ran a hand through his hair. "Coming from the man with experience."

Tuck stopped his motion. "What does that mean?"

Rave pointed to the bottle of whiskey on the counter. The only alcohol in the house, the booze that was only consumed on memorial night. "Tuck, I've watched you use the men in your unit as an excuse to not forgive."

Tuck took an angry step toward him. "They don't need forgiveness. They gave everything." His voice pitched up, a sign of losing control.

"Not their forgiveness, Tuck. Your own."

Tuck's eyes narrowed on him, red, angry.

Rave should have known this was going to happen. For three weeks they'd been acting like a family. But all Tuck wanted was for Rave to forgive his mother. He hadn't cared about Rave, hadn't cared what Sharon had put him through. "Look, I'm not forgiving her. And you're obviously not going to forgive yourself, so I think we're done here."

Tuck crossed his arms over his chest. "I think we are."

"Bye, Tuck."

Rave spun and headed out of the kitchen. He grabbed his keys from the nail hanging by the front door and headed up to his room. He'd started thinking of it as his room. He should have known the rug would be snatched from under him. Isn't that what always happened? People could not be trusted. You couldn't count on them. Apparently he was dense to have to keep learning this lesson. He sat down on the edge of the bed. Everything but a few boxes of antiquated computer equipment was gone. Antiquated. Maybe that's what he was.

Maybe he'd been a fool for hoping that a life with a family was possible. But Tuck had broken through the outer casing that kept Rave's heart safe. Just like Ashley had broken through. And Daniel.

He grabbed the two trash bags he'd stored in the bottom of the closet. When Tuck had taken the bags to toss them, Rave had said, "I'll do it." But instead of throwing them away, he'd wadded them up and shoved them under a few pairs of jeans. Maybe he had known it would end this way. Maybe he'd always known.

CHAPTER 7

He'd been so unfair with the boy. Tuck wrung his hands and paced the back porch while the sun hung high above him. He'd watched clouds gather and come closer and closer to the mountaintops across the lake. But the sun burst through with blasts of color that spread from one side of the horizon to the other. Tuck and Rave had experienced their first squall. He blamed himself. He'd just been so filled with emotions earlier, feeling like a man who needed to set everything straight. If everything could be set straight in the course of one conversation, he'd have done it long ago. He was an old fool.

Bullet had stayed near his side since the argument. Sick of stumbling over him, Tuck led him through the house to the front door because Bullet wouldn't leave the back patio. With the door open, he waited for Bullet to go. But the dog stared up at him, blinking big black eyes, tongue hanging to one side. "Go on!" It was a gruff sound, one Tuck rarely used, reserved for those rare times when Bullet did something wrong. Instead of going out, the dog cowered. Tuck grabbed him by the scruff—Bullet let out a yelp that sounded like it was coming from a much smaller dog—and shoved him onto the front porch.

That's when he noticed the empty spot where Rave had parked. Grass flattened, dying from a lack of sun and rain and utterly empty. Tuck's gaze shot to the key nail—as if the keys would be there, and the car would magically appear once he laid eyes on them. Like the driveway, the nail was empty. His own truck keys looked lonely there without their comrades. He ran up the stairs, taking them two at a time. At the top, he flipped the light switch and looked around Rave's room. The closet was empty.

"No . . ." Tuck grabbed the frame for support. He drew one steadying breath, his heart hammering in his ears and nausea working its way through him, souring his stomach. His eyes searched the room and landed on a notebook sitting beside Rave's bed. Tuck rushed to it and flipped through the pages. They were filled with song lyrics. He held it against his chest.

Tuck made his way downstairs and went to the kitchen. The lid on the cookie jar was off, and a piece of paper stuck out from inside. He snatched it, holding it between trembling fingers, and tried to make out the words.

I took two hundred dollars from the jar, along with five hundred I sent to Ashley. When I get home to Tampa, I'll send the money back when I can.

Tuck squeezed the paper until it crumpled. He held the mass to his chest. He'd thought he'd heard a car less than half an hour ago, but even if he started now, he'd never catch him. Tuck groped for the phone and called Phil. Words rushed out as he explained what happened. "I just meant to give him some space, I didn't know he meant he was *leaving* when he said good-bye."

"I'll find him, Tuck. Don't worry. If not here, back in Tampa. At least we know where he's headed."

But that wasn't good enough for Tuck. He'd head out, too. Look for Rave. Search everywhere. He was sweet on that girl, Rebecca. Maybe Rave would stop by her house on the way out of town. Even if he had a girl back home, Tuck knew a young man smitten when he saw one. He had to find him. After what happened today, there was no way he'd lose Rave. At least, not like this.

⟋⟍

"What am I doing here?" Rave asked himself for the tenth time. He barely knew Becca. And she wasn't interested in him. Still, they'd shared a few nice nanoseconds, and it seemed wrong to up and leave town without saying good-bye.

And yet, he was still in his car parked in front of her coffee shop, Sustenance, with no explanation as to why he found it impossible to go in. He glanced into the rearview mirror at his own reflection. Cautious eyes stared back at him. Fearful eyes. He blamed Tuck for that because in the three weeks he'd been in Barton, Tuck had chipped away at the stone encasing him, the rock that dispersed pain and kept hurt from permeating his flesh. He wished he'd never come.

At the same time, Rave also knew there were things about him that needed to change. Had to change if he was ever going to be worthwhile to anyone on this planet. He was going home to Ashley and Daniel. Daniel deserved better than what Rave had to offer.

He thought about them for a moment. Ash and Daniel. A new sensation entered his chest. He needed to let her know he was coming. She'd be so happy. He could practically hear Daniel squealing. In the rearview mirror, Rave saw himself smiling. His eyes searched for the pay phone he knew was there. Like a tiny sliver from days gone by, a single anchor keeping the past alive. He dug change from his ashtray and jogged the distance to the phone booth. Silently, he prayed.

"Hi," Daniel answered, and Rave smiled so big it made his cheeks hurt.

"Hey there, Rock Star."

"Rave! I'm watching *SpongeBob*. My favorite episode, where SpongeBob and Patrick paint Mr. Crab's house."

Overwhelmed, he practically blurted out the news but stopped just short of saying he was headed home. He was trying to be more responsible about things. He'd tell Ashley first. "I want to hear all about it, buddy, but first can you put your mom on the phone for a second?"

"No." No explanation. Rave could hear him crunching potato chips in the background.

"Come on, Daniel. I need to talk to her. Then we can talk for a while, OK?"

"I can't. Aunt Nicole is here. Mommy's leaving."

Cold shot into Rave's gut, but he dismissed it. She was probably just running to the store or something. "Where's she going, Daniel?"

"She's in the driveway, and Barry's picking her up. Aunt Nicole told me not to leave the couch until she comes back in."

The cold spread, chilling Rave regardless of the early-summer sun above him. "How long is she going to be gone?"

"Just for two nights."

Rave pressed his head against the wall of the phone booth. "Where are they going?"

"I dunno. Somewhere for car keys or something."

"The Keys?" His voice cracked on the word.

"Yeah. That's right."

Rave bit into his cheek and tasted blood.

"I gotta go, Rave. Aunt Nicole is coming in."

Rave started to say good-bye but heard the click before he could. He didn't blame Daniel for hanging up—the boy got in trouble for answering the phone. But he also couldn't mistake the distance in Daniel's voice. Like day by day, he was forgetting Rave, forgetting who he was and how close they'd been. Children have short memories, he supposed. And yet, he recalled every time his mother slipped out late at night and left him in the house alone.

Slowly Rave hung up the phone as if the receiver was the umbilical cord connecting him to his past life. Ashley'd played him. That was the only explanation for this. And now she was headed to the Keys on Rave's dime. With Barry. Something deep in his heart told him he'd known she was like this. She took. She never gave. Except to Daniel. Ashley was a good mom. But Rave had always assumed her preoccupation with money was in Daniel's interest. Now he knew Ashley was out for herself. She'd probably always been, but she was a chameleon—good at hiding what she wanted to hide and good at convincing everyone around her that she was sweet and innocent.

He made his way across the courtyard of the town square. The flowering trees above him had dropped white and pink blooms on the ground to be trampled by passersby. How odd to plant a tree knowing you'd only appreciate the blossoms while they hemmed the sky. Never giving a thought to them once they fell to the earth.

Inside his car, he leaned back against the headrest and closed his eyes. Where to now? Not home. Tampa had felt like home before Tuck. Before that stupid attorney showed up and ruined what semblance of a decent life he had. Now he was homeless. Again.

He brushed a tear from the side of his face. It had collected in the outer edge of his closed eye and ran from his temple through his hairline to the corner of his ear. Another followed.

He'd been here before. But it had been a long time. He could start over somewhere. Maybe head east to North Carolina's shoreline. But shoreline meant ocean, and ocean made him think of Daniel and endless numbers of sand castles and shell collecting. No, he couldn't go to the beach. Not for a long, long time. He'd head west. Rave sniffed, swiped his eyes to remove any remaining moisture, and threw one last long look toward the window of Sustenance. He didn't need to say good-bye. After all, he owed her nothing.

∽

"You think you can will that young man to come inside?" Alexandra Sheffield stood behind Becca, her wide hands clamped on Becca's shoulders and staring out the same window she'd redecorated earlier in the day with the new coffee flavors and the new book club books.

Beyond the window, beside the town square, Rave sat in his car looking . . . lost. Why Becca's heart was so drawn to him, she couldn't say. There was something damaged, shattered, about him. And yet, he was made of iron-clad pieces that could easily be forged anew. It was a strange mix, to be sure. Somewhere between haunted and hunter. His eyes were the color of the sky at night, endless and powerful. There was depth to Rave that she rarely found in young men her age, an old soul filled with ageless wisdom.

"He's been out there for at least fifteen minutes. I don't know what he's waiting for." Becca gave a questioning look to Alexandra.

"Young men. I've had my share of them, and I can tell you this, they don't know what they want." Alexandra had lived a life. The kind that could make a sailor blush—if even half of her stories were true. She'd come to Barton seven years back and opened the first coffee shop/bookstore. Culture for the ladies, java for the men. On any given day, a bevy of farmers would sit at the small round tables and talk politics and almanacs. Alexandra mostly stayed out of the discussions but frequently rolled her eyes at the "Yes sir, this country's goin' to hell in a handbasket" commentary. Same conversation every day.

It had prompted her to come up with a new brew. A decidedly strong, dark coffee she affectionately called Helena Handbasket. She was—on one side—a mentor to Becca. On the other side, Becca was learning what *not* to do from listening to the worldly, uninhibited Miss Sheffield.

Becca was a good girl. She liked that about herself. It was important not to follow Alexandra's example too closely. But wisdom laced her words, and Becca found it impossible not to learn from her forty-year-old boss.

Alexandra toyed with the new streak of purple in her too-long bangs. Her hair was short and jet black, except for the chiseled bangs overhanging her forehead, the long spikes now sporting a violet hue. "Go on out. Your shift's over in half an hour anyway."

Becca chewed her bottom lip. "I really need the hours."

Alexandra nudged her shoulder. "I'll clock you out on time. Go."

Becca turned to face her. "You do realize you're cheating yourself by paying me for time I haven't worked?" She'd worked for Alexandra all through high school and took the full-time position when she graduated. Even though she'd had other plans.

"Just rewarding you for a job well done. Go. See if handsome out there can find some other ways to reward you."

Becca blushed. "Alexandra, *please.*"

Alex crossed her arms over her vintage Def Leppard concert T-shirt. "Yes, *please* usually works to get you what you want. But I'd always rather demand. That's just *my* MO. Handle him however you choose. But, if you decide you're not interested, let me know. It's been a long time since I—" She cleared her throat. "Spent any quality time with a younger man."

Becca leaned forward and whispered. "He's young enough to be your son."

Alex tossed her hands in the air. "That's it. I'm docking your pay. Pull the 'You're an old lady' card again, and I'll fire you."

Becca grinned and started to untie her apron.

Alex snagged her arm just as she was getting ready to step out. "Uh-oh."

Becca followed her gaze to the square. Her heart dropped. Blue lights flashed in the shop window. Sheriff Cogdill pulled his squad car in behind Rave's beat-up Honda.

Becca sighed, her fingers nervously twining around the apron string because the last thing in the world she wanted to watch was Rave getting arrested. Or getting a ticket. He'd been on her mind since Trini's house. The way he'd tried to act so natural while trudging through the field. How he'd kicked the ground as if he knew what he was looking for.

He'd answered her pointed—and probably obnoxious—questions. She'd made him smile.

Orley Cane, seated at the table with the checkerboard painted directly on it, pointed out the window. "I knew that boy was up to no good coming here."

Becca spun and gave him a dirty look. Alexandra took the coffeepot to his table and filled his cup. "Mind your own business, Orley, or I'll be forced to tell everyone about your secret visitor the other evening."

Orley visibly reddened. How it was that Alexandra knew absolutely everything about absolutely everyone in town escaped Becca. But she did. Oh, the stories she could spin. Becca left the window and busied herself drying the freshly cleaned coffee mugs and placing the cupcake tins in the small kitchen while keeping one eye on the happenings outside. By the time Sheriff Cogdill left, with Phil Ratzlaff at his side, Becca felt nauseated. Something was wrong. She didn't think Rave had gotten a ticket, but the heaviness of the atmosphere suggested a ticket would have been better.

Rave started the car, but the quick whir of a siren stopped him. In his rearview mirror, he saw blue lights. "Are you kidding me?" He reached to his glove compartment to get the registration.

Sheriff Cogdill leaned into his driver's window. "Hello, Rave."

"Pretty sure I wasn't breaking the law." He held the registration out to the sheriff, along with his Florida license. He hadn't bothered to get it changed to a Tennessee one yet.

"I don't need to see that, son. You're not in any trouble. Would you mind stepping out of the car?" Cogdill took a few paces back, giving him room to open the car door.

Rave took a breath and considered his options. He knew his rights. Without probable cause, a cop couldn't just detain a person. At the same time, Sheriff Cogdill didn't really seem like he was looking for an excuse to arrest Rave, so he got out of the car and propped his weight on the door, folding his arms over his chest.

Cogdill pulled his sunglasses from his eyes—eyes framed with worry or concern or some such thing. "I got a call from Phil Ratzlaff. He said you were likely headed out of town. He'd like to talk to you before you go. Thinks it might change your course."

"So, you're a glorified messenger boy? Back home in Tampa, the cops usually spend their time stopping lawbreakers." Rave could see Cogdill reluctantly absorbing the words, though he didn't like them.

"Look, kid, Phil's on the way. If you care about Tuck, give him five minutes of your time. If you don't, hit the road. We take care of our own here. Tuck's in good hands."

Something cold snaked down Rave's spine. He uncrossed his arms and planted his hands on the trunk of the car behind him. Care about Tuck? Yes. Of course he did. In the few weeks Rave had been there, Tuck had offered him a more stable home life than he'd ever known. He could go to the grocery store and buy as much meat and fresh food as he wanted. He could jump in the truck and drive all day and never worry about having enough gas for the rest of the week. Tuck was a good man, plain and simple. Caring, trustworthy, the kind of person someone like Rave could look up to.

Yeah, Rave cared about Tuck. Even though the old man was stubborn to a fault, Tuck's place had become home. And Tuck's memorial.

How he spread his emotions on the table and relived the horror he'd suffered during the war. Tuck was a man of honor. Maybe that's why he'd wanted Rave to forgive Sharon, his mother. But Rave was stubborn, too. And some people didn't deserve forgiveness.

Phil Ratzlaff came jogging across the courtyard. His brow was furrowed, his step heavy. When he finally stopped at the back of the car, Rave knew something, something really terrible, was wrong.

CHAPTER 8

"Rave?" Becca's voice interrupted the nothingness. A green apron dangled from her fingertips. He'd noticed her watching through the window while Phil had been talking. But the words from Phil's mouth had caused everything to disappear. There were no birds, no trees, just a pinpoint of focus—Phil's face, heavy with the news he was sharing—and Rave's need to lean against his car to keep his legs from buckling.

Behind Becca, the town square was quiet. A few people meandering around, but not many. And the ones who were there were going on about their business like nothing had changed in the last few moments. And yet, for him, everything had.

He stared past Becca, his gaze focused on the brick building. When their eyes finally met and held, he could see her concern. Rave tried to find his voice. "I was gonna talk to you before—" But then a fresh wave of the conversation he'd just had assaulted him again. Was it possible that words spoken so softly could be so sharp, so jagged? Rave felt a gentle touch on his arm and glanced down to find Becca's hand at the bend of his elbow.

"What's happening, Rave? Is it some news about your mother?" The wind kicked up and carried her scent. Freshly ground coffee and that strawberry shampoo.

"No."

She raised the apron in her free hand and used it to point behind Rave's car. "I saw the sheriff talking to you. And then Phil Ratzlaff."

He nodded, still dazed.

"Is it . . . is it Tuck?"

Rave pushed off the car and turned to face her. "Is there somewhere we could go and talk?"

Becca gave him a smile, a sliver of sunshine at midnight. "Yes. I know just the place." She opened his passenger door and tossed her apron inside. Becca closed the door and motioned for him to come around the car. "Let's walk. It's not far." She looped her arm through his.

Rave went willingly. She could be leading him to slaughter, and he wouldn't care. It seemed utterly unfair that Tuck was facing this. The man who'd cheated death during the war and who kept the memory of all of his men alive—no matter the personal cost to his own heart.

They walked slowly, making their way from downtown. Becca pointed ahead. "Take a right here." At the end of the narrow street, they arrived at a metal gate where weeds had grown and intertwined with the bars. It seemed like they were miles away, instead of a few blocks from the downtown area. Here, with the overhanging oaks and the tall, spiny weeds, it was like they'd stepped into another time.

Giant trees shaded the entryway, and if they were to step inside, they'd need to push their way through the overgrown brush. "Looks ominous."

Becca gave the gate a tug until some of the weeds broke loose. It moved a couple of inches, and she tossed a wide smile over her shoulder at Rave. "Help me."

He gripped the corner of the gate and pulled. It opened enough for her to slip inside. Rave glanced behind him. "Are we going to get caught doing this? I've already had face time with the sheriff today."

"No. We all own it. It was left to the people of Barton." She grinned at him from the other side of the gate, her fingers lacing the metal bars.

"So what is it?" He tried to look between the hanging branches. Beyond the gate, an area opened up as if it had once had a purpose.

Becca used her cowboy boots to tamp down the weeds that rubbed against her legs. "I call it the place where dreams die."

"Great," he deadpanned. "Field of death." He laced his fingers just above hers.

She shoved the gate open enough for Rave and motioned for him to come in. "It's not a field, it's a park."

When he didn't move, she reached around the vine-laced wrought iron, got a firm grip on his hand, and pulled. Oh yeah, he'd go anywhere with her. Rave slipped inside and tried to keep the tree branches off them while they moved deeper into the park. Crinkly summer leaves scraped his neck and shoulders. The overhang darkened the atmosphere, making the place surreal. He half expected a haunted mansion to appear before them. Once they made it through the dense foliage, the sun shone down on the octagonal park, its overgrown borders defined with a tall fence and massive trees.

The park itself looked like something out of an apocalypse movie. Cobblestone walkways wound through the landscape, visible only in snatches where the weeds surrounding them had died. In places, the terrain had busted through the creamy white stone. Wrought iron benches anchored resting spots, but they, too, were overcome by the weeds and vines that seemed bent on swallowing the foreign objects.

Becca seemed to look everywhere at once. "It makes me sad coming here."

"But you still do? Obviously you choose to come—after all, you've got to fight through the forest Ents to get here."

She turned to face him. "Is that a *Lord of the Rings* reference?"

"Tree Ents, yeah. Guess it is."

"Read it or watched the movie?"

He'd found the worn copy outside a used bookstore. It was the only thing he'd ever stolen. "Both."

Still holding his hand, Becca pulled him toward one of the benches. He didn't want to let her go. Her fingers were warm and soft and gave him a sense of stability. No matter how ridiculous that might be, still the sensation was there. Someone falling will lash out and grab air, even though it can't possibly hold them. He knew from experience.

Rave pulled some weeds and unwound them from the seating area on one of the benches, then motioned for her. "Your throne."

She sat down. He sat beside her. Before them in the center of the park, vines and ground cover were growing up through a maze of stones. Becca pointed to it. "That was to be a fountain."

"So who did this? And why abandon it?"

"A large corporation planned to build a factory here. As a show of good faith, they started work on the park—a place where factory workers could walk during lunch or on a break. The land beyond those trees was where the factory was supposed be." She pointed off to the right.

"I take it the factory was shelved?"

She nodded. "Yes. They got a better offer from a neighboring state. Tax incentives or something. Barton's older community didn't want a factory. Some of the younger generation did."

"Some, but not you?" The breeze played in her hair, making it move. Long auburn strands dancing with the wind.

She shrugged. "I mean, we could use a little help, and a factory would mean a lot of jobs, but—"

"It could potentially ruin your quaint little town?"

"Old-fashioned, aren't we?"

"It's nice, Becca. Means the almighty dollar isn't the only concern here."

Becca turned to face him, propping her knee on the seat between them. "If you go to the local café, Vernie serves you breakfast. Just like she did forty years ago. Her son runs the kitchen. Her daughter runs the business. If you need gas, Clifton Banks will wash your windshield while giving you the ten-day forecast. Everyone knows everyone's name. We know when a stranger comes to town. We know what our neighbors need. Whether it's to borrow a John Deere or someone to help shore up a shed."

"Why do I feel like we're no longer talking about factories and abandoned parks?"

She peered at him from the corner of her eye. "Perceptive, city boy. I'm trying to tell you that whatever you and Tuck are facing, you're not facing it alone."

His chest tightened. But they were facing it alone, weren't they? No one could help. There was nothing to do but wait. This was unfixable. A ten-day forecast and a top-rate breakfast weren't going to change Tuck's fate. "He's dying, Becca."

The sudden intake of air and the way her eyes filled—instantly, swimming in pools of tears, the sun glinting off the green—caused Rave to bite his cheek. When she finally blinked, those tears trekked down both cheeks, straight lines sliding, then rolling, off her jaw and onto her creamy throat.

She scooted a little closer. "Rave. I'm so sorry. You just got here. You two finally found each other and—" Her hand came up and covered her mouth. "And poor Tuck. He's suffered enough. Losing Millie."

Rave swallowed the ball of cotton in his throat. "It's his liver. It's called hepatocellular carcinoma. It's a liver cancer, and I guess Tuck had radiation treatments on it quite a while ago. They thought they got it all, but the cancer is back."

"There's nothing they can do? People survive cancer all the time."

"I guess the doctor isn't giving him much hope."

Becca took his arm and wound it around her shoulder, then tucked herself into his side. She laid her head against his chest. It should feel backward. It should feel as though he was consoling her. But it didn't. The warmth of her body pressed so perfectly against his, the feel of her shoulders rising and falling with each breath. Rave reached around her and threaded his fingers together, Becca in the tight circle of his arms. Becca consoling him.

They stayed like that for a long time. Her tears moistened a spot on his shirt, and when the wind changed direction, it caused the spot to cool. But he was in no hurry to leave. Rave closed his eyes and dropped his cheek to the top of her head. There, a few of his own tears dampened her hair.

He'd cried while holding Becca at the park where dreams die. Rave used to think tears meant weakness. But they didn't. They were a release, helping you let go of the *should have been*. Helping you process the *what was*. Each tear was a memorial. And once they were shed, the giver understood that life could be harsh, even cruel, but it didn't have to break you. Rave wasn't ashamed of tears. They were a badge that said you were strong enough to rise above your circumstances. He no longer associated them with weakness. Weak people gave up. His mom had been weak. And she'd always been too busy to cry. Busy working the angles and making a plan to get more drugs, find them a new place to live when they got kicked out of one, looking for someone to take pity on them and help financially. So it had been up to Rave to shed the tears. He'd go to his room, put his face in his pillow, and cry until his body had emptied all its liquid emotion. Then, he'd wash his face, roll up his sleeves, and figure out how to help his mom out of whatever mess she'd gotten them into.

He'd helped her because he loved her. That was the thing. He'd never stopped loving his mom. Maybe no one ever did. But he'd loved her in spite of her debilitating faults. He'd loved unconditionally. And now he needed to show the same to Tuck. Because other than being as stubborn as a mule, Tuck had shown Rave nothing but kindness.

Rave pulled onto the long dirt driveway and rounded the first turn. Up ahead, he saw Tuck's red truck off on the side of the road. Rather than slow down, Rave stepped on the gas. His bald tires spun in the mud, but he held steady until he was on Tuck's rear bumper.

He could see Tuck sitting alone in the cab of the truck. Rave got out and ran up to the open window. "Tuck, is everything OK?"

But when Tuck glanced over, Rave saw the trickle of blood on his brow.

"Geez, what happened?" Rave threw the truck door open and grabbed Tuck, clamping his palms on Tuck's cheeks, examining the inch-long cut above his eye. "You're bleeding."

Tuck halfheartedly waved him off. "Just a scratch." His eyes went wide, lips turning up at the ends, hope filling his craggy features. "You're back?" It was both a question and an answer, and it made Rave grin. He continued to hold his hands at the sides of Tuck's face. It was a snapshot of their life ahead, Rave knew. Him, caregiver to someone not used to being taken care of. He thought of Daniel and the many times Rave had held his face in the same manner, assuring him that there was no monster under the bed or no werewolf in the hallway. It was the gesture of a person who loved another. It was the anchors that held, no matter the storm.

"I'm back, Tuck." Rave had to swallow a few times before he could say more. "I'm back for good. I swear."

Tuck's chin quivered. He pulled away from Rave's touch. "It's not fair for me to want you here. To have to watch—" Tuck's shaky voice cracked. He drew a long breath. "I wanted to be the one helping you."

Rave itched to reach out and hug him, but he wouldn't. "We're family, Tuck. We help each other. If you swear to me you'll do what the doctors are telling you to do, I swear I won't go anywhere."

Tuck frowned. "They don't know everything."

"They know more than we do about this. And I know how stubborn you can be. So, we follow the doctor's orders."

"You're stubborn in your own right. Anyone ever tell you that?"

"Yeah. Starting with kindergarten and pretty much for the rest of my life. Now I know where I get it. Let's take you home and get that cut cleaned up."

Tuck nodded. "I learned my lesson. Don't tangle with an angry bee."

Rave jogged back to his car and followed Tuck to the house. In the downstairs bathroom, Tuck sat on the edge of the tub while Rave cleaned the wound. "A bee, you say?"

Tuck grunted. "I was holding a notebook you'd left behind, thinking it might have some clue about where you'd have gone before leaving town. A bee came in the window and landed on my forehead. Without thinking, I swatted at it. Bee high-tailed it out the passenger window, but the edge of the spiral on the notebook caught my brow. Bled like a stuck pig."

Rave hadn't realized he'd left anything behind. Washing the line of mostly dried blood from beside Tuck's eye reopened the wound. Balls of fresh blood appeared and started trickling down his temple. "Starting to bleed again."

"Stupid medication makes my blood thin. I swear, if I didn't know better, I'd say they are hurrying to get rid of me."

Rave chuckled. "I think I saw some butterfly bandages upstairs."

Tuck raised his brow. "Spread a little super glue over it."

Rave stopped midturn. "No. I think we'll stick with Neosporin and bandages."

"Spoil sport," he grunted.

"Stubborn old man."

Rave got the antibiotic cream and bandages and finished working on Tuck's brow. "Good as new."

Tuck gave him a crooked grin. "If only that were true."

Rave poured them each a cup of coffee and followed Tuck to the back deck. They sat on the lounge chairs and watched the sun dip lower and lower where the lake beckoned it home.

"I'd still like to teach you about electrical."

Rave glanced over. "You'd be up to that?"

Tuck's face scrunched. "I was up to it yesterday. Other than the opinion of a doctor who looks young enough to still be in high school, I'm fit." But the words held no real conviction. Tuck was far from fit, and this was far from fixable.

Tuck's fingers threaded through the handle of the mug. From the corner of his eye, Rave watched. "Tuck, what are the treatment options?"

The older man was heavy with the news he'd gotten, no matter how much he tried to show he wasn't shaken to the core by the diagnosis. "It's inoperable. Got lucky last time around. This time . . ." His words trailed off.

No options? That seemed inconceivable in today's age of medicine and technology. That also meant there was nothing Rave could do to lift this burden. What he could do was help carry it.

Rave opened his mouth to ask what Tuck needed, but when he glanced over, Tuck's pale blue eyes were solid on him. It was Tuck who spoke first. "I'd have never hired Vin and never sent Phil to ask you to come meet me if I'd known."

Rave frowned.

"I meant to help make your life better, not saddle you with something like this."

Rave placed his mug on the small round table between them. "Didn't we already have this conversation?"

"It's important to me that you know. I didn't bring you here to babysit me into the cemetery."

Rave shrugged. "Then I won't. We're in this together, Tuck. Thick-headed as you are, I'd think you can at least understand that. I've been here almost a month, and until our fight, I was planning to stay. I'm not here out of some sense of duty. I'm here because I want to be. Got it?"

The lines of age deepened on Tuck's face. "I don't know why." He shook his head helplessly. "I sure don't know why."

Rave leaned back in the seat, resting his head. It had been a long day, and the fatigue of it was taking a toll.

"What I said about your momma. I had no right. You got a good heart, boy. Who and when you forgive is up to you."

Rave tilted his head and peered at Tuck with one eye. "Or *if* I forgive."

Now it was Tuck's turn to lean back. Rave watched the smile slowly spread across his profile. "Oh, you'll forgive her. One day. Because you got good blood flowing through your veins, and good blood always does the right thing. Sooner or later."

"Mom had the same blood. She never made good on it." Maybe he shouldn't be pointing that out at a time like this, but Rave wasn't perfect. He didn't want Tuck to have unrealistic faith in him.

"Whatever demons drove you momma to her death were ones too big for her to fight alone. She was an incredible young woman at one time. Best and brightest in her class."

His mom had been a good student? Rave's head filled with questions. Thoughts about his mother, the relationship she'd likely once had with Tuck and Millie, and who she'd been before the drug abuse. She'd no doubt burned that bridge long before Rave was born. Addicts scorched their way through friends and family, leaving the remnants empty and branded. That's how it was. And yet, Tuck still wanted to see the woman forgiven. "I said things I shouldn't have, too. I'm sorry, Tuck."

They were silent for a long time. Finally, Tuck said, "Are we going to the swap meet tomorrow? We've got a whole truckload sitting inside the barn."

"Do you feel up to it?"

"Yes, sir. Think we'll do as well as we did the other two times we went?" Tuck gave a lopsided grin.

"I can't see why not. We've got the same kind of stuff."

"Afterward, we'll have us a good lunch at Vernie's café. I'd also like to stop off and buy us a couple of cell phones. Then we'll come home, and I can rest up for the memorial."

Saturday night. Of course Tuck would still want to have the memorial. But it took so much out of him, Rave hated to think about it. Well, the memorial would be vastly different now, in light of the liver disease. Maybe it wouldn't be as hard on Tuck.

At 8:00 p.m. the following evening, Rave came down the steps. He'd changed into a pair of sweatpants and a T-shirt he'd bought at the swap meet earlier in the day. They'd sold most of their wares, third weekend in a row. He thought about the day while he readied for the memorial. His mind turned to Becca and when he'd seen her earlier. She'd brought a cup of coffee out of Sustenance for him and one for Tuck. Tuck took one sip, wrinkled his nose, and asked who put candy in the java. Becca laughed and kissed his cheek. Tuck went three shades of red before saying he could get used to the brew and the attention.

Rave turned off the stairwell light and came to a stop at the table. He first noticed the shot glasses sitting like tiny monuments before each empty seat. His heart rate kicked up.

Tuck came out of the kitchen carrying the bottle of whiskey.

A humorless laugh escaped from Rave's mouth. "You're not planning on drinking that, right?"

But the confused look on Tuck's face told him that he was. "It's memorial night."

Rave grabbed it from him. He set it on the table hard enough to make the shot glasses quiver. "Your liver is failing, Tuck. People with liver cancer don't drink half a bottle of alcohol in one sitting."

Tuck's spine straightened, his jaw setting in that way it always did when he was readying for a battle. "I'm not changing my memorial just because some wet-behind-the-ears doctor thinks I should. I owe it to these men—"

Rave raised his hands. "You owe it to *them*? What about me, Tuck? Don't you owe me anything? Like the right to get to spend as much time with you as we have left? You're dying. This isn't about someone wanting to take away one of your freedoms. This is your life. And this"—Rave raised the bottle to eye level—"this is poison for you."

The hard frown around Tuck's eyes softened. But only for a moment. "You . . . don't understand. I know you don't, because you've never been in a war. These men, my friends, died. Some of them died in my arms. Some of them died carrying out my orders. A man never forgets that."

Rave pushed the bottle farther away on the table and moved to look Tuck in the eye. "I understand, whether you believe it or not. A military conflict is not the only kind of war, Tuck. I feel like I've logged more combat hours than most soldiers. But my war was right here. Watching my mother slowly kill herself. I won't do that again. I won't watch someone I love put poison in their body. Never gonna happen. If you do this, this way, you do it alone."

Tuck's face hardened. "You swore you'd stay."

"As long as you were following the doctor's orders. You want to call him? Get his take on this?" Rave wouldn't back down. There was no retreat from this stand.

Tiny cracks appeared in Tuck's armor. His gaze darted around the room, falling one by one on the empty chairs. "How will I honor them?" The words were so soft, so sad, they broke Rave's heart because it wasn't just a question; it was a plea. Honoring the men was one thing, but trying to carry a burden from so long ago was a far different thing.

Across the room, the wall clock ticked. "Do you wish you'd died instead of them?"

Tuck opened his mouth, but words didn't form.

Rave pulled two chairs from under the table and sat in one. He motioned for Tuck to take the other, but when his grandfather didn't move, Rave stood and gently coaxed him into the seat. It was quiet for a long time. Off in the corner of the room, Bullet lay sprawled on his dog bed. There seemed to be no breeze outside, and Rave could see the leaves shining with the last drops of the setting sun touching their tips. It was as if the whole world around them waited to hear what Tuck would say. His voice was gentle. "I'm happy I'm alive. And that's part of the problem. I feel bad because inside I know it could have been me. There's even a part of me that wishes it would have been. But then I think about the good things in my life, and I know I've helped some people along the way, and I start comparing those men—those men who died—to myself. Would they have made the same kinds of choices?"

Rave understood. "Somewhere in your head you're trying to justify the why. But you can never reconcile those two things, Tuck. Because we don't pick the *why*. All we get to choose is the *what*."

"Explain what you mean." Tuck's watery eyes were so penetrating, Rave had to blink to break the intensity before answering.

"What do you choose to do *now*? What did you choose after you came home from the war? You found Millie. Made a life, a pretty good one, I'd guess."

Tuck smiled at the mention of Rave's grandmother. "It was a first-rate life, boy. A first-rate life."

Rave grinned. "I know it was. And I know my mother caused you a ton of heartache. She had to have. But you got me in the bargain. Took a while, but we found each other. And now I have roots. All because of you. All because you made it back. It's time to stop letting the war kill you slowly, Tuck. A memorial is a tribute. Not a funeral."

All the air hissed from Tuck's lungs. "I don't know any other way to do it."

Rave squeezed his shoulder. "Tonight, we use water, not whiskey. But I'll start working on ideas of how we can honor the men." Rave's heart was pounding because a renegade thought came into his head and almost shot right out of his mouth before he could stop it. *Don't do it. Don't go there. It's not your war.* "And Tuck?"

Tuck looked bewildered, all the things Rave had mentioned dancing like fireflies in his eyes. He looked childlike, and it made Rave want nothing more than to protect him, to put his mind truly at ease.

"Tuck, I swear when you're—no longer able to do the memorial—I'll continue it. For as long as I live, the men will be properly honored."

There was the sound of Tuck's voice, deep in his throat, then a cracking and a release. Old men weren't supposed to cry, but there at the dining room table with the glasses spread for the memorial, Tuck broke down. His shoulders curled forward, his hands partially covered his eyes and mouth, and his tears flowed freely.

Rave's heart broke along with his grandfather's. For so long, Tuck had carried this pain. Was Rave really able to help? It seemed such a monumental task, and what if he let Tuck down? Maybe he wasn't strong enough, brave enough to do what he was promising. Rave's own eyes glistened as he listened to the haunting sound of an old man's profoundest pain sneaking out from the deepest cavern of his heart.

Tears were not weakness. Tears were a release.

Rave scooted his chair closer and draped an arm around Tuck's shoulder. He stayed quiet, listening to the dragonflies outside kissing the dining room windowpanes as years of guilt and worry and shame fell from Tuck's shoulders and landed on the floor. Beyond the sliding glass door, the sun was setting, dropping embers of gold on the lake. Rave had never made so bold a commitment. But as time passed and tears fell, he knew one thing. This promise he'd keep. He had to. Through the glass, Rave stared up at the darkening sky. *If you're up there, Grandma Millie, I could use a little help down here.*

ᔥ

Tuck woke up early Sunday morning. Unusual for him because the memorial typically took everything out of him, and Sunday mornings were meant for recuperating. But not today. Through groggy eyes he could see a figure moving from one side of the room to the other. He tried to focus.

A scent—magnolia perfume and Jergens cold cream—entered his nose. He breathed it in, drawing a lungful of the air that was rich with . . . Millie. He was holding the pillow against his chest, his grip tightening, tightening until he heard music.

It wasn't music. Someone was humming. Again, the image passed him and went to the closet door.

Annie Baker has the same dress as I do, but she says it's not church-appropriate, so she won't wear it on Sundays. Can you believe that, Tuck? The woman who prances a steady stream of gentlemen through her house at night is worried about appearances?

"They're all hypocrites, Millie." Tuck's words were sleep-slurred.

She stopped at the edge of the bed. With her hovering over him, he could smell the Aqua Net hairspray. *Not all are hypocrites. Pastor Keith is a gem. And his wife, LaDonna, she came straight over to compliment me on this dress the first time I wore it. Annie Baker says the split on the skirt is too high. What do you think?*

"The split in the skirt is my favorite part of that dress."

She swatted at him, the air moving above his head, filled with the scent that was unmistakably her. Tuck drew it into his lungs. "Don't go today, Mills. Stay here. Stay home in bed with me, and I'll see if I can't effectively change your religion."

Tuck Wayne! I swear there is going to be a special place in heaven for women who've had to handle men like you.

"Well, I'd sure like to know the address on that street. Think you can put in a word with the big guy for me?"

You can tell him yourself. You're going to church with me today.

Tuck pushed the pillow away. "Millie Wayne, you made me a promise that you'd never ask me to go again."

Oh, I'm not asking you. I'm telling you. Get up. Get dressed. Fix breakfast. You're taking my grandson to church.

Tuck opened his eyes to find himself alone. Across the room, a closet door hung open, one side gaping and empty. Millie's side. He'd never been able to bring himself to fill her space with his own garments, but he'd moved her things—other than a few sweaters and overshirts—to the sewing room.

Tuck huffed and dragged himself up out of bed.

Within an hour, he was banging on Rave's door. The boy opened the door, his blond and brown hair tousled and his eyes still sleepy. He wore a T-shirt and flannel pants, and Lord help him, the boy looked just like he did as a child. Years melted away, and Tuck's mind had gone back in time, twenty years ago, with his grandson waking up. Tuck tried to turn away. But his feet were lead. He should have told Rave. He should have told Rave the truth.

Tuck's chest squeezed. A shaky breath drifted from his mouth.

Rubbing one eye with the back of his hand, Rave said, "Are you all right?" The words were groggy, as if his mouth hadn't become fully operational yet.

Tuck clamped his back teeth together, memories and ghosts from the past flooding his senses, throwing him off. "You need to get dressed." It was a gruff command.

Rave shook his head to clear it, eyes focusing in. "What's wrong?"

"Nothing. We're going to church." The words sounded so foreign, even Tuck didn't recognize them.

With a yawn, Rave mumbled, "Thanks, but I think I'll pass. Church isn't really my thing."

Tuck had already started to walk away. He spun on his heel and pointed a finger at Rave. "If I have to go, you have to go."

Rave ran a hand through his hair. "Dude, you don't have to go."

Tuck turned back around and headed for the stairs. "Oh, yes I do. She's making me."

Rave hollered after him. "What? Who's making you? Trini?"

"Your grandmother, Millie."

CHAPTER 9

Church bells rang, and Tuck and Rave found themselves sitting stone-faced on a padded burgundy pew. With his back arrow-straight, Rave wouldn't have thought it possible to straighten anymore, but when he saw Becca walk in, her arm laced around Trini's, he did just that. His jaw went slack, his mouth fell open.

She was headed for the center, but when she saw him—and paused in the middle of the aisle to shoot him a winning smile—Rave's palms grew sweaty. She veered, dragging Trini along and maneuvering around a crowd of people to come sit by them. Trini stepped over Rave to get to Tuck.

Becca sat down by Rave. She wore a light-blue summer sweater that hugged her shoulders and a darker blue skirt that hit just above her tanned knees.

"Hi Rave, you look great," she whispered as the congregation settled into the remaining spots. Her feet were clad in cowboy boots.

"And you look incredible."

She smoothed her skirt.

He leaned closer. "Are you blushing?"

She waved him off. "I'm not used to being hit on in church."

"I wasn't hitting on you. Wait, if I was, did it work?"

Her eyes narrowed.

"Becca, do you want to go out with me?"

"No." She flashed him a perfect smile. A smile meant for someone who deserved her. An intimate smile. A smile that could wake you in the morning and kiss you to sleep at night. His thoughts trailed off, and he wondered if it was a sin to have these kinds of images surging through his system while inside a church house.

Well, sin or not, he couldn't help himself.

When the singing and the sermon were over, Becca angled to face Rave. "So, what do you think?"

"I already told you. You look incredible."

"Not about me. What did you think of the sermon?"

He shrugged. "It was OK. I mean, he kind of hammered that thing about not letting competition get the best of you."

Becca folded her hands in her lap. "Well, he had no choice. It's the one thing he really struggles with."

"Huh?"

"Pastor Keith is our star hitter on the church league softball team. He played in college, so he's a bit *too* competitive sometimes. I'm the pitcher. Anyway, we have a championship game today. It was supposed to be a couple of weeks ago—we usually play on Friday evenings—but it got rained out. Now, the opposing team is coming here—a bit of a grudge match for Pastor Keith—it's a buddy from college who heads up the other team."

Rave shook his head. "Are we still talking about church?"

Becca laughed. "What did you expect? A monk who lives alone and took a vow of silence? That would make for boring sermons, wouldn't it?"

His brows rose. "I'm . . . speechless."

Trini leaned over Tuck and shook Rave's sleeve. "You and Tuck are staying for the picnic lunch. Pastor Keith needs all the support he can get before the game. We need to be here when he mops up the field with that poor excuse for a deacon from—"

Becca leaned over Rave and hissed, "Trini! Did you not hear one word of the sermon?"

"I hope that Craig Allestaire eats a mouthful of dirt." She thrust her fist into the air. "The Lord wants vengeance. I don't care what you say. That's in the good book."

Trini held her Bible up as proof.

Rave liked how Becca leaned over his lap to reprimand Trini.

Becca exhaled forcefully. "She's misquoting."

Trini shoved a pointed finger at Becca's face. "And she's Miss Manners, obviously."

Becca pressed a hand to Rave's thigh. "I hope you didn't have other plans. Looks like you two are staying for the picnic."

Actually, Rave wouldn't have it any other way.

Tuck had to admit, it felt good to be walking with Trini's arm threaded through his on the way to the picnic. But he knew what this was about. They'd known each other for a few decades, and the way she was acting, well, he knew she knew. "Who told you?" Tuck said.

She stopped filling her red cup with sweet tea and set it beside the drink station. Her arm tightened around his, and she pulled him away from the group waiting for drinks. "Becca told me. She was there when Sheriff Cogdill pulled over Rave."

Tuck frowned. "Rave got pulled over? He didn't tell me that part."

Trini pointed to a shady spot where there was more privacy. "Well, he'd been trying to get up the nerve to go into Sustenance and talk to

Becca. Sheriff spotted him. Asked him to wait to talk to Phil before leaving town."

Tuck fought back the emotion welling in his heart. "I sure got a lot of people lookin' out for me." And now they'd be looking out for Rave. If Tuck could only turn back the hands of time and bring Rave here sooner, back when they would have had years together instead of months. Tuck was all right with the fact of his mortality, but the thought of leaving Rave stabbed at his heart. Too many had left Rave already.

Trini squeezed his arm a little tighter and led him to a park bench under the giant oak tree in the churchyard. "You sure do, Tuck. But you haven't let many people in. You've been a good neighbor to me. Always there when I need you. But you've never really let me repay your kindness."

Around them, the sounds of a church picnic filled the air. Ladies laughing, children running around in a never-ending game of chase, men greeting one another with backslaps and man hugs. For a few moments, Tuck took it all in. The way the sun bounced off the giant cross on the steeple, the scent of fresh baked goods and newly cut grass, the feel of Trini beside him, staying close, keeping a point of contact on his skin at all times. Like a dream, almost; if she were to let go, he'd dissipate like fog. He forced his mind back to their conversation. "I only did what any good neighbor would do."

She laughed, and the sound rolled over him, clean water on a wound. "Not many neighbors would show up at all hours of the night, guns blazing and scaring away degenerates."

Tuck threaded his hands together on his lap. Trini's arm was fastened around his, and it felt good to have the touch of female flesh against his rough skin. "Millie made me come today." He practically whispered the words.

He felt Trini lean away from him, and when he looked over at her—expecting to see shock—he saw only her sweet smile. "I expect she did. And it's high time."

"I should have—" His throat closed on the words, making them impossible to speak until he swallowed. "I should have come with her when she was alive."

Trini patted his upper arm with her free hand and looked up into the swaying leaves of the oak tree. "She's here, I'd suspect. In the warmth of the sun and the fresh of the breeze. We don't lose the ones we love, Tuck, we just don't see them for a little while."

When Tuck lost Millie, he'd thought he'd die. Like the best part of him was already gone and what was left was just a shadow. But then, he'd sat on his porch and watched a massive storm front rolling in. He could swear he saw Millie in that vibrant, wild, blue-gray storm that rode the horizon and engulfed his house and the mountains around. Within the curtain of rain spilling over his roof, overflowing the gutters, he felt Millie. Right there. And she'd been with him since, in the softness of a setting sun, in the pristine beauty of a freshly fallen snow.

Someone was making his way to them. As he neared, Tuck saw it was the pastor. Tuck started to stand, but Keith motioned for him to remain seated. The two men shook hands. "Glad you came out today, Tuck."

"Good sermon. I enjoyed it." Tuck nodded as if the words needed a boost. He actually *had* enjoyed the sermon.

"Thank you." Pastor Keith put his hands on his waist. "Millie sure loved a get-together like this. She was always telling me we needed to have more picnics."

Tuck nodded. "Millie was a social creature at heart. She loved everybody, and everybody loved her. Sometimes she'd bring me home a plate lunch from the gathering."

Keith smiled and dropped a hand to Tuck's shoulder. "LaDonna and I speak of her often. She was an angel, Tuck. Just wanted to make sure you knew how fond of her we all were. The world became a sadder place when she left it."

Tuck rubbed a hand over his chin. "I know my world did."

"Well, if there's anything you need, anything at all, please, don't hesitate to call me."

Tuck turned to Trini. "Blabbermouth."

Keith laughed out loud. "Aw, I wouldn't blame her, Tuck. She told me in confidence so I could pray for you and Rave."

At the mention of his grandson, Tuck scanned the crowd for the boy. Off to the left of the picnic, Rave and a smiling Becca sat on a checkered picnic blanket. Keith's words warmed a place inside him. "You'd do that? Pray for him?"

Keith shrugged. "Of course, Tuck. That's what all this is about. We're family here. We may not be blood kin, but we're kin just the same. You won't have to face this alone. Neither will Rave."

Thousands of pounds lifted off Tuck's shoulders right there under the oak tree in the church lot. Just knowing that Rave would have people to lean on made the coming months almost bearable.

Keith lifted his chin. "Now, what immediate need do you have, and how can I help lift the burden?"

Tuck was a man who believed in folks putting their proverbial money where their mouth was. He crossed his arms over his chest, not bothering to remove Trini's hand. "You mean that, preacher?"

Keith smiled. "With all my heart."

Tuck nodded, straightened a little. "Well, sir, it involves whiskey and a memorial to the men I served with during Vietnam."

The preacher's brows went up, his chin went down. He blinked. "Is that right?"

Tuck nodded. "Yes, it is. Have I lost your support?"

"Not at all. I'd say this request is just getting interesting."

Rave had never seen a spread of food like the one that filled three long picnic tables. Becca had pointed out to him all the award-winning recipes while he drooled like a Doberman over the dessert table. Now she sprawled on a picnic cloth—checkered red and white, just like in the movies—and watched him eat two plates full of food. She had a few veggies and some dip on her plate but had barely touched any of it. "So, tell me about Ashley. She's the one you left behind, right?"

Rave ran a hand through his hair. "She had already dumped me. The more I find out about her now, the more I realize I was blind. Does that make any sense?"

Becca crossed her legs, tucking her flowing skirt around her. "Sure it does. When Michael left for college, I believed we could do the whole long-distance thing. But all I did was sit around thinking about how he was missing out on college life."

Rave frowned.

"It's a rite of passage, isn't it? The frat parties, the girls." Becca corralled her hair by sweeping it over her shoulder and clamping a hand around it. "It just seemed wrong that he was weighed down with a girl back home."

"Wow."

She searched his eyes for an explanation. "Was that sarcasm?"

"Um, let me think." Rave tapped his chin. "Yes. It was sarcasm."

Becca's cheeks reddened.

Rave set his plate aside and moved closer to her. "Weighed down? With you? Sorry, Becca, but any guy would be lucky to have a girl like you. And what are you even talking about, *rite of passage?*"

She opened her mouth, but he cut her off.

"Are you saying guys deserve to get to go off to college and act like idiots? Sleeping with as many girls as they want and partying every night?"

Becca dropped her head.

"That's pathetic, Becca. That's not a rite of passage. That's indulgence. It doesn't make someone a better man. It certainly doesn't build character. Any guy with half a brain would wait for you. You're worth it."

"He's a good guy. I didn't give him a choice."

Rave reached over and touched her leg. "There's always a choice, Becca." His fingers grazed her skin for a moment, but then he dropped his hand.

"It was too complicated. I don't need complicated. I need easy. Simple. There's a lot going on with my family—my dad is in a new job."

"You want to talk about it?" he said.

"No. We weren't talking about me. We were talking about you."

Rave leaned back. "Ashley is working her way out of my system."

Becca bumped his shoulder with hers. "You sure about that?"

He drew a long breath. "Trust me on this one. Funny how blinded we are until we get some distance."

"But you're not over her. You still seem so sad."

He wasn't over her. Rave reached for his lemonade. "It's not just Ashley. She has a little boy. He's like . . . well, kind of like my own kid, except he's not. I was with her when she went to the hospital to have him, and I've been in his life ever since." At the hospital, she'd even told the nurses Rave was the father so he could have access to the nursery whenever he wanted. Even though it was a lie, it had felt really good to be called Daniel's father.

"It's him you miss?"

Rave dropped a hand to his chest. "Yeah. It kills me. But, I mean, I miss her, too. She was a friend for a long time. Then we became more. It was pretty easy for her to let go, but I still feel—"

"Kind of abandoned?"

He wouldn't have used that word. But yes, he felt abandoned by Ashley. Even though he knew what really mattered to her now, and he understood that people like that only ever did what was best for themselves.

Becca scooted even closer. "Michael is in his second year at the University of Kentucky. It's in Lexington."

"So you guys haven't been together for two years?"

Her right shoulder tipped up. "We tried to pick up last summer. It worked until he left again. I told him not to let me know if he was coming home this summer."

Rave cleared his throat. "I wish I could say I'm sorry, but if you were taken, I doubt we'd be sitting here having a picnic together. It's dangerously close to a date." He winked.

She pressed her fingertips to her heart. "It's nothing like a date." But a tiny dimple appeared at the edge of her mouth, conspirator to her staunch reserve. "Do you like living with Tuck?"

"He's the best man I've ever known." Rave could say that honestly and with absolute confidence.

"My dad's the best man I've ever known." She smiled. "But I do love Tuck."

"He does a memorial for the men he served with in Vietnam."

"Like once a year or something?"

"Like twice a month."

"Wow." Becca's eyes rounded. "That's incredible."

Rave nodded. "Like I said, best man I've ever known. Hey, you need to eat. I'm not about to let all this food go to waste."

She squeezed her hands into fists and released them. "I'm always too nervous before a game. Can't eat a bite."

"You know what? I have a remedy for that." Rave took her by the hand and lifted her from her spot on the red-and-white blanket and then dragged her to the corner of the church, away from peering eyes. On one side of them was the parking lot filled with cars but no people, on the other, an empty field. Without allowing himself to consider the repercussions—'cause not considering was what he did best—Rave stepped in closer to her, until his thighs rested against hers.

Little pants of hot air slipped from between her lips. She threw a look left, then right.

"No one's watching," he purred.

She clenched her hands at her sides and squeaked, "This isn't helping my nerves."

"It will." Using an index finger, he moved the long strands of hair from her throat until it toppled over her shoulder. The neckline of her blue sweater skimmed her collarbone, creating for Rave an almost irresistible temptation to trace the edge of fabric. His eyes did what his fingers shouldn't.

She was breathing hard now, fuller breaths than at first, and knowing he'd had that effect on her created a sizzling ball in his stomach. His eyes trailed up and locked on hers.

She swallowed.

Rave hooked his thumb and finger around her chin and slowly tilted her head up and back as if he was going to point out something in the sky. The length of her tanned throat filled his vision. She moved willingly, no resistance, no restraint. With painstaking slowness, he brought his mouth closer and closer to her throat. But she held her ground, her hands flattened on the solid wall behind her as if it anchored her. Rave drew in a deep lungful of air and blew it over her throat. Her body went lax, her eyes closed.

He drew in another, surprised by how shaky his own breathing had become. This time, after he released the hot breath against her throat, he dropped a kiss on the spot where her pulse throbbed.

Her eyes opened. They were glassy and far away.

Rave grinned.

"Is that how you calm nerves in the city?" Her voice was rough.

He tipped one shoulder in a shrug. "Seemed to work."

Becca focused her attention on the barren field beside them. "I like it," she whispered. "It's better than what we do here in the country."

Rave planted a hand on the wall behind her, not moving closer, but also not moving away. "What do you do here?"

"Muck out manure from horse stalls. It works, too, but it smells worse."

Rave dropped his hand. "Well, at least I smell better than dirty horse stalls."

Her green eyes flashed. "Decidedly."

"You have a wicked sense of humor, redneck girl."

"And you have a strange sense of calm for a guy who wants to kiss me."

He moved a millimeter closer. "Who said I want to kiss you?"

Becca pushed herself off the wall and moved toward him until her cheek touched his. "You did," she whispered.

Magnets were peculiar things. Flip them one way, and they repelled each other; flip them over, and they created a bond not easily broken. Her cheek was velvet-soft against his. Her flesh warm from the sun and from the heat they'd generated. Rave tried to force his mind away from this girl, this girl who was so unlike him and yet such a perfect fit. He tried to think of Ashley. That's who he was in love with. That's who his heart belonged to, even if she'd never be his. Even if she was a liar and a user. But the image of Ashley refused to materialize.

There was only Becca. Becca with her auburn hair and cowboy boots. Becca with her fierce attitude and jewel eyes. But what if Rave was just using her? What if this was his way of getting over Ashley? The thought caused him to take a step back, breaking the contact.

Her emerald eyes narrowed. "You got a problem, city boy?"

Nervous energy flew off him in waves. "I don't . . . I don't want to hurt you."

She crossed her arms over her chest and lifted one foot until it rested against the wall behind her. "You planning on hurting me?"

He shook his head and brushed a hand over his face. "No. Absolutely not. But—" How had he so quickly lost control of this situation?

She drew a breath and let it out slowly. "We're just friends, Rave." But she didn't look at him when she said it. Her gaze was focused on a faraway spot on the barren field.

"Yeah," he agreed, but his heart wasn't in it.

"You want to hear some good news?" Her voice was just a little too cheery.

He tried to focus. "Sure."

She motioned for him to follow her back to the picnic area. "I'm not worried about the game anymore."

Rave chuckled and offered her his arm. "I told you it would calm your nerves. And you didn't even have to resort to manure."

CHAPTER 10

"That girl of yours sure knows how to pitch."

The game had been a shutout with Becca, dressed in her softball uniform and her hair tied back in a bandana, throwing a no-hitter. Rave had never dated a sports girl. Of course, he wasn't *dating* Becca, but that didn't keep him from feeling the pride—and also the pinch of jealousy—when the game ended and a steady stream of softball players, *guys*, came over to congratulate her with hugs.

She was elated at the eleven-to-nothing score.

Tuck set a plate of leftovers in front of him. Trini had fixed them up with the goods. "She was tough out there. Trini told me she had a partial scholarship to the University of Kentucky her senior year."

Rave stopped moving, the fork halfway to his mouth. He could smell pot roast. "Kentucky, huh?" Made sense, that's where her boyfriend had gone. "What happened?"

"Her daddy lost his job. They were looking at losing their home, and Becca decided to stay here and go to work full-time for Alexandra, who owns Sustenance. She helped pay the mortgage until her dad found work. They're still paying off the debt."

If he could admire her any more than he already did—unlikely—that bit of trivia tipped him right over the edge. "Does she still want to go to college?"

Tuck grinned over a spoonful of mashed potatoes. "Don't know. She's your girl, maybe you should ask her."

Rave liked the sound of that. His girl. But she wasn't. "Saw you talking to the preacher."

Tuck placed his spoon on the plate. "Yes sir, I did. I told him about the memorial. Asked him to help out."

Rave wasn't sure why Tuck would do that. He'd already told him he'd be doing the memorial as long as he lived.

"Now, don't go getting all concern-faced."

Rave bit his cheek. "Don't you trust me with it?"

"Just the opposite, boy. I trust you completely. But . . ." There was a long pause as Rave watched a barrage of emotions over Tuck's features. "It's a heavy burden to carry. I carried it alone for too long. Good memories are pillows. They bounce around inside you, giving your soul a soft place to land and rest. Hard memories are like daggers. They stab the soul until it can no longer bleed."

Rave leaned forward. "But they're not my memories, Tuck."

Tuck shook his head. "That's where you're wrong. They are. Because you chose to become part of them. They take a toll on your spirit. They bleed away your life. I've been worrying over this. And I didn't have an answer. I don't want to see you carry this burden alone. The preacher said he'd pray for us. And I believe he will. There's a better way, Rave. There's a better way to honor the men than what I've been doing."

"What is it, Tuck?"

He shook his head. "I don't know. But I believe we'll find it."

Rave reached over the table and gave Tuck's hand a squeeze. "Then we will."

"Are you still wanting to be an electrician?"

Tuck had given him a series of books that Rave had been sifting through at night. He'd found the work interesting, intriguing, and in some ways like a puzzle that needed to be put together. "Absolutely."

"Good. Come with me. I've got to show you something." Rave followed Tuck out the front door, and the two waited while Bullet hopped into the cab with them. Tuck drove from the house down a back path that Rave had assumed was only used for farm equipment a lifetime ago. Deep in the woods, they arrived at a small clearing and a cabin that rested against a backdrop of mountains. A narrow stream appeared beyond the shack as Rave hopped from the truck and looked around. Wildflowers grew in bright purple and yellow pops of color. Tuck stopped at the foot of the two steps leading to a narrow, covered porch. "This is where I fell in love with Millie." His fingers traced the line of a sunflower petal. "She used to gather these wildflowers and tie them with a dark scarlet ribbon. Always the same color. Always left for me to find on the rocking chair."

Rave could imagine his grandmother as a young woman clipping flowers and leaving them for Tuck. Rave's eyes fanned over the cabin with its tin roof and wooden shutters. He'd lived in worse places. "This is a pretty cool place, Tuck."

But Tuck was lost to the memories. Finally, he turned to Rave. "It's your first project. Wiring needs redone. I'll help and instruct as you go, but you'll have to do most of the work."

Surely Tuck wasn't serious. Rave didn't know enough to start a real project. "But I've only been reading the books."

"And have you learned anything?"

"Yes. I understand the concept. But am I ready to take on a job?"

"Nope. That's why you're gonna do it. When this is done, I'll call Brice and see about getting you on at his company. Sound like a plan?"

Rave nodded and couldn't suppress the grin that appeared on his face. "Yes, sounds amazing." Together, they entered the small cabin. Once inside, it occurred to him that Tuck was pushing things into high gear. Rushing the training, choosing someone to help with the memorial. The realization stole the excitement from his new job. Tuck was preparing to leave him.

☙

May ended, and Tuck's strength stayed the same as when Rave had first met him. They worked on the cabin, bringing it back to life and running out the forest critters that had taken up residence. June was warm and beautiful in the Smoky Mountains. Rave missed surfing, and every windy day reminded him of the waves he wouldn't conquer. But life was good. Ashley had called a few times and let him talk to Daniel. Rave never mentioned that he knew about Barry and the trip to the Keys, but his mood toward her was friendly, nothing more. She didn't mention the state of her love life, and Rave didn't ask. Rave had seen the real picture of Ashley—the one she'd always tried to hide from him. Ashley was a girl with a backup plan. Always. Maybe that was how she made it through life. Rave was her backup plan if things didn't work out with Barry. With each passing day, the love he'd had for her had died a little more.

The wind around the hillsides picked up the cool of the water. He'd spent many an evening with Becca, sitting on the pier near her house. He'd end each night asking her if she wanted to go out with him. She'd smile and say, "No." Her eyes would blink, and in them, he'd see the same emotion he felt whenever they were together. Like what they shared was too delicate to mess up with simple things like dating. It was precious, and one wrong move could cause it to disintegrate as fast as tissue on a water spot. He believed with all his heart this was the reason she said no when he'd ask her out.

He'd been working on ideas for the memorial for Tuck's men. It was a cool Saturday, and they were just closing up shop at the swap meet when Becca came running out of Sustenance. She jogged over, her hair flying in the breeze, and Rave clutched his chest. It was in that moment, the moment his eyes landed on hers and her mouth slipped into that perfect smile that he knew. He'd fallen for Becca. They weren't even dating. They hadn't really kissed. But his heart had already betrayed him. Her cheeks were flushed from the jog over, and she was breathless. "Hey."

He was breathless, too. "Hey."

There was a grin, a knowing grin, on her face. She had a secret and was bursting to tell it.

Rave frowned. "What?"

Becca licked her lips—which made all his other thoughts fly right out of his head. "I'm waiting," she said.

He glanced around. "For what?"

Her brow tilted seductively. "For you to ask me out."

He rolled his eyes. "Becca, will you go out with me?"

"Yes."

He went back to packing up the tools Tuck had spread on their swap meet table until her single word registered. "Wait a minute. What?"

She rose up on her toes. "I said . . . yes."

"But you're supposed to say no."

She cocked her hip. "You want me to say no?"

"No!"

Her smile returned. "Then pick me up at eight at my house." Becca turned and ran back to Sustenance, leaving a gaping Rave behind. Everything in their relationship tipped on its axis. She was changing the rules. Changing the game. They were actually going on a date. Rave couldn't be happier.

Tuck made his way over to Rave. "Looks like you seen a ghost, boy."

Rave closed his mouth. "A miracle is more like it."

Tuck followed his gaze to the shop across the square. "Becca, huh? She's your angel. Just like Millie was mine. What do you say to burgers and fries for lunch at Vernie's? Then maybe we can stop off and buy those cell phones we've been talking about getting for a month."

They'd tried once before, but all the information thrown at Tuck had completely worn him out. He'd left the place with a handful of pages of printed information that quickly found their way to the floorboard of the truck. Still, Rave knew Tuck would go the cellular route when he was ready. "That sounds great, Tuck."

Tuck opted out of the cell phone purchasing and spent most of the rest of the day chattering about the swap meet. Rave had little to add to the discussion. He was still shell-shocked by the conversation with Becca. He started to tell Tuck several times that he'd be taking Becca on a date later, but each time he'd started to, something stopped him. He wasn't a big believer in omens, but going out with Becca—it just felt like he'd jinx it if he talked about it. At seven o'clock, he slipped upstairs to shower and change his clothes. He'd bought his own cologne, so he splashed it onto his neck and chest. It was nearly eight when he headed downstairs to tell Tuck he was going out. At the foot of the stairs, he saw it.

There, Tuck was setting out the shot glasses and filling them from a pitcher of water. Tuck looked up and grinned. "Hey, you dressed up for the memorial."

Rave grabbed the banister because the room had suddenly gone into a tailspin. How could he forget? How could he forget tonight was the memorial?

Tuck placed the pitcher on the table. "You feeling OK, son? You look a little sickly." Tuck sniffed the air. "You stink pretty, though."

"I'm—I'm all right. I just, I need to make a call before we get started."

Tuck grinned. "Phone's in the kitchen. It's on the charger 'cause I forgot about it last night." They really needed to get cell phones. Tuck had insisted that Rave keep all the cash from the swap meets, and now he had plenty to get a phone on his own, but the idea of a *family* plan—something he'd never experienced—had kept him from moving forward alone.

Rave made his way into the kitchen and grabbed the phone. It was dead. He placed it on the charger and stared across the kitchen, where the light over the stove flashed 7:52. He'd just tell Tuck they needed to start the memorial a little bit later tonight. No problem. He could run over to Becca's—it was only ten minutes away—and explain. They could go out tomorrow night. Or the next or whenever she wanted to. But not tonight.

Tuck came into the kitchen. "You ready?"

Rave brushed a hand through his hair. "Tuck, I need to tell you something."

Tuck nodded. "I know what it is."

A breath of relief left Rave. "You do?"

Tuck placed a hand on his shoulder. "Sure I do. You want to lead the memorial tonight. It's why you've been so quiet today. It's why you dressed up."

Cold shot from Rave's head down his spine.

Tuck's watery blue eyes misted. "I know you're nervous. I know you want to honor the men the same way I do." Tuck's chin quivered. "Rave, you're afraid of letting me down. You could never let me down. I'm so proud of you."

Rave's eyes closed. He swallowed past the tightness in his throat. He'd *already* let Tuck down. But he wouldn't make it worse. "Let's get started, Tuck. We don't want to keep the men waiting."

CHAPTER 11

An insistent knock on the front door caused Rave and Tuck both to rise. No one had ever come to the door during the memorial, so Rave didn't know what to do. He looked to Tuck for the answer. Tuck hooked a thumb toward the door. "You gonna get that or should I?"

"I'll get it," Rave said. It was 8:31. He knew the time without looking at the wall clock because the last thirty minutes had seemed like an eternity. Becca would never forgive him. His gaze had gone to the clock every two minutes. With each passing one, he knew Becca floated farther and farther away.

He opened the door and there she stood, eyes wide. "Is Tuck OK?"

Her concern caused him to glance back at his grandfather. "Yes."

She grabbed Rave by the upper arms. "And you? Bleeding anywhere?"

"No."

She shoved him away. "Then you better have one heck of a good reason for standing me up."

Rave moved forward, trying to muscle her onto the front porch, but she pushed past him. He tried to catch her, but he stumbled over Bullet.

"Hi, Tuck," Becca said.

He stood at the table, one hand resting on the back of an empty chair. "Hello, Becca."

"How are you feeling?"

Rave rubbed a hand over his face and followed her in.

Tuck drew a long breath. "Feeling good. Getting tired. It's been a long day, and we're only halfway through the memorial."

Her gaze shot to Rave, then to the table, then to Tuck. Understanding dawned. Rave watched it wash over her features. "Actually, Tuck, that's why I'm here."

She sent a stern look over to Rave. He didn't know what to do, what with his heart pounding out of his chest, so he just split his glances between Becca and Tuck. She offered Tuck her perfect smile. "If it would be all right, I'd like to stay for the rest of the memorial."

A frown deepened the lines on Tuck's face. "You would?"

She nodded. "You know my dad was in Afghanistan. One tour with his reserve unit. He doesn't talk about it much, but I think maybe war is war. If I'm not intruding, I'd really like to stay. It might help me understand some of the things he went through."

Tuck pulled out a seat for her. "It'd be an honor to have you."

They both sat down while Rave struggled to understand what had just happened.

When Rave finally joined them, Tuck pointed a finger at him. "You did good. Now, I'll take it from here."

Tuck began a story about Joe Malfree, the medic. Rave had heard it more than once, but with a new audience, Tuck seemed to insert details Rave had never known. Since the burden of the memorial would one day fall to him, he needed to remember these side notes.

Becca interrupted his thoughts and Tuck's words. "How did the medic not get shot? I mean, if the bullets were flying, and he's standing over the guy that was just hit, he'd be a target."

"Sometimes I'd think Joe was impervious to bullets, like they bounced off of him or something. It was crazy. He'd stand in the exact spot where one of the men had gotten shot and—" Tuck shook his head. "I don't know, I can't explain it."

"Were you able to call in an airstrike? You said the radio was damaged." Becca was on the edge of her seat, eyes wide, forearms locked on the tabletop.

Tuck nodded. "We finally got air support. We were fighting uphill, plus we were pinned down. Worst-case scenario. The airstrike was going to be danger close."

"Is that a military term?" Becca again. Rave might as well have been invisible. "I've never heard my dad use that one."

Tuck nodded. "It means the airstrike is in dangerously close proximity to where your unit is."

Becca blew out a breath. "If they were off by one degree—"

"Yes, ma'am. Radio controller had a high-stress job in a high-stress situation. I can't tell you how many times he saved our bacon. In those moments, most of us just had to point and shoot. But the Band-Aids and the radio operators—those were true tactical positions."

"Band-Aids, is that what you called the medics?"

Tuck nodded.

Rave looked from Becca to Tuck and back again. She was leaning forward and hanging on Tuck's every word. She was either the best actress on the planet, or she was genuinely intrigued by Tuck's stories.

They were amazing, no doubt. Even though Rave had heard them multiple times, he still found them astonishing.

Time passed, and as the hours slipped by, Rave could see Tuck's energy waning. When the memorial was over, Tuck yawned. "I'm headed to bed. You two enjoy the rest of your night."

He started to walk toward his bedroom, but Becca stopped him. She placed a kiss on his cheek. "Thanks for sharing this, Tuck."

He leaned closer and whispered in her ear, "Sorry I messed up your date." With Rave so close by, he easily heard the words.

"You knew?" Becca hissed.

He glanced at Rave, then back to her. "A boy don't look at a girl like that unless he's truly smitten with her. And Rave doesn't dress up for the memorial. Or put on cologne. I hope you two can still have a nice date."

Becca reached out and hugged him. "We already did."

Tuck went to bed while Becca helped Rave clear the table of the shot glasses. Once Tuck's door was closed, Rave said, "I'm so sorry, Becca."

She winked. "It's sweet, Rave. You weren't willing to leave him alone. You're a good grandson."

"I was so excited when you said you'd go out with me, I forgot it was memorial night. And that ancient cordless phone is dead half the time." Rave went into the kitchen and left the shot glasses by the sink. He opened the fridge and found a pitcher of iced tea. "Can I pour you some?"

She chewed her bottom lip. "Should I go home now?"

"No. Let's sit out back and watch the lake for a while. Give you time to process everything you heard tonight."

She followed Rave with Bullet just behind them. Rave scooted the two lounge chairs together, and Becca sat on one while he took the other. "It's not too late, if you'd rather go to town, get some food or something."

But Becca had already rested her head against the lounger and closed her eyes. "No. This is perfect."

"Did it help you understand more about your father?"

Becca looked over at him. "It really did."

"I didn't know your dad was a veteran."

"Lots of vets in town. I don't know why they don't reach out to one another. They're all carrying the same kinds of burdens, even though years and technology separate their journeys."

Rave watched the beams of the moon splash across the dark water.

Becca took a drink of her tea. "I wish there was a way to unify them. Did you know that during World War Two Barton received national attention?"

Rave leaned forward.

"Barton was a small town back then."

Rave chuckled. "Smaller than now?"

She gave him a mock glare. "Way smaller. In fact, every family in town had sent a firstborn son to war. One by one, they were all killed in action. Barton became known as the Firstborn Miracle Town."

Rave sat up so he could look at her fully. "Why would it be considered a miracle town if all the firstborns had died?"

"Because of the town's spirit. Barton didn't allow the tragedy to dampen its spirit, its zeal for life and for supporting the young men who were still over there. Lots of second- and third-born sons were still fighting. Instead of the town wallowing in its grief, it banded together and began sending multitudes of care packages not only to our young men but others. The fire spread, and soon towns from hundreds of miles away were sending care packages to GIs they'd never met. The boxes all had one thing in common: they all said, 'From the Firstborn Miracle Town.'"

Rave let the story saturate him. Why hadn't he heard that before? He'd been there almost two months now and had never heard that. "How did you know about it?"

"We learned it in school. I'm sure there is information on the Internet. Also, the town library has an area devoted to it. It's sort of our town's big claim to fame."

"It seems like everyone should know. I mean, that's a really big deal, Bec. There should be a plaque as you enter town or a monument or something."

"More than a dark corner of the library?"

"Yeah." For a town to have the grit to lose so much but still honor the men who continued to fight . . . it was inspiring. Like Tuck's memorial was inspiring. Why didn't everyone know about things like this? Before coming to Barton, Rave had given little thought to the men and women who'd died for his country. Now they filled his mind. He pushed to his feet and paced the porch. Bullet sat up and watched him. "Tuck has a memorial for the men he lost, but no one knows about it. I just wish I could do something. I wish there was a way to make their sacrifice known."

Becca stood and walked to him. "Can I help?"

For an instant, the idea was gone. There was only her and Rave and a moonlit night, and they were alone. She smelled like soft flowers and woman and strawberry shampoo. Without warning, the desire to kiss her swept into his system, stealing its way through every nerve ending and settling around his heart. Rave reached out and ran a hand through her hair where the soft breeze had tumbled the strands.

When she didn't move away, but rather leaned closer to him, Rave stepped in and pressed the lower half of his body to hers. They were less than a breath apart, and when Becca's tongue darted out to moisten her lips, he knew she knew his intention. His lips met hers gently, and he gave himself a moment to drink her in while their mouths mingled. Then, the timbre of the moment changed. He captured her head in his hand, deepening the kiss. She was soft against him—a woman's flesh, so different from his own. But she wasn't weak. She was strong. Powerful. A force in her own right, and the feel of her mouth on his only added to her power. He could drown in the sea of Becca. Still, this was their first date. And their first real kiss, and though he'd love nothing more than to continue on this track, he knew he shouldn't. With reluctance, he broke the kiss.

Her breathing was jagged. He liked that. Becca licked her lips again and flashed a quick smile. "You . . . you didn't answer my question about helping."

Rave drew her closer and tucked her beneath his arm. "You can help. I wouldn't have it any other way." She pressed her head to his chest, and Rave buried his nose in her hair.

"Thanks," she whispered. "I'll set up a meeting with the mayor."

Rave cringed. "What? Why?" He was a street kid from Tampa who'd spent his adult life washing dishes at a greasy spoon. He wasn't someone who waltzed into the mayor's office for a chat. He wasn't someone who walked into *anyone's* office for *anything*. She wrapped her arms around his waist. "We have to start somewhere."

༄

Tuck used the key around his neck to unlock the door to Millie's sitting room. He didn't look at the unfinished paint or the empty, etched water glass. He went straight to the closet and grabbed the photo albums. Unable to take this particular trip down memory lane in the room where Millie died, he carried the albums to his bedroom.

Tuck fought the onslaught of emotions as he went through the photos. Three albums full of pictures. Pictures that hadn't seen the light of day for years.

Rave was living at his home now. But the young man remembered nothing of the life they'd shared when he was a baby. When Sharon and Rave lived there under the same roof. In the room that became Millie's sitting room after Sharon broke their hearts and fled with two-year-old Rave.

Tuck ran a thumb over the grinning baby face in one photo. He didn't know what to do with the photographs now. He couldn't leave this life without Rave knowing the truth. He couldn't leave without asking the boy's forgiveness for never wanting him to be born.

Tuck wiped a fresh batch of tears from his face and stared at the child in the photograph. A white T-shirt and striped pajama pants, hair tousled and sleep still in his eyes. Just like he'd looked that Sunday morning weeks back when they'd attended their first church service.

But in this photo, a coastal breeze pressed against them. Rave had wanted to see the ocean. He was only two. His momma, a few years into her drug-addicted lifestyle, had been doing better—or so they thought—and so Tuck and Millie loaded Sharon and Rave into the car, and off to Florida they went. They'd gone straight to the Gulf of Mexico when they arrived. Millie had said to let Rave sleep, but Tuck nudged the little guy until he woke. "Are we there?" were the first words he'd said.

Tuck had taken him in his arms and carried him down the long wooden boardwalk that led to the water's edge. Rave had pointed out palm trees as they went. He'd never seen a palm tree before and asked Tuck if they were magic trees.

The ocean slapped at the shoreline, and Rave stood in awe of the massive body of water. His bright eyes the size of saucers when he said, "Big, big, big."

Tuck grinned.

Tiny toes wriggled into the sand. Then fingers followed, his striped behind still in the air. "Oooohhh." Rave held his hands out and scrubbed them together, watching the bits of sand catch the light from the sun. Behind him, Millie and Sharon watched as they made their way to the shore. Millie snapped picture after picture. For the briefest of moments, everything was right with the world. His daughter was off the drugs. His beautiful little grandson was experiencing a first. Tuck was so filled with love, it felt as though the moment could last forever. He hadn't known. He hadn't known that drug addicts were expert liars. He hadn't known his daughter was just as bad off as she'd been before, and this was a last-ditch effort to coerce more money from Tuck and Millie. He hadn't known that in three days, when they returned home, he'd have to take drastic actions.

And he hadn't known those actions would have devastating consequences. Sharon had overdosed, nearly died. Then left the hospital before she'd been released. Tuck was going to have her committed and take steps to get custody of Rave. But Sharon found out. And she ran. And though they'd searched for a year to find her, she'd completely dropped off the grid. With the grandson Tuck and Millie had grown to love.

The same grandson he hadn't wanted Sharon to carry to term.

All those memories chewed away at Tuck now. How could he have thought he deserved to raise a child he'd never wanted to be born? The pregnancy had been a dangerous one, just as the doctor said it would be because of Sharon's malnourishment. Cocaine had become her drug of choice, and the risks to an addicted mother included heart attack, seizure, and stroke. The doctor had warned she might not survive. The risks to the fetus were just as dangerous. But she'd refused to abort the child.

In the two years they'd gotten to know baby Rave, they'd loved him more than life. It was when Sharon nearly died from the overdose that Tuck knew he had to step in. But for all his good intentions to do what was best for two-year-old Rave, Tuck had forced Sharon's hand. And because Tuck had, Millie died with a broken heart, never knowing what had become of her daughter and grandson.

Tuck placed the albums in a stack and carried them back to the sitting room. He closed the lid on the box where they lived. He was too tired to approach this subject today. Soon. Soon, he'd tell Rave everything. And he couldn't wait too long, because Tuck knew time was running out for him.

∞

Rave had expected a more presidential office for the town's mayor. He'd never been in a mayor's office before, but he had envisioned a palatial room with a sturdy mahogany desk and thick-framed licenses and diplomas.

This room was on the smallish side and spartan. One desk, a row of filing cabinets, an American flag in the corner, a few family photos. The desk was littered with papers and manila folders. One window looked out over town.

The assistant outside had instructed them to have a seat, but Rave crossed the room and stared out the window. Below, the courtyard was a bustle of busy townspeople. It was different from the weekends, though. Local traffic, not the visitors drawn by the swap meet.

Off in the distance, Rave noticed the place where dreams die and wondered if his gaze trailing there was a bad omen. This felt like an insurmountable task. Would the mayor even want a monument or a plaque at the edge of town? They'd shut out an entire factory. Why would they listen to one street kid who wanted to honor his grandfather?

Behind him, he heard Becca stand and the swoosh of someone coming into the room. Rave turned as she introduced herself. "I'm Mayor Calloway." Brisk steps brought her to Rave's feet. Her hand was outstretched, her white shirt peeking from beneath a red blazer. She was around forty and attractive, and tall heels highlighted a set of slender legs beneath her knee-length black skirt.

Rave shook her hand. "Rave Wayne, Miss Mayor. Or is it Mrs.? Or—"

She grinned and pumped his hand. "Madame Mayor is proper, but you can also call me Mayor Calloway."

Mayor Calloway faced Becca. "It's nice to see you, Rebecca. I've missed our chats."

Becca hugged her and turned to Rave. "I did a job shadow for school here. Municipal work is actually pretty cool."

Mayor Calloway motioned for them to sit down. "Well, I've never been interested in taking my politics to the next level, but I adore being part of my local government. Becca was a natural fit here. I hated for the job shadow to end."

Rave looked over and gave Becca a smile.

"My assistant briefed me on your thoughts and concerns. From what I understand, you'd like to see a commemorative plaque honoring our Firstborn Miracle Town veterans. Is that right?"

Becca looked at Rave to answer. But instead of speaking, he rose and walked back to the window where he could see the town. The flowering trees, the courtyard, the square. "No, ma'am." The problem was, all too often he spoke without thinking. In fact, he'd made a career of it. The germ of an idea had been planted when he first glanced out this window. Instead of dying—like any ridiculous idea should—it had taken root. Then, with no encouragement from him, it had quickly grown with grander thoughts watering it, making it expand.

Becca stood and moved to Rave. She put a hand on his shoulder. "Rave? What do you mean, no? This is why we came here."

Ideas were dangerous things. They crashed through good intentions and common sense. Passion lit his words when he said, "Bec. It's not enough." His brow furrowed, his hand touched her arm. "Don't you see? It's not enough." His voice was soft, far away, but it held the power of perfectly placed bombs.

The atmosphere in the room changed. The mayor slowly rose to her feet, her eyes ablaze with curiosity about what manner of thing could cause a young man practically to burst with desperation.

"This town is full of veterans, Madame Mayor." He'd made a choice to call her by her proper name—and he watched the admission flicker in her eyes. She knew he meant business. "Look out there. How many families were touched by the Firstborn during World War Two? How many veterans are walking your streets today who put their lives on the line for our freedom? Madame Mayor, two Saturday nights a month,

I sit with my grandfather at his dining table while he honors the men who died in Vietnam. And Tuck's—" He had to swallow before he could finish. "Tuck's dying now. Who'll honor the men? Why haven't we honored them already?"

The mayor's eyes glistened. "What do you have in mind, young man?"

He reached over and took Becca's hand because he'd gone rogue on her, and that wasn't fair. Still, she couldn't escape all the blame. She was the one who'd given him the strength to do this. "The place where dreams die."

The mayor frowned and looked at Becca for an explanation.

Becca sucked in a breath. "The park. A memorial park for our veterans."

Mayor Calloway crossed her arms over her chest. "The park on Tenth Street?"

Becca squeezed Rave's hand, excitement flying off her in waves. "Yes, ma'am. It's owned by the city. And no one is using it."

Mayor Calloway's eyes narrowed, her sharp mind visibly clicking off ideas. "How committed to this are you two? Because this would be a huge undertaking. The town of Barton doesn't have the staff to accomplish it."

Becca took a step toward the mayor. "What about a committee? Couldn't you call for a volunteer committee? We could get donations to help with the cost."

Mayor Calloway nodded. "I can present your suggestion to the council. At the end of the day, they would say yes or no."

Rave couldn't help but notice the minuscule smile on the mayor's face. "But you're on board with this idea, right? We have your support?"

She considered him. "Yes, Rave. You have my support. It's time we had a place to commemorate our men *and women* who died in combat."

His cheeks burned. "Yes, ma'am. I didn't mean any disrespect. It's just that Tuck talks about the men who were with him. That's the only reference I have to work from."

She tilted her head. "Forgiven."

Rave rubbed his hands against the thighs of his pants. "So, you'll talk to the council? We don't need to do a presentation or anything?"

Her gaze narrowed on him again. "Have you ever considered politics? I think you'd be a natural."

"Not even for a second." Rave tried to swallow, but his collar was choking him. Or maybe that was fear.

The mayor crossed her arms. "Well, you'll get a taste. No, I don't need you to address the city council . . . unless you want to."

"No thanks. I'm nervous enough just being in your office."

She chuckled. "You have my support, Rave, as long as you're both willing to be on the committee."

His hand grew sweaty in Becca's. "What? No one wants to listen to a couple of kids." And though Rave didn't consider himself a kid, he knew people like Mayor Calloway did.

"That's my final offer," she said, then sat down.

Rave and Becca looked at each other.

Mayor Calloway continued. "You're the ones with the vision for this, so you need to see it through. Also, you might talk to Pastor Keith about volunteering for the committee. That's if the city council agrees to the restoration of the park."

Becca sat down. "Pastor Keith lost a brother in Afghanistan, didn't he? My dad told me that."

Mayor Calloway nodded. "He's expressed an interest in doing something for our local veterans. He made a point to speak with me just a few days ago. I even asked him why now. He said he'd had a nice chat with Tuck Wayne at church a few Sundays back. He mentioned something about whiskey and a memorial. I don't know how the whiskey fits into all this, but it would seem our good pastor has a soft spot in his heart for the veterans. My guess would be that his conversation with Tuck stirred up that burden."

Rave sat down, mostly because he was the only one still standing, but a little bit because his knees were weak. Someone was watching out for them, plowing the ground before they ever planted a seed. "Do you really think we could do this?"

The mayor nodded. "I really do. You'll need the town's support, no question. It'll be a lot of people hours to get this rolling, but yes, Rave. I think you can."

Two weeks passed before Rave got word that the city council was willing to consider handing over operations of the park if a suitable volunteer committee emerged and had the means to care for the park. By suitable, he figured they meant more people than two twenty-somethings with an idea. They'd talked to Pastor Keith, who said he'd spread the word to some of the men and women in town he knew would be interested. By the time Rave was able to meet the city council members, he had a list of a dozen businessmen and -women who believed in the project. For now, he was keeping it from Tuck, but once it went public, he'd have to tell him. The only reason he was waiting was because he'd started sketching ideas in a notebook, and he wanted to have something concrete to show his grandfather when the time was right. Tuck had good days and bad days now, thanks in part to a new medication the doctor was trying on him. Sometimes he had energy, and sometimes he stayed on the couch watching old Westerns. When they finally found the right combination of medications and the right dosage, Tuck's energy began to return.

They'd settled into a nice routine of early dinner and spending time in the kitchen talking about everything and nothing. Becca came by whenever she wasn't working, and the three of them would swap stories and laugh until they cried. Sometimes, Tuck would ask why Rave didn't spend more time with Becca. Rave would wink and say, "Priorities, Tuck. Got to keep my priorities in order."

But Becca had become a constant in Rave's life. Though Tuck didn't realize it, once he was asleep, Rave and Becca spent long evenings on the front porch listening to the crickets or sitting on the back patio looking out over the lake. Sometimes they'd talk, sometimes they merely sat there, wrapped in each other's arms. They'd also gone out on a few dates, which was nice, but Tuck was always in the back of Rave's mind. He didn't know how long they had. And Tuck had spent enough time alone before Rave came to Barton.

Friday morning, Tuck and Rave had just launched into a conversation about spaghetti Westerns when Rave heard the knock on the front door. He told Tuck he'd get it. On his way, as he passed through the living room, he counted off the items in his head for today's swap meet. Everything was loaded in the truck. When he tugged the door open, his heart stammered to a stop. His gaze landed on her first—the long blonde hair, pushed forward by the summer wind, the hopeful eyes. Beside her, the little boy Rave adored. "Ashley? *Daniel?*"

He leaped into Rave's arms, a squeal ripping through the air and settling in Rave's ears.

"What—what are you guys doing here?" Rave hugged Daniel so hard, he feared he'd hurt him. But Daniel only nuzzled closer, wrapping his arms around Rave's neck and blowing little-boy puffs of air on his throat. Emotions surged, and Rave squeezed his eyes shut, hoping, praying that he wasn't dreaming. He'd had too many dreams lately where what he loved slipped silently through his fingers.

When he finally opened his eyes, Daniel lost interest in him and reached down for Bullet. The boy turned into squirming knees and elbows to get out of Rave's grasp and introduce himself to the dog who weighed half as much as Rave himself.

Ashley's hands were crossed in tentative fashion over the waist of her beige summer dress. It was one of Rave's favorites on her, and he had to consider the irony of her now standing at his door in a garment he used to love to try to get her out of.

His eyes met hers, and she smiled. Sweet, innocent. Two things she wasn't.

"Can we come in?" she asked.

Daniel was already in. Flat on his back and getting a tongue bath from Bullet. Deep belly laughs rumbled from him, causing both Rave and Ashley to watch. Was there anything happier than a child with a dog?

"Yeah." Rave motioned for her to come inside just as Tuck came out of the kitchen.

"Truck's ready. Who was at the—" But Tuck looked up and saw them standing there, and he stopped dead in his tracks. "Oh."

Rave tried to breathe, but the air had gone stale. "Tuck, this is Ashley and Daniel."

"Nice to meet you, Ashley. Rave's told me a lot about you."

She smiled, blinked several times, looking angelic behind those dazzling blue eyes, her oval face filled with hope. Show. This was a show, and Tuck was the audience. "Your home is lovely."

Tuck's brows rose slowly. "You think?"

Oh, come on, Tuck. Don't fall for this.

"Yes, I do." She took a tiny step forward.

Tuck grinned. "In that case, I won't hold your bad judgment against you."

Rave bit his cheeks.

Ashley visibly stiffened.

Tuck was no one's fool. "Well, I'm sure you have a lot to talk about. I'll head on over to the swap meet. If I don't see you there, Rave, we'll catch up later."

Concern pinched Rave's gut. "Tuck, you can't unload everything by yourself."

He waved a dismissive hand. "I'll get Buck and Rowdy to help me. Like as not, they'll be hanging around waiting to talk to you. Take your time."

Rave nodded. Tuck left. The air was thick. Thick and muggy for June and still surging through the open door. He motioned for Ashley to follow him, and they sat on the couch. Rave's system boiled with questions. But he'd be patient. He'd see just how she planned to let this play out.

"I'm sorry I didn't call," she said.

"I'm uh—surprised to see you." Rave clenched his hands on his lap, an attempt to squelch the jitters that racked his system. As happy as he was to see Daniel, the boy and his mother were a package deal.

Ashley scooted closer to him and touched his leg. Her hand lingered, and he ignored the sensation it sent through him. And the longing. "Rave, you need to be in Daniel's life. You're such an important part of it."

He bit into his tongue until he tasted blood, willing her hand to move off him. "Really? Because it seemed pretty easy for you to replace me with Barry."

She jerked away from him. "I should have listened to you about him. But I told you, we're done. I knew—I knew—the day he refused to help with the bills that we couldn't count on him. He took the paternity test, and he's not Daniel's father. Daniel deserves better than that, Rave. We deserve someone who won't let us down."

He deserves better quickly became *we deserve someone.* "So, you and Barry broke up?"

She flashed a frown. "Yes. Weeks ago. I told you that when you sent me the money for rent."

Rave bristled. A sudden rush of anger drove him off the couch. Bullet noticed and sat up, but Daniel scrubbed at the dog's ears, and he turned into a melting ball of fur. Rave turned his fury on Ashley but lowered his voice so Daniel wouldn't hear. "You're lying, Ash."

Her eyes widened. "Rave, listen to me. My sister has taken a job working on a private yacht. Her leaving made me realize how important you are to me. And Lord knows you're the sun and moon to Daniel. We need you, Rave. I've—I've come here to stay."

What? *What?* As much as he'd love to see Daniel on a daily basis, he wasn't about to move them into Tuck's house. His thoughts went to Becca. The girl who was everything he'd needed and nothing he'd expected. The room darkened around him to one tiny pinpoint of light. In the center was Ashley. And she was pleading.

"We've already rented an apartment downtown. It's small, a single bedroom, so Daniel doesn't have his own room, but he said he didn't care. As long as he could be close to you."

Rave's heart might as well be ripped right from his chest.

Ashley moved close to Rave. She whispered, "He's started referring to you as Dad."

Rave spun on her with anger that was clouded by the love he felt for Daniel. As if on cue, Daniel threw his arms around Bullet and uttered, "Dad, Dad, Dad."

Rave pulled a deep breath. "You moved here?"

"We got in yesterday. I wanted to surprise you. I've already got a job at the café, Vernie's? It's on Main."

Frustration caused his eyes to close. "Yeah, I know where it is."

"Anyway, I was hoping you could keep Daniel during my shifts. You know, like old times?"

Keep Daniel. Rave's gaze went to the beautiful little boy rolling on the floor with Bullet. Keep Daniel. The desire to maintain a relationship with the little boy he loved overwhelmed his senses. There'd been a Daniel-shaped hole in Rave's life. He couldn't deny that.

Ashley must have known he was softening. She stepped closer and wrapped her arms around him. He remained stiff, motionless. Moments ticked past, Rave trying, trying to make sense of all of this, Ashley desperate for him to just give in.

"I'm sorry about the Dad thing," she whispered, scooting her agile, soft body against his stern one. "I've told him not to, but he'd found out that Barry might be his father, and when he did, he came to me and said, '*Rave* is my daddy. Rave. Not Barry.' He's called you Daddy ever since."

The very idea toppled Rave's equilibrium. There was nothing he'd love more than to be Daniel's daddy. But he wasn't. And he never could be. He'd have to go back to being just Rave to the little guy.

Her hands moved rhythmically over his back. She pressed against him. "Rave, can we just start over? I made a stupid, horrible mistake with Barry. And I realized, I love you."

The air left his lungs. A punch to the gut would have been better. A fist to the face. A kick to the ribs. This, this was what pain was made of. The mix—anger, regret, frustration—all making an explosive cocktail. "Ashley."

She smiled up at him, feigning innocence and exuding hope.

"I'm with someone else."

Her hands dropped to her sides. Her face hardened. "Break up with her. We're here now. *We're* your family."

"You're the one who pushed me away, Ash. You forced me to stay away from Daniel. So, don't think for one second that you can walk right back into my life like that never happened." He reached out and cuffed his hands around her wrists. Rave leaned so close to her face, she barely had room to blink. "You gutted me that day." The words were a growl. They came from deep inside his soul, and they left no room for argument.

Understanding dawned. She'd burned a bridge that could never be rebuilt. Her gaze shot to Daniel, her eyes welling with tears. "What are we going to do?" She said it to the air, to the house, to anyone and everything except Rave.

He released her wrists. "I'll give you enough money to get back to Tampa." It broke his heart to say it because the idea of having Daniel close by was a temptation he could barely resist.

She shook her head, hopelessly. "No. I walked out on my job to come here. There's nothing for us there anymore. Nicole's gone, working on that stupid yacht." She sank into a nearby chair. Her hands were trembling as she wound them together. "We're alone. Daniel and I, we're completely alone in the world."

Rave clenched his teeth until they ached. How many times had his mother told him that they were alone in the world? Of all the things he feared, having Daniel grow up like that topped the list. Without her sister, Ashley really had no one.

He'd regret this—he knew that already. "Look, Barton is a nice town. Good for raising a child. Ashley, if you've already rented a place, you might as well give it a chance. Stay for a while, see how things work out."

Hope filled her features again.

He needed to squelch it. "But you and I—we will never be a couple again. You need to understand that. I know you didn't spend the money I gave you on rent. I know you left town with Barry and went to the Keys."

"You don't understand," she said, rushing toward him.

He held a hand up to stop her. He'd not get sucked into her lies again. "It doesn't matter. Even if the trip was strictly platonic, and you didn't use my money. It made me realize I didn't love you. It also made me realize I was already falling for the girl I met here." Most of that was true. He hadn't really known Becca long enough to have fallen for her then, but he'd instinctually known she was a cliff, and he was about to take the dive. Even now, he was still falling.

"You're—in love with her?"

This was what Ashley needed to hear to back off. To know there was no way he'd get back together with her. "Head over heels." *If she'll even have me after learning you're here.*

Ashley combed her fingers through her long blonde hair. "I'm scared, Rave. I don't know if I can do this on my own. I've always had your help. And Nicole's."

He moved to the spot where she sat on a worn armchair. "You're not alone, Ash. You know I love Daniel. I'll keep him while you're at work. But it's important that you know my commitment is to him."

She looked crushed. But Ash was strong, iron strong, and she wouldn't stay in a state of defeat for long. He'd derailed her plan, sure. But there was a bright spot in all of it. She'd get the help she needed from Rave. And with any luck, Rave could keep Becca.

"Mommy, can we get ice cream now?" Daniel's head rested on Bullet's stomach. The dog was in his glory, with a small companion giving him heaps of attention.

Her shoulders hunched forward. "I've been promising him we'd take him for ice cream."

Rave scrubbed his hands through his hair, an attempt to calm the zinging nerve endings in his system. All it accomplished was messing up his hair. He faced Daniel. "Sure, Rock Star. We can go get ice cream."

CHAPTER 12

From the story Becca got from Alexandra, who'd heard it from Buck who heard it from Tommie, Rave and some mystery girl were at the ice cream shop on the other side of the square. Becca was working, so right now, she couldn't be bothered with gossip like this. Still, her skin went clammy, and her hands started trembling. She should have known not to fall for a guy so soon after having a broken heart. All the pieces weren't fully healed, and that made the blow that much worse.

Alexandra took the stack of dirty dessert plates and mugs from her hand. "Go see what's going on," she said with little emotion in her voice, though her eyes were filled with compassion.

Becca shrugged. "I don't own him. We're not married."

Alexandra set the dishes aside and took Becca by the hand. She led her into the small, hot kitchen. "You're falling for him, Bec. And he's a guy with a lot on his plate right now. He needs you. And you need him. Don't let some other girl steal your happy ever after."

Becca stared up at the ceiling. Is that what Rave was? Could he be? She considered the possibility of him as her happy ever after. They were light and life to each other, that was certain. But forever? She didn't know. Forever had always seemed so far away. And with the thought of him sharing an ice cream cone with another girl, forever seemed like a lonely, desolate place. She stripped off her apron and tossed it to Alexandra. "Be right back."

Alexandra gleamed with pride. "Take your time, sweetheart. I'll hold down the fort."

By the time Becca jogged from Sustenance across the courtyard to Mel's Ice Cream Shop, a bead of sweat from the blazing sun above trickled down her spine. Another appeared on her temple. She brushed at it, splitting her thoughts between how she could effectively break up with him and at the same time give him a chance to explain. This was madness, she decided. Breakup. That was the answer. But when she rounded the corner and saw the beautiful blonde sitting beside Rave, all she felt was jealousy. It raked over her head and clawed down her shoulders. Her teeth clamped down, her hands clenched.

Just as she prepared to turn on her heel and not give him the satisfaction of knowing what she'd seen, a little boy appeared at their table-side. His hair was blond, his face smeared with mint-green ice cream. He hugged Rave and carried his cup and spoon to the trash, then disappeared on the other side of the table.

This had to be Daniel. And that meant the young woman beside Rave was Ashley, the one who'd broken his heart.

The strangest sense of both defeat and calm washed over her. Her gaze dropped to the concrete and stayed there. A breeze blew the scent of freshly baked waffle cones in her direction, and though waffle cones were her favorite, the sugary, almost nutty scent left her feeling nauseated. Something prickled across her shoulders, and Becca knew she needed to get out of there quickly . . . before Rave turned and noticed her. Without glancing up again—after all, she didn't need to, the image of the pseudo–happy little family was seared into her mind—Becca turned to leave.

Rave's voice stopped her in her tracks. "Becca!" He was coming over. She could hear his footfalls and the lilt and fall of her name as he jogged to her.

She straightened, checking her armor, and turned around.

He reached her and took hold of her forearm. Rave glanced over his shoulder. "This probably looks bad."

She bit into her cheek. "Is that Daniel? He's a beautiful little boy, Rave."

Rave nodded but didn't release her. "I didn't know they were coming. She's planning on staying here."

Becca bristled.

"I mean, not with me. I told her about you. I told her that she and I were over. Really over. For-good over."

Becca's skin was on fire. "I get it." But when she looked at the pretty blonde, the girl whose smile was too sweet, whose eyes were too understanding, Becca knew that Ashley was willing to battle to the death for Rave.

"Bec, I know this is a lot to ask, but will you come over and meet Daniel?"

Stake her claim? No. She wasn't like that. She couldn't very well go meet Daniel with a pure heart. It would be about marking her territory for Ashley to see. She was shaking her head when the girl rose and started toward them. Becca pulled to get away, but Rave held on.

When he realized his mother was moving, Daniel made his way toward Rave and Becca. "I'm sticky, Rave." Daniel touched the tips of his fingers to his thumb.

Ashley smiled, stopped at Rave's side, and cocked a hip. Her blue eyes were kind at first glance, but Becca could see the boiling lava just below the surface. "Hi."

It was all too friendly. Becca wasn't used to games. She didn't play well. And she was certain Ashley was an expert.

"Hi," she forced out through a tension-filled throat. "I'm Becca."

Daniel bent down and flattened his hand on her cowboy boots. "I like your boots. Mommy says it's too hot where we live for cowboy boots, but I want them anyway. I'm Daniel."

She couldn't help but like the grinning little boy. Becca dropped to her haunches, where she could look him in the eye. "It's nice to meet you, Daniel. I'm Becca."

"Are you the Becky Rave said he loves? He told Mommy that when my ice cream was melting."

The ground shifted, and Becca fell off her haunches and onto her butt. A rock bit into her left cheek. Heat snaked up her throat. He'd told them he loved her.

Ashley's voice was tight when she said, "Daniel and I have moved here. It's really important to me that Daniel has a relationship with Rave. If this is home for Rave, then this is home for us." She scooped Daniel into her arms. "Maybe we can go buy you some cowboy boots now, Daniel. I'm sure Rave will know where to go."

But Rave wasn't paying attention to Ashley. He dropped to his knees and angled Becca's chin up so she had to look at him. "I'm sorry you found out this way," he whispered.

Found out which part? That his gorgeous ex and her irresistible son were there or the fact that he loved . . . loved . . . loved Becca? She leaned closer to him, ignoring the pain in her left butt cheek. "We don't know each other enough to be in love," she hissed.

Rave's eyes sparkled. "Then deny it." A half grin, that sexy smile. *Dear God, strike me dead right now.* Her hands closed in the gravel. She couldn't. She could neither deny nor quantify what she felt for Rave. It was without explanation.

Above them, Ashley grew impatient, like a prize racing horse, stomping at the ground to be turned loose and angry that no one cared enough to open the gate. Her irritation was palpable.

Except Rave didn't seem to notice. His eyes and focus were on Becca. Completely and utterly on Becca, which meant there was not even an ounce of attention going to Ashley.

Becca shouldn't like that, but God help her, she did. She liked that Rave was oblivious to everything else. Everyone else. Right now, Ashley didn't exist. And the emotions that passed between Becca and Rave were intensified by his single-minded focus. A swirl of emotions blasted her. She thought of when she'd said a final good-bye to Michael. How she'd felt seeing all the posts of him hanging out with other girls at frat parties, the beach bash they'd had on the campus lawn, girls in bikinis hanging all over him posing for pictures. It had hurt so much. Too much because it wasn't just the betrayal. It was a life she'd never get to live. Her choice, of course. It had been her choice to stay behind and help her family, but seeing a world she'd never know unfold through the photos splayed across a buffet of social media sites had left her empty. It was all too big, and it hurt too deeply. And then summer had come, and they'd picked up where they left off. But then he went back to school, and once again she had to relive the same hurts.

Gravel stuck to her palms as she shifted to put her hands on her lap. She and Rave must look like quite a spectacle right now, her sitting cockeyed on the ground, him on his knees before her. She'd known no one like Rave throughout her lifetime. He was . . . different. Hiding the stars in his gaze and a lifetime of hurt he refused to unleash because that would be weak. Still, she should say something. "Rave, this is—"

He reached out and grabbed her hand, bits of gravel transferring to him. His touch stopped her words. "I know. It's danger close."

Becca blinked. How'd he know that's what she was going to say? It had been weeks ago that Tuck had told them about danger close.

Rave turned her hand over in his and brushed the bits of gravel from it. He dropped a kiss in the center of her palm.

Above them, she heard a frustrated huff from Ashley, who then spun on her heel and walked back to the ice cream shop's outdoor table.

"Please, Becca." The world was in his voice. Promise, hope, all the things a girl could want rounding out the words and making them seem as real and absolute as the rocks she sat on.

She was shaking her head. She hadn't even realized it until she watched the horror skate over Rave's features. His grip on her hand tightened. "Don't answer now," he pleaded. "Meet me later. Think it over, Bec. I know what I'm asking. I know it's insensitive and unfair. But I've lost so many people in my life, and I've been able to move on each time, but I don't think I can lose you."

Did she really mean that much to him already? She knew she did. Because Rave was a unique human being, able to give all he had to those he loved. She'd never met anyone like him, and that alone should terrify her. But it didn't. It made her feel privileged to know him. "I'll meet you later."

A smile of relief spread across his face. He reached for her other hand and pulled them both to a standing position. They were nose to nose when he said, "Come to my house tonight. Seven. Promise me you'll be there."

"I will."

He leaned in and kissed her forehead. And somehow that light brush of soft lips against her flesh felt more intimate than if she were standing there naked.

Rave turned her by the shoulders and—carefully—dusted the gravel from her backside. Her face flushed, heat streaking to her cheeks. "I'm usually pretty sturdy. I didn't mean to fall off my boots." *When Daniel told me you loved me.*

He gently guided her so that they were eye to eye again. "I'll catch you."

Rave had picked at his dinner, too nervous to eat a full meal.

"He sure is a good-lookin' boy," Tuck said to Rave as they cleared the dinner plates. They'd started eating earlier in the evening because some of Tuck's meds couldn't be taken on an empty stomach.

When he'd returned home, Tuck had been full of questions. *Yes, Ashley is staying. No, there's no chance we will reconcile. Yes, I'm thrilled to have Daniel here.* But the one question he couldn't answer was, how does Becca feel about all of this? When he told Tuck she'd be there later to discuss things, Tuck had told him he'd better make it a good night.

Tuck had scratched his head and asked if Rave knew anything about boats. He did. He'd had a friend who worked at the marina, and the one big perk was taking the rental boats out when it wasn't busy. So Tuck showed him around the dock that sat on the edge of his property. The boat was an older-model runabout, but it was in good repair. Apparently, the neighbor who shared the dock kept it up and seaworthy. Or in this case, lakeworthy. Rave had a map that would lead him to a cove where Tuck used to take Millie for romantic evenings.

Rave had hit the grocery store and grabbed a picnic basket of things for them to nibble on. For Rave, this was going to be either the night that began what he hoped to be a deeper, more exclusive relationship, or it would be the last night they'd be together. Either way, he'd resolved to make it special. Memories, he'd learned, were the cornerstones of life. A person could survive almost anything if the memories they kept in their hearts were good. Sometimes memories were all you had.

Becca arrived right on time, and her being there—and all that rested on the decisions she'd make tonight—worked its way through his body like a sudden illness. She kissed Tuck's cheek when she entered the house and told him he looked handsome.

Tuck hooked his thumbs in the bib overalls he wore and preened. He'd been staunch with Ashley's disingenuous compliments, but with Becca, he was putty. When Tuck slipped into the kitchen to give her and Rave a chance to say hello, Becca's eyes lit. "Guess what?" She dropped her voice and stepped closer to Rave, who tried—unsuccessfully—to pay attention to her words rather than the sensation coursing through him. She'd dressed for a date. A good sign. Her torso was covered in a soft black summer dress, and her signature boots were on her feet. Her hair was different. She'd curled it or something, since the long locks were twisted and twined, like they could set their own course, and the world would follow. He supposed the sun and wind prayed for a chance to invade those long, beautiful strands. He certainly did.

Becca came closer. She smelled like strawberries and cream. "Rave, I heard from the mayor. It's a go. All of it. Pastor Keith has agreed to head the committee—but only if you won't. He wasn't sure if you wanted more or less control."

It took a few moments for it to sink in. The memorial park was actually going to happen. That worked well with his evening plans, too, because he'd already intended to tell Tuck tonight. It was only right that Becca be there, and since he didn't know what their future held, tonight might be the only chance. "It's happening." Those were the only words that formed, though his mind crackled with thoughts.

"It's happening," she confirmed.

Without meaning to, he grabbed her in his arms and spun her around.

She laughed and gave him a hug before pushing away from him. "Something else."

When she headed for the front door, an unrealistic rush of panic gripped his chest. But she only stepped out for a moment and reentered carrying a round tube. "I know I probably shouldn't have done this, but I gave your drawing to Ellen Kirsch."

He'd given one of the early sketches of what he'd like to see at the park to Becca so she could think about more ideas.

"Ellen's an architectural engineer, and—the best part—she was in the Marine Corps." Becca opened the tube and pulled out the contents. When they heard Tuck rustling around in the kitchen, she grabbed Rave and dragged him onto the front porch. She handed him one side of the large paper and unrolled the entire thing.

Rave could hardly believe what he was seeing. "It's the park." From the tall fence and wrought iron gate to the cobblestone streets to the large fountain in the center with water cascading over a mound of carefully placed boulders. In the drawing the weeds and the brush were nowhere to be found. Large planters filled with colorful flowers sat beside the many benches, and the massive trees had been trimmed back to allow ovals of shade between the areas of bright sunlight. "It's amazing."

Becca nodded furiously, a sparkling pink smile on her mouth. "It's just the beginning. I told her you had other ideas, but she said it would be fabulous to have a visual, even if it's going to evolve. This way, we have something to show people."

Rave couldn't stop staring at the paper. Only a short time ago this whole thing was a dream, nothing more than an idea. Now, it was alive, breathing, growing. His thoughts turned to his grandfather. "Let's show Tuck."

Becca nodded and let go of the paper. Rave carried it inside, and they called for Tuck to come out from the kitchen to the dining table. Rave used a heavy mug to anchor one corner of the page and a book to anchor the other.

"What's this?" Tuck leaned over the page with curiosity.

"Tuck, we've been working on something. I didn't want to share it with you until we knew if it was going to happen or not."

Tuck frowned.

"I know I made a promise to continue the memorial, but—well, it just wasn't enough. I want your men, and all the men and women who've served, to be honored. So we went to the mayor."

Tuck's frown increased. "You spoke to the mayor about my private memorial?"

Rave had practiced saying this a million times, but now that he was, it all seemed to be coming out wrong. His words rushed to fix the damage he was doing. "Tuck, there are a lot of people who feel the same way you do. I wanted to help unify—"

Tuck rubbed a hand over his mouth. "They don't understand."

Becca lightly touched Tuck's arm. "My dad does. He was in a war, too. He still has nightmares, still has bad days."

Rave swallowed. "We felt like it was time for this town to rally around its veterans."

Tuck took a marginal step back. "Who's doing this?"

Becca pointed to Rave. "Your grandson. This whole thing was his plan. I got him an appointment with the mayor, and let me tell you, he gave one heartfelt plea for Barton to turn over the park to us."

"What? What do you mean to *you*?"

Becca smiled. "The mayor spoke to the city council on our behalf. The council agreed to a committee that can oversee the restoration of the park. Rave and I will be on the committee. So will Pastor Keith, and he would like for Rave to chair the committee. The park will be incredible. It'll be a place of reflection and remembrance for all veterans and their families. Rave did this because of you, Tuck. But because he loves you so much, now all the veterans will benefit from his goal to honor you and your men."

Tuck's eyes softened. "Because you love me?" He looked straight at Rave, his watery blue eyes filled with too many emotions to count.

A relief-filled laugh escaped Rave's mouth. A single tear accompanied it, sliding down his cheek. He sniffed and brushed at it. For all of Rave's life, he'd never had a male role model. No father figure, no man to look up to. Now he had all of that and so much more. "Yes, Tuck. I love you."

Tuck sucked a quick breath. When he reached for Rave, he was trembling. "I love you, too, boy. I love you, too." They came together in an embrace that had both men sniffing away the tears.

Maybe grown men weren't supposed to hug. Maybe they weren't supposed to cry, but nothing felt more natural to Tuck than this, having his grandson wrapped in his arms and feeling wave after wave of love for him.

When Tuck released Rave, Becca patted the old man's shoulder. "It's quite a good grandson you've got there."

Tuck nodded. "So much more than I deserve."

From the other room, they heard Bullet bark and then the unmistakable sound of someone knocking on the door. Repeatedly. Without stopping for even a second.

Rave rushed forward, meeting the panicked knock with a brisk stride. He tugged the door open and found Trini on the front porch.

"I thought you'd never answer," she said, blowing past him to come inside. Her energy had Bullet turning circles again and waiting for attention. He stomped his feet and whined.

Trini pointed at Bullet. "Sshh," she commanded, and the dog instantly cowered.

"Wow." Rave closed the front door. "I've never seen him listen to anyone that fast."

She went to Bullet and rubbed his head. "Knows who's boss."

There was not a person in the room who doubted Trini's statement. Trini was boss. Period. All five feet one inch of her. Whether she was at home, at church, at a restaurant, at the feed store. When Trini entered the room, she was in charge. "Now," she said, opening a bag hanging from her forearm. "I expect you kids are leaving. Is that right?"

Tuck grinned. He wasn't sure what would come next, a lesson on date etiquette or a sermon. Either way, Trini had both young people's attention.

"Yes, ma'am. I'm taking Becca out on the boat."

Becca squealed. "The boat? Awesome."

He faced her and leaned closer. "I thought we'd watch the sunset and talk."

If Tuck wasn't mistaken, Rave was very hopeful about this boat trip. Tuck understood why. Becca was a special kind of girl. The kind who only comes around once in a lifetime. Like a comet. You get one shot, and if you miss it, it's gone.

He thought of Millie. How he could have driven right past her that clear, sunny day when she'd gotten stranded, when she'd stood at the edge of the road taking out her aggression on the flat tire by kicking it with the toe of her platform-sandaled foot. Though he'd not been much of a praying man throughout his lifetime, he'd more than once thanked the good Lord for the infidelity of Millie's boyfriend. If not for his alley-cat ways, Tuck wouldn't have met his Millie.

Trini reached into her bag. Her white locks were pulled back with a headband. "I've got some playing cards, a bag of microwave popcorn, and duct tape."

Rave's brows rose. "Duct tape?"

Trini waved it through the air. "In case this old scoundrel tries to get away," she joked.

"Scoundrel, you say?" Tuck's knuckles went to his hips, but he'd be a liar if he said he didn't enjoy the goading. He didn't want folks treating him with kid gloves or like an invalid. "You better have something stronger than duct tape if—"

Trini put a finger to her mouth. "Sshh."

Tuck shut up. Just like Bullet had. Hmm. Guess she really was the boss.

Trini turned to Becca. "You two kids go on. I'll keep Tuck occupied."

Tuck frowned. "I don't need a babysitter. I'm a grown man. Lived alone for years."

Trini faced him. "I thought I told you to hush up. Now, I'm here, and I'm staying. I've got a purse full of poker chips, and the cash to back it up."

Tuck ran a hand through his hair. He did enjoy playing poker. "Blackjack?"

"Texas Hold'em."

Tuck closed one eye and pointed a crooked finger at her. "All right. But if I catch you cheating—" he teased.

"I'd renounce my poker title if I even thought I'd *need* to cheat. You're out of practice, Tuck, and my card-shark teeth are sharp."

Tuck turned to Rave and Becca. "You two better go on before it gets serious in here."

CHAPTER 13

Rave and Becca stepped outside onto the front porch. It was a perfect June evening with a soft breeze whispering through the quivering leaves of the trees. Inside, they could still hear the trash talk passing between Tuck and Trini.

Becca stopped at the top of the steps.

Rave turned to see why. "What's wrong?"

"Rave, let's invite them to come along." Her hip was cocked, her hand on the banister, her forehead puckered in a concerned frown.

He cast a glance to the door. Had Becca seen something he'd missed? Trini and Tuck seemed happy to stay behind. "Why?"

She tipped her head back, and the rays of the early evening sun kissed the highlights on her face. "I don't . . . know." Becca toyed with the edges of her sundress.

Rave stepped up the stairs to her. "What's wrong, Becca?"

She looked at the front door. "It's just that, well, Trini likes Tuck."

"Yeah."

Becca rolled her eyes. "No, you're not getting it. She *likes* Tuck."

Oh. Oh! Rave might be slow, but he wasn't blind. Of course, Trini liked Tuck.

Becca chewed her cheek. "She has for a long time. And now, now I think she feels like time's running out."

Rave pressed a hand to his stomach. "I feel the same. But they looked pretty happy to stay right there." Besides, there were things he had to discuss with Becca. Maybe this was her way of putting off the inevitable.

She sighed. "I remember losing my grandpa. He had an opportunity to come to the lake with us just a few days before he died. No one knew anything was wrong, but he stayed home. And I remember looking through all the pictures my mom took that day and wishing we had pictures of him. Wishing he'd gone with us."

"I don't think we have a camera here, Becca. Unless you brought one."

She shook her head. "We don't need one. Memories are pictures. They're stored in the part of your mind where happiness lives."

That was something Rave understood. "Tomorrow I buy a camera. Or a cell phone with a good camera in it. Tonight, we'll take memory pictures."

"I can invite them?" Her face glowed.

Rave nodded. "But what about the things we need to talk about? Ashley isn't going away, Becca. We have to deal with this."

She spun from him and sat down on the porch swing. "So deal with it."

Right now? He'd rehearsed this differently. After nibbling on cheese and crackers and watching the sun go down. He'd imagined the gentle rock of the waves and the warm sun on her skin. "Uh."

"Deal with it," she repeated, as if he'd forgotten what he was supposed to do. When he still didn't speak, she added, "I'm waiting."

Instead of sitting on the swing, Rave dragged a chair over so he could sit with his knees brushing against hers. When he placed his hands over her knees, Becca stopped the swing's motion and swallowed hard.

Rave dived in. "When you can see someone for what they really are, it removes their power. Ashley used to have power over me. I see that now. I thought she loved me, but she only craves more. She's like an addict in that respect. I won't turn Daniel away. I know he needs me, and I love him. But Ashley won't ever come between us—us meaning you and I."

A soft chuckle escaped Becca's mouth. "Yes, I know what *us* means."

"I know you've been through a lot with the college boyfriend and with your family. I know you passed up a partial scholarship to stay here and help with bills. You've sacrificed a lot for the ones you love, and Becca, I know it's not right for me to put you in the center of all of this. But you've taken up residence in the spot that's in the center of my heart. Right or wrong, my world is orbiting around you. You're *already* at the center of all this. I'll never hurt you. I'll do everything in my power to protect you. And Becca, if you give me the chance, I'll love you."

Her eyes filled with tears, and he wasn't sure if that was a good sign or a bad sign until she threw her arms around his neck. "I'll love you, too," she whispered in his ear. A moment later, he dragged her off the swing and onto his lap. Perched just above him and with the wind tossing her hair onto his throat, she bent and kissed the edge of his mouth.

Hunger churned inside, rushing to life like a wildfire. He tried to still himself, but his flesh quivered in response to her touch. "Kiss me again," he growled.

This time when she bent, he moved at the last possible moment, causing her full lips to press onto his. Soft. Warm. Perfect. It defied words. He decided to call it home. She tasted like home. And it wasn't nearly enough. He parted her lips gently, nudging them with his own. The kiss deepened, and his hand came up and thrust into her hair, capturing her, planning to never release her.

When they finally broke the kiss, he pulled her forehead to his and closed his eyes. Becca was breathless. Rave was the same. "Are you sure you want to invite them along?" As he asked, he wove his fingers through hers.

Becca cleared her throat. "I think we might need a chaperone."

He kissed her throat. "We're adults. We don't need a chaperone."

She drew a shaky breath. "Then why do I feel like a teenager on her first date?"

"Is it a good feeling?" he asked, pressing his lips against her collarbone.

"A little too good, I'm afraid." He heard the tension in her tone, so he stopped.

"I'll never push you, Bec. We've been taking things slow, and if that's what you need, that's how we'll continue." That wasn't really what he wanted, but it couldn't all be about him. Rave wanted this to last. He'd like for it to last a lifetime, and things that had staying power also required good sense. And patience.

"Rave, I know I'm changing the subject here, but I think you should head the committee."

He closed his eyes for a second and tried to access a picture of himself in charge. "Or you could."

She cast her eyes heavenward. "I'm being serious. This is your vision. And like you said, who wants to listen to a couple of kids?"

"So my being the head of the committee helps how?"

"It gives you a louder voice. The decisions about the park will be made at your discretion. Pastor Keith believes in you. And so do I. And this is for Tuck and his men."

Head a committee. No. That was as far from his nature as . . . as spending every other Saturday night reminiscing about the Vietnam War. But she had a point. Plus, this wasn't about him. This was for Tuck. One side of his face slid into a smile. "You make a convincing argument.

OK. I'll do it. For Tuck." Rave rose from the seat, lifting Becca with him. "Come on, let's go see if we can ruin that poker game."

Tuck was surprised to get the offer from Rave and Becca. Trini had won two hands in a row, and he suspected she was sitting on a royal flush when the kids came back into the house. He and Trini were reluctant at first to go along on the boat ride. But after a little coaxing, they agreed. What Tuck couldn't understand was why Rave and Becca had invited them. Why did these two kids want a couple of dried-up raisins tagging along? By the look on Rave's face, whatever the boy needed to talk to Becca about was done. Rave had spent the entire day with his face pinched in a frown. It hurt Tuck to see him like that. He remembered Millie walking around the house with that same look after Sharon left. It broke Tuck's heart then, and it still did.

But the kids had been gone just a few minutes when they returned and asked Tuck and Trini to go. Now, the four of them were on the boat and headed toward the cove. The sun was still up but riding low on the horizon, like it was tired, like it would soon succumb to gravity and land—like a dropped ball—on the lake's edge. Maybe it would bounce, or maybe it would scorch the water, and they'd hear the sizzle from here. Tuck had to laugh at himself. Such musings for an old man with a death sentence. He had months, a year at most. That's what the doctors had said. For the first time since Millie died, Tuck had something to live for.

The water was smooth glass with the only breeze generated by the movement of the runabout. Rave was at the helm. Becca at his side. Tuck knew her daddy used to have a boat, but Becca must have been an avid fan, the way she hopped onto the deck and untied the ropes like a pro. The two young people gleamed.

Trini, sitting beside Tuck in the front of the boat, leaned closer to him and whispered, "They're holding hands."

Tuck tried to wave it off—as if it was none of their business, and they shouldn't notice, but when Rave released Becca's hand and slipped an arm around her shoulder, Tuck couldn't help the words from zipping out of his mouth. "Look, look."

Luckily, the two kids were too engrossed in what they were doing to notice the audience watching their every move. This was a memory Tuck would cherish for his remaining months. But as he scooted closer to Trini, a renegade thought struck him. It had come from somewhere deep within, a knowing, a premonition.

With absolute certainty, Tuck was sure he had a lot less time than that.

Two major things happened for Rave over the next few weeks. First, Ashley began to comprehend Rave's level of commitment to Becca. Rave wasn't trying to rub it in her face, but it was vital that she understand. Her attempts to drive a wedge between them became fewer and fewer. Finally, by around mid-July, she ceased completely and had even gone out on a few dates with guys in town. To Rave's delight, he could concentrate on the things that mattered: Tuck and his health, Becca and Daniel, and of course, the memorial.

The second thing that happened was a series of committee meetings that had the memorial park beginning to feel as real as the picture Rave had in his mind. The town had rallied and started working on the place. Weeds were pulled, trees were trimmed. Becca met Rave there after work every day. The two of them digging in to whatever project was on the day's schedule. A few trees were being moved, the wrought iron fence was being power washed and cleared of debris. It was beginning to look like a clean slate.

Tuck hadn't seen the park yet. Rave wanted to surprise him with it. The committee had settled on a ninety-day completion schedule. It was ambitious, but it was possible. Still, Rave wouldn't wait that long before taking Tuck to the park. He just wanted it to have a sense of the veteran devotion they were all putting into it.

They'd had a total of six committee meetings in the last three weeks. They'd planned to get together once a week while the memorial park was in the main stages of work. But once a week became twice a week when three unplanned meetings happened. The first came when the owner of the local lumberyard wanted to inform the committee that he'd decided to donate an almost unlimited supply of materials. The second was to accept an offer from a local granite contractor who wanted to donate granite slabs that could be etched and used as memorials for veterans of each war fought by American soldiers.

The last meeting was to accept a check from a wealthy businessman who resided in Memphis but had been born in Barton. His grandfather was one of the firstborn killed in action during World War II. The soldier's wife had been pregnant, and that baby grew up to be the businessman's father.

If materials and volunteer labor kept up, they'd meet their ninety-day completion window. The townspeople of Barton had surprised them all, and help had come pouring in as soon as word of what they were doing began to spread through town.

To his surprise, Rave had actually enjoyed being on the committee. Heading it, even. It suited him to be the voice of reason when the conversations got heated—which they did now and then—mostly because of a local businessman named Tom Blythe. He'd volunteered for the committee and filled the last open spot. Rave wished he'd known more about the man before being on the committee with him. Not that he could have stopped him from volunteering, but it would have prepared Rave for dealing with the self-centered, egotistical Blythe.

Now Blythe had called an emergency meeting of the committee, and Rave could only guess what it was about. First, Blythe contacted Pastor Keith and must have been miffed at the fact that he'd have to go through Rave to make the impromptu meeting happen. Rave agreed to the gathering and called the other members.

Over the last weeks, in Rave's free time, he'd been learning about the wars in which American soldiers had fought. Sure, he'd learned some of that in school, but now he felt connected to it, a part of it. Most mornings, he and Tuck worked on the cabin. By noon, Tuck was usually ready to rest, and Rave would head into town to meet up with the day's volunteers at the park. Ellen, a committee member and the architectural engineer, had become something of a forewoman on the job site. Having been a marine, she was great at organizing the day and delegating the work. She'd also suggested creating an all–combat veteran advisory board that could be consulted on events to be held in the park. Rave loved that idea.

Though Rave was the head of the committee, he led in a gentle way. Since he was young, he had been careful not to cause friction. But friction could be Tom Blythe's middle name. There was a slickness to him that Rave didn't trust. He didn't so much feel threatened by the guy as watchful about his true motives. Everyone else on the committee was in sync. Tom was not. He was the perpetual devil's advocate and seemed to glory in that title. But it didn't matter; they were a team and Rave was their captain, not their king. If Tom had some great news about a fat check or donation, well, Rave would gladly give him the floor for an hour so he could preen about how no one else but him could have accomplished it. Different personalities had different needs. Some people thrived on constant praise. Some shriveled to dust without it.

The committee had gathered in a meeting room inside the courthouse. Tom, dressed in a red tie and a white button-down shirt that stretched over his wide stomach, stood to address the group but waited until every set of eyes was on him, a tactic used to establish control. No one else stood up when they had the floor. Rave thought it was silly. And by the looks on the other committee members' faces, everyone agreed. The room was cooled by an ancient air conditioner that hummed and gave out the occasional groan as they waited. Even so, Tom's face glistened with a sheen of sweat. His small, round eyes occasionally darted to Rave. The cracked concrete floor of the courthouse was in need of a polish, but the space was clean and always available for these after-hours meetings. Rave usually found it a comfortable place to be. Tonight, not as much.

Tom cleared his throat. "So, we've got a lot happening in town with this memorial. I'm so glad we thought to do it."

Pastor Keith leaned forward on his forearms. "Agreed, Tom. Everyone in town is getting on board with the plan. I'm certainly glad Rave had this idea. And certainly glad he spoke to Mayor Calloway about it."

Becca reached under the table and squeezed Rave's hand.

Tom sucked his teeth, obviously not appreciating the interruption. "As I was saying, I've been talking to folks in town, and I realized something. I believe we're thinking too small." He paused for effect.

Too small? The project had evolved from a simple monument to an entire park complete with seven-foot-tall granite monuments.

"In fact, I think we owe it to the people of this town to honor not only our veterans."

Ellen Kirsch tilted her head. "What do you have in mind, Tom?"

He raised and dropped his hands, but there was a dramatic flair to his actions that had Rave's flesh crawling.

"Well, what I propose is this—and a lot of people in town agree—we not only honor our veterans but open it up to all public service personnel. Firemen, law enforcement. My problem with this whole thing is why not honor everyone who puts their lives on the line for us? There would be some logistical changes, of course. I mean, we'd need to reorganize this group. Maybe select a new chair—after all, we're talking a much bigger commitment. I think it'd be in the memorial's best interest to have an established businessman as the chair."

"Someone such as yourself?" Pastor Keith asked.

Tom's eyes widened as if surprised. "Never thought of that, but someone." He motioned around the room. "Several of us are qualified." His emphasis on the word *qualified* spoke volumes. Rave wasn't. That was the point.

The room was quiet. Rave could feel the atmosphere changing, and not in a way he liked. It felt as though the memorial garden was slipping through his fingers. And he could do nothing to stop it. His throat constricted. Maybe Tom was right.

Becca leaned over to him. Her teeth were gritted. "Put an end to this."

And that's when it hit him. Tom didn't care about veterans or fire-fighters or law enforcement. He cared about control. He wanted to be in charge, no matter the cost.

Tom rocked back on his heels. "I think we should put it to a vote right now."

Rave stood up. "No."

Tom blinked twice and chuckled, but it was a tense sound filled with shock. He hadn't expected Rave to buck. Or to stand up to him.

Unlike Tom's, Rave's posture was loose, comfortable.

"Well, young man, can you give us a reason why?"

Rave glanced down at Becca, who smiled up at him. "Sir, I can give you twenty-nine reasons why."

Tom waved his hand in front of his face dismissively. "Twenty-nine? What's that?"

"That's the number of firstborn killed in action during World War Two."

Tom's face scrunched for a moment, but he quickly recovered. That was a number he should have known.

Rave continued. "And if that isn't enough, I can give you 33,652. That's the number of US battle deaths during the Korean War."

Tom's eyes narrowed on Rave.

"And another 47,500 killed in action during Vietnam. And the last statistic—almost 7,000 killed in Iraq and Afghanistan."

The room was silent, but Rave could see the frustration in Tom's face. "Mr. Blythe, I truly appreciate your suggestion. And I whole-heartedly agree that our local law enforcement and the fire department should be honored. But this isn't the place for that. This is for the men and women who died on foreign soil so that we could *become* firefighters and cops. This is for them, the ones who didn't get to come home. And it's for the men and women who held their hands on battlefields and in combat hospitals while they died."

Tom looked away from Rave and studied the other faces at the table. He knew his hold was slipping. Beads of sweat dotted his forehead. For a moment Rave thought he'd relent, but Tom's chin jutted forward as he said, "I called for a vote."

CHAPTER 14

Becca's heart was so happy, it could burst. "Unanimous. You should be proud of that." But she already knew Rave was proud of it. The council had stood behind him a hundred percent, causing Tom Blythe not only to leave angry, but to forfeit his place on the committee altogether.

Becca stepped through the courthouse door and into the cool evening. "Admit it. You didn't mind seeing Tom go."

Rave slipped his hand into hers. His smile was a devastating slash that made her heart skip a beat. "His heart wasn't right. He needed to go."

They walked beneath the giant tree downtown that held as much mystery as it did summer flowers. "You know," Becca said, "they say that couples who kiss under this tree are destined to stay together forever."

Rave stopped and pulled her into his arms. "Is that so?"

"That's what they say." His hands roamed over her back, creating a zinging sensation in her flesh. The breeze was still, only the tiniest of winds rustling the very top of the tree. Evening lights lit the darkening streets as town folded up for the night. Becca breathed it in, all of it. The whisper of fluttering leaves, the scent of freshly mowed grass, the man before her. There were moments in life that instantly had a full range of emotion attached—even if the moment was just beginning. Right here, right now, Becca felt complete, like everything was right with the world. Rave's fingertips grazed the ends of her hair. Every sensation intensified because somewhere deep in her spirit, she knew this moment—or the moments following—were about to change everything for her.

Rave lifted her chin and dropped a kiss on her mouth.

How he could so easily leave her feeling dizzy, she didn't understand. "That's a dangerous thing you're doing, Rave. Tempting fate."

He leaned again, this time brushing his lips across hers, then trailing little kisses from her cheek to the sensitive spot below her jaw. "Not tempting, daring."

"You'll be stuck with me. Forever is a long time."

He leaned back so he could look her in the eye. "When are you going to figure out that's exactly what I want?"

Under normal conditions, she wasn't a highly emotional person. Becca had always prided herself on her straightforward reasoning and sensibility. But Rave made her want to dream, to hope, to soar. Here she'd been thinking she was stuck in a town that couldn't let her fly when all along her wings were waiting to swoop into town and sweep her off her feet. "Thank you, Rave."

He guided her long hair over her shoulder. "For what?"

"For being my wings." He pulled her into an embrace. She pressed her ear to his chest and closed her eyes. There wasn't anything that felt more right than this moment. This place. This man. Rave was an old soul, damaged but stronger for it. He was gold, refined by the hottest of fires. Tempered into a rock-solid combination of determination and empathy.

When her eyes opened, she saw the silhouette moving in the shadows beyond the tree. Gooseflesh broke out across her shoulders.

Rave must have noticed. Of course he did. There was little that slipped past him. "What's wrong?" he whispered.

When the silhouette took form—Ashley, standing alone, the pain and sadness in her eyes tangible—Becca opened her mouth. She snapped it closed when Ashley shook her head and mouthed, "Please, no."

"Nothing," Becca said, a little too cheerily. "Rave, I want to stop by Sustenance. Alexandra is there baking for tomorrow morning. I need to talk to her."

He threaded his fingers through her hair. "I'll go with you. Then walk you to your car." Usually, she loved having his hands dig through her hair, but right now, with Ashley watching, Becca just wanted him to stop.

"Actually, I'm going to help her for a while. Go home. Isn't Daniel staying the night? Didn't you promise him you could make a fort out of quilts in the living room when you got home from the meeting?"

"He promised to be a good boy for Tuck. They're watching a superhero movie." Rave kissed Becca's cheek. "But if I didn't know better, I'd think you're trying to get rid of me."

She stretched up on her tiptoes to kiss his cheek in kind. "That's because I *am* trying to get rid of you. Now, go."

His brow furrowed. "Everything OK?"

"It's great, Rave." That wasn't a lie. For her, everything was perfect. But the small blonde standing alone in the shadow of the mighty oak, well, that was another story. "I just need some girl time."

"I'll call you tomorrow." Rave gave her one more peck before darting off toward Tuck's Chevy.

Becca watched his taillights disappear before looking over to the place where she'd spotted Ashley. The girl looked helpless as Becca walked over, each step a warning that she should mind her own business. But Becca knew she couldn't do that. She was likely the cause of the pretty blonde's misery. Ashley had dropped onto a park bench. Her knees were bent, pressed to her chest. Her arms wrapped around them. Red-rimmed eyes made contact as Becca neared. She'd been crying.

"Ashley, what's wrong?" Becca sank beside her slowly because of all the people in the world, Becca was probably the last she'd want to confide in.

Ashley shook her head. "It's *all* wrong."

Becca wanted to reach out, reach over, but she figured that might not be well received.

Ashley pointed down the road where Rave had driven away in Tuck's truck. "He's really into you."

Becca swallowed. "I'm sorry, Ashley. Is that why you're upset?"

Ashley pushed the hair from her face where it had stuck to the tears on her cheeks. "It's that and everything." She shook her head. "This town, this place. I don't belong here."

Becca turned to face her. "No one belongs anywhere until they make it their home."

"I've tried. It's not working. I just need to go."

Panic set in. Rave would die if he lost Daniel again. "Please. Daniel loves it here. It's already starting to feel like home for him. It can be for you, too."

Ashley hugged her knees. "I came here for Rave. And he's with you now. I just need to go somewhere and start over."

Becca's stomach roiled. She was losing this fight. "Ashley, you've got to give it a little more time. I know it's scary being alone, but Barton is a great town. I promise it'll get better for you."

"This is already July. In less than two months I have to get Daniel enrolled for school. But there's nothing here for *me*."

Becca threaded her hands together for fear of lashing out and grabbing Ashley to plead with her not to go. "But there will be. In time. If you stay here, we can help you. Rave and I. You're not alone here, Ashley."

She sniffed. "I have a job opportunity somewhere else."

Becca could no longer stop herself. She placed a hand on Ashley's arm. "Please don't take it. It'd kill Rave. Please."

"Winter will be here soon, and I don't even own a coat. Neither does Daniel."

"I know Rave wants to take him school shopping. He already mentioned it a couple of times. Rave will make sure Daniel has winter clothes. And as for you, I've got a great winter coat I can give you—I mean, if you wouldn't be offended by a hand-me-down."

Ashley laughed without humor. "I wouldn't. My whole life has been hand-me-downs."

Becca smiled. "My mom works at a thrift store in Crowder, just a few miles down the road. It's kind of an upscale place, designers you'd like, I swear. Maybe we could go over there tomorrow and pick out some fall and winter clothes for you. She gets a great deal on what she buys."

Ashley stared straight ahead for a long time. Around them, the town square was quiet. A lone car drove past. "Why are you doing this?"

Becca sighed. "Because I know what it's like to feel left behind. A couple years ago, my then boyfriend went to college without me. And since we're on the subject of boys, I can tell you what guys in town are OK and which ones are trouble."

Ashley rolled her eyes. "I already met trouble. One of the reasons I'm out here alone tonight."

"Who?"

"Glen Cogdill. I figured going out with the sheriff's son couldn't be a bad idea."

Ugh. Glen had been a troublemaker since elementary school. "I'm glad you realized differently. Glen is all trouble. He couldn't be more different from the rest of his family."

"You know them well, I guess?" A couple walked past, and Ashley ducked her head while Becca gave them a quick smile.

"Really well. It was Glen's older brother that went off to college."

"You were dating him?"

"Yes. And he and Glen are different as night and day. But there are some really good guys here, Ashley. Good-hearted guys who will treat you well."

"Right, and that's why you latched on to Rave as soon as he hit town."

The words cut. Becca wouldn't deny their sting. She also wouldn't apologize for her feelings. "Actually, I tried not to be interested in Rave. But it's inexplicable. I couldn't fight it."

"And you think there's an inexplicable for me here in Barton?" The tiniest bit of hope lifted her words.

Becca smiled. "I believe there could be. If you stay."

"So this job opportunity, you think I should pass on it?"

Becca nodded. "You're already building a life here. You've got a job and a cute little apartment; you have Rave and me to help with Daniel. Yes. I think you should pass on it."

Ashley stood up from the bench. "OK."

"There's always time down the road to change your mind if things don't work out, Ashley."

"You're right. Thanks, Becca."

"There are six more weeks of summer. Maybe you can reevaluate then." In that time Becca could introduce her to everyone, give Ashley a sense of family, of home.

For a few long moments Ashley stared at Becca. "I get it."

It felt as though she'd said the words to herself. Becca frowned. "Get what?"

"Why he fell for you. You're authentic." Ashley nodded. "He deserves that."

Becca watched her walk away, off toward the apartment complex just a block down. Becca couldn't have said anything else if she had to. Surprise had stolen her words.

Becca's dad was awake early the following morning and sitting at the kitchen table when Becca grabbed her keys to head out.

He smiled at her. "You work today, Pumpkin?"

"Nope. Spending the day with Rave." Rave had called her at 6:30 a.m. and told her to get to his house pronto. Tuck was making pancakes, and if she cared about spending the day with them, she'd better show up in time for breakfast.

Becca's dad nodded, his mouth pressed into a line.

She placed the keys on the table and blew out a breath. "What is it, Dad?"

She was in a hurry, but there was always time for her father. Breakfast might have to wait. Rave had also promised Daniel a fishing trip. She knew Ashley was working the early shift at Vernie's. That gave Becca time to go out on the boat but be home in time for Ashley's shift to end and to take her over to Crowder. Becca had already called her mom to let her know they'd be coming and to please set out some of the nicer items for Ashley to consider. "Look, Dad, I know when something is bothering you."

He leaned back in the chair, his broad shoulders rising and falling. "The young man you've gotten involved with has a lot of grown-up problems."

Her mind clouded. "What's that supposed to mean?"

He raised one hand. "Stepson, ex-girlfriend."

She leveled him with a look. "He's a good man, Dad. One of the best I've met, and until you get to know him, it's pretty unfair to pass judgment."

He closed his green eyes, a mirror of her own in color. "True. I just want you to be careful."

"You do realize I'm not in high school anymore, right?" She knew he meant well, but really? He was treating her like a child, not an adult. Two years. For two years she'd been helping with bills and carrying some of the family burden. Had he missed that?

"I didn't mean to upset you."

She looked away. "It hurts that you don't have more faith in me. In my judgment."

He offered a sad smile. "I do, Bec. You've got a good head on your shoulders."

"Then know I'm using it."

His voice was toneless. "I've watched Rave at the memorial park. I can understand what you see in him. Forgive me for being a father."

A grin appeared, even though she didn't want it to. Honestly, his words had stung. More than she cared to admit. But this was her dad, her hero, and at the end of the day, he only wanted what was best for her. That fact alone made it easy to forgive his nosiness. "Deal. I'm going fishing with Rave, Tuck, and Daniel. Be home later."

"Have fun, baby girl."

She shook her head, kissed his cheek, and left the house.

She arrived at Tuck's place, inspected the quilt fort, ate a hearty breakfast, and was waiting for Rave to come downstairs after taking Daniel up to change his syrup-stained shirt when the doorbell rang. Bullet jetted past her and went straight to the window.

Rave had Daniel in his arms when he hollered down to Becca, "Can you see who that is?"

Becca pulled the door open to find Ashley on the other side. First she smiled and waved for her to come in, but Ashley's somber demeanor created a flash of apprehension that ran from Becca's head to her heart.

"Sorry to just drop in."

Becca shot a glance over her shoulder at Rave. "I thought you'd be at work," he said as he let a squirming Daniel out of his arms to go hug Ashley.

"Something's come up. I need—"

Tuck strode out of the kitchen with a cooler hanging on his forearm. He stopped just inside. All eyes were on Ashley, and if Becca wasn't mistaken, both Rave and Tuck had a sense of what was happening.

Becca took Ashley by the arm and led her to the couch. "Come in and sit down. We can all chat for a while." She hoped the others didn't hear the desperation in her voice, but Becca knew exactly what this was. Ashley wasn't at work because she was planning to get Daniel and leave.

Becca tried to take a calming breath, but it came out in a shudder. She glanced at Rave. He stood over the couch like he knew her plans. Like he'd lived this before, maybe several times, and like he'd quite possibly come apart at the hinges if he had to suffer it again.

Deafening quiet pressed the air around them, causing it to tingle. Ashley finally spoke. "Rave, I—"

He sank onto a nearby chair, his tanned face white, his fingers tight at his sides. "Just say what you have to say, Ash." Daniel found his way to the floor, where he and Bullet wrestled.

She forced out a breath. "I have a new job. I've been invited to work with my sister, Nicole, on the yacht. It's a great opportunity, Rave, and it'll give me a chance to put some money away for winter. Vernie said the diner slows down through January and February."

Rave looked at Daniel.

The look wasn't lost on Ashley. "It's six weeks of work, but it will pay for my apartment until March. The problem is, I can't take Daniel this trip."

Rave leaned forward. "This trip?"

"The yacht has a regular crew and a seasonal summer crew. I can work summers, and the money is great, but they won't let Daniel go until next year."

Rave brushed his hands through his hair. "Ashley, you'd be away from him for a month and a half."

Daniel was happily playing on the floor with Bullet and apparently not listening to the conversation. "I know I would. And the thought of that kills me, but, Rave, you said I should try to make a life here. I'll be back in time to get him enrolled for school, and the money from the yacht will take some of the pressure off. Plus, I'll get to be with Nicole. And Daniel will be here. With you. Unless you don't want to keep him."

Rave reached out and grabbed her hand and squeezed. "Of course I can keep him, but Ash, you've never been away from him for more than a couple days. I don't think you realize what that would be like."

Ashley cast a long look at her son. "I know he'll be too busy here to miss me. Lots of parents have obligations that take them away from their children. I'm trying to do what's best for both of us. I want to make a life here, Rave. I'm doing the best I can."

When Rave started to shake his head, Ashley pointed a finger at him. "Of everyone in the world, you of all people know how much I love him. This isn't like what happened with your mother."

Of course that's what he'd been thinking. That was why he'd sensed the change before she'd even admitted it. Becca's heart broke for all of them. Especially for the four-year-old on the floor. Rave leaned closer and whispered, "You'll miss his birthday."

She drew a deep breath, but with it, her eyes filled with tears. "I know. But I'll celebrate with him when I get back." Her chin quivered, and Becca knew just how difficult this decision must have been for her.

Rave rubbed his hands over his face.

Becca dared not say a word. Even though she wanted to tell Ashley everything would be OK, it wasn't her place.

"Rave," Ashley said, using a tone that had likely gotten her whatever she'd wanted from him once upon a time. "Last night, Becca reminded me that it's never too late to reconsider my options."

Rave's gaze shot to Becca and held. "You encouraged this?"

Her mouth opened, but nothing came out.

Ashley leaned back on the couch cushions. "She encouraged me to stay. She said she wanted to help me make a life here. But it made me realize that I really don't belong here. At least not yet. I need these six weeks. If you can give me this, I swear I'll stay here for all of Daniel's kindergarten year. I'll give Barton a real chance. Besides, I'd never want to uproot Daniel in the middle of a school year."

Rave lifted and dropped his hands. "You know you can count on me, Ash. But just know that being away from him will be devastating for you."

Despair skated over her features. "I know."

Rave's steel-cold eyes softened. "But as long as he's here, I'll take good care of him. He's in good hands."

"He's alive because of you, Rave. You've always been there for him. For both of us." She brushed her hands over her thighs. "Now I need to tell my little guy good-bye."

"You have to leave now?" Becca blurted. She hadn't meant to, but the words shot right out of her mouth before she could stop them.

Ashley nodded. "My sister sent a plane ticket for me. The yacht leaves Miami tonight. There was a direct flight from Gatlinburg. A car is picking me up at my apartment in an hour."

Becca glanced at Rave, trying to digest all this.

Ashley continued. "I'll have my cell phone, but it won't work on the water. There's a satellite phone I can use once a day." She pulled a slip of paper from her front pocket and handed it to Rave.

He stared at the paper but said nothing.

Becca moved to place a hand on his shoulder while Ashley called Daniel over. She sank onto the floor and pulled him onto her lap. "Listen, buddy. Something came up, and Mommy is going to have to go to work for a long time."

"I thought you were already at work, Mommy."

She rubbed her hand slowly over his head, smoothing his hair. "I know, baby. But I have to go out of town. You're going to get to stay with Rave while I'm gone."

Rave cleared his throat. "That's right, Rock Star. We're going to have lots of fun." But the words were flat, and Becca squeezed Rave's shoulder to let him know she understood.

"But will you be back in a jiffy?" His bright blue eyes pleaded.

Ashley hugged him hard. "No, Daniel. It won't be a jiffy. But I'll be back in time to get you ready for school. You're excited about school, right?"

He worked his mouth. "I guess."

"I want you to be a good boy for Rave. Promise you'll mind. I'll try to call you every night before bed."

"OK, Mommy." He hugged her, his eyes squeezing shut as he did.

Becca fought tears as Ashley held her son to her. "I love you."

"Love you, too, Mommy."

"I'll bring you something special when I come home."

"OK." But it sounded automatic, like there was too much weight on the little boy's shoulders to answer with any excitement.

Ashley kissed his forehead, his cheek, his hair. "Come on, let's get your things from the car."

CHAPTER 15

"I just think it's time I took you to the doctor instead of Phil." Daniel was already asleep when Rave launched into the argument about Tuck's doctors and why he should be going with him. For the second time in as many weeks, Tuck had gotten his medications mixed up.

"What about Daniel? Can't just leave him to fend for himself."

"No, we can't." Daniel had been with them for two weeks. Four more weeks and Ashley would be home. True to her word, she'd called every night. Even if the chats were short ones, Daniel loved listening to her tell stories about seeing dolphins and watching the night sky from the deck of the yacht. And just like Rave had expected, the separation was harder on Ashley than she'd ever thought it would be.

But they were all adjusting. Daniel went with Rave and Tuck whenever they were going to work on the cabin, and he pounded nails into a two-by-four using a little tool kit Rave bought at the lumberyard while Rave rewired, and Tuck watched and instructed. It was late July and though it was hot outside, with the windows open and the breeze working its way inside, the cabin temperature was tolerable. But only in the mornings, before the sun moved higher in the sky and the shade from the trees and the mountains shrank.

Rave had Daniel twenty-four, seven. He'd be lying if he said he didn't love it. Their days off had been filled with fun and discovery. Becca joined them whenever she wasn't at work, and the three had done everything from picnicking at waterfalls to swimming in streams. It was almost perfect; if it wasn't for Tuck's illness, life would be golden. But there was an illness and Rave knew he needed to know more about it. "We wouldn't be leaving Daniel alone. Becca volunteered to watch him so I could take you to your appointments."

Tuck frowned. "They're during the day. She'd miss work."

"I told her that. She said it was no problem. Things are slowing down at the coffee shop." Rave poured a glass of iced tea and sat down at the table where Tuck was laying out his meds. "I know you're a private person, Tuck. But I want to do this. Not just for you, for me. I worry about you. Knowing your doctor's recommendations will help me rest easy. OK?"

Tuck shook his head no but grumbled an almost imperceptible, "OK."

When the doorbell rang, Tuck and Rave looked at each other. "I didn't know we had a doorbell," Rave said, rising to see who it was.

"Most folks knock." Tuck shrugged and followed him with Bullet in tow.

Rave pulled the front door open. His sudden gasp drew all the air from around him. A wave of shock hit him full force, then trickled from his shoulders down, like an earthquake shifting the very ground where he stood. For a solitary second, his vision darkened. Rather than pass out right there in the doorway, he forced all the air from his lungs. He groped for something to hold on to and found only the edge of the door he'd opened. There, standing on the other side was the one person he'd never expected to see. She wore a white shirt and jeans. Her hair was longer, fuller, as was her face. The dark circles beneath her eyes were gone, and she looked healthy. A woman he'd known from so long ago. A woman who'd been slowly killed by the drugs in her system. Or so he'd thought. She was dead. Except she wasn't. She was right there in front of him. Rave stumbled backward. "Mom?" No, it couldn't be her. Sharon Wayne was gone.

And this was just a dream. He'd lived it many nights. Many times, and he'd wake with his hands aching, clutching the covers, trying to cling to something that was long lost.

Her eyes widened. "Rave?" There was hope in those words. Hope and life. When she reached a hand toward him, he jerked away, emotions surging from the deep basement of his heart. Her face, the face of his mother . . . staring at him, looking as surprised to see him as he was to see her.

Her fingertips hung in midair, waiting, wanting, but understanding filled her eyes. "Rave, how did you get *here*? It's so good to see you." Each word was a breathy whisper.

Rave shook his head. This wasn't happening. It wasn't possible. He willed himself to wake from this nightmare. Outside the crickets hummed, the air was crisp, cool off the surrounding mountains, the world was neither dreamlike nor nightmarish. It was normal. All normal except for his long-dead mother standing in the doorway.

She took a small step forward. He shuffled back. "Rave, I have so much to tell you. Honey, I'm so sorry for leaving you in Tampa."

When the room slanted to one side, he groped for a better hold on the door, needing something to stabilize him. But the words entered his ears first, then his mind and then his heart. On autopilot he repeated them. "You're sorry for leaving me in Tampa."

She nodded, her dark hair moving around her face. "Yes. So sorry."

His fingers clutched the wood of the doorjamb. "How about being sorry for not coming back? How about being sorry for the fact that I had to quit school and get my diploma online because my mom ditched me just when things were starting to feel like they might be OK? How about being sorry for the fact that I was homeless within two weeks after you left?" He knew his voice was rising, his blood starting a slow boil as the years unfolded before him anew.

Concern furrowed her brow. "The Dawsons kicked you out?" She shook her head. "I thought they'd let you stay."

His mother had rented the Dawsons' pool house, and in exchange, along with the five hundred a month his mom paid them, Rave took care of their pool. The older couple had taken the two of them in and for the most part treated them like family. Until they realized he'd not be able to afford rent.

"Surprise, Mom. People let you down." All this time, he'd assumed that she'd gone off and died somewhere. That she'd ended up overdosing, and the only comfort in that was that perhaps her passing had been a peaceful one. But instead, she'd been alive all these years. Since he was barely seventeen, she'd been out there somewhere and had never even tried to return to him. And that meant she had—in every sense of the word—truly abandoned him.

Her face clouded, tears filled her eyes. "I can never say I'm sorry enough."

"Right." Strength came back to him. Rave had made it on his own. He'd survived. He hadn't needed her. "So don't even start. Apologies from you are worthless. You haven't earned the right to them." Behind him, something moved, drawing Sharon's attention. Rave turned to see his grandfather releasing his hold on the kitchen door and taking a cautious step forward.

"Sharon?" Tuck whispered, and a trembling hand came up to cup his mouth. Tuck looked old, frail, worn down by the disease that was working to kill him and by the daughter who stood before him, the daughter he'd made peace with burying long ago.

"Dad?" She leaned forward, but wouldn't take a step. Fear, maybe, or dread. Tuck would certainly slam the door in her face if he was standing close enough.

But he wasn't, and what he did shocked Rave. Tuck, with outstretched arms, rushed toward the door. He grabbed her in an embrace, and Rave could hear both Tuck's and Sharon's voices tripping over emotion-filled words.

When spots appeared before his eyes, Rave released the breath he'd been holding.

Sharon was sobbing when Tuck leaned back and cupped his hands around her cheeks. "You're alive. You're really alive."

"Dad, I—" But each word caught in her throat. "I'm so sorry. I'm so sorry about everything. Especially about Mom. Oh, God, I'm sorry about Mom and that I wasn't here for you."

He held her at arm's length and studied her face. "You're not using?"

She shook her head. "No. Clean for three years."

Rave took a protective step toward Tuck. "Three years, but you didn't bother to try to find either of us?"

Her eyes were pleading when she said, "I couldn't, Rave. I was in prison."

Rave swallowed. That wasn't what he'd expected to hear. "And that fact is supposed to excuse five years with no word from you?"

She shook her head. "No, Rave. Nothing excuses that. When I left, I believed I was doing the right thing. That's the thing about addiction. It rules you. It convinces you. I believed the Dawsons would make sure you were all right. I was wrong about everything." Her glances were split between father and son. "But how did you end up here? I figured I'd find you in Tampa."

"I don't owe you anything. Least of all an explanation," Rave spat.

Tuck hooked his arm around Sharon's waist and ushered her to the couch. "I had a private investigator search for him. Your momma came to me in a dream and told me he was alive. Then I dreamed about him. He was holding a cross, and I knew it had once belonged to you, Sharon. That cross helped me find him. *You* helped me find him."

Rave remained standing.

His mother and grandfather sank onto the sofa. Sharon touched Tuck's cheek. "I'm also the reason he grew up not knowing you. I can never restore what I've taken."

Tuck took her hands in both of his and cupped them like they were a priceless treasure. "You're here. You're clean. That's what matters now. And you're really OK?"

Rave crossed his arms over his chest. It hurt to see Tuck's face, so filled with hope—hope that would be obliterated in a matter of time—so he turned away. Rave knew his mother. She'd many times over the years said she was done with the drugs. She'd made promises in the past, and every single one had been broken.

Sharon nodded. "I'm really good, Dad. I'm going to work for a couple who do missionary work for half the year in the jungles of Peru. I leave in about a month."

"Until then?"

She glanced over her shoulder at Rave. "I was hoping to spend some time here. With you. I can't believe Rave is here. It's like a dream."

"We'll get a room ready for you, Sharon. Your mother would be so happy."

What? No. There was no way she'd stay here, take advantage of Tuck, insinuate herself into their lives only to let them down. Rave had lived this too many times. And so had Tuck. Had he forgotten? What was wrong with Tuck to be so willing to invite her into their world? Rave stepped toward them, his face hot. "She's not staying here."

Tuck stood, his brows dipping into a deep frown. "She's my daughter."

"And she's done nothing but hurt you. If she stays, I go."

Sharon stood and stretched a surrendering hand toward both of them. "Please don't do this." She turned to her father. "Dad, I've got a motel room in town. Just let me stay there. This has to be difficult for Rave. I won't make matters worse."

Rave moved around the edge of the couch to stand at her feet. "You made matters worse by showing up."

Her eyes pressed shut. He'd hurt her. Good. She needed to feel what they'd felt for all those months, for all those years.

Sharon's reaction fueled Rave. "You were dead, Mom. That was the best thing you could have done for us. But you couldn't even get that right."

Tuck raised his voice. "That's enough!" The tone was sharp, final. So severe it sent Bullet scurrying under the edge of the end table in the corner.

Sharon's lip quivered. Her hand came to rest on her father's arm. "He's right, Dad. About everything. And I don't deserve the forgiveness you're offering. If it's selfish to be here, I'm sorry. But now that I'm well, I had to come."

"Here?" Rave interrupted them. He pointed to the floor. "You had to come here? Where there was someone who could take care of you instead of trying to find your son in Tampa. You'll never change."

Sharon drew a breath. "I was going to Tampa next. I was hoping to—"

Rave snapped his fingers. "Think fast, Mom."

"I was hoping Dad would come with me. It was time the two of you met."

Rave inched closer to her. His voice dropped. He knew that she knew how to say all the right things, the things people wanted to hear, needed to hear. Rave had started to build a real life in Barton, a life far from drug addicts and all the pain that went along with that world. For the first time in his life he felt as if he had a future, for the first time he felt like he belonged. And now she was here, and bit by bit, he'd lose each of the things he'd been fighting to have. Because when you were part of a drug addict's world, you eventually were consumed by it. Addiction was a monster with teeth. And it was never satisfied until it ate everything. "You're what you always were. A liar. And I'll never trust you again. And I will never forgive you for what you've done."

Rave stormed to the front door, whipped it open, and left. The door slammed closed behind him, its echo vibrating into the yard. Where Sharon Wayne was concerned, his heart was as closed as the door. He'd made it to his car when he realized he couldn't leave. He had responsibilities. Daniel was asleep upstairs. So Rave sat in his dark car—something he'd done many times over the years—something he was used to. Many hours had found him alone in a hot vehicle, waiting for his mother. He'd sit outside a crack house waiting for her to stumble out so he could drive her home. That had started when he was fourteen. When most kids were just learning how to drive, he'd been practicing evading the cops on the way back to their place. He'd have to practically carry her inside, then deposit her on the bed before making his bed on the fold-out couch. He'd leave a glass of water on her nightstand. He'd smooth her matted hair and cover her if she felt chilly.

But here in Barton, Rave had gotten to feel what normal was like. Tuck and Becca, fishing, learning a trade, and a life that held promise. A home and Daniel. Now Sharon Wayne was here. How much of his life would suffer the consequences of being connected to a drug addict? Sharon had a way of ruining everything she touched. And for the first time, Rave had things to fight for.

An hour later, the front light came on, and Rave could see the silhouette of Tuck and Sharon on the porch. They hugged, and she made her way to her car—a newer-model Toyota with Texas plates. Where'd she get the money for the car? Was it a rental? Had she flown or drove, and why did it matter to him? It didn't. That was the thing. It couldn't matter because if details about her mattered, then that meant *she* mattered, and Rave couldn't face a realization like that after all she'd done.

After her taillights disappeared down Tuck's dusty road, Rave opened his car door. Tuck stood waiting for him on the front porch, his hand resting on the banister. "Figured you were close by," he yelled to him when Rave stepped out.

Rave slid his hands deep into his pockets. "How'd you know?"

Tuck hooked a thumb over his shoulder and gestured to the house. "Daniel's here. It's not in your nature to run away, boy."

A humorless laugh slipped from Rave's lips. "Then you don't know me as well as you think."

Before Rave could rise to the top of the steps, Tuck stopped him by placing a hand on his shoulder. Rave looked up to the deeply lined face of his grandfather. He looked tired, worn out, but at the same time, there was a light in his eyes Rave had never seen before. "Tuck, what is it?"

Tuck's mouth pressed into a straight line. "Have you ever heard about the empty chair?"

Rave frowned, the weight of Tuck's touch coupled with the desperation in his voice causing a bead of panic to trickle over him. "No."

He squeezed his grandson's shoulder. "I first heard it from your grandma Millie. It was springtime, and the flowers were just starting to bloom. She'd gone to Gatlinburg to an antique shop where she'd found two rocking chairs. Come on."

Rave frowned but followed his grandfather to the barn. They wound their way around an almost impossible array of metal parts and boxes that had been overloaded with junk. There was a narrow path to the back corner and there, a green tarp hid a chest-high bundle.

Slowly, Tuck folded the tarp back, its old plastic cracking as he went and bits of dust floating in the air then settling on the ground. Beneath the sea of green sat two rocking chairs. "It's time we put these back on the porch." Tuck lifted one, and Rave followed his lead, carrying the remaining chair. They were works of art, with their long, narrow spindles and perfect wood. But as Rave wound around the path from the back corner of the barn, he knew these chairs were much more than that.

Tuck placed the chairs beneath the lantern-shaped porch light so its illumination held them. Rather than sit, Tuck went into the house and returned with a hand towel. He approached the rocker he'd carried and used the towel to wipe down each spindle, the long slender arms, the narrow legs, even the rockers.

Without a word, Rave took the towel from him and wiped down the second chair. It was just as he ended that the towel scraped against something on the underneath side of the seat. "Go on," Tuck encouraged him. "See what it is."

With careful hands, Rave turned the chair until he could see the bottom. There, taped to the seat was an envelope. The tape had yellowed, but its grip was firm.

"Open the envelope, slide out the page."

Rave did as instructed, his fingertips careful because the paper was old and brittle, rough with age, and felt as though it could disintegrate in his hands. It was a single folded piece of paper.

"Read it," Tuck said.

The ancient page popped as Rave unfolded it to reveal faded script of what looked to be a poem. At the top, handwritten in beautiful script, was a date, 1918.

"Near the end of World War One," Tuck added.

Rave read,

> Off in the distance, burning bright
> One flickering candle lights the night.
> Its flame is small but ever true
> It points the way for me and you.
> For we were warriors in our day
> Until the fight took us away.
> A whisper on the quiet air

Says leave behind your empty chair.
Let the fallen not be forgotten
For no greater gift has man to give.
Our sacrifice has been for nothing
If those beside us do not live.
So, brothers, when you go back home,
We pray you live the life we won't.
Love the woman of your dreams.
Find your hope. Find your peace.
And never forget our hearts are there
Even though we left an empty chair.

"Is that what war is like?" Rave gently folded the paper. For all the memorials he'd shared with Tuck, he'd not heard sentiment like this before. Perhaps it was because it was a message from a fallen soldier to the ones who survived.

Tuck nodded, his watery eyes far away. "I remember thinking that if I didn't make it home, the ones who did had better live a life worth living. In a way, they'd be living for all of us."

"So, when you were the one to come home—"

"I knew I needed to live. Just didn't quite know how. My family didn't make it any easier. But then one day I saw Millie." He ran a hand through his springy hair. "Ah, she was a beauty. Kicking that tire like a wild thing. Beating her fists on the hood."

Rave stayed quiet, letting his grandfather's memories soak into the air around them.

"I made mistakes, Rave. Oh, too many to count. Where Sharon was concerned. I didn't give her much choice but to run. In the twisted mind of an addict, she felt she was doing the right thing. For everyone."

Something about this story didn't sit well with Rave. There was a crack in his grandfather's voice, a clip to his words. "Tuck, is there something you're *not* telling me?"

Tuck shook his head, little jerks back and forth. He busied his fingers by taking the towel from Rave and brushing the dust off. "I'm saying that a man has to make a choice whether he can forgive or not. If he doesn't, then that pain grows and sprouts roots, and one day it'll take over, choking the life from him. Forgiveness is like fresh mountain rain. It erodes away the sorrow and cleanses the land. Forgiving those we love is easy when we don't base that decision on what they will or won't do."

But how was that even possible? When a child burns his hand on a stove, he knows not to touch the stove again. Rave shrugged. "I guess I don't know what you mean."

"Rave, you don't have to believe that your momma has changed in order to forgive her. Forgiving and forgetting aren't the same. Forgiving her doesn't mean that it all disappears. Fact is, you'll still be angry with her, you'll still be unwilling to trust. And that's OK. Forgiveness is the first step. It's not the whole thing."

When Tuck motioned for him to, Rave sat down. The chair cradled him, a perfect fit.

Tuck drew a deep breath and slowly sat down, too. "I remember the day Millie told me she'd be leaving behind an empty chair. She'd had a dream. In the dream, she was gone, and I was alone. She saw me standing over her grave and crying."

It was hard for Rave to breathe. As much as he loved reminiscing with Tuck, hearing him speak of Grandma Millie always caused his heart to close off. Rave reached over and placed a hand on his grandfather's forearm where age spots and wiry hairs mingled.

"Millie made me promise never to do that." Tuck used his free hand to swipe at his eyes. "And I never have. But when I got home from her memorial service and saw these two chairs sitting on the porch, I broke down. Cried harder than I ever have. Yelled at God. Told him he was unfair to take her and leave me. Went inside the house planning to find her Bible and throw it out."

Rave's brows rose. He wasn't much of a spiritual man, but throwing away a Bible?

"It was open to a page Millie had marked with a little crimson ribbon. That thin, narrow strip reminded me of the ribbon she used to tie wildflowers with. I started reading and didn't stop until the next morning. Read that whole thing over the next three days. Still wasn't keen on going to church, but those words gave me strength. Helped me understand forgiving." Tuck pushed his rocker into motion.

Rave did, too, and the two of them sat on the porch with the crickets and the frogs accompanying the gentle sighing of their rocking chairs. "Thanks for sharing that, Tuck." But Rave wasn't sure he could open his heart enough to forgive. Maybe not ever. He'd like to, for Tuck's sake, but where his mother was concerned, a part of his heart had died.

"One day, Rave, I'll leave an empty chair. But don't do what I did and hide it in the barn. Sit here with Becca or Daniel or maybe even with your mother. There's nothing sadder than a chair with no one to sit in it. I spent too many years in solitude. Learn from my mistakes. Be a better man than I was."

Rave squeezed Tuck's arm. "You're the best man I've ever known. If I'm half the man you are, I'd count that as a success."

Sharon Wayne brushed at the tears as she drove toward the motel. Happy tears for her father, who was glad to see her. Tears of pain for Rave, who had cut her over and over with his words. She deserved it, that and worse. But it still hurt. And yet, through his pain-filled comments, there was something in his eyes—some tiny spark that let her know he was glad—if even the tiniest bit—to know she was alive and not using.

It was still hard to fathom that Rave was here. They'd found each another, even though she'd worked to keep them apart. It was a miracle.

The air in the car was cool, but she put the windows down and let the July breeze comfort her. Once she reached town, she drove to the high school. Memories flooded her as she took in the brick and concrete building. It was here that it had all began. Her addiction. Her life as a user and a liar. The only good thing that had come from it was Rave. He'd been her angel. And so much more than she deserved.

The school had been updated but still looked as it had twenty-three years ago. She'd been a star basketball player back in those days—something Rave had never known about her. She'd planned to study engineering. But a knee injury in a championship game sent her first to the hospital, then down the road to addiction. But she could only blame herself. As the knee healed, she found that the pain meds made life easier. Took the edge off. There had been so much stress, much of it self-inflicted, but still, so much pressure to perform. Basketball was out. She was a senior, and all her plans were now in the toilet. Until she met Jorge.

He'd graduated a couple of years before her and still hung out at the school. Wherever kids were, Jorge was. He'd eventually overdosed at age twenty-five. But by then, she was an addict. Not that Jorge was to blame. Sharon had been looking for an escape. She'd always been such a perfectionist. And once her body was broken, perfection was no longer an option.

Now that she thought about it, it seemed stupid. She'd had everything going for her. Everything. So what if she could no longer play basketball? There were plenty of dreams she could still achieve. Sharon propped her elbow on the windowsill and wiped the remnants of tears from her face. That was all behind her. She was clean, and though the memories were hers, she felt strangely disconnected from them. Like they'd happened to someone else. Or to her, but in another life. She scrounged around in her bag and found her cell. Moments later, she was talking. "Maria, how are you and Don?" The two had a prison ministry, and that's where Sharon had met them. Maria had taken her under her wing. Long counseling sessions turned into plans for the future. It had always been Sharon's hope to return home. In her most vivid dreams, she'd reunited with Rave, and the two had moved here to be with Tuck. But Maria had warned her not to put all of her trust in people she'd not spoken to in years. Sharon needed a plan for the possible future that didn't include the people she'd hurt in the past.

"We're fine, but the question is, how are you? Did you get to speak with your father?" Maria's faint Hispanic accent rounded each word, causing Sharon to smile.

"You won't believe it. Rave is here. It's like my biggest dream has come true."

"Oh, Sharon." Maria knew what this meant to her. Other than talk of work, Rave and Tuck were all Sharon spoke of.

"Rave is angry. He may never forgive me."

"He will. He needs time," Maria assured her. "And he needs to know that you are not the same mother who left him."

Sharon drew a deep breath. "Is it even right to expect him to forgive me? He said he thought I'd died, and that was the best thing I could have done for them." As long as Sharon lived, she'd never forget those words.

"Like I said, he's angry. He has a right to his anger. Don't try to take it from him. Just give him time to see who you are now. You knew this would be hard."

"Yes."

"And your father?"

Sharon smiled. "So forgiving. He's just happy I'm alive and not using. He looks older than I'd anticipated. There was no anger, no adjustment time for him. He looked in my eyes and knew I was no longer an addict and drew me instantly into his arms."

"Sharon, he knew you before. That's why it was easy for your father to embrace you." There was a pause before Maria continued. "Rave has never known anyone but addict Sharon. He's being introduced to a stranger. Trust is not an easy thing to offer."

She knew that. They'd discussed it many times. For the course of Rave's whole life Sharon had been an addict. "Well, I've got my work cut out for me."

"Speaking of that, shall I bump your mission trip to next year?"

Sharon could hear her thumbing through papers, probably the Peru schedule. "Not just yet. I need a few more days to know if my being here—really being here—is good for the two of them. They have a very nice dynamic. I don't want to ruin anything. I've already put them at odds with each other. Plus, you're counting on me."

"We're counting on you to get your new life started in the best way possible. Whether that includes Peru or not. Besides, as long as we know within two weeks, we can sub in a replacement. Tiki is ready to go at a moment's notice."

"Thanks, Maria. I don't know what I'd do without you." Sharon hung up the phone and drove straight to the motel. She was exhausted. Even with her soul aching, hope filled in the hollow places in her heart. Maybe she'd see her family intact after all.

The doctor had given Tuck a thorough exam, but Rave only felt slightly more informed about Tuck's condition than before they came. He'd expected to accompany Tuck and to come away with a complete understanding of the disease, the prognosis, the meds. That didn't happen. Now, as the doctor shook Tuck's hand, Rave's panic grew. "Is there anything else we should be doing? Anything that can help his energy level?"

Tuck's mouth dipped into a frown. "I have good days and bad days."

Dr. Voight glanced down at the chart. "Eat right. Plenty of fluids to offset the medications. And just wait. Tuck's on the donor list." He shrugged. "That's about all we can do at this stage. We're closely monitoring the cancer. It hasn't spread from the liver."

"Donor list?" Rave shot a glance to Tuck.

"For a liver transplant," Dr. Voight explained.

"Thanks, Doc." Tuck quickly shook his hand again and headed for the door. "We'll see ya next time."

Rave planted his feet at the exam room door. "Stop. Tuck, what is he talking about?"

Dr. Voight, who had seemed all business up to this point, paused. It was the kind of pause that said there was much to discuss, and he wasn't certain Rave was the one to discuss it with. His gaze hesitantly went to Tuck. "Have you not talked to your grandson about this?"

Tuck huffed. "Isn't there some law? Hippo or something?"

Dr. Voight laughed. "HIPAA. Yes, of course. However, when you arrived today, you told me we could discuss the details of your illness openly with Rave."

Tuck's head dropped. "That's 'cause I wasn't planning on this coming up."

Rave was putting the pieces together. "Tuck, you're on a liver transplant list, and you weren't going to mention it to me? Why?"

"Didn't want you to worry."

Rave turned his attention to the doctor. "What would this transplant do for Tuck?"

Dr. Voight shrugged. "It's a cure. A transplant means we remove the cancerous organ."

"Wait, is that—" Rave took a small step toward the doctor. "Is that something I could do for him?"

The doctor's brows quirked. "If your blood types are compatible. Close family is typically the best match for living donor transplants."

Tuck squared his shoulders. "Now stop right there. There's no way I'm letting them cut you open for me. Never gonna happen, boy, so get it out of your head."

Rave ignored him and faced the doctor. "What would I have to do?"

"Blood type first, then we'll do a fairly lengthy series of tests. If you were to pass, it's a week's stay in the hospital for the donor, longer for the recipient. But we've had tremendous success with living donors. There's a much higher rate of success, in fact."

Tuck's fists dropped to his waist. "This is not going to happen."

Again, Rave addressed Dr. Voight. "But everyone only has one liver. How does this work?"

"The liver has two sections. We remove the left lobe and use that for the recipient. The liver immediately begins to heal. Eventually it will completely regenerate."

"So, I'm giving something that is going to grow back after?" Rave turned with exasperation toward Tuck. "How could you not tell me this, Tuck? I've been looking at the possibility of losing you when I had the answer all along?"

Tuck's shoulders curled forward. "I'm an old man, Rave. I've lived my life. Surgery comes with risk. And I'm not willing to take that risk where you're concerned. Your life is just getting started. Please don't make me choose."

"Choose what, Tuck?"

"Don't make me choose to remove you from my life."

All the air left Rave's lungs. The room spun. His face heated. "You'd do that?" Tuck couldn't be serious, but the stubborn look on his face told Rave he was. It was like a punch in the gut. Tuck was good at giving. Look at all he'd given to Rave. But he was lousy at receiving. Especially at receiving help.

The corner of Tuck's mouth ticked. "I stood on a battlefield too many times and watched people who should live die. Those were my men. My soldiers. And though I did everything I could to protect them, I still lost them. I won't lose you, boy. I won't."

"You will if you force me out of your life." Once again, Rave felt like he was locked in an impossible situation—one that would cause him to lose everything no matter what he did.

Tuck squared his shoulders. "Like I said, don't make me choose."

CHAPTER 16

In silence, they left the doctor's office. Rave wanted to be angry with Tuck, but how could he be? Tuck loved him enough to be willing to push him away just to keep him safe. Maybe Tuck wasn't recognizing the advances in medicine. Sure, there was always risk, but the reward by far outweighed those risks. When Rave got home, he hugged Daniel a little tighter. Moments like this made him realize how hard this whole thing must be on Tuck.

Later that night, Ashley called to talk to Daniel. Rave had been a little concerned because they hadn't heard from her in two days. Daniel's mood deteriorated when he didn't hear from his mom. When Daniel was finished, she asked if Rave had time to talk for a while. He said yes. "I know you, Rave. What's going on?"

Did he want to share this with her? No. But the weight of all that had happened in the past two days was as heavy on his shoulders as a soaking wet blanket. "My mom is alive."

A rush of air over the phone. "Rave, that's great. Is she—you know, all right?"

"She's not using. I wouldn't let her stay with us. She's got a room at the motel."

"Oh geez, Rave. Not that roach motel. It should be condemned."

He closed his eyes. "Better than her last address. She's been in prison."

"Good, Rave, if it got her straightened out. Is she really straightened out?"

He nodded. "Yeah, seems so. She looks healthier than I've ever seen her—full cheeks, no gray tone to her skin. You can't fake those things. But that doesn't mean I trust her. And it doesn't mean she won't go back to using."

"If you believe she's clean, get her out of that fleabag motel. In fact, I've got an idea."

He closed his eyes. He knew Ashley well enough to know the change in her tone. Somehow, she could see a way to profit from this situation. "I can't get her out of the motel, Ash. I don't want her here. Maybe that's wrong, but it's how I feel."

A long pause. "How long is she staying?"

"About a month. Tuck's really glad to see her." Even though he didn't trust Ashley, she'd known his mother back when he and Ashley were friends long before she ever got pregnant with Daniel.

"Go get her, Rave. She can stay at my apartment. I was thinking maybe she can kick in on the rent while I'm away. It costs the same as the motel. I checked when Daniel and I got to town. That would really help me financially."

"Ash, I'm not sure—"

"Just stop, OK? You're not that guy. You don't leave your mother in a place like that when there's no reason. Go, Rave. You'll never forgive yourself if you don't."

Maybe she was right. He already felt bad for the way he'd treated his mom. Even though she didn't deserve any better. "Stupid conscience. Are you really sure this is a good idea, her staying in your place?"

"Are you afraid she'll fall off the wagon and sell my stuff to buy some drugs? I don't have anything that's worth anything, so good luck to her. My important papers are in a locked box in the top of the closet. If you're worried, grab the box and leave it at your place. But I don't think you should. I think you should give her a chance. It's what you'd want Daniel to do if she was me."

He knew she was right. He'd want Daniel to give Ashley a chance—even if she blew it. Rave's eyes drifted shut. "All right. I'll do it, but I don't have to like it."

"One other thing, Rave." There was another pause. He knew Ashley. Maybe too well.

"What is it?" His tone was flat. More surprises he didn't need.

"It's just that . . . well, I kind of feel like life is giving me a second chance here."

He couldn't explain the tension that gripped the skin around his shoulders.

"Rave, I started life so young, getting pregnant with Daniel. And he's the light of my life, but—"

Through gritted teeth, Rave asked, "But what?"

She blew out a breath. "I just wanted to say thanks for letting me do this. I needed this. I'd forgotten what it felt like to not spend every waking moment thinking about someone else." Before he could answer, she added, "Take care of Daniel for me."

"He's the very best part of my world right now."

Ashley said good-bye and hung up. The wall clock ticked. Bullet nudged Rave's leg. The dog had grown accustomed to long evening walks where Daniel ran off his impossible four-year-old energy and Bullet hunted for stray bunnies. Always searching, never finding.

As they were headed out the door, Becca arrived. And Rave's heart stuttered when she stepped out of her car and ran toward him. Outside, the air was a perfect mix of summer and evening, the setting sun casting long shadows on the green grass around the house. Trees swayed with their own song, each one with a voice, each one harmonizing.

Becca threw her arms around his neck and kissed him. It was quickly that her lips met his, her body pressed to him and even more quickly that she moved away. His hands found their way around her waist, the material of her sundress still cool from the air-conditioning in her car. "What was that for?"

She grinned up at him. "Because I missed you that much."

"You saw me three days ago." His grip tightened around her. "And this is how much I missed you." He pressed his mouth to hers and deepened the kiss before she could stop him. Her intake of air pulled the oxygen from his lungs, creating a desperation in his chest. Heat fanned out from the flame in his belly.

"Eeeewwww, gross." Daniel pointed at the two of them, and Rave laughed.

Becca blushed.

"Dad, can we go now?" Daniel didn't always call him Dad, but it was common enough that he'd stopped correcting him. Daniel and Bullet ran ahead.

Becca and Rave fell into step behind the energetic boy and the lumbering dog. She bumped Rave's shoulder. "You all right?"

"Still not sure about the dad thing."

"People in town assume he's yours. Maybe that's for the best. I mean, with Ashley gone. Little towns love gossip. I'd hate for innocent Daniel to be at the base of their nosiness."

"Yeah." Rave had to agree. Still, he wasn't Daniel's father. "Becca, we need to talk."

She dipped her head. "Sounds bad."

"No. No, it's good. Amazing, really. But I need you on board with this."

For the next half hour, he explained the procedure to her. What would be expected of him as a donor, what the recovery time would be.

216

She had a lot of questions but gave her unwavering support . . . just like he knew she would. "When will you do it, Rave?"

"Well, I have to wait until Ashley's back. And I have to convince Tuck. He's so stubborn." Rave shook his head. "But I'm going ahead with the tests. Made my appointments already."

"Can you do that? Without Tuck's consent?"

Rave shrugged. "Of course. I don't need his consent to be a liver donor. I just need his consent to be *his* liver donor."

Her grip tightened on his hand. "It's a really brave thing to do, Rave." But her grip didn't let up, and he knew she was sensing the risks associated with the surgery.

He stopped and turned to face her. "Hey, I'll be fine."

She nodded but didn't make eye contact.

He tilted her chin. "Becca, I'll be fine."

"I'm really proud of you for doing this. I just don't want anything to happen to you."

He pulled her into his arms. There, with the sun's last rays sliding behind the mountaintop, Rave silently made three promises to Becca. He swore he'd be OK after the surgery. He swore he'd love her always, and he swore he'd never leave her with an empty chair.

From the window above, Tuck watched them. A young man, the woman he loved, and a beautiful little boy trying to keep up with the dog. His hand rubbed over his chest, its familiar ache still there, but different now. For years since Millie died, he'd looked out this window to the empty road. The empty chair. Inside, the half-empty closet. Closer yet, his empty heart.

It was being filled now. Filled with Rave and Becca. Filled with Daniel and his eternal questions and inquiries. He'd heard Tuck mumble about the cookies he was baking taking too long, and Daniel had informed him that maybe he needed some time flies. He'd asked him to explain. Daniel told him he didn't know how they worked, but he knew that time flies when you're having fun. Maybe he could go on the computer and order some time flies.

Tuck's life and his heart were full with memories. And now he knew Sharon was alive and well. What a beautiful way to leave this world.

Cowardly is more like it.

He turned to the empty room. "I'd have thought you'd be ready to see me, Mills."

Not when there's a fighting chance for you. Look out that window. That boy still needs you, Tuck.

He knew he did. "But I miss you, Millie."

I miss you, too. But you've got unfinished business here.

He clenched his hands. "How do I tell him? How do I tell my grandson I'd encouraged his mother to abort him? Millie, Rave talked Ashley into *keeping* Daniel when he wasn't even his flesh and blood. He valued that unborn life. How could he ever forgive me for not valuing his?" But there was only silence in the room. For a long time, Tuck stared at the stack of photo albums he'd removed from the top of the closet in Millie's sitting room. The albums that starred Rave as a baby. When he could no longer take staring at the memories from so long ago, Tuck dropped his face in his hands. He cried silent tears because he knew Rave couldn't forgive that. Just like Rave couldn't forgive his own mother.

You'll find a way, Tuck Wayne. You always do.

He swiped his eyes. "I love you, Millie."

But Millie was gone.

∽

Becca stood at her car door with Rave pressed against her. He'd put Daniel to bed and now the two of them were alone. "This is dangerous, you know?" She'd fallen hard for Rave. Maybe too hard.

Rave leaned back to look at her. "What? The fact that it's a gorgeous summer night, and the woman I love is perfectly wrapped in my arms?"

Was it normal to feel this good? This whole? And most of all, was it a prelude to disaster? It seemed as though whenever things were going great for Becca, some unforeseen hand slashed through her reality and dropped a giant load of yuck.

Becca was tired of yuck. She was a happy person. A smiler, as her dad called her. He sometimes told her that her smile could calm seas and stop storms. All she knew was that life was better when one chose to see the good in it. Besides, there were plenty of people only seeing the bad, and she liked to be different from the crowd.

"So, I know this is a weird time to bring it up, but there's something else going on in my world," Rave said.

"Beyond Tuck and the donor thing?"

Rave nodded, and Becca sensed the heaviness. She placed a hand to his cheek. "Something's wrong, isn't it? Why didn't you tell me?" Gob of yuck, getting ready to fall.

"Yesterday I found out my mom is alive. She's off drugs and staying here in town for a month."

Becca shook her head to clear it, wondering which part she'd heard wrong. "She's *alive*?"

"Yeah."

Her free hand cupped his other cheek. "Are you OK?" Becca's gaze shot to the house. "Oh my gosh, and Tuck! Is Tuck all right with this?"

Rave grinned. "You're beautiful."

She squeezed her eyes shut. How could he be talking about how beautiful she was when life had just thrown him yet another curveball? "Rave, please stay on topic."

"I'm still in shock. Tuck is really happy to see her. For him, all the years of pain and betrayal just . . ."

"Just what?" Becca pressed.

"Disappeared, I guess. He thinks he's dying soon, and I suppose it'd be more important to make your peace than to hold to your principles of not forgiving someone who hurt you. Especially someone you love."

"Everything's a risk, isn't it?"

Rave pulled her to him. "Seems so."

"Your mom got here yesterday? Did she call you and let you know she was here?" She had so many questions. Best to start at the beginning.

"She showed up on the doorstep. We had no idea she was coming. She's at the motel in town." Rave's demeanor changed as he was talking, evidence of the toll his mother's arrival was taking.

"Ugh. That awful place?" Becca wished she hadn't said that the moment the words left her mouth. More problems, he didn't need.

Rave chuckled. "Don't worry. I'm going to move her out of there. She'll be staying in Ashley's apartment."

Something cold zipped into Becca's stomach. "Ashley?"

Rave brushed a hand through his hair. "Yeah, I talked to her earlier this evening, and she insisted. She shares your opinion of the motel."

Becca wanted to correct him and tell him that she and Ashley had nothing in common. But what really bothered her was that Ashley knew about Rave's mom before Becca. That felt out of balance, but she tried to ignore it. Ashley called frequently to talk to Daniel. It wasn't like Rave had called her to share his news. Was it? Becca shook off the feeling. Rave and Ashley were over. Still, she wondered why he hadn't called Becca when he first found out.

Rave slid a hand down her arm. "You OK? You seem a little distant all of a sudden."

"I'm just wondering why you told Ashley before me." This was something Becca needed to know because she was diving in headfirst with Rave. There were some things in a relationship that needed to be between the couple first. Not the couple and the ex. Becca wasn't trying to be possessive, but if Rave's natural instinct in a crisis was to run to Ashley, that was something Becca needed to know.

"Becca, I'm sorry. She called a few hours ago, and I guess she could tell I had a lot on my mind. When she asked what was up, it never occurred to me not to tell her what was going on."

Becca chewed her cheek. "If you would have called me, I would have come over. There's so much on your plate with Daniel, Tuck, and even the memorial. And now, your mom is here."

He grinned. "I've got strong shoulders."

"I know. But the best part of a good relationship is having someone to lean on."

Rave's look was unreadable. "You're right. I should have told you first."

"I'm not trying to make things more difficult for you. But we're still finding our way as a couple. I want us to have a solid foundation."

Rave's brows tipped into a frown. "So do I, Becca. And Ashley is a—complicated—ex. I handled it poorly. From now on, you know things first. I swear."

The frustration she'd felt moments ago melted, leaving a warm pool of affection in its place. Yuck obliterated. Becca threaded her fingers together at the back of his neck. "Now, are you going to kiss me good night, or do I have to beg?"

There was a growl deep in his throat, one that sent a fresh flash of heat down Becca's spine. "Bad word choice?" she said in a small voice.

"Yes, if you're afraid of being danger close."

She pressed into him. "I'm beginning to like danger close."

"You know, you don't have to leave. Daniel and Tuck are both in bed. They've been asleep for over an hour." Slowly, Rave moved away from her, but only enough to slip his hand down her arm and grasp her fingers. With a fear-destroying smile, he tugged her gently toward the house.

It was then that they heard the scream.

CHAPTER 17

By the time Rave and Becca made it to Daniel's room, Tuck was already flipping on the light. He hurried over and dropped to the edge of Daniel's bed.

Daniel's head thrashed against the cotton blanket. His face was covered in sweat, and his brow was furrowed. Tuck wasted no time scooping the mound of blankets and boy into his arms. "He's having a nightmare," Tuck said over his shoulder. He held Daniel close and rocked him.

Rave stuttered to a stop at the foot of the bed with Becca at his side.

"Sshh. It's all right," Tuck whispered, moving his craggy hand over Daniel's head. "It's all OK, Daniel."

A whimper came from the child, and Rave moved forward, wishing he could soothe Daniel, but Tuck had him bundled against him so completely, there was little Rave could do but stand beside Becca and watch.

Tuck cradled Daniel's tiny head against his chest. He nodded to Rave. "He'll be all right. Just frightened."

Rave offered an uncertain nod. Tuck looked perfectly at home holding the little boy. Did this kind of wisdom come with age? It certainly didn't look like the first time Tuck had done this. It probably wasn't. After all, Tuck had raised Sharon. Still, those protective instincts must have come to Tuck instantly and without a second thought for him to have so readily scooped Daniel into a sheltering hold.

Daniel's eyes finally opened.

Rave dropped to his knees so he could look at Daniel eye to eye. "It's OK, buddy. Just a bad dream."

Daniel's mouth turned into an upside-down bow, and giant tears filled his eyes. "But it seemed soooo real."

Rave kissed his forehead. Tuck kept his grip on the boy swallowed in blankets, one leg dangling off the edge of the bed. Tuck whispered, "That's the thing about dreams—they seem real, but they're not. You're OK. Rave is here, and I'm here, and we won't let anything hurt you."

Daniel blinked up at Tuck. "You promise?"

Rave had never taken notice of the differences between Tuck and Daniel's skin, but now the dissimilarities were glaring. One lined with age and spots, one so new it nearly glowed. They were the very contrast of life and death. Seeing them made Rave realize the mortality Tuck was facing. It brought it too close to home, like a sudden slap in the face. A rush of emotion surprised him—a runaway thought urging him to fly downstairs and call Tuck's doctor and set up the transplant for the immediate future. But he knew that was impossible. He'd have to wait until Ashley returned. There was no other way.

Tuck adjusted Daniel on his lap. "Now, do you want to talk about that dream?"

Daniel chewed his cheek, causing his little mouth to quirk from side to side. "I guess. In my dream my mommy went away. And she never ever came back."

The following morning Tuck called Sharon and asked her to come over. Becca, Rave, and Tuck had talked late into the night about Daniel. Tuck knew Daniel was feeling abandoned by Ashley. Even though she called frequently, it wasn't the same as her being there in the flesh.

Tuck knew, because years ago, when Rave was a baby and his mother lived with Tuck and Millie, Rave would have the same kinds of anxieties. Sometimes Sharon would disappear for days, once for three weeks. And every time, little Rave was left to wonder if his mother still cared. But Sharon was different now. Tuck knew that as well as he knew his last name.

Morning sunshine filtered through the sliding door, lifting some of the heaviness from the house. This house had seen too many sad days. Too many hard days. It was time for some good memories again. "I called your mom. She's coming over." He said this in a matter-of-fact tone as he watched his grandson pour a cup of coffee for each of them.

Rave walked toward him but stopped just inside the living room. "She doesn't need to be here, Tuck. You said we'd spend the day thinking of ways to help Daniel with how much he misses his mom. Pretty sure we can do that on our own."

Tuck's eyes narrowed slightly, and he crossed his arms over his chest. "Yep. And of all of us, Sharon is the only one who has raised a small boy. Like it or not, she may be able to help."

Tuck watched Rave chew on those words and swallow them—bitter as they tasted, he knew Rave couldn't argue.

The two men sat in the living room instead of on the back deck, their usual habit. "Daniel still sleeping?" Tuck asked.

Rave nodded. "He'll probably sleep late. It was a long night for him."

"For all of us." Tuck didn't mention the mysterious sensation he'd had after Daniel told them about his dream. Tuck couldn't allow that notion to take root. It was just a dream. The dream of a small boy who missed his momma. Nothing more.

They'd barely finished their first cup of coffee when the phone rang in the kitchen. Rave stood and crossed the room. He didn't say it, but Tuck knew he was hoping it was Sharon canceling her visit.

"Ashley. I'm surprised to hear from you so early."

The boy talked on, and Tuck tried to eavesdrop. He mostly failed and cursed his bad hearing on his old age. He'd barely made out one word of every three. He stood when Rave returned from the kitchen.

"The yacht is in dry dock. Something wrong with the engine." Tuck could see Rave sorting through the details and that he didn't like the picture it drew.

"Does that affect Ashley's job?"

Rave forced a hand through his hair. "Yeah. It'll be a few weeks before the boat is seaworthy. Her boss has paid the crew for the entire season."

Tuck should feel relieved. He didn't. He knew there was more going on. "So, is she coming home?"

Rave shook his head. "No."

Tuck had left the front door open, but the knock on the door frame took his attention away from Rave. A tentative-looking Sharon stood on the other side of the screen door. His heart leaped. It was still hard to believe she was really there. His girl. His daughter, the one he'd given up hope of ever seeing alive again, as real as the floor beneath his feet and the roof above his head. He motioned her in. Her eyes skated to Rave, and in them was the hope that Rave, too, would welcome her.

But Rave dropped silently onto the couch. Tuck gave Sharon a quick rundown of what had transpired last night and how Rave had just gotten off the phone with Ashley.

Sharon and Tuck remained quiet. It seemed as if a silent conversation was going on in Rave's head. Finally, he said, "I told her that Daniel had done really well with her being gone until lately. I told her about his nightmare. I said, 'Maybe it's good that this boat breakdown happened. He's really missing you.'"

Tuck folded his hands in his lap. "What did she say?"

"She said she met someone in Costa Rica. He's a friend of her boss, and she and this guy hit it off instantly. She's traveling with him to Bermuda for a weeklong conference."

"Instead of coming home early." Tuck was getting the picture. Sharon was, too, if the saddened look on her face was any indication.

Rave shook his head. "It was a weird conversation. She kept talking about how she needed time. Time to be herself. She said she had an amazing opportunity to travel and see some of the world—"

"Some of the *world*? How long is she planning to be away?" Tuck's hands grew clammy around the coffee mug.

Rave was pale. "I—I don't know. She swore she'd be home in time to register him for school, but she said it . . . almost like an afterthought."

Sharon scooted forward on the chair. "But she will come home eventually, right?"

Rave's eyes were empty when they landed on her. "She will. Ashley wouldn't do that to Daniel. She adores him." But there was the smallest hint of uncertainty. When Rave heard Daniel moving around upstairs, he excused himself and left Tuck and Sharon to talk.

Sharon's gaze landed on her father. "Do you believe Ashley will come home?" It ripped at her heart to see her son hurting so deeply and not to be able to comfort him. It was, however, a cage of her own making. Still, a mother's love ran deeper than any ocean.

Tuck gave an almost imperceptible shrug. "I don't know her well enough to say. Rave wants to believe in her."

"But is he setting himself up for a fall?"

Tuck rubbed his face. "Let's not talk about this now, Sharon," he said, his voice cracking as he fought a sudden surge of emotion. "You're here."

She stood from the chair she'd been sitting in and dropped onto the couch with her father. "I'm so sorry it took me this long to come home." It was a statement meant to cover a multitude of feelings. She was sorry for this and so much more. All she put her parents through, for keeping Rave away, for not being the kind of daughter they deserved.

"Do you want to talk about prison?" Tuck asked.

She could. And probably needed to so that Tuck wasn't forever wondering about the details of her incarceration. "I was picked up one too many times for drug possession. Finally, I got a judge who wanted to make an example of me. It was a blessing in disguise. If not for prison, I wouldn't have survived much longer on the streets."

Tuck reached for her hand, held it between both of his.

"The funny thing was, all along while I was on the streets, I kept telling myself that I was doing the right thing. For you, for Rave. Leaving him, staying out of your life. In the addled mind of an addict, it made perfect sense. Now it sounds as crazy as it was." She glanced up the stairs. "Do you think I've lost him for good?"

"No." Tuck squeezed her fingers. "No, Sharon. But it's going to take time. He's got a good heart, and whether he wants to admit it or not, he loves you. Always has. Always will."

"Sometimes love isn't enough."

Tuck closed one eye. "Love is always enough. It's the mortar that holds life together. As you earn Rave's trust, he'll remember that."

Rave and Daniel appeared at the top of the stairs. Sharon glanced up at them and smiled. Her heart nearly burst, seeing her grown son holding the hand of a small child. She'd missed so much of Rave's life. She could only pray he'd give her the chance to be part of it again.

"Hello, Daniel," she said. "Are you hungry for breakfast?" One thing she knew about little boys, they were always hungry.

"I guess," Daniel answered, casting a look up to Rave.

Sharon could easily see the battle going on in Rave's mind. Finally, he relented. "Daniel, has anyone ever made you pancakes shaped like Snoopy?"

Daniel's eyes widened. "No. Can you really do that?"

"Well, I can't," Rave said. "But this is Miss Sharon. She makes pancakes shaped like all kinds of cartoon characters."

Rave had extended an olive branch. Sharon would grab it with both hands. "Would you like to help me?" She reached toward Daniel.

"Sure!" Little-boy excitement chased away the last of the sleepiness on his face.

"Come on, let's make some pancakes."

Daniel grinned and flattened a hand on the banister as he bounded down the steps.

Rave had a faint smile on his face. When his gaze locked with his mother's, the smile faded.

While Daniel ate a mound of pancakes, Rave and Tuck discussed their original plans for the day. They were canceled now, all of them deciding that giving Daniel a day of fun might be the best medicine for a lonesome heart. Rave had invited Becca, who had called back and asked if Trini could come along. Sharon remembered Trini from years ago but wondered what Rave's relationship with Becca was.

"Rave's redoing the wiring in the cabin, Sharon. That's where we were headed today." When Tuck pulled a large pill case from the kitchen cupboard, Sharon frowned. That was a lot of pills. Too many for any healthy seventy-six-year-old. Tuck had gone on chatting about the cabin as he downed a handful. When he was finished, he looked her straight in the eye. "Nothing to worry about," he said, under his breath. "Old men get sick. Back to what I was saying . . . Rave's doing a fine job on the wiring at the cabin."

Sharon turned to her son, her mouth dry and her heart heavy. She needed to form words. "When did you start learning about electrical work?"

Rave downed the last of his coffee and stood to put the mug in the sink. "When I got here."

The words themselves weren't combative. It was the way they were delivered. Flat eyes, stiff posture, no emotion. Sharon gripped her own cup a little tighter. She knew this would be difficult. It was going to be a long journey to Rave's heart. She only hoped it wasn't too late to find the way.

Sapphire Springs and the gorgeous falls that dumped thousands of gallons of water into its gurgling pool used to be one of Sharon's favorite places to visit. She'd sat at the base of the falls once, her life ahead of her, her hopes and plans glittering diamonds in a sea of possibilities. Life had changed. What had once been hope turned to despair. Wrong guy. Wrong crowd. An injury that left her an orphan to the sports dreams she'd had.

Sharon turned her thoughts from the past to the present. To the boy who'd grown into a man. To the grandfather she'd kept from him. She couldn't help but smile at Tuck. He'd situated himself on a park bench near the edge of the falls. Trini Barton sat beside him. She'd been a friend of Sharon's mother's years ago, and although the woman had certainly aged, she still had a childlike sparkle in her eye and a bounce to her step. It was good to see Tuck happy. He grinned now and again when Trini said something particularly snappy. His crooked grin, that single front tooth just a bit longer than the other.

An ache so deep it could grow legs and walk away settled in her stomach. She'd missed so much. And Tuck was sick. How sick, she didn't know and wouldn't press because there was a marginal strip of justice being doled out to her. She hadn't been here. She hadn't been the one available when a diagnosis came. Oh, God, she didn't want to lose her father. Not now, not after finally finding her way back home.

The sting of oncoming tears caused her to stand and walk away from the group. Becca and Rave held hands with Daniel and once even swung him out over the water as if to drop him in. He squealed and yelled, "Again!" But Rave shook his head. A loving but wise, fatherly decision. Again, Sharon was painfully reminded of how much she'd missed. How much she'd traded for a drug that could only give her a momentary release, followed by years of heartache. But she was here now. That's what she had to concentrate on because rehashing the mistakes for too long could only make her bitter. Bitterness was something she'd fought all her days in confinement and something she refused to allow into her heart.

She was strong now. She could do this. Whatever Tuck needed. Whatever Rave needed, whether he agreed to allow her to be part of his life or not, she'd be here to help. For the first time in her life, Sharon knew she wouldn't let down the people who needed her the most.

She heard someone coming up behind her and turned.

Tuck opened his arms, and she found a place against his chest. Closing her eyes, she relished the feel of her dad's arms around her. No matter how old a girl got, she was never too old for her father's arms.

"I still can't believe you're here," Tuck whispered.

"I can't believe how good it feels to be home. But Dad, I need to know how sick you are."

His mouth pressed into a flat line. "Plenty sick. Cancer."

No. No, not now that she was finally home. "Is it . . ."

"It's localized in my liver. As long as it doesn't spread, there's still hope."

Sharon's mind clouded. Cancer always spreads. That's what it does. "What can we do?"

He cradled her closer. "We can live, Sharon. We can live every single day to the fullest. Let's not dwell on it, OK?"

She drew a steadying breath, but her heart was breaking. "I'll try to concentrate on being home."

He leaned back and looked at her. "You know, folks remember who you were back in high school more than they remember what you became after you got out."

Whether they did or didn't was something she knew she had to face. If they remembered the basketball star with the bright future, wonderful. If they remembered the injured senior who slipped right into drug use and eventually abuse, well, that was OK, too, because she'd learned in prison a person can't live her life in fear of what people thought of her. "Thanks, Dad."

"Transitions are tough. Having some friendly faces will make it easier." His brow furrowed. "But do you really have to leave in a few weeks?"

Her gaze trailed behind them. It all depended on Rave. "I can't stay if Rave doesn't want me here. It's not fair to him." At the same time, she wasn't about to leave if her father was sick, maybe dying.

"Rave has more strength to forgive than he knows. He's an amazing young man."

She looked across the stream where Becca and Rave stood arm in arm, staring up at the gorgeous falls. "He is. I'm not going anywhere as long as the two of you need me, Dad."

He gave her a crooked smile. "Better cancel that trip, then. I have a feeling we're going to need you for a long time."

Becca remembered days like this back when her grandmother was alive, and her family would take all-day trips to the park or a favorite fishing hole. Sometimes they'd all pile into her dad's boat and float along on Lake Tears. They ate lunch and caught fish for dinner. But that was before her dad lost his job, and they had to sell the extras. The boat, the four-wheeler, all gone. Not that any of them had time for those things anymore. They were all working and helping each other stay afloat.

This had been a great day. Even though there was tension between Rave and Sharon, the buffers of Tuck, Trini, and Becca herself had created a nice insulation, so all could enjoy Daniel and his first trip to Sapphire Springs. There was no more mention of Ashley. And Becca hoped maybe they'd all overreacted to Daniel's dream and the phone call from Ashley. Becca could certainly understand a young woman falling hopelessly in love. After all, she had with Rave.

They'd gone back to Tuck and Rave's house and had dinner, a perfect ending to the day. Becca was planning to leave soon when the night took a horrible turn.

It was after dinner that Tuck's illness was brought with resounding immediacy to the forefront of their minds. Everything had been fine. Sharon had left an hour before, and Rave and Becca were finishing up the last of the dishes when Tuck came into the kitchen, lost his balance, and nearly collapsed. A mug he'd been holding shattered to the floor as if its purpose had been to punctuate the cancer that sought to destroy Tuck.

Becca sat with him on the couch while Rave tried to get ahold of Tuck's doctor. They were waiting for a call back when Trini arrived.

Straightaway, she plucked the phone from Rave's hand and redialed the doctor's office. She placed her hand over the receiver and pointed to the kitchen. "Rave, go get your grandfather's medications."

When the doctor's service answered, she started talking. She talked and talked and talked until finally, they told her they'd call the doctor immediately and have him call back within the hour. When she hung up the phone she said, "You have to be your own advocate these days. If Tuck has another one of these dizzy spells, we're taking him to the ER." She spun and pointed a finger at Tuck, who was shaking his head. "Like it or not."

"It was just a spell. I probably stood up too fast or something. I'm fine."

Trini was wearing jeans with the bottoms rolled up to midcalf. She had on plain white sneakers that looked like their sole mission was to absorb the green from the freshly mowed grass. Even though she was in her early seventies, she liked her jeans and her sneakers, and Becca thought she was one of the most inspiring women she'd ever known. Trini was a force of nature.

When Becca's family had fallen on hard times, it was Trini who'd found work around her house to keep Becca's dad busy. Trini would load him up with fresh vegetables from her garden and send him home with meat from her freezer because it was going to get freezer-burned if someone didn't eat it. Meat—she'd explained—didn't always agree with her. Becca had learned that this wasn't true. She'd seen Trini work her way through ribeye steaks like a hungry lumberjack.

She was the closest thing to a grandmother that Becca had, and it helped to know she was here with Tuck when they all needed her most.

Becca slipped into the kitchen and used her cell to call her parents and tell them she was staying at Tuck's place for the night. Her dad was silent on the other end of the line. "Dad, it's fine. Tuck is having a rough night. I want to be here." She was an adult. She didn't need their permission or their blessing, but Becca cared about what her parents thought of her.

"And Rave is there, too?" her dad asked.

She stared at the ceiling. "Yes. Of course. He lives here."

"This young man knows I have a variety of guns and know how to kill with my bare hands, right?"

"Funny, Dad." She glanced at Rave, who'd just entered the kitchen and rolled her eyes.

"Shall I tell him I know how to make a body disappear?" His tone was flat but edged with humor.

"And shall I tell him you're really just a giant teddy bear who likes chick movies and sipping tea in the afternoon?" Her tone matched his.

"That was a particularly low blow."

"It was. Don't make me rat you out. Love you, Dad."

"Love you, too, Bec. Give Tuck our best, and be careful." It was a father's warning to a grown daughter. She loved him all the more for it.

She hung up the phone and replaced it in the kitchen. When she returned to the living room, she was stopped by the heaviness that lingered there, the tension thick. She took a delicate step closer to Rave, who'd left the kitchen when he realized she was on the phone. "What did I . . . miss?"

Rave's hands were on his hips. "He wants me to call my mom."

Tuck's eyes were hopeful, the brackets around his mouth deep. "I'd like for her to be here. I'd like for you to give her a chance, Rave."

Rave pulled a steady breath. "Tuck, you can't just throw her into every situation we're facing and expect all the things she's done to disappear."

Tuck nodded. He looked tired. Worn out by the day and the dizziness and the weight of unforgiveness that hovered in the room. "I know. I just want you to agree to give her a chance."

Trini wasn't speaking. Like Becca, she didn't want to get in the middle of this delicate conversation. Becca's gaze trailed to Rave. His fists found their way to his waist and even before he spoke, a challenge was in the air. "And I'd like you to agree to me being a donor for you."

Becca's eyes widened. Rave was smart, really smart, to think on his feet this quickly. Her gaze trailed to Tuck.

Tuck huffed. It was evident what Rave was asking, and really, could Tuck say no? Becca figured the one thing Tuck wanted more than anything was to see his daughter and grandson reunited. This might be the only way. "You give your mother a chance. And I'll be open to you being a donor."

"Then I'll give her a chance. But no promises, Tuck. I'm not sure I can ever let go. I'm still so angry at her. When I see her, I want to put my fist through the wall. Like I said, I'll give her a chance, but I can't promise much more than that."

Tuck came closer and extended a hand for Rave to shake. "That's all I'm asking, boy. We agree to take it one day at a time." They shook hands, and then Tuck surprised them all by drawing Rave into a hug.

Sharon arrived within the hour. Rave opened the front door to her, noticing first the dark circles under her eyes—lack of sleep, he assumed, but who knew? After all, this was Sharon Wayne, lifelong drug addict.

She swallowed and smiled. The dark disappeared. Just lack of sleep. Or waking after so little sleep. Whatever. It really didn't matter to him. "Is Dad OK?" she asked.

No, Rave wanted to say. *He's sick. He's dying, and you weren't here for him. And neither was I, because you kept us apart.* Rave forced the renegade thoughts down. He'd told Tuck he'd give her a chance. For the sake of his grandfather, Rave was going to do that. But only baby steps. That's all he was capable of. "He's upstairs changing clothes. He'll be down in a few. He can explain."

A look of horror washed over her face.

A stab of regret pricked Rave's heart. He quickly washed that away with a fast rundown of the things she'd done, the things that could have kept this awkward meeting from ever happening. When the moment stretched without further explanation, she held out a grocery bag. "I bought these for Daniel after I left earlier."

Rave took the bag and looked inside to find coloring books, puzzles, crayons, and washable markers.

"I know he'll probably need supervision with the markers, but they were always . . ." Her voice faded away.

Rave's gaze returned to her.

"They were always your favorite." It seemed as though the words had fought to stay inside her mouth, a battle lost; they slipped from her lips only to die in the encroaching air around Rave.

"Thanks." His voice was clipped. He started to put the bag of books on the coffee table, but a shiny gray cover on one caught his eye. He slid his hand inside and tugged at the book until he could see the entire thing. "*Creatures of the Deep.*"

"It's all underwater pictures—sharks, dolphins, and stingrays. Colorful fish, too. I hoped he'd like that one." Her voice was tentative with each cautious word.

But coloring books and markers didn't erase what he'd lived through. Markers only covered things, made them look less lifeless. And that's how Rave felt. Lifeless where his mother was concerned. "Like I said, Tuck will be down in a few minutes." Rave turned from her.

She followed him deeper into the house. "I'm glad you called."

"Yeah, about that." Rave spun and took a step landing at his mother's feet. "He made me call. I don't want you here, Sharon. But it's not up to me. Tuck is sick. Really sick. And if you have any thoughts about backsliding, you need to either leave or not do it until—" *Until he's gone.* Those were the words that stuck in his throat and refused to come out.

Her face darkened. And Rave knew he probably should have been a touch gentler in telling her. Tuck was her dad, after all. Her only living parent. But right on the heels of that thought came another. His only living grandparent—whom his mother kept away from him, telling him Tuck was dead.

Her brow furrowed. "He told me at the waterfall," she whispered, so many emotions gathering on her face that Rave had to look away.

Behind them, Rave heard shuffling and the unmistakably cheery timbre of Becca's voice. "Trini's in the kitchen making cookies. I made fresh coffee for when your mom arrives—" She came into the living room. "Oh, hello again, Sharon."

Rave couldn't help but smile. Becca always made him smile, even in the tensest of moments. When she looked up into his eyes, all the frustration of having to explain anything to his mother melted. He squeezed her hand. She squeezed back. And for a few glorious moments, it was just the two of them.

Sharon sighed. "You two really are great together."

When Rave questioned her with a look, Sharon went on. "I watched you today at the waterfall. You're fortunate to have found each other. That kind of emotion is rare." Her voice got quieter. "Once in a life-time." At that, she turned away.

Rave had to wonder if *she'd* had a once in a lifetime. He'd never thought about it before. When he was a kid, she'd just been his mom—a woman with poor judgment and an addiction she couldn't control. She'd found the loser guys. The no-goods. She'd let them into her life but had protected Rave if they ever acted like they'd turn their anger on him. For all her failings, she had protected him in ways that he'd never even thought about until right now. This moment. With her eyes misty and her heart bare. There was much about his mother he didn't know.

Becca spoke up. "Daniel went on and on about what an amazing day it was."

Sharon smiled. "He reminds me of Rave at that age. Curious about everything. Fearless. Little-boy excitement is contagious."

Rave busied himself sifting through the mail near the front door. He didn't want this kind of attachment to his mother. She always left. Eventually, she always left. He didn't want her chatting about Daniel and what an intelligent little guy he was. Rave didn't want her knowing these things because knowing meant contact and contact meant future failure. He couldn't allow his mother to fail him again. And more important, he couldn't allow her to fail Tuck.

Becca and Sharon sipped coffee while Rave roamed the living room like a caged cheetah.

"Any word from Ashley about her plans?" Sharon said when the room grew heavy with the quiet.

Rave stopped pacing. "We were gone all day. You were here all evening. So you already know the answer to that."

Sharon swallowed hard. "I just thought . . ." But there were no words to complete that sentence because all three of them knew she was trying to approach the *is Ashley really coming home* question.

Rave moved to sit on the couch beside Becca. "She's trying to give them a better life. Ashley would make any sacrifice for her son."

The comparison was not lost on Sharon. She bit back a painful smile.

Rave instantly felt bad. Then he felt angry for feeling bad because she didn't deserve to be here. She didn't deserve Tuck's forgiveness, and she didn't deserve to step back into their world like nothing ever happened. He'd told Tuck he would give her a chance. But he would also protect Tuck.

"Rave, can you tell me if Dad's cancer is terminal?" Her eyes were pleading. Impatience crackled around her.

"If he wants you to know, he'll tell you."

She nodded slowly, gaze dropping to the floor.

Rave knew he wasn't making this easy on her. But why should he? When Tuck rejoined them, dressed in jeans and a blue flannel shirt, he hugged Sharon, then explained that he'd had a dizzy spell. Nothing to worry about, but he'd wanted her there. They all sat quietly for several minutes, then Sharon spoke up. "Dad, are you sure we shouldn't take you to the emergency room? Just let them check you out. I know we'd all sleep better."

"Pfft. Emergency room, my rear end. They ought to call it a-grow-old-and-die room. Or a we'll-get-to-you-if-you-don't-bleed-out room. I've been poked and prodded enough."

Becca curled her feet under the afghan on the couch. "Should we call the answering service again?"

At that moment, the phone on the wall sprang to life. Tuck stood to answer it, but Rave got there first. He was done with feeling like an outsider to his grandfather's condition. Liver cancer was nothing to mess with. And Tuck was failing right before his eyes. With the medications spread on the coffee table before them, Rave ran through the list of drugs while the doctor listened. "Tuck, where are the pills for tomorrow night?" Since the doctor had added more medications to Tuck's routine, he'd purchased a pill holder that had separate morning and night spots for each day of the week.

Tuck scratched his head. "They're not in there?"

"No. When did you take your meds tonight? Before or after dinner?"

Tuck's face scrunched into a frown. "Good Lord. Both." He rubbed his hands over his face. "I was getting ready to take them early, but I got distracted helping Daniel with his shoelaces. Had one in a knot. But I—"

Sharon stood and put an arm around her father's shoulders. Then she stepped away from him, toward Rave, and reached for the phone. "Rave, can I speak to the doctor?"

He recoiled.

She leaned closer and whispered. "Drug overdose is something I know a little bit about."

Rave hesitated only a moment longer and then handed over the phone. He was at Tuck's side in less than a heartbeat while Sharon talked to the doctor and explained what had happened.

She listened, nodded as if the doctor could see her, and addressed the group in the living room after hanging up. "He said you'll be OK, Dad. No need to go in. We just need to make sure it doesn't happen again."

A collective sigh passed through the room. "How could I be so stupid? Where was my mind?" Tuck scratched the thin spot on his hairline.

Sharon shook her head. "Dad, I show up out of nowhere, a ghost, someone you thought had been buried long ago, and you're wondering where your mind was? It was distracted. That's all. Your doctor said to skip your morning meds tomorrow. By tomorrow evening, you can resume your regular schedule."

Rave had to admit he was surprised that she took the blame for this. Sharon Wayne had never assumed responsibility for anything back when . . .

Back when she was a drug addict. She wasn't anymore. At least, she wasn't right now. Time would ultimately tell how committed she was to staying clean. Still, he wouldn't take a risk that made himself or Tuck collateral damage.

Sharon's cell phone rang. She looked at the caller ID and answered. She stepped away from the group and chatted in perfect Spanish while Rave could only watch in disbelief. When she hung up, he spoke. "You know Spanish."

She nodded. "Yes, learned in prison. It was a prerequisite for going to Peru next month."

When he stared at her, mouth gaping, she said, "I'm not the person you knew, Rave. I'm trying to become the best version of myself. And right now, that's a person who hopes you can one day forgive me."

Forgive her. That was a long way away. If it was even possible.

Rave and Becca left the house in Tuck's Chevy early the next morning. They'd kept a close eye on Tuck, all of them staying awake late into the night. Sharon had ended up sleeping on the couch. Becca had curled up on Rave's bed, but Rave had stayed in the armchair at Tuck's side, watching him breathe and only dozing for a few minutes at a time. Tuck suggested the two young people get some air, so they went to town and picked up breakfast at the drive-through.

Rave drove them to the corner of the square, where he parked in the early-morning shade of a flowering tree. "I need to check in at the memorial park. They've added some flowering plants, and Carr's Landscaping has offered to run irrigation throughout the park."

Becca picked at her biscuit sandwich. "That's fabulous. Wait, why didn't I know about this?"

"Pastor Keith called me this morning." After talking to him, Rave had tried to call Ashley to check in. There'd been no answer.

Becca took a drink from her lidded cup of coffee. "I vaguely remember hearing the phone ring."

Rave wasn't hungry, but he tried to eat.

Once they finished their food, Becca opened the truck door. "Shall we walk to the park? It's a gorgeous morning." She didn't wait for him to answer.

Rave got out and looped his arm through hers, and they headed toward the memorial park. It was halfway to completion now—a marvel, considering that only a short while ago, it was as abandoned as the desolate streets of a ghost town. Often, he'd drive by to find people he didn't even know spreading mulch or planting flowers. The gate was always left unlocked now so local citizens could have access. They paused at the gate. Rave didn't want to go in because he was getting anxious about getting back to the house. Everything looked in order.

"Rave, since last night when Tuck had his dizzy spell, I've been thinking."

"About?" Rave was listening, but his gaze roamed over the park. Off to the left, the first of the tall granite slabs had been installed. They would surround the fountain with a wide walkway between each slab and a massive open area with room to roam. The fountain, the centerpiece and, in his opinion, the masterpiece of the park, had yards of space around it where families could enjoy the spray of the water. There were even a few picnic areas in this central section of the park.

"Well, I know we talked about Tuck waiting until the park is farther along to see it, but . . ." Becca's voice trailed.

"But what if Tuck is running out of time?" It had been on Rave's mind since last night.

She dropped her head. "Yes."

"I know. Sometimes I forget he's not invincible. He's even been working alongside me at the cabin. Until last night, his illness seemed pretty far away. And it brings up another question."

Becca looped her arm through his.

"The transplant surgery."

Becca nodded slowly. "Are you afraid you're waiting too long?"

Rave pulled her closer. "Everything is depending on Ashley coming home when she's supposed to. I've tried to call her, and she's not answering. We only have a few more weeks before she's due home, and I can't escape the feeling that she's putting me off."

"Rave, let's talk to Pastor Keith. He said he'd be there for you and Tuck. Maybe he'll have some ideas."

"Unless he can clone me, I'm not sure he can help." Without discussion, Rave and Becca both turned from the memorial park and headed back to Tuck's truck. The park was looking incredible. They should be proud, but right now, all Rave felt was fear of the unstoppable future.

"And what about your mom helping with Daniel? She seems great with him."

She *was* great with him. Right now. But what if she slipped? What if she had a bad day and went looking for drugs? "I can't take a chance like that with Daniel. I'd never put him at risk."

"Well, you know I'm here to help as much as I can."

"I know. I love you for it." He opened the truck door for her and helped her inside. Together, and with more hanging on their shoulders than any two twenty-somethings should have, they drove back to the house.

⌒♋

Sharon had spent the better part of the day coloring on the floor with Daniel. She used to do that with Rave, so long ago. She assumed he didn't remember. But midday, she'd caught him standing at the top of the stairs watching them. The look in his eyes was haunting. For a moment, his heart was open to her. She could feel it. And she wanted nothing more than to run up the stairs to him and hold him in her arms. But she didn't. She glanced down at Daniel, and when her eyes went back to Rave, he'd closed off the emotion. She gave him a sad smile and returned to coloring.

Daniel had finally tired of coloring, so the two of them had walked the property looking for wild blackberries. At first, Rave had been reluctant to let Daniel go with her, but Tuck had coaxed him, and finally he'd agreed.

At one point, they'd turned down the winding path and landed at the cabin door. She knew Rave and Tuck were fixing it up. Maybe Rave planned to move into it one day. She hoped. That meant he planned to stay in Barton. Whether she was able to be in his life or not, she liked the idea of her son living here. When they returned home, she found her dad asleep in the recliner and Rave and Becca gone.

She slipped inside, hoping not to wake him. Sharon pointed to Tuck and made a "sshh" sign by slipping her finger to her lips.

Daniel nodded and tiptoed past Tuck. Daniel looked so adorable, his shoulders hunched, his hands clutched in concentration. It reminded her of the many times she'd watched Rave sneak through the living room on Christmas Eve, hoping to catch a glimpse of Santa. She'd never had much money, but she'd always tried to keep the magic of Christmas alive for Rave. Heaven knows she'd destroyed most of the magic of his childhood.

As soon as Daniel was beyond the recliner, he bolted into the kitchen, where Sharon had told him they could wash the blackberries and make a cobbler. There were barely enough. But baking always helped her think, and when she'd mentioned the idea to Daniel, he'd gone all round-eyed and said, "Really? Really, I can help?"

She'd propped her hands on her hips. "Not just help, you can do the whole thing. I'll just supervise."

They were just getting started when a groggy-looking Tuck came into the kitchen. "Sent Rave to the store. We'll fix dinner here, and then he can take you over to Ashley's place."

Sharon chewed her cheek.

A grinning Daniel looked over from the kitchen chair that sat propped at the sink. "I'm making cobbler. It has blackberries and sugar in it."

Tuck walked over and looked into the sink, where the pitiful pile of berries sat under streams of running water. He raised his brows and glanced at Sharon. A moment later, he dragged a shiny new phone from his pocket. "Rave bought this. One for him, too. I still haven't mastered it, but maybe you could give him a call." He lowered his voice. "Pick up some extra . . ." His words trailed off, but he nudged his chin in the direction of the berries.

Sharon's hands grew sweaty as she took the phone. After a few crushing moments, she held the phone back to him. "Maybe you should call."

"He'll come around. You'll see. Needs time is all. He's a good boy, Sharon."

Daniel looked up with a mouthful of berries. "I am a good boy. Miss Sharon told me when we were picking berries, and I promised her I wouldn't go too close to the river."

Sharon went to him and gave him a hug from behind, maneuvering around the chair back. "You, sir, are an amazing boy."

Daniel giggled. "I'm not a sir."

She leaned back where she could look at him. "Well, you're not a ma'am."

The giggle became a full belly laugh, prompting Bullet to come prancing in to see what he was missing.

Sharon scratched Bullet's ears. It was so easy with dogs and children. They held so little resentment, so little bitterness. If only she could turn back the hands of time and do things right. But she couldn't. One thing she'd learned from Maria and Don and her long years away was that a person couldn't change the past. She can only control its effect on the future.

She had a future waiting for her in Peru and Texas. She had a job and a life plan. But she'd give it all up in an instant to have her son and her father. She just still wasn't certain that was a possibility.

∽

After eating dinner and a delicious cobbler prepared by Daniel, Sharon followed Rave to Ashley's apartment. It was late in the day, and although she'd felt so at ease with Daniel and her dad, Rave's reappearance at the house had made her stiff as a poker.

"Rave, are you sure about this?" Sharon asked when Rave used his key to unlock the front door.

"Mom, this is the last request Ashley gave me before going off on her 'romance adventure.'" He made air quotes when he said the last part. "She wanted you to stay here." He flipped on a couple of lights but hovered near the front door.

Sharon nodded. "I know, but she could show up at any time and—"

"It's going to be a while. I could tell by her tone. She's always been so ready to jump into a romance, and this guy is rich and obviously into her. She's a big believer in fairy tales."

The apartment held an old loveseat and a recliner that must have been made during the seventies. Still, it was better than the motel by a wide margin. Simple, old, but clean. "And you, Rave? Do you still believe in fairy tales?"

He leveled her with a look. "I had too much reality thrown at me while growing up to believe in happily ever afters."

She knew he didn't really believe that. Even as he said it, his eyes told her the truth. In the deepest part of his heart, Rave still believed that life could be happy. If a person only gave himself a chance. She'd pushed this conversation enough. Sharon turned their attention back to the one of the two things that always made Rave smile. "Daniel is so amazing, Rave. Such a smart little boy. Inquisitive. He asked about everything while we were looking for blackberries." Sharon placed her suitcase on the floor while Rave changed the setting on the air conditioner. She'd hoped they could bond over Daniel. It was common ground, and after all, he'd left the little guy alone with her, so maybe some of the outer crust that kept Rave distanced was starting to crack.

But when he looked over his shoulder at her, that hope dissolved.

"Should I make us some tea?" she asked.

"No. I need to get back."

As he opened the door, she stepped beside him and said, "Rave, have you considered what you're going to do about Daniel if . . ."

He closed his eyes. And closed the door. "I'm not giving up on Ashley. She's had a momentary lapse of judgment, but that doesn't mean she won't come to her senses quickly."

But Rave needed to think about what could happen. "You're not Daniel's father. Unless . . ."

"I'm not. And I'm still not sure why Tuck felt at liberty to discuss any of this with you." He wanted to run. She could see it.

"Social services will step in as soon as they discover Daniel was abandoned."

He spun around. "Stop it. You haven't earned the right to do this. And Ashley didn't abandon him. She left for work."

"Work that she no longer has. Social services will look at it as if she'd left him weeks ago." She didn't flinch or move away. This was bound to get sticky. She wanted to prepare Rave for it.

"Social services never stepped in to take me away from you." But as he said it, she knew his mind had been roaming over this territory. What would he do? What *could* he do?

"Our situation was different. You were my son."

A sound escaped his mouth that was part laugh, part huff. "Yeah. *Were.*"

Rave stepped out and closed the door hard behind him. She'd never heard a lonelier sound.

CHAPTER 18

A week passed before Rave called Pastor Keith. He'd dialed Ashley's number and left multiple messages, but there'd been no response. Rave sat on the couch with Tuck waiting for Pastor Keith to arrive.

Tuck rubbed his hands on his thighs. "You know there's no way I'll let you be a donor for me now that we don't know about Ashley."

"Why would you say that?" Rave's thoughts had been scattered by the what-ifs. If Ashley wasn't there to help with Daniel, how could Rave move forward?

Tuck leaned forward on his knees. "Rave," he whispered, "if Ashley really is gone, Daniel needs you more than ever now. We can't just abandon him for the week you'll be in surgery and recovery."

Rave's chest pinched. Was he really going to have to choose between his grandfather and Daniel? This was an unbearable situation. "I'm still moving forward with the donor plans. It will work out."

Tuck shook his head, his mouth a straight line. "Already *is* worked out."

Rave trapped Tuck in his gaze. "Listen to me, *I* need *you* more than ever if—" He had to swallow before continuing. "If Ashley doesn't return. There's a way, Tuck. I just don't know what it is yet."

Pastor Keith knocked and entered when Tuck yelled for him to come in. "So sorry. For all of you. LaDonna gives her best and made you a casserole. Three hundred twenty-five degrees for twenty minutes." He set the dish on the table just inside the front door and sat down on one of the easy chairs.

Tuck nodded at him. "Thanks for coming, Pastor."

His smile was warm, his dark hair shining with some kind of gel or product in it. Rave grinned. "New haircut?"

The pastor nodded. "Yes. My barber, Mark, put a handful of some strange paste in it. Said it would make me look dapper."

Tuck rubbed a hand over his chin. "It does."

Pastor Keith's gaze drifted around the room. "I'd like to know what I can do for the two of you. There's a lot on your shoulders right now."

Tuck shook his head. He was a proud man and one who didn't rely on outsiders for help.

Rave was a realist. Without help, Tuck wouldn't survive this. "Daniel's not my son."

Pastor Keith's eyes rounded for a few seconds. "I assumed—"

"Yeah." Rave sliced a hand through his hair. "Everyone assumes. And now I'm starting to worry that Ashley isn't going to come home."

"That does complicate things."

"Or *when* she's going to return. I know Ashley loves Daniel. She's just had a momentary lapse. The problem is, we're three weeks from school starting, and I can't register him. If she's not back—"

"You're worried social services would step in? Rave, if Ashley doesn't return, are you thinking of raising Daniel?" Keith asked.

Rave thought of a world without Daniel. The very notion stole the warmth from his bones. "I've always felt like he was my own son. But for now, I just want more time to figure out what to do. Giving up on Ashley doesn't feel right. If the circumstances were different—"

"Could he start school late?"

Rave had considered that. "It's not really fair to him, is it? Beginning with a disadvantage. Daniel's fifth birthday is coming up. I'm not sure his mother is going to be here for it."

"Ashley really has had a lapse of judgment." Pastor Keith steepled his hands and stared up at the ceiling. "Did she leave any instructions, anything written about Daniel's care? If so, we might be able to use that to get the enrollment process started."

Rave shook his head. "No. I mean, I've taken care of Daniel lots of times."

Pastor Keith gave an affirming smile. "Let's concentrate on what we can do."

"There's more." Rave locked his fingers together as if the motion could keep him from coming apart. "I'm planning to be a liver donor for Tuck. Our appointments and hospital stay are all scheduled. It's for four weeks from now, a week after we thought Ashley would return."

"God bless you, Rave. That's a very brave decision." Keith leaned forward.

Tuck spoke up. "It's not happening now. No way. Not with this new situation with Daniel. Rave can't do everything. He can't be all things to all people."

Keith nodded, rocked back in the easy chair, and scratched his chin.

Rave stayed quiet. He was done arguing about this with Tuck.

"No. Rave can't," Keith said. "At least, not alone. The church can help with Daniel's care while you two are in the hospital. Also, when you get home. We'll arrange meals to be delivered for the first couple of weeks. But I warn you, we've got some top-notch cooks in our congregation. You may get fat."

"Why would you do this?" Rave hadn't meant to say it. He was thinking it, and before he could stop the words, they slid out of his mouth.

"The real question is, why wouldn't we, Rave? Now, we'll need to be delicate with the Daniel situation. I don't want people in the congregation knowing he's not your son. Though my flock is a loving one, it'd only take one busybody with a cell phone to make a call to social services suggesting that his mother has abandoned him. For now, we keep this between us."

Tuck rubbed his hands over his springy hair. "This is an awful lot to ask of you, Pastor."

Keith stood and offered Tuck his hand to shake. "Then it's a good thing you don't have to ask. But Rave, you need to remember, the paternity situation with Daniel is bound to come up sooner or later if Ashley doesn't return. I'll start doing some research for you on becoming a foster parent. Also on adoption. We need to know our potential options. This won't be something you can run from. It'll have to be dealt with eventually."

Rave thanked him and nodded. He knew it would, but right now Daniel needed him. And it just wasn't in his nature to let the little guy down.

Rave had to give props to his mother. Sharon had made a trip to the local nursery and bought an array of flowers for her and Daniel to plant in the yard. She knew how to keep him busy and engaged, and though Rave hated to admit it, she'd been a needed distraction. Daniel had been used to talking to his mother on an almost daily basis. Now, it had been days since they'd heard anything from her.

She'd called a couple of times—for no longer than a minute or two—always with a bad connection. Rave had pressed the issue of when she was coming home, but her answers were always vague. He had to accept the idea that she might not be planning to come home before school and certainly not before Daniel's birthday.

Pastor Keith arrived the next day just as Sharon was leaving to take Tuck to the doctor. It pinched a little that Tuck wanted her, not Rave, along for the visit, but it was Tuck's life, so he wouldn't say anything. Tuck had, in fact, had Sharon take him to the last two doctor visits.

"You look concerned, Pastor Keith." Rave shook his hand as he came up the steps.

The man sat down on one of the rocking chairs on the front porch. Rave took the other. The chairs were getting lots of use now, with so much to look at in the yard. Daniel would sit on Rave's lap and stare out at the visiting butterflies and honeybees by day and the fireflies as the sun was setting. The immediate view from the front porch was the array of colorful blossoms that spread from the banisters to the towering oak trees anchoring the edge of the yard. Lush green and pops of color—red, purple, yellow—even some tiny blue flowers mingled with the mass. Beyond the flowers, a late-summer lawn continued to stay green—as if it were competing with the flowers for attention. All in all, it was a perfect place for a small child to forget the sorrow life had handed him.

"Rave, I've been doing some checking about what might happen if—well, if it comes to light about you and Daniel before Tuck's surgery."

"And?" His heart thudded against his ribs.

"There was a similar situation a few counties over. A young woman's sister needed a transplant, and the older sister became a donor."

Rave leaned toward him in the chair.

"The older sister was trying to get custody of a child. I don't know all the details, but the judge ruled that because she'd put her life on the line, she wasn't putting the child's best interests at heart."

"But—"

Keith shook his head. "I know. I know. It's completely twisted. But now, there's a precedent set. I'm afraid it could harm your case if it ever comes to that."

"Maybe it won't. Maybe nothing will come to light until after the surgery is all over."

Keith nodded. "Maybe. But it's a huge risk to take. You could lose Daniel. And not just for a short time. Forever. Having no definitive word on Ashley has bought you time, but if you choose to go through with the surgery while being the interim caregiver for Daniel, well, I'm afraid that's something the courts couldn't overlook."

Rave rubbed his hands over his face, wishing all this would just disappear.

"Rave, there could be another way."

All right, he had his attention.

"I would imagine your mother could also be a donor match for Tuck."

Rave stopped rocking. "Keith, my mom is a recovering drug addict. There's no way they'd let her be a donor. She spent years destroying her body—I'm sure her organs—it's not a possibility. And even if they would let her, they'd put her on meds to counteract the pain. That's what first got her hooked. She's clean now for the first time in twenty years."

Keith nodded. "I guess I'm grasping at straws."

"You did the right thing letting me know. Let's not share this with Tuck. He's got enough."

Keith stood and shook Rave's hand. "The memorial is coming along. We've set almost half of the granite monuments."

"I haven't been out there for a week." Rave's time had been split between Daniel and Tuck. Mostly Daniel.

Pastor Keith paused to smell a large purple flower. "Stop by. It'd do you good."

Rave nodded. "I'm taking Becca to the outdoor movie tonight."

"Oh yes. The Barton Betterment Society is hosting that, right? You kids have fun. Do you have childcare for Daniel?"

"Yes. Tuck will be home, and Trini is coming over to play poker. Daniel will be asleep before we leave."

Rave followed the pastor to his car. Keith turned. "I know things seem bleak right now, Rave. But keep the faith."

"I'm trying. Truly. The only good news is . . . things can't possibly get worse."

Rave was wrong.

CHAPTER 19

It was almost dark when Rave and Becca arrived at the outdoor showing of the '80s classic *Stand by Me*. The square had been draped with small, round, overhanging lights that lit up the area and gave it a warmth, despite the chill that snaked through the surrounding buildings.

Rave and Becca spread a blanket and watched the movie while eating popcorn, drinking root beer, and trying to forget all the sorrow beyond the protective bubble of the outdoor cinema. When it ended, the crowd of around a hundred people cheered as the credits rolled. Becca knew everyone there, so it took them a good thirty minutes just to make it across the square and to the truck. All the parallel parking spots had been filled, and Rave judged the space between Tuck's truck and the cars in front and behind. There was no way he could shimmy out of the parallel spot. He shrugged. "Looks like we'll have to stay for a while."

Becca tipped a shoulder. "Fine with me. I'm having an amazing night."

The blanket was over Rave's arm so he tossed it in the back of the truck and pulled her to him. "We could make out in the truck."

She giggled and swatted at him. "In the middle of town? That would certainly end up on the Internet."

"Not if we fog up the windows quickly." He kissed her before she could protest. Becca wound her arms around his neck. Beyond them, something was happening. Rave had spent enough time on the streets to know when the atmosphere changed. He ended the kiss and looked toward the spot where the giant projector screen was being removed.

A crowd of people was making its way toward Becca and Rave. They didn't seem threatening, but his senses went on high alert. Rave's gaze skated over the crowd as he looked for familiar faces. He found none.

One guy seemed to be leading the pack. Tall as Rave, but thicker, with broader shoulders, and stocky. The family resemblance was unmistakable. This had to be the sheriff's son. And that meant he was also the brother to the guy named Glen who liked to tear up Trini's field.

Becca stiffened and pulled away from Rave slightly. "Hi, Michael."

He smiled, hands in the pockets of his jeans. "Becca, you look great. Kept your hair long. Glad you didn't cut it."

She nodded, and Rave watched the tension enter her features. "Are you in town for long?"

"Couple weeks."

Suddenly she grabbed Rave's hand and pulled him to her side. "This is Rave." That was all she said, but when he glanced down at her, her smile said everything her mouth hadn't.

It was a moment before Rave realized the guy had moved closer. Rave's attention sharpened. But when he looked up, he found kind eyes and a hand stretched toward him. "Nice to meet you."

Rave shook his hand.

He leaned closer to Rave. "Listen, my dad told me about Tuck. He's a really good man. I hope everything works out."

Rave nodded, swallowed the wad of cotton in his throat. "Thank you."

Michael turned to Becca. "Good seeing you, Bec."

She smiled. "You, too."

The crowd started to walk off just as someone yelled across the lot. "Michael, come help the ladies with the popcorn table."

He chuckled. "Not sure what I got myself into volunteering." He jogged off. The crowd followed.

Rave pointed. "So, he's the guy."

Becca nodded. "Yes. I told him I didn't want to know when he was coming. I'm as surprised as you are."

"And he's really Glen's brother?"

She gave him a sidelong glance. "What do you know about Glen?"

"I know he likes to party."

She pointed her index finger into the air. "Right. Trini's field. The two brothers couldn't be more different."

Rave nodded toward Michael, who was disassembling a popcorn table with several gray-headed women instructing him. "Michael looks like his dad."

"Acts like him, too. Glen is their polar opposite." Becca reached down and took Rave's hand. "We don't always turn out like our parents."

"And sometimes our parents change."

Becca leaned closer. "Your mom?"

He nodded. He'd been watching her. She was becoming . . . the best version of herself.

Sharon meandered the darkened streets of her hometown until the journey ended at the marvel that was the memorial park. *My son did this,* she thought as she entered through the main gate. Her gaze went instantly to the center, where water cascaded over rocks, creating something both powerful and at the same time serene.

It still felt strange to be home. The place where she'd grown up. She knew these streets, every oak tree that lined the sidewalks, every street lamp that illuminated the storefronts. For the first time in a long time, Sharon sat down on a park bench and let her guard down. She'd made progress with Rave. Her heart broke over the burden her barely grown son carried. Still, there was only so much she could do. Only so much he'd allow her to do.

Tonight, at the outdoor movie, she'd watched Rave and Becca from the safety of the flowering tree. She made sure they never saw her. But she'd gotten to watch her son with the young woman he undoubtedly loved. The measure of a mother's sorrow was in direct relation to the sadness of her child. For once, Sharon could smile while looking at Rave, instead of regretting all she'd put him through.

She'd heard someone else creak the gate open but hadn't bothered to turn around until she noticed the crunch of footfalls coming closer. Maybe someone else was doing a little late-night soul searching. But when she turned, she knew that wasn't the cause for this interruption.

Sharon stood from her spot on the park bench. "Marty?"

He was dressed in his sheriff's clothes. She supposed that's what he wore most of the time now, a badge on his chest, a gun on his hip. So different from the T-shirts and Wranglers he used to wear when they'd spend long evenings together cramming for a geometry test or a history final. She was more accustomed to seeing him in a letterman's jacket and high-top sneakers than the attire of an officer of the law. His hair was a little thinner, but still wavy and cut now in a shorter style. He used to keep his hair long. Of course, that was the style back then. "It's late to be out here alone, Sharon."

She glanced around the darkened park, half of it shrouded in shadow, half of it a black-and-white snapshot of the park in the daytime, complete with flowers and plants framing each monument. "Is it unsafe?"

His gaze narrowed, but not before a smile changed his face. "Well." Marty Cogdill made a show of placing his hand over his gun and puffing his chest. "I'd say you're safe enough as long as I'm here."

She placed a hand on her heart and spoke with her best Southern accent. "Why thank you, Sheriff. I suspect a little lady such as myself should be more careful."

Marty stepped closer. "You always were safe with me, Sharon."

She nodded but couldn't hold his gaze. Her long hair fell forward as she searched the ground for some anchor, some rock to plant herself on. Her attention strayed to the fountain, the safe, solid fountain. "Is it too late to say I'm sorry?"

Marty sniffed. "It's never too late." When the silence between them thickened, Marty passed her and sat down on the park bench. "Were you at the movie tonight with Rave and Becca? I saw them before getting called to a house across town."

"I didn't . . . I didn't let them know I was there." Shame pried at her vanity, but she'd long ago learned the value of honesty over pride. "Things are still . . . rocky . . . with Rave."

"He'll come around."

That was what she prayed every night. Every day. Every moment. Not so she could finally put the person she had been to rest, but so she could help him carry some of the burden. "He's pretty stubborn. Gets it from Tuck."

Marty threw his head back and laughed.

She peered at him from the corner of her eye. "What?"

"It's difficult to believe that you see stubbornness in him and think it came from anyone but you."

She laughed, too. And it felt so good and so right to be able to just let go a little bit. A lifetime ago, Marty had known her. And it was nice to drop back into that familiar comfort. With Rave, she was careful. Even with Tuck. But with Marty, it just felt like she could be herself.

Her best version of herself—which, as she always told Rave, was the goal. "We're all cut from the same cloth."

"An unguarded strength can become your biggest weakness. Sharon, I know it's been a long time, but I want you to know I would have helped you."

She breathed in the honeysuckle on the air and the fragrant flowers at their feet. Even the freshly turned earth hinted of new beginnings. "I didn't want help. I wanted to drown in the void."

"It's one of the reasons I went into law enforcement."

At that admission, Sharon pivoted on the seat.

"I needed to know there were ways to help people who were addicts. If I couldn't help them directly, I'd work to get the dealers off the streets."

Her heart swelled with this new knowledge. "I'm sure you're amazing at your job."

"Too good. Ran my wife away with my dedication."

"You and Holly split up?"

He nodded. "Few years back. She travels with her work, so the boys grew up living with me."

Sharon's mind went back to high school. "Holly worshipped you. I can't imagine her ever leaving—"

"Apparently I'm not idol material. What was once worship over years became dissatisfaction, which quickly turned into all-out disdain. It wasn't her fault. She'd never really had my whole heart."

Sharon tried to swallow, but there was only cotton in her throat.

Marty's gaze was intense. "I should never have pushed you away. Maybe—"

She placed a hand flat on his leg, stopping his words. "Don't, Marty. You did the right thing."

"I gave you an ultimatum."

Sharon's tongue moistened her lips, her mouth had gone dry with the gravity of the conversation. She figured she'd eventually run into

Marty, but she hadn't expected them to dive headlong into this discussion so quickly, if at all. "And I chose the drugs. It was inevitable. One of the things I've learned on this journey is that you can't live in the 'what if' world. There's nothing but sorrow there. Your past has only the power you give it. Right now, I'm choosing to live in the moment, with one shoulder slanted toward the future. That's the best we can do, I believe. Live for now and stretch for tomorrow. And in this moment, my son needs me. Even if all I get to do is color on the floor with little Daniel, that's enough—because it's what I'm able to give."

"Your philosophy has changed."

She chuckled. "It needed to. If I couldn't do something perfectly, I wouldn't try at all. If I couldn't master it, I wouldn't tackle it. Now, I've come to understand the beauty of rest, the awesomeness of doing something even if you aren't able to do it well. There is just as much pride in a job done as in a job done perfectly. I let go of that perfection pressure. Pressure kills. It kills slowly, but it's still a murderer."

"Is it OK to tell you I'm really glad you're back?"

When her hand heated, Sharon glanced down and realized she'd kept her fingers on Marty's thigh. She snatched it away. "Sorry."

A gentle smile spread across his face. "Can I walk you home?"

She didn't answer. Instead, she gave a last look to the memorial park.

Marty stood. "Your son, he's a pretty amazing young man."

Sharon stood, too. "Yes, he is."

They fell into step beside each other, her shoulder brushing his upper arm now and then. The comfort of an old friend—but they'd been so much more. They passed beneath the flowering tree downtown, where the streets were littered with the last bits of trash from the movie. She wondered if he'd pause beneath it. But he didn't. His step had faltered, but only for a moment, and she knew it was ridiculous to think that after all this time, he'd remember that beneath the tree, when it was barely high enough to stand under, they'd shared their first kiss.

When they reached her place, Marty said, "Are you here for good, Sharon?"

A direct question. "I hope to stay. I'm here until Tuck has his donor surgery. Then it all depends on Rave. I won't make his life more complicated. And a new liver means Tuck's cancer is cured. There is a job waiting for me in Texas, but—"

"But you'd rather stay here." He didn't move toward her, but he did lean. Ever so slightly, in her direction.

"Yes. To be with Tuck for the rest of his life. To have my son again. To have my hometown." Still, she had to remember that Rave might not ever be OK with her being there. He had a right to his emotions. And she had a place to go, a mission to accomplish if it was in his best interest to leave. But either way, she'd make frequent trips home. And once Tuck was feeling up to it, she'd bring him to Texas to visit as well.

But in the end, she'd learned that life wasn't perfect. She'd no longer try to make it something it could never be. Instead, she'd started to think of life as something like perfect. Not perfection. But something so close that in its purest sense, it was its own kind of lovely. Something *close* to perfect. Something close to beautiful. A new kind of happy.

Tuck arrived at Trini's just before noon. The early August sun was warm, but not unbearable, prompting him to ask her to go on a picnic. He hadn't meant to, really. She'd called earlier to check in on him, and he'd yammered on about the yard with its new flowers, the feel of an early fall bite in the morning air, and before he knew what he was doing, he'd said, "Let's go on a picnic."

Everyone else was busy. It would only be the two of them. Trini had agreed and told him to meet her at noon. He'd arrived ten minutes early to find her swinging a broom at the air.

Tuck stepped out of the truck and headed for her. She was at the side of the house and even from the front yard he could hear her cursing.

"Lost your marbles, Trini?" he asked as he neared, careful not to get in the trajectory of the broom.

"Dad-blasted wasps. Weather is turning, and they're coming into the house." She brushed her free hand across a sweat-glazed forehead. Some of her hair had slipped out from her headband. She looked pretty, though. He'd always liked a woman a little more on the tousled side, a little less on the perfect side.

"So the sensible idea was to come outside and kill every last one?"

She pointed to the top of a tall window. "They're coming in around the frame. Did it last year, too."

"You got a tube of caulking around here?"

She rested her arm on the top of the broom. "There's some in the garage. I don't know if it's any good. Been there for months."

Tuck angled toward the garage, and Trini followed him. After a few minutes of looking around, he found the tube and a caulking gun half buried under the garden tools. "Where's your ladder?"

Trini pointed to a corner where the ladder lay on its side behind boxes marked Christmas Decorations. When Tuck started to pull the ladder from its spot, Trini placed a hand on his shoulder. "Maybe we should wait on this. Becca and her daddy are coming over next Sunday. He can take care of the wasps."

Tuck gave her a crooked smile. "You really want to battle them for several more days?"

She huffed and took the loaded caulking gun from Tuck so he could concentrate on the ladder.

Within a minute's time, he had the ladder situated under the window and was climbing up. "Careful," Trini said.

He stared down at her. "You do realize I was an electrician for thirty years. This isn't my first time on a ladder."

Trini positioned herself opposite the wall, dutifully gripping the metal sides.

But everything happened so fast.

First, as Tuck was readying the caulking gun, two wasps came jetting out of the wall. He glanced up at the sound of their buzzing just in time to see them headed straight for his face. Pure instinct caused him to swing the caulking gun. He lost his grip, and the gun went flying. He reached for it, knowing Trini was below him. Then he saw sky as the ladder tipped.

The strangest thoughts whisked through his mind as he felt his body slamming into the ground. Something hard bit into his side. For an instant, he was back in Vietnam. But that moment passed. He was not there. He was on the ground, and Trini was above him, screaming. He wanted to calm her, but he couldn't move. What was in his side? The pain was unbearable.

There'd been a time when he was OK with leaving this life. A time when he'd thought Millie was waiting—right there on the other side of Glory—arms outstretched, ready to welcome him. But then he'd found Rave, and Sharon had come home. And leaving this earth and Rave and Sharon behind was unthinkable. It was also unthinkable to know that if he stayed, Millie would remain waiting. At least for a little while longer. How could living be more complicated than dying? Tuck wanted to live. But around him, the world was growing foggy.

CHAPTER 20

Rave sped into the driveway of Trini's house just as his mother was getting out of her car. She looked frantic.

In a voice much calmer than he felt, Rave said, "Daniel, stay in the truck with Bullet, OK?"

Sharon rushed to him. "Trini called me. I got here as quickly as I could."

The ambulance was just arriving, and rather than find Tuck, he motioned for them to follow him around the side of the house, the place where Trini said he'd fallen.

A sound somewhere between a scream and a cry ripped from Sharon's mouth. "Dad!"

She dropped beside him. He lay on the ground, and Trini was on her knees alongside him. He wasn't moving, and Rave had to bite back his own emotions. There was blood on the edge of Tuck's mouth.

The paramedics were already beginning to work on him, but Tuck wasn't responding. Around him, Rave heard the words, "We've got a pulse."

Rave tried to breathe, but everything was disappearing, his focus becoming small. He drew a breath, and with it, strength, and he rushed forward.

Sharon gripped Tuck's hand. "He's not moving. Rave . . ." Her panicked eyes searched him. When the paramedics moved her aside, Rave pulled her to his chest.

Trini was giving an account of what had happened. Her face was pale, and her lips had lost all their color, but she was exhibiting the kind of strength she was known for. Now Rave understood why.

"Take Trini to the hospital, Mom."

When Sharon only stared at her father, now being lifted on the gurney, Rave moved her away from the scene by stepping around the edge of the house. "Sharon!"

Eyes filled with fear and dread focused on him. "I need to drop Daniel off at Becca's house. Can you get Trini to the hospital?" He spoke each word carefully, hoping she understood.

She swallowed, nodded her head. Pulled a few deep breaths. "I can."

"I'll meet you there."

∽

Sharon met Rave in the hospital hallway. "He's going to be OK, Rave."

Rave rushed forward and hugged her. In the folds of his shirt, he could hear her sobs, her hands fisted into the cloth. He tried to be strong. So many times he'd been strong for his mother, but that was because he'd had to be. There'd been no choice. Maybe for once, he could just let go. Maybe for once, they could console each other.

"We almost lost him, Rave. I thought we had lost him. I can't—I can't . . ."

"Sshh," Rave soothed. "It's all right, Mom. We didn't lose him."

When she quieted, he released her. "Any broken bones or anything?"

She shook her head. Her makeup was smeared. "No. A pretty good bump on the head. Bruised and exhausted. They'll keep him overnight for observation. He's been asking for you."

Rave put an arm around his mom, and together they entered Tuck's room.

Emotions surged through Rave's heart when he saw Tuck stretched out on the white bed. "Are you OK, Tuck?"

"Tough as nails," he said. But when Rave had to gulp back the sobs, Tuck reached for him. "Come on, now. I'm all right. Takes more than a ladder and two wasps to put me down."

"Dad, please don't joke. It's not the time." Sharon dropped into a nearby chair, and Rave could see the toll this had taken on her. On both of them.

Tuck pulled himself up on the bed, an obvious attempt to reassure them. "The doctor says that everything can move forward as planned."

Rave nodded. "You mean your surgery?"

"Yes." His brow furrowed.

Rave felt the atmosphere shift. "What are you not telling me?"

"Rave, we need to talk. It's not about the surgery, although I'd expect it'll change things when you know the truth."

Rave glanced behind him at his mother. Eyes wide and mouth open, she didn't look like she wanted to travel down this road. "The truth about what?" he coaxed.

Sharon stood and rushed forward. "You know what, there's lots of time for discussions after you get home, Dad." Cheery, too cheery.

Rave swallowed. "Tuck, is she not telling me something about you?"

Tuck's hands spread across the white sheet. "It's about you, Rave. And I've been keeping the truth from you for long enough. Sometimes it seems better, easier, to not admit fault, but I've been harboring this since you've been here, and it's just wrong."

Rave leaned back, trying to ready himself for what Tuck would say.

"When you came to my door, that wasn't the first time we'd met."

Rave shrugged. "Sure it was."

"No. Your momma was living here when she was pregnant with you."

Rave looked at his mother's face. Had she left when she was pregnant? Right after he was born?

Sharon came around the side of the bed and started to place a hand on his arm. Instead, she closed her fingers and dropped her arm to her side. "Rave, we were here for two years after you were born. And I—I was afraid that Tuck was going to take you away from me. That's why I left, and that's why I let you think they were dead. I just—"

Tuck interrupted her. "Stop it, Sharon. He needs to hear all of it."

Rave looked back and forth between his mother and Tuck.

"When we found out your mother was pregnant, I tried to get her to—" But the words seemed to die in Tuck's mouth. His face was pale, the lines around his eyes deep with worry. "I wanted her to abort you."

All the air left Rave's lungs.

"I'm so sorry, Rave." Tuck's eyes pleaded. "And I know you can probably never forgive me."

Thoughts rushed at his mind, but all he could say was "Why would you want her to do that?"

Sharon placed a hand gently on his arm. "I was an addict. Even then. They were afraid I might not survive the pregnancy and afraid of what it would do to the child."

He stepped back. "So the sensible answer was to remove me from the equation?" End his life. That was their answer to a difficult and potentially life-threatening situation.

Tuck drew a sharp breath, then winced at the pain it caused. "I was wrong, Rave. I was so wrong, and your mother got clean and stayed clean until you were born. For two years she fought to keep her sobriety, and Millie and I were so blessed to have you in our lives. But then, we saw her slipping. I feared for your safety and made arrangements to have her committed."

"And what about me? Were you planning to dump me in foster care?"

"No. Good heavens, no. You were the light of our lives. We were going to get custody. Raise you ourselves until your momma was clean and fit." A nurse stepped in, hit the brick wall of tension in the room, and turned around and went back out.

Rave's eyes landed on his mother. "So you took me, and you ran."

Sharon nodded. "And told you they were dead. I didn't want to lose you. Not ever."

Rave tried to digest what he'd just heard, but certain phrases kept flickering before his vision. *Abort. Custody.* It was too much to take in. He slowly moved away from them.

Tuck's voice followed. "I guess there will never be words adequate. But, Rave, I am so sorry."

A humorless laugh escaped Rave's lips. How many times in his life was he going to hear the words *I am so sorry?* They were tossed around carelessly, thrown like a ball on a playground. Rave didn't know how some people could think of others as throwaways. He'd never thought of anyone like that. Had always seen the worth in a human being, no matter how ugly his soul might be.

Maybe he needed to learn the art of detachment. Maybe his heart wouldn't be broken time and again if he could master that skill. But even as the thought entered his mind, he knew that would never be possible for him. Deep within his soul, he believed in people. Even those who let him down. And potential was almost as important as aptitude, wasn't it? If a person possessed potential, there was hope. And Rave had gone through too much to give up on hope. But what he didn't know was how many times a man was supposed to forgive.

His legs carried him a few steps away from them, out of the fog of honesty. He stopped walking just shy of the door, trying to make sense of it. Trying to wrap his head around the fact that his grandparents hadn't wanted him to be born. Of course, they were trying to keep their daughter alive. Rave could understand that. And maybe if he hadn't been failed so many times by the people he trusted, he could even deal with it. But people had failed him. Over and over and over. Rave turned. His focus stayed on the white tile floor. There were bits of dark in it. He knew that was a technique used by places like hospitals and restaurants—it camouflaged the dirt. It hid the bits of trash so people would be fooled into thinking the floor was clean.

But the image of Tuck behind him filled his vision. Tuck, small and frail on the oversize hospital bed. White sheets pulled up to his chin, his face sagging as if the conversation had stolen years from his life and life from his flesh. Rave squeezed his eyes shut, then cast a fleeting glance at Tuck and his mother. "I need some time." It was all he could manage.

Neither of them moved. Tuck and Sharon remained like glass statues, as if the smallest hit could crumble them, reduce them to shards. Never ever had he seen anyone look so broken. And yet, he found it impossible to comfort them. When he reached the hospital room door, Tuck said, "Wait."

Rave turned.

Tuck winced as he removed the chain from his neck and held it out to Rave. "There's a photo album in the top of the closet. It's yours."

Rave returned to Tuck's bedside and let him drop the necklace into his hand. In his palm was a shiny brass key. The key to Millie's sitting room.

It was strange to see photographs of himself, not recognizing his own face. He'd stared at picture after picture of the little blond boy with the slightly crooked smile. Tuck was easy to recognize—twenty years younger back then, but still the same man. His mom looked like he remembered, only younger, more full of life and happily holding her little boy.

There were a few photographs of Grandma Millie downstairs in frames, but they looked posed. These photos were candid. In one, her head was tipped back, mouth gaping, while a toddler-aged Rave poured a colorful bucket of sand into her lap. Sand. Probably the first time he'd ever seen the ocean. His mom looked beautiful then—happy, glowing, almost. So there'd been a time when they'd been a real family. All of them. It both hurt and gave him hope, a strange mix of love and regret, a cocktail he had a difficult time drinking.

After spending an hour poring over the pictures, Rave went to Becca's house. Her mother offered to keep Daniel, so they drove down a winding road that ended at a waterfall. They sat at the bottom, where the spray could mist their hair and bodies while he told her what he'd learned.

Becca held his hand. "What are you going to do?"

"What would you do?"

She shook her head. "I don't know. When my dad was in Afghanistan, all I wanted was for him to come home. I just wanted him to be all right. Family is a gift. Even when they're not perfect."

Rave nodded. "Pretty sure your dad has never done anything like this."

Becca's hair glistened with tiny drops from the falls. "No. He hasn't. I'm not excusing what they did, but at each step along the way, everyone was trying to protect the ones they loved. Your grandpa was trying to protect your mom. Your mom was trying to protect you."

He stayed quiet.

She angled her head back and looked up through the haze and dappled sunshine to the place where the falls began. "Family. It's danger close."

"Yeah."

Becca scooted closer to him. "I guess you can at least be thankful that you have family who love you. They didn't have to tell you the truth. Your mom could have put all the blame on Tuck and Millie.

Tuck could have done the same. But they wanted to tell you. Maybe that counts for something."

"Maybe."

"What are you going to do, Rave?" That was the question. If he took Daniel and ran, he'd be no better than his mother. That's what she'd done. Rave locked his elbows behind him and leaned back. "I want Daniel to grow up with a forgiving heart. How can I expect that when I can't forgive my mother and Tuck? What does that say about me?"

She rolled up on one hip and leaned toward him until she could kiss his cheek. "It says you have a heart and a conscience. And in the end, you'll make the right choice."

Rave captured her by placing a hand at the back of her neck, his eyes searching hers for answers he knew she didn't have. "Will I, Becca?"

Her face grew troubled. "You love them, Rave."

"Are there limits?"

"To love? No. I don't think so."

But that's what he'd begun to wonder. If love ran out. If there was a place where all the failures gathered into one giant cocoon of dysfunction where there was no room for second chances. No place for fresh starts.

Becca's phone rang, interrupting them. She dug the phone from her bag. "It's my mom," she said as she lifted the phone to her ear. "She said she tried to call you."

With all that had gone on, Rave had left his phone in the truck.

But watching Becca, he knew something was wrong. Becca's face changed from cheery to concerned to downright afraid. Before she could say good-bye, he was rising and pulling her up from the ground. "What happened? Is Daniel all right?"

Becca gathered her things. "Daniel's fine. It's Tuck. They had to rush him into emergency surgery."

The world blackened. For an instant, Rave knew he'd already lost him. But he fought that sensation, fought it with everything in him because he knew that fate could be cruel, but it wasn't evil. Tuck would be all right. He *had* to be all right.

Halfway to the hospital, blue lights flashed behind them. "I don't have time for this," Rave mumbled. He'd been going twenty miles an hour over the speed limit.

Instead of stopping behind him, the patrol car pulled alongside.

Rave lowered his window to find a worried Sheriff Cogdill looking back at him. "Follow me," Cogdill said.

When Rave only blinked, Cogdill went on. "Tuck's in surgery. Come on."

The word *Tuck* forced Rave's mind into gear. They were getting a police escort. That was a first.

Becca was too quiet. She'd found a McDonald's napkin on the seat and had ripped it to shreds on her lap. Rave reached over and gripped her cold hand. "What are you not telling me, Bec?"

Her face was pale, lips tight. "He only has a twenty percent chance of making it, Rave." Becca covered her face with her hands and cried.

When they arrived at the hospital, Pastor Keith was the first person they saw. He stood from his seat in the waiting room and made his way to them. Before Rave could ask, Keith began talking. "He's in surgery now. He's stable, Rave, but the next several hours are critical."

Rave tried to breathe.

"Becca, your mom will be here soon. Daniel is with your dad. He's going to take him fishing. Your mom wanted to be here with you. So does Trini. She'd just made it home when we got word. Your mom's picking Trini up on the way."

After slowly ingesting the information being spoon-fed to them, Rave found his voice. "What happened?"

"There was some internal bleeding. They didn't catch it until . . ." Pastor Keith's mouth pressed into a straight line. "His stomach became distended. There was blunt-force trauma directly to the liver. Trini said he must have landed on the caulking gun. His liver has been hemorrhaging. They were unable to stop the bleeding."

The room spun. Rave needed to sit. The contents of his stomach roiled, swirling until he thought he'd lose them.

"Rave, they have to do the donor surgery now."

Rave shook his head. "How can that be? I mean, if he is in such bad shape, how can they even consider doing that?"

"The liver is a vascular organ. Their best chance is to place the new liver as quickly as possible. They're afraid he won't be strong enough for another surgery in a few weeks' time. The doctor said this was a one-in-a-million scenario, and not far from worst-case. But he feels confident that if they do the surgery now . . ." His voice trailed off.

Rave nodded. "OK. What do I need to do?" The strangest thoughts shot into his mind. How the doctor had told him that he'd need to have nothing to eat before going into surgery. "I ate breakfast. Will that be all right?"

Keith took him by the arm and led him to a nearby chair in the otherwise empty room. "Rave, you won't be the donor for Tuck."

Rave had started to sit but locked his knees. "I know I left mad, but that doesn't change how I feel about this."

Keith waited for him to sit before continuing. Finally, Rave relented. "Your grandfather doesn't need you to be the donor. There's another."

Rave knew the chances of a donor match for Tuck from the transplant list was unlikely at best and—what? It just happened to happen when Tuck was literally running out of time?

"Rave, have you ever heard of a drug called methadone?"

"No." What did any of this have to do with Tuck?

"It's a slow-acting opioid agonist. It's given to heroin addicts to help them get clean. When your mother first went through rehab, they offered it to her. She refused. She didn't know why at the time, but she wouldn't let them put her on it. Addicts who've been on methadone can never be liver donors."

"My mom is Tuck's donor." It was an answer more than a question.

"They've both already been prepped, and she'll go into surgery shortly."

"But how? I had to go through tests, a physical."

"So did your mother. Weeks back, when she first took Tuck to the doctor, she started the process. She knew the complications with Ashley could get very sticky for you. I hope you can forgive her for not telling you."

Rave ran his hands through his hair. Did love have limits? Now, he was asking that question from a different perspective. His mother had worked to get clean and stay clean. Still, she'd placed it all on the line to help Tuck, to be a donor when Rave was already a perfectly suitable donor. So, in essence, she'd placed her sobriety on the line for Rave as well. Keith's words echoed in his head. *I hope you can forgive her for not telling you.*

"Yeah," he finally uttered. In fact, his heart felt the strangest mix of both admiration and surprise. He understood why she'd hadn't tried to tell him. He wouldn't have listened. "Even after all this time, she still knows me pretty well," he admitted. "The problem is, I never got to know her. How do you treat someone who is willing to lay down their life for you?"

Pastor Keith smiled and placed a hand on his shoulder. "You start with forgiveness. Would you like to see her before she goes into surgery?"

Rave nodded. "Yeah." He wanted to see her. Wanted to hear her voice, smell the scent that was unmistakably his mother. What if this was the last conversation they'd ever have? What if he'd wasted what little time they'd been granted by holding on to his anger? What if those hurt looks on her face were the only images remaining in his mind after today? All the moments leading to this one were a blur. His heart was still at odds with his mind. His mind still held to the truth that she'd hurt him almost beyond repair. Still. He'd forgive. He'd forgive today and tomorrow, and if she ever fell back into drug use, he'd forgive her each and every day. And he'd be there to help. He'd pick up the pieces because he knew in her heart she wanted nothing more than her family. If she was too weak to maintain it, he'd be her strong arms.

◌

She was in a white holding area. On each side of the wide hallway, glassed walls separated patients. Through the sheer curtains at the foot of each bedside, people waited with their loved ones. They moved like shadows or perhaps like angels caught in sunlight around the tall, metal-lined beds. His throat closed when he stepped into her room. She was alone.

He drew a breath and moved her curtain aside.

The smile appeared immediately on her face, lighting it up against the stark white pillow. She'd already been hooked up to an IV, and other pieces of hospital apparatus surrounded her. "Hey there," she said, words soft, almost a whisper, as if she wasn't sure if he'd run the other way if she spoke too loud.

He forced his feet to move and stopped at the end of her bed. Without warning, a splash of ice-cold fear hit him. He didn't want to lose her. He didn't want to lose his mother again. "I should be the one . . ."

Her head shook slowly, spilling her hair over the pillow. Her eyes were glassy, and he wondered if they'd already given her something. "When I was in prison, I had a lot of time to think. I was a horrible mother. I'm so sorry for that. I loved you, Rave. Every day of my life,

I loved you. I wish I'd been stronger. Strong enough to be what you needed. What you deserved."

He came around the edge of the bed and took her hand. "You had a giant demon to fight. And it wasn't his first battle, and he knew how to win. You did the best you could, Mom. I understand that now." She'd been a bad mom, but Rave had never gone hungry, and no one ever laid a hand on him. For all her faults, she'd protected him in the ways she was able. A rush of self-preservation warned him not to let her back into his heart. And yet he knew it was too late. Her desire to be Tuck's donor, the way she was with Daniel. Rave needed her. He'd tried so hard to push her away, but at the end of it all, he needed her.

It suddenly became clear all she was risking by being the donor. Maybe it wasn't too late. Maybe he could step in. With anxiety pushing his words, Rave said, "Mom, you don't need to do this. There's too much risk."

She drew him closer and placed a hand on his cheek. "I've risked so much more for so much less."

"But you're clean." His voice was pleading.

"Yes. And I intend to stay that way. They've been instructed to only give me the minimal amount of pain meds and for as short a time as possible. Rave, *this* is why I'm still alive. To get to give something back to Tuck, something back to you. This isn't a risk, Rave. This is an honor."

"What about Peru? You're supposed to be leaving."

"As soon as I knew Tuck was sick, I told them to sub in one of the people on the waiting list. Peru will still be there long after this is all over. And there will still be people there who need help. But it'll only be me helping them if—"

"If what?"

"If I'm not welcome to stay here. With Tuck. With you."

As recently as a few hours ago, she wouldn't have been welcome. Now, it was what he wanted more than almost anything else. It would be his opportunity to get to know the person she had become. He grasped her hand, pressing it harder into his own flesh, capturing her, holding her there. "Mom, I didn't want to forgive you. Because if I did, it meant I had to let you in. I've kept that door in my heart closed long enough."

A single tear trickled onto her cheek.

Rave brushed at it. "Do you remember that saying you used to tell me? About the selfless act?"

"The true beauty of a person lies in their willingness to be selfless. Selflessness may require sacrifice, but it always produces the kinds of stars that shine the brightest."

"I've tried to live by that, Mom, as best I could. But from today forward, I promise to. I promise to make you proud."

"Rave, I'm already proud."

There was a time when hearing those words from his mother wouldn't have meant a thing to him. Now, it seemed like the most profound phrase he could ever hope to hear. "I love you." His voice cracked.

"I love you, too. And even though it's not right for me to ask, I hope that one day you can forgive me for not being the kind of mother you deserved."

There was suddenly so much to say to her. So much to tell her about Daniel and his life and how he used to play guitar because she'd once dragged home a secondhand guitar for him, but how he didn't play much now because his life was so full. There were a million thoughts crashing through his mind. She needed to know that he could change his own flat tire because she'd taught him how. And that sometimes the car's battery cables got dirty, and a can of soda could do the trick. There was much to say. And no more time to say it. So, he settled on, "Mom, I forgive you now."

She laughed through the tears. "Forgiveness. It changes everything."

Two nurses interrupted them. "It's time, Miss Wayne."

"Rave, take care of Daniel. And take care of Tuck."

"Please don't talk like you're not coming back from this."

But she only smiled. "No matter what happens, my heart is right here with you. Never stop shining, Rave. You're the one star that lights my world."

"I love you, Mom." The words were rushed. He'd already said them once but needed to again. Needed her to hear. It was as if the room had swallowed the words, making them fade, voiding them. "I never stopped loving you. Not even for one day, not even for one moment."

Tears trailed her temples and ran into her hair. "You're the one thing I did right in my life."

Moments later, one of the nurses told him he'd have to leave. He moved away from her bed slowly but continued to hold her hand until both of theirs were outstretched, and only their fingertips touched. It was like letting her slip away, but he knew he had to let go. Tuck was waiting in surgery and was running out of time. Rave left—no small feat with legs made of lead. He paused outside the door, leaned his weight against the cold glass wall, and prayed.

CHAPTER 21

Rave stood on the back deck of Tuck's house, watching the morning arrive. He'd prepared himself for losing Tuck—at least as much as anyone could. He'd considered what it would feel like to return home to the quiet of the house and the whimpering of Bullet, a dog with no master. Then, he'd prepared himself for losing his mother, the woman who'd done her best to raise him in the shadow of the great demon Addiction. But he hadn't prepared himself for losing them both. That realization came after the eleventh hour. They'd had only a few updates while they'd paced the waiting room. Still in surgery, still stable. It was then that the desperate thought entered his head. Like a drill on full blast, it burrowed into his psyche, making it nearly impossible to think of anything except the fact that he didn't know how to plan funerals and whether there was some kind of book that would teach him. Eleven hours of waiting, sipping cold coffee, counting the waiting room tiles. Watching as other families came and left, gathering their belongings and their snacks and board games and playing cards, watching surgeons step through the doorway and deliver wave after wave of good news. Watching people breathe sighs of relief and smile and joke for the first time in hours. Their body language changed, their hearts lightened, their loved one was going to be fine.

I'm going to lose them both. He hadn't been able to stop his mind from straying onto that path. It had so taken over that when the surgeon stepped out and said they were both in recovery, and things looked good, Rave had shaken his head, confused. Surely, he'd heard wrong. The surgeon had pulled the surgery cap from his scalp, leaving short brown hairs to stand on end. He'd placed a hand firmly on Rave's shoulder. "They're fine. Both Tuck and your mother." He'd nodded as if he understood where Rave's mind had settled. Thoughts of a hillside monument in the local cemetery dissipated like fog in the sunshine.

Now, two weeks after surgery, that moment was still fresh in his mind. The surgeon had smiled, dark circles beneath his eyes smiling as well. He looked tired. "Your mother had a minor complication, a spike in her temperature, but she's stable and doing great. Tuck is one tough old guy. He came through it like a champ."

Even now, Rave replayed those moments in his head. In those eleven hours he'd learned how truly important family was. How much was forgivable . . . even if it wasn't forgettable.

Tuck had returned home yesterday after a thirteen-day stay in the hospital. For the first time, Rave sensed that life was going to be normal. Somewhat normal. At least, his normal, and that was more than he'd dared ask for. Bullet sat at his feet on the back deck with the sun casting shimmering rays on the lake behind the house. Finally Rave could put to bed those thoughts of losing everything he'd just gained. Both Sharon and Tuck were OK. Sometimes he'd catch himself saying it over and over again. *Sharon and Tuck are OK.*

He'd moved his mom into Tuck's house. She'd been in the hospital seven days, and when she was released, he knew he wanted to keep her close, keep an eye on her. He'd watched her fight the pain of the surgery with almost no meds. She was incredible.

Becca rapped on the glass slider, and when he turned, she stepped out to him. "I thought I'd find you out here." She was dressed in a light-blue sweater, thin material, but enough to keep the late-summer morning chill from her skin.

He reached out and pulled her into his arms. "You look beautiful this morning."

She batted her eyes. "I do what I can."

The sun rays gravitated from the lake to her, as if knowing she was a more brilliant canvas. He ran his fingers through the long locks of her hair where sunshine glinted off every strand. "Have you been thinking about Alexandra's proposition?" It was another thing that had happened since the surgery. Alexandra's wandering spirit had settled on an extended trip to Europe. She'd littered the entire coffee shop with booklets and tour guides, saying that as long as she knew she'd get to go, she could wait a few months.

"It's a huge responsibility."

Rave smiled. "I know. But she'll be checking in weekly. You practically run the place now."

Becca's eyes widened. "Out front. I run the dining room. She does the books. That's what's scary."

"But it won't be if you take my advice."

Becca huffed. "I don't have to make a decision today. We've had enough stress. And speaking of stress, how are you?"

Rave bent and kissed her cheek. "I couldn't have made it through this without you."

"Well, today will be the real test. A dozen five-year-olds and an ocean-themed birthday party."

"You sure your parents want to host? It sounds pretty awful."

"Eh, my mom has worked with the five-year-olds at church for years. She knows how to corral them."

"It was really nice of your parents to volunteer. I'd practically forgotten about Daniel's birthday. Some dad, huh?"

She hugged him. "You're a great dad. But with everything that has happened, it's no surprise it slipped your mind. Besides, it's all good. The party is a go, and we have a shark cake. Daniel's going to love it."

"Thanks to your mom. She even provided the five-year-olds."

Becca laughed. "Yeah, she gave out the invitations in her Sunday school class, then Pastor Keith personally invited the parents."

"I have an incredible group of people around me. They're more than I deserve."

"Life isn't about what you deserve. Life is about grace. And grace always gives more than we've earned. I'm proud of you for letting people help."

He shrugged, grinned. "No choice in the matter. Y'all are bossy."

Her eyes narrowed playfully. "And my city boy just said *y'all*, which means I've taught him something."

"I'm acclimating."

"Trini is going to stay here with Tuck while we're at the party. She'll keep us on speed dial, so stop worrying."

"That obvious?"

"Mmm." She winked. "Come on, you've earned a nice day."

⁓

Rave watched Daniel playing sea-themed party games and laugh like a five-year-old should. The absence of his mother was far away from him today, and for that, Rave was thankful. It was near the end of the party that Becca's dad took Rave into the house and down to the basement, where a perfectly appropriate man cave waited for them. "Nice big screen." Rave pointed to the TV mounted on the far wall.

Gary, Becca's dad, grinned. "It swivels. I had just finished fixing up this space when I got laid off. Dora had gotten tired of the noise and mess of Monday-night football. Down here, we can be as loud as we want and make as big of a mess as we want."

Rave nodded. "Who cleans it up?"

Gary opened a door alongside the large, spacious room that encompassed the entire basement to reveal a tidy broom closet filled with cleaning products and a vacuum. "Me. So don't spill anything."

He crossed to a small fridge and pulled out a beer and offered one to Rave. "No, thanks. Just a soda."

Gary popped the tops on each bottle and motioned for Rave to sit.

The sectional couch was comfortable, and he could imagine hanging out down here on a Monday night. If, of course, he ever garnered an invitation.

"Look, I'm not much for small talk, so I'll get right to the point."

Rave slowly set the drink on the coffee table. He knew when a rejection was coming. So many times in life, he'd seen the signs.

"Becca is a really brilliant young woman."

Rave's hands grew sweaty. He rubbed them together on his lap. "Agreed."

Gary looked up at the ceiling for a few long, excruciating moments. "Her mother and I are a little concerned that she's running headlong into life a little too quickly."

Rave bit into his cheeks. "And you're hoping I can slow her down?"

"We're hoping . . ."

Rave leaned forward, resting his elbows on his knees. "Sir, please excuse my frankness, but Becca's life first took on speed when she stayed here instead of going to college."

Gary frowned.

"She's not living the life of a college student. She's living the life of a woman dedicated to helping her family, paying bills, budgeting money. She's not a kid anymore. And I'm fairly certain she'll never be able to go back to that status."

Gary straightened. "Are you saying she can't go to college?"

Rave shook his head. "Not as a kid. That's gone. She can go as a woman. In fact, I've been encouraging her. She's so smart. Alexandra at the coffee shop is wanting to travel Europe for six months next year. She's talked to Bec about running the shop."

"I . . . I didn't know that. She never mentioned it."

"Well, it just came up recently, but when she asked me if I thought she could handle it, I said yes. But only if she took some business classes in the meantime."

Gary stared at Rave, his chin slightly cocked, his eyes narrow.

"Look, Alexandra will train her on the business stuff. But Becca needs the confidence some college classes will give her. She's brilliant. But she doesn't always believe it."

Gary leaned back. "Wow."

"I'm sorry she hadn't talked to you and her mother yet. She planned to soon."

"I guess she really is growing up." Gary leveled him with a look. "About the two of you."

Rave waited for the bomb to drop.

"We've been watching things unfold since you've been here, Rave. Your character is . . . well . . . impeccable. You'd have made a great soldier."

Something like relief rushed from his head down. Until now he hadn't had a clue what Gary and Dora thought of him. He'd brought so much drama, he hadn't dared hope they liked him . . . or thought him good for Becca. "Thank you, sir. That means a lot."

Gary stood. "We should join the others."

Rave followed him up the stairs.

Tuck and Trini sat on the front porch in the rocking chairs. The gentle swoosh of the rockers kept a steady beat. "It's getting cooler," Trini said.

Tuck nodded. "Fall is right around the corner." The last two weeks had been a blur with all the medications he'd been on. Pain meds, antirejection drugs, all of it took a toll. But he was alive, and his family was intact for the first time in two decades. Life—with all its faults—was beautiful.

Trini had been there every day to check in on him, something he'd come to look forward to. His feelings toward her had shifted. At least a little bit. Trini had always been a good neighbor and a sweet friend, but somehow, even through the fog of medication and exhaustion, he'd come to see her differently. She was a good woman. The kind you could spend the rest of your years sitting beside on a front porch rocking and maybe even holding hands.

"Sharon must have been feeling pretty good to go to the party today." Trini had brought out a carafe of hot tea. She poured a cup and held it to Tuck.

"She's in more pain than she lets on. Has been since the surgery, but she's determined. Proud of my girl." His medicine-addled mind hoped Trini hadn't picked up on his musings.

"And proud of her son."

Tuck wrapped his fingers around the mug. "They're my rock."

"I hear the memorial is almost complete. And they've set a date for the ribbon cutting."

"Two weeks from tomorrow. A congressman is going to be in town and expressed a desire to attend. Since they've set the date, now a senator is interested in coming."

"I guess you are proud of Rave. But you haven't seen it yet?"

"No. The ribbon cutting will be my first time."

Trini took the cup from his hands and set it on the ground. She grasped Tuck's hands in hers. "If it isn't too forward, I'd like to accompany you."

He gave her a sidelong glance. "I expected you'd want to be there."

She swallowed, and he watched as her lashes fluttered nervously. "I mean as your . . . date."

Tuck's brows tilted down, then up. "Oh. Like a date." Well, he hadn't thought of bringing a date, but he sure had been thinking about Trini. What would Millie say? Would she want him to move on? Knowing her, she'd likely told Trini to make the first move since Tuck was a gentleman and would probably die of old age before getting around to it.

Trini cleared her throat. "Mm-hmm. Like a date."

He grinned. "I guess nothing would make me more proud, Trini." He had a life to live. One that was no longer determined by liver cancer. He could date. Millie would want him to.

She patted his hand, then released him and sipped her tea. From the corner of his eye, he could see Trini rocking in the chair and smiling.

It was early on the following Thursday that the call came from social services. They said they were checking into a situation with a Daniel Walters, age five. They planned to send a social worker by the following morning. Rave's heart had dropped into his stomach. Tuck had called an emergency meeting complete with Sharon, Becca, Trini, and Pastor Keith. They'd all be there with him when the social worker arrived. Rave had been a wreck. He hadn't slept all night, and Friday morning met him with a slap of cold wind and the threat of losing Daniel. He'd hurried through a shower and dressed in his best clothes. He now stood by the sink, staring into a cup of coffee that had already gone cold. The last thing in the world he wanted was to lose Daniel. He'd worked so hard to protect him. Through all of this. He kept hoping Ashley would call, and maybe, by some miracle, she could talk to social services and explain that Rave was in charge of Daniel legally until she returned.

Trini had made cookies—her famous oatmeal–chocolate chip recipe—and scones. "People are easier to get along with when their bellies are full of yumminess," she told Rave as nervous energy drove him to dump the cold coffee and pour a fresh cup. He wished his stomach wasn't in knots.

Trini eyed him over the pan of cookies she'd just pulled from the oven. "You need to get ahold of yourself, Rave."

"Huh?" It took him a moment even to register her words.

She pointed an oven-mitt-covered finger at him. "I know you're imagining the worst, but we don't know what they want yet."

He placed the coffee on the counter by the pan of cookies. "I'm nervous, Trini. Scared to death, really."

She removed the avocado-green mitt and came to him. "The way you love that boy oozes from every pore. Anyone can see that. A social worker will be able to see that."

"It takes more than love, Trini."

"You've got a good home here. Working toward your electrician's license, you're an upstanding part of Barton's community. Give yourself a chance, boy. If you don't, how can you expect them to?"

When he grinned and nodded, she patted his cheek. "Now eat a cookie. They're made with love and have magic powers to calm your nerves."

He doubted that but took one and bit into it. He was just starting to feel at ease when the front doorbell rang. He turned to rush out, but Trini stopped him. "Wait, wait." She reached up and swiped melted chocolate from his cheek. "Now go. I'll bring out the cookies and scones in a few minutes."

◦◦◦

Sharon pulled her car into the small spot at Ashley's apartment. She'd already told the landlord she'd be staying on and keeping the apartment, but Rave had insisted she stay with them at Tuck's house—which had felt strangely foreign and yet oddly comfortable. It was the home she'd grown up in. But it was different now, no longer hers. Still, being with her dad and with Rave made everything right in the world.

She wasn't supposed to be driving. Not yet. But she'd woke up and realized they didn't have any of Ashley's papers that dealt with Daniel and that might be one of the first questions the social worker would ask. It wouldn't bode well for her to ask about Daniel's shot records and Rave to admit he didn't know if the boy was up to date or not. Rave had been resisting breaking open the locked box of Ashley's important papers. Sharon understood that. But this was in Daniel's best interests, and Ashley would want her son to be taken care of. From everything Rave had told Sharon about Ashley, she'd be angry if they didn't break the lock and access the papers if it meant helping keep her son out of the system.

Besides, Rave knew in his heart they'd have to at some point so they could register Daniel for school, which was only a few days away. Sharon flipped on the bedroom light as she entered and went straight to the closet. Her own clothes were still strewn here and there as she hadn't been back to the apartment since the donor surgery. Rave and Becca had stopped there and gathered enough of her stuff to live for a week or two and had then emptied the fridge of perishables and locked up. The apartment felt stuffy and lonely, and in the moment, she was thankful on a whole new level that Rave had extended the invitation to stay at Tuck's.

Sharon carried the box to the table and inspected the flimsy lock. She dug a butcher knife out of the drawer and closed her eyes for a few seconds. "Hope you can forgive me, Ashley. But I believe in my heart this is what you'd want if you knew the circumstances."

Her strength wasn't all it should be, and when she placed the knife against the lock and shoved, it slipped, practically gashing her hand open. She moved the box to the kitchen counter by the sink and used the backsplash as an anchor. She wedged the knife, tightened her grip with one hand, and with a solid motion, pounded the end of the knife with her free hand.

The lock broke free. Sharon placed the knife on the counter. Her hands were trembling when she lifted the lid. Maybe the exertion of energy, maybe the fact that she was breaking into personal records. She shook off the obtrusive thoughts and riffled through the papers.

When her gaze landed and held, her mouth dropped open. Her trembling hands became solid, granite slices strong enough to hold the entire world. "You've got to be kidding me."

Sharon gathered the box in her arms and rushed out of the apartment, leaving the lights on and the front door unlocked.

CHAPTER 22

The social worker stood at the front door with a clipboard in her hand and a phone hanging from her hip. Her glasses were dark red and rimmed a pair of observant brown eyes. She was probably ten years older than Rave. She looked kind when she smiled, and that caused Rave to take a much-needed deep breath. "Hello," Rave said.

"Hello, I'm Kristin Daus."

"Rave Wayne." He shook her hand. "Please come in." Rave's gaze went momentarily to Becca. Her smile gave him strength.

Pastor Keith was just coming out of the kitchen, wiping cookie remnants from his fingers onto a paper towel. He stopped when he looked up. "Kristy?"

Her eyes lit up. She blew past Rave and met Keith in the center of the room, arms outstretched. "Pastor Keith, it's great to see you."

Rave glanced over at Tuck. He shrugged and gave a nod and a wink. OK. This was probably a good thing, right? The phone in Rave's pocket buzzed. He'd turned it on silent. Everyone was here, so whoever it was could wait. He just wished his mom would come downstairs.

Pastor Keith and Kristin were engaged in one of those quick, catch-up conversations in which sentences were left unfinished and there were lots of interruptions with phrases like *you look great* and *it's been too long.* Somewhere along the way, Rave gathered that she'd been working in Gatlinburg but had recently relocated back home.

Pastor Keith finally addressed the waiting group. "Kristy used to be in my youth group." He glanced over at her. "Oh, sorry. You go by Kristin now, don't you?"

She nodded, all smiles. "Yes, but you can call me Kristy if you forget."

Pastor Keith took the lead introducing her to everyone. Welcomes were extended, hands were shaken. Rave shot a glance upstairs. He hadn't seen his mom all morning and figured she'd been tired and was getting a late start. Still, he'd like her down here before they started.

They all sat in the living room, and Trini brought out the cookies and scones along with a carafe of fresh coffee and a pot of tea. Kristin chose coffee and a scone, and for the first several minutes they discussed pleasantries. The weather, the fresh coat of paint on the grocery store, the downtown area's face-lift. Pastor Keith turned the conversation to the memorial park and told Kristin about Rave's involvement. He made Rave sound good, and *that* made Rave self-conscious.

Rave sat with his hands clasped between his knees, trying not to seem like a nervous wreck. When Kristin had finished her scone, she dusted her hands, took out a pen, and placed the clipboard on her lap, causing Rave to feel like he might hurl.

"We received a call about Daniel, that his mother was gone and may have abandoned him."

This was it. Rave drew a breath. "Daniel was left in my care, Ms. Daus, and Ashley has always been a loving, sacrificial mother. Yes, she's out of town now, but she'd never leave Daniel unless he was with me. There's just so much more to the story."

Kristin smiled. "There always is. Where is Daniel?"

Becca leaned forward on her seat. "My mother is watching him this morning."

Rave nodded. "I knew the conversation today would be . . . sensitive . . . I didn't want to confuse him more. I know you'll want . . . you'll want to meet him. But I thought this first meeting should be just us."

Kristin weighed him through keen eyes. "I couldn't agree more. It sounds like we have some things to iron out. No need for Daniel to be in the center of that."

"I know I should have gotten in touch with you. It's just that I love Daniel more than anything, and I don't want to see him suffer any more than he already has. He has a life here. With me and Tuck; my girlfriend, Becca; and my mom, who—"

All eyes went to the front door as Sharon came bursting through with a handful of papers in her grip. "I'm so sorry I'm late."

Rave couldn't stop the frown on his face. He'd thought she was still upstairs. Where'd she been? And why hadn't she made this meeting the top of her priority list after going on and on about how important it was to be there? Words failed him.

Sharon came to him, blocking Kristin's view. She pressed the pages into his hand with more emphasis than necessary. "Here are the papers you wanted me to retrieve from Ashley's apartment." Her wide eyes shot down to the paper on top. "Daniel's shot records are here and of course"—she squeezed Rave's hand so hard the knuckles cracked together—"his birth certificate." Her eyes dropped to it, and Rave's followed.

There, on the page in front of him, he read the words on Daniel's birth certificate. Mother—Ashley Lynn Walters, father—Rave Matthew Wayne.

Kristin interrupted them. "So, I take it Daniel lived with his mother—she had custody?"

Rave had no words. His mind raced to understand what he was looking at. His name. His name on Daniel's birth certificate. The silence stretched. Finally, Pastor Keith stood and took the paper from Rave. Accustomed not to reacting in delicate situations, he cleared his throat. "Rave and Ashley had a good relationship, even though they were no longer a couple."

"That's good," Kristin said. "Stability is of the essence. It certainly looks like Daniel has a solid family unit around him. Rave and Ashley were never married?"

Pastor Keith nudged Rave's shoulder, forcing him to answer. "No, we never married. And yes, ma'am. He does have a stable family here."

"I'm not certain why the anonymous caller suggested we check in. But it's my duty to offer whatever help we have." But she wasn't buying it. At least not all of it. Kristin's sharp eyes behind those red glasses darted around the room, landing on faces that didn't seem able to hold eye contact with her. "Would you like some counseling for Daniel, Rave? A sudden missing parent can take a toll on a child."

He mumbled a simple, "Yes, ma'am."

She jotted something on her clipboard and held it against her chest. "What more can I do for you today?"

All eyes went to Rave. He took the birth certificate from Pastor Keith and consulted it again. Yes, right there in bold, black letters, it said he was Daniel's father.

Kristin gauged the reactions around her, then squared her shoulders. "Before Daniel's mother left, had there been a custody hearing of any kind?"

Cold shot down his back. "What? No."

"No court order? Am I to understand that Daniel's mother and you had always been on good terms where Daniel was concerned?"

"We were always on the same page. Daniel came first, always. For both of us."

Kristin's chin tipped back. "Mr. Wayne, may I be frank with you?"

Her smile was gone, and that scared Rave. "Yes." It was a tentative agreement at best.

She used her pen to point at the paper. "That's Daniel's birth certificate, am I correct?"

"Yes." He didn't dare say more.

"And your name is on it?"

He had to give it another glance before answering. "Yes, ma'am."

She clicked her pen. "Then you are responsible for this child, Mr. Wayne. Food, shelter, love, clothing, education. All on you. I realize Daniel lived with his mother much of his life, but that's not an option if she's gone. If you don't step up and take over complete care of this boy, he's going to go into the system. Is that something you're prepared to do? Give up your son?"

He blanched. "No. No, of course not."

"Then I'm not entirely sure what the problem is here. This boy is your responsibility now. Yours and yours alone. Raising a child well is a selfless act. Are you ready for that?"

"Yes, I am." He looked at his mother. "In fact, my mom taught me that the true beauty of a person lies in their willingness to be selfless. Selflessness may require sacrifice, but it always produces the kinds of stars that shine the brightest."

Kristin smiled and gave those words time to sink in. "Then I think we're done here." She stood. "I'll send you a schedule for some possible times for counseling for Daniel. And, Rave, I'm not supposed to tell you this, but keep him in church. Being there will be paramount to his healing. Plus, Pastor Keith is an amazing influence." At that, she looked over at Keith and winked.

Once she was gone, and Rave had watched her pull out of the driveway, he turned to the others in the room. But he still couldn't find his words. They bounced around, jumbled, in his head, colliding with the very real and legal fact that Daniel was his.

Sharon launched into the topic, waiting on Rave only a moment before she began. "I woke up in the middle of the night thinking about how important it would be for Rave to be able to answer all of the social worker's questions. How would it look if he didn't know when Daniel was due for his next set of shots or where those records even *were*? I broke into Ashley's important paper box, and there inside was the birth certificate listing Rave as Daniel's father."

Becca sucked a breath. "Rave, you didn't know?"

He shook his head. "No. I never—I never knew."

"How did this happen?" Becca held the corner of the page. "Is that your signature?"

An explosion of joy shot through the confusion that still held his thoughts captive. "It's close enough. I didn't sign this."

"Ashley forged your signature?" Tuck said.

"I guess." His mind took him back four, now five, years ago, when Daniel was born. "At the hospital, we told them we were a couple. She didn't want to be alone, and I was her best friend, so we pretended."

"But the hospital wouldn't take it upon itself to just put you on the birth certificate." Pastor Keith had been quiet since Kristin left.

"No. But Ashley—Ashley always had a backup plan. I guess she told them I was the father. If she ever needed to disprove it, all it would take is a paternity test. But if things didn't work out, she'd have me as a backup. I guess I was always Ashley's backup. I guess this is the one time I can be thankful for that."

Tuck nodded. "Still, why not *tell* you? You've only wanted what was best for Daniel."

Rave shrugged. "I don't know. She was hoping Barry was the father because he comes from money, but the paternity test determined he wasn't. If he'd been the biological father, I guess she'd have taken legal action to get this changed. Maybe she figured it would be easier if I didn't know."

Tuck stood slowly and put a hand on Rave's arm. "Well, that boy's yours now. If not by blood, by contract. You reckon this is the end of it?"

For the first time since he'd gotten the news about Ash, Rave's shoulders weren't aching under the weight of uncertainty. "Yes. Even if Ashley returns. This is the end of it. Now that I know, she won't deny me any rights to him."

Sharon stepped closer. "He's not only *Rave's*." A broad smile appeared. "He's *ours*. All of us. And together, we'll raise him. You're not in this alone, Rave. Not that you couldn't handle it. Lord knows you practically raised your own mother. But you have us. And we won't let you down."

Rave looked out over the crowd of people gathered for the ribbon-cutting ceremony. It had been five days since the social worker left the house, and the weight of losing Daniel had been removed from his shoulders, allowing him to concentrate on today. His throat tightened. Over three hundred people had arrived, half of them filling the chairs and the rest standing like guards behind them. Three hundred people. Tuck would be so proud. At the thought of his grandfather, the tightness in his throat became painful.

Becca reached over and took his hand. "Thinking about Tuck, aren't you?"

Rave didn't trust his voice, but even if it broke, it didn't matter. This was the woman he loved slipping her hand into his. "He'd have loved seeing this."

She smiled. "I know. I wish things were different." It had all happened so quickly. Tuck was fine. He'd had a good day on Friday after the social worker left and was just turning in for the night when he'd collapsed. They'd rushed him to the hospital, and there they'd watched and waited while his body began to reject the new liver.

Rave had wanted to cancel the ribbon cutting but knew he couldn't. After all, this wasn't only for Tuck. It was for Tuck's men and all those who'd served. His gaze wandered to the front row, where Daniel, dressed in a suit, sat in a chair swinging his legs.

"You ready to speak?" Becca smiled up at him, and if a man could look into a face like that and not feel bulletproof, well, there was something wrong with that man.

Rave had been in front of microphones plenty of times, but never for this purpose. Never to address an audience of hundreds that included a congressman and a senator.

He stood and walked to the podium. Rave cleared his throat. "I was asked to open the ceremony today. When the committee first asked me to do that, I declined. I said, 'This is a day about our veterans. What could I possibly have to say that would honor them? I've never served. I've never fought on foreign soil and watched my best friends die. How do I have any right to address this group of men and women?'

"The Firstborn Veterans Committee is made up of a dozen men and women from Barton. We also have a twenty-member advisory board consisting of combat veterans. It was the advisory board that asked me respectfully to reconsider. When I asked them why, the head of the board, Mr. John Kidd, told me simply, 'Because you understand REST.'

"That's an acronym for Remember Every Soldier Today. That's what my grandfather, Tuck Wayne, taught me. That's why we're here today. And that's why this memorial was built."

The mention of Tuck made his throat tighten again. Rave removed his gaze from the crowd and focused on the long, straight road beyond the parking area. Far away, flashing lights caught his attention, their blue glow drifting through the trees, probably headed to the highway.

"Tuck's not here today. I wish he was. He'd tell you all how important it is for a soldier to be remembered. His words would be more eloquent than mine." Rave placed his hands flat on the podium. "Last week, Tuck was rushed to the hospital. He'd so been looking forward to this day. He hadn't seen the memorial park yet, but in the hospital I described it to him. When I told him about the wrought iron rocking chairs at each monument, well, Tuck cried. He said those seats meant the men and women who died would always be in our hearts, in our lives, and sitting right there in the empty chair beside us. Tuck told me that when a soldier dies, he doesn't leave an empty chair. He just leaves a spot for another to come and rest. My grandmother used to leave a bouquet of flowers tied with a crimson ribbon on the rocking chair for Tuck. To him, it meant that things were still beautiful even though they were dead."

People in the audience were wiping tears. Becca smiled. But beyond it all, past the rows of seats and the people standing, past the park and the tall fence, a set of blue lights stopped. When the vehicle came into view, Rave could see it was the sheriff's car—lights still swirling—stopping just beyond the gate of the memorial park. He watched Sheriff Cogdill step out, go around his car, and help someone from the passenger's seat. When a white head of springy hairs appeared over the top of the patrol car, Rave's heart leaped. Still dressed in his hospital pajamas and with the sheriff's coat over his shoulders, Tuck made his way into the park.

Rave drew a breath and continued. "As I said, Tuck was rushed to the hospital last week after a complication from surgery. But those of you who know Tuck, know he is one tough soldier. And it takes an awful lot to keep him from honoring the soldiers he lost."

The doctors hadn't warned them that signs of transplant rejection were fairly common. They hadn't told them that antirejection meds could be adjusted. An increase in those antirejection drugs saved Tuck's life. At first, Tuck's body had warred against the new liver. But the doctors began to modify the medications, and once Tuck's mind understood what the real enemy was, he forced his body to cooperate. He fought like the soldier he was. Maybe not the way he'd fought in Vietnam, but with all the passion of a man who had a lot to live for.

Phil Ratzlaff, standing on the back row, rushed to Tuck's other side, and he and Sheriff Cogdill helped him make his way forward. Even from the podium, Rave could see Tuck's amazement at the park.

Rave found it nearly impossible to continue speaking, but he wanted to give Tuck a few moments—his first moments experiencing the park—to take it all in without the prying eyes that would soon be aware of the pajama-clad soldier making his way forward. Some of the men and women standing had looked back when they noticed the lights, but most kept their eyes on Rave. "I was told once by another committee member that this whole thing started with me. But that's wrong. This whole thing started with my grandfather, a man who has held a memorial twice a month since the time he left Vietnam."

Rave lifted a hand and gestured to the back of the park where Tuck had finally paused in the sea of people. "Ladies and gentlemen, my grandfather, my hero, Tuck Wayne." Rave motioned to the back of the crowd, where Tuck stood, Phil on one side and Sheriff Cogdill on the other. The applause of the crowd drowned out any more words. Then those seated began to stand. A standing ovation for the soldier who'd returned home to feel not only abandoned by his country but by his family. The soldier who never abandoned his men.

EPILOGUE

Eleven years later

There were certain moments in a boy's life when he knew without a doubt he was a man. Rave's first came at age fourteen, when he had to drag his mother out of a crack house. Then again, when she'd left him in Tampa, and he'd become homeless. He'd worked hard and found a suitable if imperfect place to live.

Both of those times, he'd had to shed a certain amount of innocence to step into the shoes—ill-fitting as they were—of a man. And in retrospect, he could be proud of that. But never had he been more proud than today. Even over the years and all the times he'd addressed a crowd standing here at the podium of the memorial park.

Today was different. Today was the memorial for Tuck. As he stood in the early-winter sun with the tiny bits of snow sprinkled across the ground of the park, Rave thought of all the moments that had brought him here.

In the front row, Becca sat with her arm around Millie, their six-year-old daughter. His baby girl was the spitting image of her auburn-headed mother and sat with skinned knees dusting her winter dress, bony legs hidden to midcalf by her favorite pair of dress cowboy boots. Her feet swung forward and back, the rhinestones on her toes catching the light of the sun. Beside her, their son, Daniel, now sixteen, produced a colorful sucker for his little sister. Though Ashley had eventually returned to Barton, her stays were for short spurts only. The wife of a world-traveling entrepreneur, she allowed Daniel to continue to live with Rave—just as it was supposed to be—while she and her husband traveled the globe. Sharon sat beside Daniel with Sheriff Cogdill on her other side. His mother and the sheriff had rekindled a long-ago romance that had them both smiling and happy. His mother had never gone back to using drugs.

"Over the last several years, Tuck has given me five letters. Each one marking the important days of my life. The day I married Becca; the day we moved into Tuck's house and he moved into Trini's after the two of them ran off to Vegas to get married. The day my son, Daniel, graduated from middle school; the day our daughter, Millie Elisabeth, was born; and the last one was left for me to read today. He made me promise to read it here."

Rave drew a shaky breath and opened the envelope. He began.

"Dear Rave,
I guess to tell you I'm proud of you would seem silly since I make a point to tell you every time I see you. It's hard to imagine not spending long fishing days with you and discussing your next electrical job. But I guess I've kept Millie waiting long enough. She never was the most patient woman.

When you first came into my life, I was being swallowed by my grief. Grief for your grandma, grief for the men I served with. But you came along and stood beside me, took my burden, carried my yoke.

302

Because of your dedication, the memorial grew into something everyone could be part of. You made that happen, Rave.

But there's something that's been bothering me. Something we need to clear up. Right about now, I'm sure you're looking out at a crowd of our friends, at the monuments you helped erect and that have stood the test of time for these past years, at the rocking chairs, because no one should grieve alone. I'm so proud of what you've done here. But Rave, this place, these stone tablets, they aren't the memorial."

A chilling wind stole the warmth from his body, and Rave had to take several breaths before continuing, because the next three words blurred. He blinked and let the tears fall as he tried to concentrate on the page.

"You're the memorial."

His hand trembled, and he squeezed the paper in an attempt to get control of his emotions.

"You're the legacy I leave behind. For the worth of a man doesn't lie in stone monuments. It doesn't lie in bank accounts or assets. It lies in the lives he's touched, the people he's helped shape, the change he's created. You're my legacy, Rave. And it's a beautiful one. I don't know why God granted me such a gift."

A hush came over the crowd. Even the wind seemed to stop.

"Make me a promise, Rave. Live life to the fullest. Love in the fiercest way you can, and REST. If you do those things, then I've succeeded at life. Because life's true value lies in souls, not in things. And the best memorial a man can leave behind is one of flesh and blood. It's been an honor to be your grandfather."

ABOUT THE AUTHOR

Photo © 2016 Melinda Hanks

Heather Burch is the bestselling author of the novels *One Lavender Ribbon, Along the Broken Road, Down the Hidden Path,* and *In the Light of the Garden,* as well as several acclaimed young adult novels. *One Lavender Ribbon* was in the top 100 bestselling books of 2014 on Amazon. Her books have garnered praise from *USA Today, Booklist, Romantic Times,* and *Publishers Weekly.* Heather's deeply emotional novels explore family, love, hope, and the challenges of life. She tells unforgettable stories of love and loss—stories that make your heart sigh. Heather lives in southern Florida with her husband and has two grown sons who are the light of her life.

Made in the USA
Lexington, KY
16 September 2017